SHED
NO
TEARS

SHED NO TEARS

A NOVEL

CAZ FREAR

HARPER

An Imprint of HarperCollinsPublishers

This is a work of fiction. Names, characters, places, and incidents are products of the author's imagination or are used fictitiously and are not to be construed as real. Any resemblance to actual events, locales, organizations, or persons, living or dead, is entirely coincidental.

HarperCollins books may be purchased for educational, business, or sales promotional use. For information, please email the Special Markets Department at SPsales@harpercollins.com.

Originally published in Great Britain in 2020 by Zaffre

FIRST U.S. EDITION

Library of Congress Cataloging-in-Publication Data has been applied for.

ISBN 978-0-06-297985-8

20 21 22 23 24   LSC   10 9 8 7 6 5 4 3 2 1

To Reggie, Flynn & Lucie

The "Roommate" case: 2012

From Wikipedia, the free encyclopedia

Contents [hide]

When the first blow lands, it's almost a relief.

A karmic debt paid.

A maneuver, at least.

She battles at first, of course; kicking and clawing and begging and bargaining all the way from the cold kitchen floor, where they first bounce her skull, through the hall, across the driveway, and into the boot of the waiting car.

A car she knows well.

A car she's sat in maybe ten, fifteen times—always the passenger, but always firmly in the driving seat. Queen of the world. Top of her game.

Tonight, the gun glinting in the midnight light signals that, for her, the game's now up.

She had this coming. She accepts this. She knows she created this whole sordid mess herself. And yet she'd prayed that they'd stop at a beating—because a beating she could take; bruises fade, fractures heal, even the worst scars can be covered with makeup. And God knows she'd taken enough beatings in her life and still lived to tell the sorry tale.

She won't live to tell this one.

She doesn't deserve to. Even by her standards, this one was cruel.

And she is sorry. She knows they don't believe her, but maybe if there's a God upstairs, He will.

Maybe next time around, she'll come back as a better person.

This time around, there was only ever one way this mess was going to end.

1

We'd prayed for rain for weeks. Or maybe it was months? It's hard to remember a time when griping about the heat wasn't a national fetish. When days weren't spent sighing and swearing and spraying yourself with Magicool, and nights weren't spent tossing and turning, wondering if sleep was now a pleasure of the past.

And then there were the arguments. *Christ, there were the arguments.* Civil war over air-con settings. Men carping at women, jealous at the sight of us drifting around in lightweight dresses while they sweated buckets in the same suits that saw them through winter. Old versus young: Steele and Parnell crowing that *this* was no way near as brutal as the summer of '76, when the rivers ran dry and the asphalt melted, and using your hose was a crime routinely punishable by social death.

Of course, we—"The Young"—stated long and loud that, as *we* weren't even twinkles in our parents' eyes in 1976, "The Olds'" point was entirely moot and, frankly, not helping. *You can only play the hand you're dealt,* we'd endlessly argue, and we'd been dealt *this* cursed summer. The paralyzing heat wave of 2018. We were living through it, sweltering through it, surviving it—*just*—with the aid of desk fans and ice packs, and the constant yet sagging hope that it might one day rain again on England's green and pleasant lands.

And now here, on a grassy dirt track, running alongside a remote field in the molten heart of Cambridgeshire, our prayers are finally answered.

"Fucking rain," I say, scowling at the sky. All our sweaty, parched misery forgotten in an instant.

"You don't get rain in London, no?" DC Ed Navarro—our crime scene guide, *and boy, does he resent it*—is smirking in a way that makes me want to to flick his pale, waxy face, like a boiled potato with a goatee. "Because seriously, you're looking a little frazzled there. Do you want to go and sit in the car for a bit?"

"Why, is it acid rain?" I bite back.

He rummages in his pocket, retrieves an opened packet of Polo mints. "Not that I'm aware."

"Well then, I reckon I'll survive."

"Ah, come on, Kinsella, this is bliss," DS Luigi Parnell raises his hands, letting the rain patter off his palms: pennies from heaven. "It's not even that heavy. And remember what the boss says, 'It's good for the garden.'"

"I don't have a garden." I lift my plastic file of crime scene photos above my head, a macabre makeshift umbrella. "I do have frizzy hair, though."

Immediately, I regret saying it. Holly Kemp doesn't have to worry about frizzy hair anymore. Or the fact that her cheap cotton work shirt is getting more see-through by the minute.

Holly Kemp hasn't worried about anything in a long time.

"So, yeah, this is where we found her."

Navarro nods toward the deep ditch at the side of the track, then leads us to a gap in the covering hedgerow, presumably cut away to give Forensics easier access. Just yesterday, a crime scene tent would have stood here, preserving evidence and privacy for the army of white suits going about their crucial black art, but we're quick to get them down these days. It's not "resource efficient"— to use the term à la mode—to keep them under guard for a second longer than necessary.

Money. Budgets. PR. Stats.

The four horsemen of modern policing.

"Well, of course, *we* didn't find her. Lady Persephone III did— that's a dog, before you ask." Navarro pops two mints in his mouth, not bothering to offer them around. "Honestly, I don't know what planet some people are on. What's wrong with Patch or Rex or Rover all of a sudden? Proper dog names."

"I like it," I say, just to agitate him. In my defense, we're under strict instructions from DCI Kate Steele to play the agitators today. The standard "up from London" arseholes who think the rest of the force are an *el cheapo* version of the mighty Metropolitan Police. Steele's hoping a blast of belligerence might put a rocket up their backsides.

"So, any danger of a postmortem?" asks Parnell, casualness spliced with scorn. "It's been over forty-eight hours—*well* over forty-eight hours."

Navarro widens his stance. "Hey, hang on a minute. It's been over forty-eight hours since we contacted you about the locket, but we only got her back to the morgue last night. You can't rush forensic archaeology—it's a fiddly business." Parnell pulls an unimpressed face. I opt for *majorly* unimpressed. "And, look, we've got a back-log, OK? Our pathologist's run off her feet."

I fold my arms, giving up on my file-cum-umbrella. "Whereas ours just sits around sharpening her rib-cutters, waiting for a body to roll in."

"Bodies, actually." Navarro looks more sad than defensive. "There was a pileup on the M11 a few hours before this. Two cars, five teens, four dead—two from the same family." He raps a knuckle on his forehead, knocking out the thought. "I knew one of them—not well, mind. I used to coach him at SoccerTots. But I'd see him in the pub sometimes, acting the big guy, getting the pints in. They grow up so quickly and then bang . . . gone."

And then *bang*, the "up from London" arseholes feel like bona fide lousy arseholes. We offer quick but sincere condolences, Parnell catching my eye to convey that Operation Arsehole is being immediately stood down.

I bring the conversation back to safer ground—the dog with

the dumb name. "You know, we really should be shaking Lady Persephone III by the paw. She did what we failed to do. She found Holly Kemp. Poor soul's been missing for years."

Nearly six years, to be precise. Six birthdays. Six Christmases. Six anniversaries spent wondering if this is the year you get "closure"— that storybook notion they talk about on TV.

"Er, *we*? What your lot failed to do, you mean?" Navarro can't stop himself—the pissing contest between forces is as predictable as it is puerile.

I let the dig pass, mainly because I feel heartsick about Navarro's ex-SoccerTot, but partly because it's fair enough. This is on the mighty Metropolitan Police, no question.

"So, how in God's name did she lie here for so long, unnoticed?" I ask of no one in particular.

"All this," says Navarro, drawing a semicircle on the drizzly horizon, "belonged to an old farmer, Johnny Heath. He died a while back, but he'd let the field lie fallow for years; more to do with bad health than good crop rotation, I think." The reference is lost on me but I nod sagely. "His son lived in America. Didn't even bother coming home for the funeral, so they say. And he never got round to selling the place when the old man passed because he was making a king's ransom on Wall Street and didn't need the money. So after Johnny died in 2015, the whole estate just sat here. The son paid a local to cut the grass a few times a year, but that's about it."

"And the tractor wouldn't go anywhere near the ditch," says Parnell.

I pull a photo from my file. "And even if it did, she was well hidden."

Twigs and branches and bracken and logs. It was the logs that were the chilling detail; the logs that proved this wasn't some tramp looking for shelter who'd died of hypothermia in the night, or a binge-drinking casualty, staggering home across the field. The logs were placed on top of the body, no doubt about it. They'd covered it, cocooned it, made sure that a grieving family didn't get closure any time soon.

"So, to finish the story . . ." Another mint in his mouth. "The son's luck ran out in the US of A a few months back—redundancy, he says—and lo and behold, suddenly he's Old MacDonald. Over here like a shot, talking about organic farming, setting up a shop for fools with deep pockets."

"So is the dog his?" I ask, giving up on Lady P's full title.

Navarro nods. "She'd been scrabbling around the same spot for days. He didn't think much of it until a few days ago when she wouldn't come when he called. And then when she wouldn't respond to the whistle either, he knew something was up. The whistle always works, apparently."

"A whistle? So she's a puppy. He's training her." Parnell fancies himself as a bit of an expert, having walked his kids' dog twice in the last year.

"Got it in one." Navarro wipes the rain from his face with his shirt cuff. I'm past the point of caring about my halo of fuzz. "He thought he'd mastered it too. But, you know, give a dog a bone . . ."

Not *a* bone, it turned out. *Bones*. One hundred and eighty-nine of them, which, according to my GCSE B in biology, means seventeen are missing. Lost to foxes or scattered by starlings, we'll assume. An almost entire female skeleton left to decompose in a ditch, miles from where she was last seen.

6 Valentine Street, Clapham, South-West London.

Six years ago, the press dubbed it the ultimate "House of Horrors." More recently, an estate agent called it a *stunning, characterful midterrace home, with a newly extended kitchen and a real oasis of a garden. Seldom do properties such as this make it onto the market.*

Which is true, if a little sugarcoated.

"So why here?" I ask in place of *Why do we do this job when it's all dead SoccerTots and bones and standing in fields in the bloody rain?* "And I don't mean, why not Valentine Street? I mean, why here—Caxton? Why this spot, specifically?" I do a slow 360, taking in our surroundings, which to be frank aren't much. Apart from the three of us standing here like peasants in a Constable painting and a rusted tractor in the next field, there isn't a single point of interest as far as the eye can see. Just a vista of bleached land and a temporarily sullen sky. "OK, sure, you're off the beaten track a bit, but you aren't exactly sheltered. Even at night, you'd have to feel slightly exposed."

Navarro shrugs, as though the methods of a killer aren't his to judge.

"Ah, come on, Ed, help us out," says Parnell, all chummy now. "You know the area. If you were going to bury a body, would you really do it here?"

"Maybe. We aren't exactly spoiled for choice around these parts. There aren't too many wooded areas, and The Fens, just north of here, is a completely flat landscape." The smirk is back. "Do you know what my guv'nor says? He says FENs stands for Fucking Enormous Nothing."

I smile. Parnell laughs generously. "Fucking Enormous Nothing, that's a good one." He's back to business quickly. "But seriously though, there must be somewhere safer than this? Somewhere more secluded?"

Navarro considers it this time, rubbing at his goatee. "Me, personally, if I'd killed my sister-in-law—which would be an honor and a privilege, I tell you—I wouldn't bury her at all. I'd weigh her down and throw her in the Ramsey Forty Foot—it's a big drainage dike about twenty miles north of here."

Dragging him from his daydream, I say, "You know, you both keep using the word 'buried,' but she wasn't buried, not really."

"Well, she wasn't under the ground, no," Navarro concedes. "But he did a thorough job of hiding her."

I step closer to the ditch, peering at the space left, the nothing-ness. "Hiding is different from burying, though. Hiding's quicker. This person was in a rush."

"Hold on, 'this person?'" Navarro's eyes narrow, piqued and suspicious. "Look, I know we're skirting around this until we get dental records back, but this *is* Holly Kemp. The locket, it's engraved HOLLY. It's got photos of her parents inside. It's *hers*. And she's one of his, isn't she?" We say nothing. "Well, my guv'nor spoke to the DCI who headed things up back then and they're still convinced. He admitted it, right?"

He, Christopher Dean Masters, did indeed admit it. And then he denied it, then admitted it, denied it, then admitted it, and so on and so on, until the original investigators stopped giving him the airtime and the warped satisfaction.

"Believe me, I wish she was one of ours. Our clear-up stats aren't great at the moment." This should rattle my cage but depressingly, I hear him. Too many cases and a major drop in the number of murder detectives makes you clinical—brain-fried and clinical. "I thought she *was* one of ours, actually. The minute the call came through, I said, *That's Ania Duvac, that is.* I had a £10 bet with Jonesy, our exhibits officer." He clocks my expres-sion and his face flushes—boiled potato to raw beetroot with one misjudged admission. "Look, it wasn't my idea. Jonesy'd bet on two flies crawling up a wall. He's got a real problem, that one. Anyway, I knew I'd lost my tenner the second I got here. Ania only went missing last September, see. You'd expect to see a bit of muscle tissue still attached." He smiles to himself. "The lads think it's weird, but I've got a real interest in this type of stuff. I know a thing or two about decay."

Fair play to him. It's more than I do. You see, policing is generally a conveyor belt of firsts. You walk your first beat, make your first arrest. You brace yourself for the first time you shatter a heart with the words, "I'm so sorry to have to tell you . . ." And despite what the old guard say—the know-it-alls, the thirty-year-service brigade, the retired peacocks propping up the bar at so-and-so's leaving party, regaling anyone naive enough to listen about the time they met the Kray twins—you never *ever* stop learning. There's no finite number of head-fucks this job can serve up. Today, for example, despite it being four years since I first joined Murder, since I crouched over my very first corpse at my very first crime scene, *this*—Holly Kemp—is my first set of bones.

No blood. No wounds. No gag-reflex smell.

No small but poignant detail to connect you to your victim.

I admit it. I'm finding it hard to connect with just bones. With a skeleton laid out like a science project, or a cheap thrill on the ghost train. Holly Kemp's photo is all I've got to gauge the essence of who she was. The "famous" photo. The classic news feed fodder. The one of the home-dye blonde with the duck-pout lips. Tan straight out of a bottle. Teeth straight out of a Colgate advert.

And "tits straight out of a catalog," according to Navarro. They found implants among the bones. Silicone's a hardy bugger to break down.

As are rubber soles.

"Did I see something about footwear?" I rifle through my file, looking for the relevant printout.

"You did," confirms Navarro. "There was a trainer—pretty distinctive, actually. Possibly custom-made. A photo's been sent to her mates—they should be able to ID it, hopefully." There's a spark in his eyes; morbid curiosity. "Odd though, isn't it? The trainer."

"Yeah. No. Maybe." I let him read what he wants into my airy nonanswer.

"Thing is," he goes on, the mints click-clacking against his teeth, "there were a few scraps of fabric too, sticky patches melded with the bone. Jeans, probably, as they found copper rivets—you know, the tiny bits of metal you get on the pockets?"

I shoot a fidgety glance toward Parnell, who quickly looks away.

Navarro spots it. "Oh, I know what you're thinking. You're thinking the same as me. I mean, it's hard *not* to think it." He pauses, and for a moment there's only the dripping-tap trickle of the weakening summer rain and the soft, tidal rush of motorway, God knows how far away. "The others . . . they were naked."

The others.

Strangers in life, bound together in death.

Names on a Wikipedia page.

The victims.

2

I let the door slam hard and stomp through the heart of MIT4 base camp, Parnell hard on my heels, whistling a radio jingle that had plagued us the whole way back to Holborn HQ. Detective Sergeant Pete Flowers visibly jolts at the reverberation, dropping his soup spoon and splattering fiery red liquid onto his starched white shirt.

"Jesus, Kinsella!" He lurches for a tissue. "Close the door, why don't you?"

"Oh, shut up, Sarge, I'm cranky." I'm also tired, straggly haired, and surprisingly still damp, despite a two-hour journey that should have been less had Parnell—who has the thirst of an elephant but the bladder of a pygmy shrew—not needed to stop at every motorway services from Caxton to eternity. "Send me the dry-cleaning bill," I add—I may be cranky but fair's fair. "Although not that one by the station. Eighteen quid for a suit! We should be arresting those crooks, not giving them our money."

The main benefit of having worked with the same crew for four years, bar everyone knowing how you like your tea, is that rank often goes out the window. In a day-to-day sense, anyway. In the sense that you can tell a sergeant to "shut up" without them frothing at the mouth. Around eighteen months ago, I'd been seconded to City Hall to work on policy and planning in the mayor's office—great for my CV, not so great for my boredom threshold—and I'd missed the freedom to be tetchy. The safety to be myself.

Or at least the disinfected version I let others see.

The room's quiet, the only energy coming from a flickering strip light that Facilities promised to fix back when Noah built the ark. Apart from Flowers, our resident slab of testosterone, there's only two other people here: DC Renée Akwa, currently curling her lip into the receiver of her phone, and DC Ben Swaines.

I can't actually see Ben Swaines, but as the air-con's set to Baltic, it's a dead cert he's here.

"I swear that man's part polar bear." I adjust the thermostat to something more considerate then fling my bag on my desk. "Hey, Ren, where is everyone?"

Renée lowers her phone. "Don't know. Out making more use of the taxpayers' money than me, with any luck. Twenty minutes, I've been on hold. Twice to the wrong department. Haringey Council, who else?"

"Ahhh, Haringey on hold . . ." I've had my own share of mind-numbing stints. "Mozart's Symphony No. 40 in G Minor. Am I right?"

"Spot on."

Steele's office door flies open. Her petite, pristine presence gives the room some instant zing.

"Well, well, well, the wanderers return." Her scarlet mouth dips as she looks us up and down. "Bloody hell, guys. Here I was, bragging to Tess about my Cat-and-Lu dream team, and then in you trot, looking like you've been camping for a week."

Tess? I glance through the blinds, spy a platinum-blond bob and a Grande Starbucks Something.

"We got soaked." I walk in and perch against a filing cabinet, offering "Tess" a generic smile. She's in her midforties at a guess, and in her prime for damn sure. Sleek and elegant in a cream tailored shift dress. And not one you'd throw in the spin wash either.

"Soaked?" Steele grins as Parnell troops in behind me. "What happened, Lu? Did you leave the sunroof down in the car wash again?"

He laughs, nodding at "Tess" in a way that suggests a faint history. "Rain, would you believe? Do you remember it? The wet stuff."

"Well, I hope you brought it back with you," says Steele. "My hydrangeas are knackered."

"Tess" stretches forward, wrapping her French manicure around her Starbucks. "You still like your garden then, Kate?"

I reach across Steele's desk, snatching up a magazine blotted with coffee cup rings. "She still likes buying *Gardeners' World* and using it as a coaster, if that's what you mean."

Steele grabs it off me, clouts me on the shoulder. "Tess, meet DC Cat Kinsella. Cat, meet Detective Chief Inspector Tessa Dyer. You and Lu know each other, right?" A nod from Dyer. A "vaguely" from Parnell. "Tess headed up the Roommate case. She's popped in to give us the scoop—or 'the skinny' as the kids say—on Holly Kemp."

The Roommate's last victim.

"So how'd you get on in the sticks?" she carries on, introductions complete. "You must have ruffled someone's feathers. I got a call just now—the postmortem's happening this evening."

"Only one feather," I tell her. "A guy called Ed *Navarro*." I drawl his name in a dud Texan accent. "Sounds like a gunslinger from an old Western, don't you think?"

"You're thinking of *The Guns of Navarone*, and that's a war film, not a Western."

Dyer's laugh fills the room. "God, you haven't changed a bit, Kate."

Steele sits down. "Well, I'll be honest, Tess. I can't say the same about you. I hardly recognized you."

Dyer shrugs, but there's a glint of triumph in her powder-blue eyes. "Ah, you know, working in Lyon, you have to up your game. French women are a different breed."

Steele explains. "Interpol, no less. Four years."

"Wow."

"Not as 'wow' as you'd think, Cat." My name trips off her tongue with an easy warmth. "You're not making arrests. It's all about information-sharing, greasing wheels, coordination between member countries. You actually have very little power."

Meaning it's high on pomp and protocol, low on kick-ass glory.

"So when did you get back?" asks Parnell.

"Late last year. I'm with SO15 now."

"Counter-Terrorism, eh? 'Making the World a Better Place'—isn't that the latest slogan?"

Dyer's eyes flick skyward. "Yeah, although 'Plugging the Leak with Your Little Finger' might be closer to the truth."

"At least you're trying to stop bad things happening," I say. Flashes of our visit this morning: Parnell and I staring uselessly into a scooped-out ditch. Holly Kemp's bones packed into Tupperware boxes—life at its most extinct. "All we do is mop up the mess." Steele's face is a picture—*Portrait of a Pissed-off Woman.* "Sorry, that sounded worse than I meant, boss. It's been a long day."

"It's about to get a whole lot longer, m'dear." She doesn't elaborate and I don't ask. I'll find out soon enough. "So, Tess, any superintendent plans on the horizon?"

"You never know." She gives a cryptic smile, then tosses the question right back. "You never fancied it? The way Olly talked about you, I thought you'd be commissioner by now."

It might just be me, in fact there's a very good chance it is—when I'm tired and cranky, I have a high frequency for slights—but I sense something sharp in Dyer's statement. An acidic little jab. Steele doesn't look bothered, though, and that's good enough for me.

"Oh yeah, so who's this Olly then?" I say, grinning. "Another paid-up member of the Kate Steele Appreciation Society?"

Steele likes that, blows me a kiss for my efforts. "Detective Chief Superintendent Oliver Cairns. Actually, *Retired* Detective Chief Superintendent Oliver Cairns. He was my mentor way back and Tess's—well, not quite so way back, let's leave it at that." She turns back to Dyer. "And in answer to your question, Tess—no, I've never fancied it. I've thought about it over the years, of course I have, but I like it at the coalface. This lot think I'm bone idle as it is, sitting on my arse planning for divisional budget meetings. And anyway, I think Olly had higher hopes for you than he ever had for me."

"I doubt it." Dyer frowns over the rim of her coffee. "You scaled the heights quicker. You were thirty-six when you made DCI. I was thirty-eight." She makes a joke of it, muttering "Dammit" under her breath, while I silently calculate that I've got roughly a decade to get my act together. To become the kind of woman who plans budgets while wearing chic bespoke tailoring.

"Ah, but I didn't have two small kids," says Steele, gracious to the last. "You trumped me there. And thirty-six isn't any great shakes these days, not with all these fast-track schemes. Look at my Lord and Master, Blake. He made superintendent before he could pull his own pants up."

It's unfair but it's funny and funny wins out. Steele likes Blake, really. And a DCI like Kate Steele needs a DCS like Russell Blake—someone who'll give her carte blanche as long as she at least pretends that he's the one in charge.

"So have you seen Olly lately?" Dyer asks Steele.

"You must be joking. I haven't seen my own husband in broad daylight for the past ten days." Eyes down, she catches a memory. "I suppose it must be around two years, give or take. His retirement party, probably."

"Oh, you went? I'm glad. He'd have appreciated that." Dyer's voice is soft, a little gloomy. "I really wanted to get back for it, but you know how it is . . ."

Steele flaps a hand. "I wouldn't worry, you didn't miss much. Flat prosecco and DAC Dempsey making jokes about golfing holidays. Did you ever hear anything like it? Olly wouldn't know which end of the bat to hold." Parnell opens his mouth. "And yes, I know it's a club, Lu. It was a joke." Back to Dyer. "I heard he'd not been well."

"Well enough to be meeting me for a drink or five tomorrow. After band practice, of course."

Steele leans back, smiling. "God, I'd forgotten about that. Him and his bloody pipe band. So he's still big in the Emerald Society?" She stretches an arm across, grazing my elbow with the tip of a mauve fingernail. "Here, you could join that, Kinsella. It'd be right up your street, all that Irish stuff."

"Oh, here we go. You know, technically, I'm not even half-Irish, boss. My dad was born here, which means . . ."

But she's not listening anymore. A quick glance at the time and Steele's face is wiped clean of smiles and replaced with the kind of focus that gets you DCI rank before your thirty-seventh birthday.

"Right, *mes amis*, I'm due at a 'Policing After Brexit' workshop in an hour, lucky me, and Tess isn't going to make superintendent lounging around with the likes of us, so let's crack on, OK? And you—sit down." I sit, assuming that's aimed at me, given the clipped maternal tone. "Now obviously we're all familiar with the Roommate case, but one thing's for sure—if I have to go in front of the media once we get Holly Kemp's PM results back, I want to be more than familiar. I want to be clued-up. And you pair should be too." She raises a hand to Dyer, effectively offering her the floor. "So clue us up, Tess."

In truth, "familiar" is still a slight stretch for me. Sure, I had a skim through the case file last night. I scanned the Wikipedia page, did a quick Google search while my prawn bhuna was cooking—Parnell's big idea: spicy foods cool you down, *allegedly*. And, obviously, I was aware of the case back in 2012. But only in the way you're aware of an interest rate rise or a senior royal wedding. It's important, yet distant, and you really couldn't give a fuck.

Sounds harsh? Well, don't judge me. It wasn't long after my mum died. While Holly Kemp and "the others" were living out their final months in blissful ignorance, Mum was on her final straight too. A slow, merciless straight that altered me forever, the grief a cancer of its own. So, by the time the news broke that London had a new monster to revile and four victims to mourn, I was so mired in my own despair—in senseless guilt and ferocious drinking—that the details of the Roommate case slipped me by. In fact, *life* slipped me by. I cared for nothing except anger and white wine oblivion. Aliens could have landed and I'd have neither noticed nor cared.

Until I saw the advert.

MAKE LIFE MORE MEANINGFUL
MAKE LONDON A SAFER PLACE
JOIN THE METROPOLITAN POLICE

The girl on the poster even looked a bit like me. A less grief-haggard version, anyway.

It was fate.

And a middle finger to my dad, who'd only ever made London worse.

"God, where to start?" Dyer says, with the faux modesty of someone who knows exactly where to start, every word, every beat. "The media called Christopher Masters 'The Roommate' on account of several adverts he placed on various sites. *Roommate wanted—female, age 20–35, for quiet, respectful, friendly house near Clapham Common. Double room. Bills, TV, Wi-Fi included, £600 per calendar month.*" All this, right off the bat, the words seared on her brain. "Masters owned a hardware store, had done since the nineties, but he was a keen handyman too—*no job too big or too small*, that kind of thing—so when he and two cousins inherited 6 Valentine Street from an aunt, he swooped quickly, suggesting he renovate the house in exchange for an increased share of the profits. He started the work in autumn 2011 but it was a big job, the place needed gutting. And what with running the store as well, it was still only half-finished by February 2012, which was when he

placed the ad and began luring young women to the house. Tortur-
ing them. Strangling them."

"Do we know if he actually killed them there?" I ask, mentally
sifting through the facts I gleaned last night and coming up blank.
"I know the bodies were found in Dulwich Woods. Well, except
Holly Kemp's, obviously."

"We know he definitely harmed them there. We found the
blood of two of the victims in the house. Apart from that, though,
we don't *know* much. He led us to the bodies in Dulwich Woods;
he gave that up within an hour of arrest, but he wouldn't say why
he did what he did or give us any sequence of events. Just that
he'd 'felt like it.' There's a theory his ex-wife's recent engagement
might have sparked something."

"And he completely refused to say anything about Holly Kemp?"
asks Parnell.

"At the time, yes. He admitted being at the Valentine Street
address on the day she disappeared, but that was it. He got more
talkative over the years, though: 'I killed her. I didn't. I killed her.
I didn't . . .'" Her face roars with anger. "*He killed her.*"

Steele jumps in. "Park Holly for a second. Tell us a bit about the
others first, Tess. While we've got you here, we might as well get
everything from the horse's mouth."

Dyer nods. "Sure, no problem. So Bryony Trent was the first.
She was twenty-four, a live-in shift manager at The Cross Keys
pub in Clapham North. She was last seen on Friday 10th February,
leaving the pub around five p.m. We got one sketchy CCTV sighting around five fifteen p.m., heading in the direction of the Common, but it was lashing rain that day and it wasn't much use—her
umbrella didn't help either; it made it even harder to pick her out
again. According to cell site analysis, her phone was switched off
twenty minutes later. We never found her phone or her bag—same
with the others. When we got her phone records back, though, we
did find a pay-as-you-go number that nobody seemed to recog-

nize, dialed the day before. Problem was, no one knew she was flat-hunting, so we missed that early lead. She hadn't said anything as she didn't want her boss to know she wasn't happy until she was ready to leave—basically, until she'd found a new place to live."

She comes up for air, pausing for any questions. I'm swaying between having none and having a barrage. Steele gives Dyer the nod to carry on.

"OK, next, Steffi König; twenty-nine, German. She'd been in the UK for six years, working for an event management firm in Clapham Old Town."

Steffi, not Stephanie. I might have only scanned the internet and taken a cursory flick through the case file, but she's certainly been Stephanie in every report I've read. *Steffi* implies attachment, a pained affinity, a genuine care. It suggests Christmas cards exchanged with the family and a DCI who'll never forget.

"She was last seen on February 16th, leaving her workplace at around four thirty p.m. It was her break—a late one because they had an event in the evening—and while she usually stayed in the staff canteen, she said she had to pop out that day. Again, CCTV wasn't much help because of bad weather and bad luck, and cell site analysis was as much use as it ever is in a big city. Her phone pinged off a tower on the west side of Clapham Common just after five p.m., but it was hard to narrow it down to anything helpful; the mast covered a few hundred square meters." Or a few standard-sized football pitches, to use Parnell's metric system. "Phone records gave us a vague link, though—she'd dialed a pay-as-you-go number the day before, like Bryony Trent. Different number, but the call was of a similar duration, and it was made a similar length of time before she went missing. And then, of course, we got our break with Ling Chen."

Dyer shifts in her chair, her back ramrod straight; the memory of that break still fresh.

"Ling was the eldest, thirty-three. She was last seen on the morning of Tuesday 21st by her boyfriend. They were having problems.

He was pressuring her to get married and she wasn't keen—in fact, she was planning to leave him, was flat-hunting on the sly. She'd mentioned to a colleague that she was viewing a place in Clapham that afternoon, and sure enough, the same pay-as-you-go number that Steffi called showed up from the day before. To cut a long story short, we eventually found the Valentine Street address scrawled on the back of a pizza flyer in the recycling bin at her friend's house."

"But not soon enough to save Holly Kemp."

There's nothing accusatory in Steele's statement. We've all been there, Steele probably ten times over. The torment of realizing that if you'd only known X, you could have done Y. It's pointless persecution and yet we can't help but indulge.

"Sadly not. It was Friday the 24th before the friend made the connection—that Ling was at her place when she'd made the pay-as-you-go call. Holly was last seen on Thursday the 23rd at around four p.m., so she was almost certainly dead by then. And in any case, she hadn't even been reported missing by the time we arrested Masters on the Saturday. Her boyfriend waited until Sunday because, and I'm quoting here, 'she's a mad bitch, unpredictable.' He'd assumed she'd gone on a long weekend bender, but when she still hadn't surfaced by Sunday, he got worried, called us."

Parnell's voice is a squeak. "I should bloody well think he was worried! Hadn't he seen the news?"

"I don't think he was 'the news' type, Lu. Anyway, her friends proved to be more help than him. It was her friends who told us about Holly's plans to go to Clapham that Thursday. And the CCTV snatch of her coming out of the Tube proved she got there."

"Her friends knew she was flat-hunting?" I ask.

"No. She wouldn't say why she was going. She was being very elusive, all 'watch this space.' Apparently that was typical of her. She was a bit of a drama queen."

"A nicer way of saying 'a mad bitch.'"

"Yes, well, Spencer Shaw—the boyfriend—wasn't exactly a nice guy. He'd served six months for conspiracy to commit burglary not long before he met Holly. He'd been working as an estate agent, casing houses, getting the layout, selling the information on for a tiny cut."

A "*tsk*" from Parnell while Steele mutters "*the little shitbag.*" It doesn't matter how often we deal with death and devastation, there's still something about this type of chickenshit delinquency that never fails to make you fume. It's the barefaced cheek of it. The mindless entitlement. It's the family left feeling scared in their own home, all because some faceless coward fancied a new pair of Nikes.

"He must have been a suspect?" I say. "For Holly, I mean. Anyone who takes three days to report their partner missing might as well slap the cuffs on themselves."

Dyer nods. "Oh, definitely. It was a huge red flag. And just because she'd gone missing from Clapham, that didn't *prove* a connection to Masters. There was no pay-as-you-go number in her phone records, for a start, although Spencer Shaw had a theory about that. He said Holly was always misplacing her phone, borrowing someone else's. But we checked her nearest and dearest's phones, didn't find anything . . ." She drags a finger across her lips, wrestling with something. "You know, even after Serena Bailey, I still wasn't comfortable closing Spencer Shaw off, but I . . . well . . . I was told to close him off. Masters was our man. Serena Bailey proved it." Her chin lifts, confidence swiftly restored. "And she did. I was being overzealous about Shaw, I can see that now. Serena Bailey changed *everything.*"

Serena Bailey, or as immortalized in folklore: The Witness.

This bit I am familiar with.

On Monday 27th February, hours after Holly's photo appeared in the *Evening Standard*, Serena Bailey, a primary school teacher, contacted police to say she'd seen Holly walking up the path of

6 Valentine Street on the day she went missing. She'd later ID Christopher Masters as the man who opened the door and beckoned Holly in.

Bailey's account was explosive. One hundred percent dynamite. It didn't matter now what Masters confirmed or denied: CCTV footage put Holly in Clapham and an independent eyewitness put her quite literally on his doorstep. It was obvious to any right mind that Holly was Masters' fourth victim.

Any right mind except the Crown Prosecution Service.

"I still can't believe Bailey's sighting wasn't enough," says Parnell.

"Oh, don't get me started." Dyer's mouth is a tight line. "Forget that a young woman is seen entering the house of a killer and then never seen again—if you can't make the forensic link, jog on, as far as the CPS are concerned. Don't muddy the waters for the other three. Come back when you've found her body. Which we obviously tried to do—all of Masters' haunts, every house he ever worked on, every wooded area inside the M25 . . ."

"Well, don't hold your breath for a forensic link now, not after all this time." Steele delivers a dose of gloomy realism. "Although a matching cause of death would be something. *If* we get a cause of death, that is."

I blurt it out. "Holly wasn't naked, you know? They found remnants of fabric, a trainer."

"It's different, I'll give you that," Dyer concedes. "Although I'd be wary of reading too much into it. Masters' crimes were obviously planned and he used an identical method of killing, but he's not what we'd call a classic 'organized offender.' They go to great lengths to conceal their crimes, whereas Masters didn't seem to care. He invited them to his house, handed out his address. He left DNA on the bodies, there was blood in the house. All this suggests an element of disorganization and that makes him much harder to read. Disorganized offenders don't always follow patterns."

"Doesn't the different body dump site niggle at you, though?" In for a penny, in for a pound. Like the boss said, while we've got an audience with Dyer, we might as well milk it.

"Seth and Emily are on that," says Steele. "They're heading up to Newcastle first thing tomorrow. That's where the ex-wife lives now. Maybe she'll be able to give us a link to Caxton, or even Cambridgeshire would do."

Dyer observes me across Steele's desk. "What niggles at me, Cat, is that the bastard's dead, and even if we get something to prove Holly's case once and for all, he's never going to be punished."

Ah yes, *that* small detail. Christopher Masters was murdered in HMP Frankland last year. One less monster in the "Monster Mansion," as it's unaffectionately known.

"You could argue Jacob Pope did the job when he plunged that metal shank into Masters' lung."

I'm briefly shocked by Parnell, usually our straight-shooting purveyor of fair criminal justice. It's not that he never *thinks* these things, of course. We all *think* them. We just don't say them. And the reason we don't say them is that we don't actually believe them. It's just our inner animal rearing up. Our angry child kicking out.

But I know what Parnell's doing. He's testing Dyer. Getting the measure of her.

He gets bugger all.

"Shall I pass on your thanks, Lu?" Dyer aims her coffee cup at the bin; a perfectly executed lob. "I'm visiting him later."

"And Cat's going with her." Steele turns to me, grinning. "Sorry, I told you your day was about to get longer."

"What's that in aid of?" asks Parnell, his eyes shuttling between Steele and Dyer.

"Jacob Pope always said he killed Masters because he couldn't bear his bragging," explains Steele. "Well, let's see if he bragged about any day trips to Cambridgeshire."

"So we're going all the way to Frankland? Two hundred and

fifty plus miles?" I frame it as a question rather than the plaintive whine it genuinely is. "That's me in the bad books, then. I'm supposed to be at Victoria Park by seven p.m. A picnic."

Steele laughs and stands up, quickly followed by Dyer. Side by side, Dyer's practically Queen Kong to Steele's Tinkerbell, but then fooling people with her size has been Steele's stock-in-trade for years. If push came to shove, my money would be on the warrior pixie, every time.

"You're in luck, Kinsella," she says. "Pope was moved to Belmarsh after the Masters 'incident.' You'll be there and back in a few hours." She opens her door, casting another look over me. "Although you could do with going home and getting changed first. Your clothes are damp. I can smell them from here."

"Go home? I live South-West, boss. Belmarsh is South-East. It's a massive detour."

I push myself off the wall, my limbs like bags of cement. I'm lacking the energy for a picnic, never mind a playdate with a killer.

"Borrow something of Emily's then. God knows, she's got half of Topshop under her desk. And you're roughly the same size."

Roughly. In the way a square can be roughly the same size of a circle.

"Sod that, I'm not risking Emily's wrath." *Or one of her bandage-wrap dresses.*

"I thought the ice had thawed between you pair?"

"There was never any ice, for God's sake," I say, not quite truthfully. "We're just different people, that's all." I could add, "In the sense that she's lazy and I'm not," but Dyer's presence stops me. I wouldn't snipe about a colleague in front of a stranger and, more importantly, I don't want Dyer thinking I'm difficult. Her opinion matters, almost instinctively. "Honestly, I'll pop out and buy something. Easier all round."

Steele's hand's on my back, ushering me out the door. "Your choice, but one way or the other, tidy yourself up. The only reason you're going is that you're female and you're nearer Pope's age, so he might take a shine to you, might speak a bit more freely. There's less chance of that happening if you smell like a wet dog."

Parnell won't be happy. It hasn't been a year since I was last used as bait to draw a confession from a woman-hating narcissist—a woman-hating narcissist who, rather unfortunately, decided against confessing in favor of spitting in my face. To hear Parnell tell it, and he is fond of telling it, it was the worst atrocity ever to sully our fine station. A despicable act that still turns him purple from the collar up.

He's a good man, Parnell. A protector. A real rock.

And in a turn of events I still can't get my head around, this good man now knows the other good man in my life.

Whether this is a good thing?

The jury's still out.

Parnell stays silent until we're back at our desks, facing each other across the partition that stops my mess becoming his mess. It's obvious he's itching to say something, though. It's in the twitch of his jowl and the clicking of his tongue. Those familiar little tics that signal he's about to pour forth.

Assuming today's Sermon at the Desk will be on the perils of making yourself pretty for Category A killers, I cut him off at the pass with a short, sharp request.

"Look, take it up with her, OK? I just follow orders."

He makes a noise I take to mean "since when?" but he's smiling. I've read him wrong.

"Hey, hold your horses, *touchy*. I wasn't going to say a word about that. One: nobody listens, and two: there's a very big difference this time. You won't be on your own. You'll have Dyer *and* a guard in the room."

"She's impressive, huh?" I say. "Dyer."

"You're telling me. Did you see the way she aimed that coffee cup in the bin? She wasn't even looking. She practices, I bet."

"The boss said you knew each other?" I'm trying to play it cool but I admit, I'm hungry for scraps—cases, commendations, career trajectory, even previous hairstyles will do.

Parnell disappoints. "We sat on the same HR org chart once upon a time, but I wouldn't say I know her. I know the name, the face. I know she took down some major players pretty early in her career." He slaps his hands together gleefully. "Anyway, forget her, I'm more interested in this picnic. You're not usually one for the great outdoors. You must have it *reeeeeal* bad, is all I can say." I ignore him, busying myself with online banking, checking I've got enough spends for an emergency clothes spree. "I mean, clearly Aiden's got it bad, the poor sod. I could see that the second he plaited your hair in the pub."

"God, not this again!" I keep my eyes on the screen, but even my bank balance can't stop me smiling. "It was too hot to wear my hair down and I'd sprained my wrist playing frisbee. Who else was going to do it for me? You?"

"Would if I could, kiddo. But, you know, four boys; I haven't had the training. I can no more plait hair than I can lick my own elbow."

I laugh, which is a miracle in itself given the state of my overdraft. "Yeah, well, neither can Aiden. It fell out after two minutes, remember?"

"Ah, but he tried, and that's the whole point. It's a sign. It's a bright sign."

Picnics. Plaits. The perfectly brewed tea I wake up to most mornings. So many bright signs blackened by one very bad thing.

The thing Aiden can never know.

The thing he could never, ever forgive.

"So have you told her yet?" Parnell's lowered his voice, although there's really no need. Renée's still on the phone and Flowers is swooning over a travel website—booking a flight to Antarctica, if he's got any sense.

"Told who what?" I fan myself with a stack of overtime forms.

"Jesus, it's hotter than the sun in here now. Has our air-con got any other settings than North Pole and Club Tropicana?"

"Don't change the subject. You know who I mean. Have you told Steele about Aiden? I thought when you mentioned the picnic . . . about being in the bad books . . ."

"Well, you thought wrong." I fan myself quicker, stress relief as much as anything. "Look, I haven't decided when—*if*—I'm going to tell her. It's still early days, there might be no point." I used to find lying difficult—every childhood fib, every teenage bluff would feel wrong and inedible, like soil in my mouth. These days, the lies come easy. One after the other, word after honeyed word. "I only told you because you're a nosy bugger."

And because it was time. Time to give Aiden *something*. Time to give him a small window into who I am, beyond his lover and his mate and the girl who'd lasso the moon to make him smile.

But in place of the moon, I gave him Parnell. I gave him laughs over pints with the only father figure in my life.

Except my own father, of course. Persona non grata *again* since the beginning of this year.

"That's not fair, you know? I'm not nosy. Aiden's a really nice bloke, one of the good ones as far as I can tell, and I'm happy for you, that's all."

Bless him, he looks it too. All puffed up and proud, the archetypal Papa Bear. God knows how he'll make it through his eldest son's wedding next month. He got teary enough showing me photos of the cake.

Still, I opt for the windup. "Oh, do me a favor. You've met Aiden twice, for a total of three hours." Two televised football matches, to be precise. "You've no idea if he's one of the good ones. He could be a prick of the highest order for all you know. For all *I* know, for that matter."

Parnell leans in, the tip of his finger pointing over—*infiltrating*—my side of the partition. "You take it from me, Kinsella, if a man's prepared to plait your hair in public—or try to—then he's one of the good ones. And what's more, if he'll plait your hair in public, then he'll lay on a bloody good picnic, I'm telling you. Oh yeah, I can see it now. It'll be all canapés and petit fours." He smiles, misty-eyed and amused. "Ah, to be in the first throes again . . ."

Not quite the first throes. Not even our first picnic. It's been over eighteen months since Aiden first sat across from me in this very station, handsome and heartsick, trying to make sense of the news that his long-disappeared big sister, Maryanne, was dead.

And Parnell knows this, of course. Parnell worked Maryanne's case too. But what Parnell doesn't know is that we've barely been apart since. That we swapped numbers within days, fluids within weeks, house keys within months. Parnell thinks we've been together for the grand sum of eight weeks. And the convoluted lie I told—because convoluted is king, I learned that from Dad— about me and Aiden bumping into each other on the bus, and the bus breaking down, and the rain forcing us into the pub, and the chat flowing until dawn, *blah-di-blah-di-blah*, is frankly the least of the lies I've told to my sergeant-cum-father-figure. And it doesn't come close to the lies I've told Aiden about my dad or Maryanne.

About Dad *and* Maryanne.

3

London has its own velocity. A pulsing rhythm best played at high tempo.

Unless you're trying to get somewhere, of course.

"Two miles in twenty-five minutes. Ridiculous. Another thing I miss about Lyon."

Dyer's scowling at the traffic but I'm not missing anything right now. Not Parnell's burger-scented Citroën, with its kid paraphernalia strewn across the back seat, nor the hurly-burly of the office, where we left Flowers arguing with everyone about whether "Roommate" should be one word or two. No, for me the crawl toward Belmarsh is a welcome afternoon respite, and quite a deluxe respite too, due to the swankiness of Dyer's car. Sleek and elegant, like the woman herself. Although away from the office—away from Steele, at a guess—she's not quite so refined.

"I hate this fucking heat," she says, one willowy arm jutting out the driver-side window. "You can't sleep. You're not hungry."

"Everyone's got their feet out."

"Exactly." She drags her eyes from the road ahead, landing them squarely on me. "Nice suit, by the way. Although not the best color for a heat wave, I wouldn't have thought."

Black, as most of my work wardrobe tends to be, which means I'm being slowly cremated as we inch through Woolwich, past the cheap high street stores and their displays of flimsy summer rags. In fact, the contrast of the black fabric and the signature pinkness of my skin immediately brings to mind the image of a burned sausage, and I must be starting to smell like one too. I reach into my bag and then spritz myself with something unpronounceable, a word conjured up by marketeers.

Dyer flaps her hand, diffusing the sickly sweet scent. "Jesus, I know Steele said to tidy yourself up, but I hope that isn't for Jacob Pope's benefit."

"Christ, no," I say, mortified. "I'm just trying to get through it. It's my boyfriend, you see. He travels a lot for work and spends half his life in Duty Free, buying me perfume I don't need."

"Tough life you've got there. Does he have an older brother, by any chance?"

I glance at her left hand, at the narrow gold wedding band. "He does, actually, but he's in Canada."

"Even better. I like Canadians. They're laid-back, uncomplicated."

"You're out of luck. He's Irish, not Canadian."

"That'll do. The Irish are the same."

They are, and Aiden's a shining example. Although who knows if his brother is? His sister certainly lacked the "uncomplicated" gene.

As does Jacob Pope. Keen to show off my rush-job research, two-thirds of it gleaned in the queue at H&M, I say, "He's some work, eh? Killing his girlfriend because she neglected to mention she's a cousin of a 'business' rival. That's callous."

And childish, to be flippant. A devastating version of playing dens with your mates. *You're our friend, not their friend. Bang bang, you're dead.*

"Ah, but have you seen him?" Dyer's tone is playful, her face pure disgust. "Gorgeous cancels out callous, apparently. He can't keep up with all the marriage proposals and naked selfies he gets sent, so they say."

I have no words. There's nothing that explains that level of lunacy—or loneliness, if you're being charitable. A minute passes—maybe two car lengths, at best—before I can think of anything to fill the silence. Maybe I do miss Parnell after all. The inane chat. The incessant whistling.

"Do you honestly think he'll be able to tell us anything?" I say eventually. "From what I read, Pope isn't shy. If Masters had bragged about where Holly was buried, Pope would have said after he murdered him, surely? I mean, he practically wanted a medal for the murder. If he helped us find Holly's body, he'd have been angling for a knighthood."

"Parnell thinks he deserves a medal," she says, tip-tapping the steering wheel, eyes locked on the car in front, on its tasteful bumper sticker—*If you're gonna ride my arse at least pull my hair.*

I shake my head quickly. "No, he doesn't. He was seeing how you'd react. He likes to know who he's working with."

"Well, he should have a rough idea. We were part of the same unit back in, God . . . 2009, I think." She wrinkles her nose. "Although, I suppose I was on Organized Crime, Parnell was on street gangs. Completely different focus. We only knew each other to say hi."

And we're off again, inching a few meters closer to Belmarsh. It'd be quicker to fly to Brazil.

"But you and Steele go way back?"

Horns blare in the distance. Something going on up ahead. Probably some daydreamer taking more than half a second to get their head into gear as the lights turn green. A crime in this city. A breach of the London code.

"Well, that's the thing, we never worked together either. We just kind of know each other because we both worked for Olly Cairns, both made big strides under him. The top brass used to call us his 'alumni.' Olly joked we weren't Charlie's Angels, we were Oliver's Army."

The thought fascinates me. The idea of Steele as a work-in-progress. In my mind, she's always been the finished article, the fully formed Cop Diva, careering out of Police Training College with a warrant in one hand and a suspect's testicles in the other.

"It was Olly who started the Cardigan Kate thing." Dyer throws a look over, checking I know the reference, which I do. "He's such a windup merchant. It's not like she even wore them *that* often—she's always been a stylish one, Kate—but you know how these things start. Once he said it, it stuck."

"We call her Kate Kardashian now. The glossy hair. The designer shoes."

"You're a braver woman than me." So speaks the woman giving the finger to a tanker driver. "I bet you don't say it to her face."

"I don't, 'cos I'm scared I'll catch her in a bad mood. Some of the others do, though. She thinks it's hilarious."

Dyer smirks. "Isn't HRT a wonderful thing?"

I laugh, knowing it's something Steele would say herself, but there it is again, that prickly undertone. One snidey little quip dressed up as a joke that says, *"I'm younger than her, more game for a laugh."*

I'm better?

She'd have a bloody hard job.

"Do you want some advice, Cat?"

Not really, but when you're in a confined space with someone three ranks higher, there's only one career-savvy response. "Of course, ma'am."

She nods, happy I've played along. "OK, well, it's like I always used to say to my boys when they were scared of a spider—'Remember, it's more scared of you than you are of it.'" I try not to look baffled. "Steele," she explains, "she thinks very highly of you. She told me about a couple of your cases, said you've got great potential." She glances in the rearview mirror, as if seeking permission from her own reflection to get to the real point. "Maybe she's a bit scared of that potential, though. Scared you'll surpass her, that you won't always think of her as near-divine." I'm still not sure where this is headed so I smile inanely. *Was there advice in there?* "Don't be intimidated by her is all I'm saying. Respect her, but don't be held back by thinking you're less."

And don't tell her you're dating a victim's brother just yet.

For a mad, dumb second, I think of asking Dyer's advice on that. I nearly do too, but she cuts in again, saving me from myself.

"And I think you should take the lead with Pope, OK? Let's see some of that famed Cat Kinsella potential."

There are very few places that can't be cheered by the sun, or at least elevated a little above the gray of their norm. From graveyards to building sites, from car parks to schools, *everywhere* looks better with a shot of vitamin D.

And yet Belmarsh on a summer's day is as bleak as Belmarsh on a winter's morning. The high stone walls. The razor-wire fences. The sense of hopelessness that clouds all beauty. The inherent jumpiness that chills the air, even when temperatures tip past thirty.

I don't like prisons, which might seem as obvious a statement as "I don't like raw chicken." But it's not the obvious things for me; the nerves, the fear, the pin-sharp awareness that on a good-to-bad-guy ratio, you're seriously outgunned. It's more the realization that in my world, all roads lead here. That my job, my vocation, is geared toward *this*—these concrete volcanoes, these boiling pots of rage. And don't get me wrong, *this* is what most deserve. While a few might deserve better, there's plenty who deserve worse.

Still, it's hard to feel good about it. To bask in the grimness and consider it a job well done.

"Twenty minutes," warns Dyer as we're processed through reception; bodies and fingertips scanned, clothes searched, possessions locked away. "Pope'll want to chat. We're a novelty, remember? A break from the routine. There's a chance he'll say anything to keep our interest, so be mindful of that. If we've got nowhere in twenty minutes, we leave."

We're led across a courtyard at the heart of the redbrick fortress—

four three-story blocks, each split into three separate wings, where overworked prison officers do daily battle, curtailing the movement, whims, and demons of far too many prisoners.

"Oh, we get all sorts in here," explains our bald, insufferably chatty PO, as we trail him through a series of locked gates and doors until we reach House Block 1, the home to Belmarsh's long-terms and lifers. "We're a high-security prison, see, but also a local one, which means we get the lot—shoplifters, terror suspects, debt-dodgers, pedophiles. I've worked with them all." Halfway down a corridor, we come to a stop outside a door. His hand hovers over the handle, key primed by the lock. Lowering his voice, he says, "Give me a lifer, like your boy in there, any day. They're not just passing through, see. They're trying to make some sort of a life for themselves, so they tend to keep their heads down, toe the line."

"By killing another inmate?" says Dyer, pleased to shut him up.

The PO shrugs. "Whatever he did up North, he's been a good boy here."

Presumably, on account of being a good boy, Jacob Pope isn't in handcuffs. Just the standard maroon tracksuit and a pair of trainers so white they're luminous. He stands up as we walk in, a shocking show of chivalry given the lack shown to his girlfriend.

Tall and lean, with eyes the color of spring grass, Jacob Pope could have been a model. He could have been anything, if you ask me. Men this handsome tend to have an easy ride through life, picking the low-hanging fruit and the highest opportunities, but unfortunately for Pope, he picked crime, or crime picked him, and twenty bad decisions later, he's eating his porridge next to a serial killer.

We shake hands, introduce ourselves. Pope sits only after we do, the overhead light illuminating one singular imperfection—a small but angry gash across the center of his forehead.

"What's that, Jacob?" I ask, tapping my own in the same spot.

"Were you talking instead of listening?" His face is blank. I let out a little laugh. "Sorry, just something my grandad used to say. It means have you been fighting?"

He's smiling too. "Good one. 'Talking instead of listening.' I'll have to remember that." He extends his arms above his shoulders, pushing up and down. "Not fighting—bench-pressing. There's only two things keep you safe in prison and it ain't the screws, I can tell you." I look intrigued although I know the answer. "Good hearing and a good physique. Can't do much about the first but plenty about the second. And this . . ." He traces the cut with his index finger. "Did one too many reps, got a bit shaky, dropped the weight."

"Ouch." I grimace. "Taking the old 'no pain, no gain' a bit too literally there."

"Ain't that the truth? Screws weren't too quick to help me, though—that's another truth for ya. Makes me miss the Mansion. Who'd have thought a London boy would prefer it up north?"

He's definitely a London boy. I looked it up on the way over. But he isn't quite the gangster boy the *ain't*s and *ya*s would have you believe. Daddy worked in shipping, while Mummy did the school run back and forth to Kingston Grammar—the school he was finally expelled from for biting a teacher on the face.

"You preferred Frankland to here?" I ask, all casual curiosity, like I'm after holiday recommendations. "'Cos you must have known they'd move you after . . ."

"Preferred's a bit strong," he says, talking over me. "You're just swapping shit for shite, really. Food's as rank. Mattress is just as lumpy. It's good that my mum's nearer for visits, but I got more respect up there, you know—and they'd have carried me down J-wing shoulder-fucking-high for killing that bastard Masters, that's the truth. Proper fucking nuisance, he was." His fingers open and shut, miming mouths snapping open. "Never shut up, did he? On and on and on and on."

"What about?"

"Loads of things. D'ya know he once told me that he nearly let that Stephanie one go. She was a bit chunky for him, that's what he said. He was going to say, 'Sorry, I've just let the room, you're too late,' and let her get on her way. But then he saw she was wearing these sexy red heels and he thought, *fuck it*, just like that. Mad, innit? Those shoes got her killed."

Dyer's chewing the side of her cheek, channeling waves of pure hate across the table.

I move things on. "Did he ever talk about Cambridgeshire? Ever mention a village called Caxton?"

He shakes his head, uninterested.

"OK, so what else? You spend a lot of time cooped up in your cells, the chat must be flying when you get together."

"We call them rooms now, not cells. The word 'cell' is dehumanizing." He's saying it to wind me up but I apologize immediately to avoid giving him the satisfaction. "Look, he talked about anything and everything. If it wasn't his sick fantasies, it was DIY, or fishing, or the problem with multiculturalism."

"I've worked with a few people like that. I didn't stab them through the lung though."

"Then their fantasies weren't sick enough."

"Care to share them?" I say it brightly, showing no fear, no hesitation about the filth he might divulge.

He grins. "I know what this is about, you know. It's about that Holly Kemp."

His eyes glint with the glory of having the upper hand for once. When your life revolves around being told what time you can eat, shit, and sleep, the power must be intoxicating.

Dyer speaks suddenly. "Clever old you, Jacob. Although seeing as the Governor told you the reason for our visit, I'm not exactly bowled over by your powers of perception."

I'd almost forgotten she was here. When she'd said "take the lead," I assumed she'd be on percussion, at least. Up until now, I've been standing at the mic, solo.

Pope's just as surprised. "Oh, so she speaks then? Detective Chief Inspector Tessa Dyer. Chris always said you were a hard bitch."

Dyer smiles at the compliment. I smile inwardly at the "Chris."

Not Christopher. Not Masters. Not "that bastard."

Chris.

An *in*.

Pope folds his arms high across his chest, his biceps like battering rams. "You know, Dyer, I don't have to talk to you if I don't want to. And I'm missing Association for this, so I'd be a bit more pally if I were you, like your mate here."

Association: the two-hour window where inmates are allowed to mingle, playing pool, having chats, having full-scale brawls if the wrong slur is thrown.

Dyer looks at me, jerking her head toward Pope. "And to think, that PO said he was a good boy."

I look at Pope, jerking my head toward Dyer. "And to think, *she* said it was a waste of time coming to see you. Said you'd be all hot air, just desperate for company. But she's wrong, isn't she? *Chris* told you something about Holly. You might have found him annoying, banging on all the time, but you were friends, weren't you? Initially, at least."

I hope I'm right about this. And I hope against all hope that Dyer doesn't mind being made the stooge—that I've read this right, cast us in the right roles.

It feels weird without Parnell. Like tangoing with a new partner.

"Friends? Let me tell you something, I've been locked up for nearly two years now, and I'm still working out what the word 'friend' means in here. We chatted, OK, passed the time, played a few cards. He taught me ten-card rummy, although he didn't teach me how to win. Still say those cards were rigged, the wanker."

"But you didn't kill him over a card game." I open my notebook. "*I couldn't take it, listening to him, what he did to those girls.* Which girls, Jacob?"

He hesitates, head tilted. "OK, what's it worth? 'Cos I want Enhanced Status."

"Ah, come on, mate, reason with me here." The "mate" tastes like grit but it feels right to throw it in. "You killed another prisoner. Enhanced Status, extra privileges, that's going to be a long road, I'm afraid. We'll see what we can do, but . . ."

"I want extra visits for my mum and more time out of my room."

"We're going." Dyer pushes her chair out. "Thanks for your time, Jacob. Enjoy the next thirty years."

Pope's hands are on the table, long fingers splayed. He stares at them for what feels like a century, weighing things up. Dyer's on her feet. I fiddle with my notebook, playing for time.

It pays off.

"You'll see what you can do, right?" I neither yay nor nay but something in my neutral face reassures him. "Look, first he says he did kill her, then he says he didn't. Reckon he only said he did to wind *you* up."

Dyer sighs, one eye on the door. "Yeah, we know that, Jacob. He'd been playing that game for years. But we came here for detail. If you don't have any . . ."

He puts a finger to his lips, shushing her. "So I say to Chris, 'Seriously, mate? Holly Kemp was seen on your fucking doorstep and then she goes missing. Bit of a coincidence, nudge nudge.' But he says, 'That bitch made that up.'" Serena Bailey, presumably. I think about clarifying before deciding it's not fair to introduce her name to this animal. "Then a few weeks later, we're watching TV—the weather, although God knows why—and that one with the long blond hair and the massive tits comes on, and he leans over and says, 'Looks a bit like Holly, doesn't she? Only her tits were fake, which was a bit disappointing.' And then he starts going on about how they felt, how they stayed rock-hard, pointing upward, even when he knocked her on her back."

Dyer sits down again, her mouth pursed, contemplating something. Eventually, "Did Masters ever talk about friends, people he was close to on the outside?"

It's not the question either me or Pope are expecting, although it's a good one. We need a name—a friend, a relative, a business associate, anyone who gives Masters a reason to be passing through Cambridgeshire.

"He talked about his ex-wife a bit, his kids—'my girls.' Don't recall no one else. Doubt he had many friends. Independent sort of a bloke—I mean, *fiercely* independent. Went mad if you told him one of the crossword clues, you know what I'm saying? Wanted to do it all himself."

Dyer says nothing. My cue to take the lead again.

"So this stuff about Holly, why didn't you say anything at the time?"

"What, grass? You don't do that in here, darlin'.' You might smack someone around the head with a cue ball, but you don't grass them up."

"But when you killed him? Surely all bets were off then?"

He shrugs. "Look, they asked me why I did it and I told them—because I was tired of fucking listening to his sick fucking stories. Subject closed. No one asked for any details and I certainly wasn't giving them."

"And yet along we come and you can't be more helpful."

He gives Dyer a sour look. Me, a smile. "Along *you* come, what was your name again? Cath? Well, what can I say, Cath? You don't get to talk to many pretty young girls stuck in here. Gotta make the most of it."

I offer a small sweet grin, placing my hands together on the table. "Unfortunately, Jacob, not having access to pretty girls is the price you and the likes of Christopher Masters pay for killing them. Although at least you've got your fan club, eh?"

"*The likes of*? Do not put me in the same category as that bastard." The gangster patois slips as quickly as his smile. "Big difference between me and Masters."

"A difference in body count, sure."

He's agitated, pumping one fist on top of the other. *One potato, two potato, three potato, four.* "Crime of passion—there's your big difference. His victims had done nothing to him, *nothing*, whereas *she'd* disrespected me, told lies. And do you have any idea what my bosses would have done *to me* if they knew I'd been sleeping with the enemy? I didn't have any choice. It was the only way to prove I was still one of them." He honestly believes his own spin. "And I was drunk."

I stare at him, at the perfect skin, the grass-green eyes, at the sandy hair running a little too long, all the better to run your hands through.

He's repulsive.

"You were drunk?" I repeat, lip curled. "Do you know the last time I used that excuse, Jacob? I'd had one too many mojitos and told a colleague his ex-girlfriend was boring. You're a fucking disgrace and I hope you never see the light of day again."

"I'm sorry, it was the drunk comment, the way he just threw it in as an excuse. Oh, and what he said about Stephanie—how her shoes got her killed. Funny, I always thought that was Masters' doing."

As we head back to Dyer's car, my phone's buzzing in my hand, demanding my attention, but I'm more concerned with explaining my sweary outburst to my honorary boss for the afternoon.

And it'll only be Aiden anyway. Asking me what's the difference between a quiche and a flan, and do I want "poncey" bread or will a crusty white loaf do?

"Don't worry about it," she says. "You did well in there. Really well."

I actually blush. I'm hoping her Jackie O sunglasses will keep her from noticing.

"Did I? We didn't get anything that helpful."

"Mind if I . . . ?" She pulls cigarettes from her bag, offering me the packet. Briefly, a stupid desire to fit in, to bond, even, almost makes me accept, but the thought of kissing Aiden later stops me. "That stuff Masters said about Holly—that's something. It's more than 'I did it,' which is all he'd ever say to us."

Something scratches at me though, prickly heat on my brain. "So we believe Pope then?"

She lights up. "You don't?"

"Not sure. He gave it up quite easily. The minute I said we'd look into privileges . . ."

"In his dreams."

"Well, yeah, but he doesn't know that."

"He knew about her breast implants, though. I know the tabloids were bad but I don't remember them ever mentioning those."

We're at the car now, mercifully shaded by the branches of a huge draping willow tree. Dyer sits on the hood to finish her smoke, but I don't take it as an invitation. With my luck, I'll scratch it.

"A guy like Pope," I say, "I reckon he'd be a connoisseur. He'd know a fake pair from a real pair just by looking at her photo. And I mean, they were . . ."

"On display," offers Dyer, taking a long drag. "Honestly, it was maddening. We had other photos—cute ones from when she was a kid, sitting on Santa's knee, holding the school rabbit, that kind of thing. Papers still ran with the glamour shots."

"Surprise fucking surprise." I've sworn once in front of her, might as well let the floodgates open. "Anyway, look, I'm not saying I don't believe him. I just don't know how worthwhile it all was."

She points the cigarette at me. "Have you met many convicted killers, Cat? Conducted many prison interviews?"

"No. When I meet them, they're usually still as pure as the driven snow, protesting their innocence."

"Well then, it was worthwhile. A learning exercise."

Which is lovely, but with eight live cases and an inbox that growls at me every time I log on, I could have done with leaving the lessons for another sunny day.

Although I enjoyed it, if "enjoy" can ever be the right word. I enjoyed Dyer, anyhow. She has the clout of Steele but with a kind of head girl "cool." A heady mix. Something to aspire to.

I wiggle my phone at her. "Better check this. Someone's after me."

Someone being my sister, Jacqui. Five missed calls, no voicemail. One text.

Dad's in A&E—the Whittington. You need to get here ASAP
15:59

"Oh my God, my dad's in the hospital."

Concern floods Dyer's face—more of it than I'd expect from someone I only met a few hours ago. "Oh hell, Cat, what's wrong with him?"

"Um, I don't know. My sister hasn't said." Embarrassment bites hard. I know this isn't normal.

Give me something, Jacqs. A sprained ankle? An aneurysm?

I try calling but her phone rings out. Is this a good sign? A bad sign? Is she holding his hand while he takes his last breath? Or is she on the toilet? Paying for parking?

"Right." Dyer throws her cigarette down. "Where is he?"

"The Whittington—bloody miles away."

"OK, OK." She opens the back door and throws her bag on the seat, murmuring to herself, making some kind of calculation. "Right, get in. This is what's going to happen. I'm going to drop you at Plumstead station and you're going to get the Thameslink to London Bridge, then the Northern Line to Archway. It's the quickest way. I'd drive you there myself but it'll take too long. We'd get to the coast quicker than we'd get to North London at rush hour."

I nod, succumbing to her efficiency. Or, at least I think I nod. I feel strange, slightly outside myself.

"Unless you don't want to be on your own, of course. In which case, I'll drive you to the door."

I hear myself saying, "No, no, it's fine" but everything's not fine. It was fine ten minutes ago when I was seated across from a double-murderer. That windowless room, with its harsh lights and nailed-down table, seems like the softest, safest cocoon in the whole world, now that I'm out here dealing with the fact Dad might be . . .

God knows.

I know I should call Aiden. But if I call him, he'll want to do something. Meet me there, wait outside, buy Dad grapes, donate a kidney? I've no idea what state my only remaining parent is in.

With a kick of shame, I tap out a text instead.

Can't make picnic. Sorry.

Aiden deserves better, but even through the panic, I'm a pragmatist.

He can't be anywhere near that hospital.

Aiden can't be anywhere near my sister.

4

Hot weather always makes casualties spike and so, unsurprisingly, A&E is packed to the rafters with not just the usual mix of blood, guts, and people with minor ailments who refuse to wait two days to see their GP, but also heatstroke and lager-stroke, judging by the state of a few louts.

Right now, I couldn't care less about any of them. I only care about Dad. I want to make amends. Make promises we won't keep. I want to change his dressing, push his wheelchair, lecture him about mixing his medication with his nightly Jack and Coke.

I need to find Jacqui.

I don't spot her at first. My sister's hair has been as blond as golden wheat for as long as I remember and I'm thrown by its reddish hue. Saddened by it, even. By the fact I didn't know she'd dyed it.

She's smiling though, so that's something. I'll take that as a sign we're not orphans just yet. Her now coppery head is dipped low, headphones in, watching something on her phone. As I get closer, the smile gets wider and the screen comes into full view. An episode of *Friends* we've watched fifty times already.

I stand behind, tug a headphone from her ear. "Is that 'The One Where Monica Scares the Shit out of Ross by Leaving a Message That Their Dad's in the Hospital with No Other Frigging Detail'?"

She turns her head, but not enough to face me. "You can't have been that scared. I left the message three hours ago."

"I was inside a prison. I didn't have my phone."

She turns fully this time, her eyes rolling at my excuse, or rather the places my job takes me. Against the sterile white backdrop, her skin looks pasty, her face drawn. And the red definitely doesn't suit her, although if I'm asked I'll say it does.

"And it was South-East London," I blabber on. "It took me over an hour to get here. Someone was taken ill at Maze Hill, see, and then London Bridge was overcrowded and . . . Jesus, why am I even explaining myself? What's happened? Where's Dad?"

She's on her feet, disappearing into a gargantuan green tote bag. *Good Vibes Only!* it states, which suits head-in-the-sand Jacqui to a T.

"Car keys, car keys," she mutters, then almost as an afterthought, "He's broken his arm. And there's some bruising too. He's through those double doors. I needed a break so I came out for a bit. It's pretty grim in there." No gesture to signal where "there" might be. "Anyway, you can take over now. Me and Finn have been here for hours. Ash's working away so there was no one to pick up Finn, which meant I had to take him out of school early and the poor guy's missed his Sports Day. He'd been practicing all week for the hula-hoop challenge. He's gutted."

"Hula hoops! A broken arm!" I keep my voice down in the name of common decency but my anger could power the whole hospital. "I've been imagining all sorts, Jacqs. Car accidents. Heart attacks."

A gunshot wound, courtesy of his "boss" Frank Hickey's enemies.

She stops rummaging, amused. "A heart attack? As if! Dad's fitter than most men half his age."

Of course he is. On Jacqui's rosy-glow plane of existence, Dad's the fittest man, the kindest man, the shrewdest man. *The Man.*

"So where's Finn?" I say, looking around. The thought of seeing my barrel-of-joy nephew momentarily cools my jets.

"He's getting a Wonder Green smoothie from the kiosk."

This detail is pure Jacqui. God forbid I think she's letting him drink Coke or beer or battery acid.

"So let me get this straight before Finn gets back . . ." I try to stay calm, visualizing a great big red STOP sign—a therapist's tip for keeping it together when you're about to lose your shit. "You didn't think it would be nice to text, *There's no need to panic but*

Dad's in the hospital with a broken arm instead of, *Dad's in the hospital, you need to get here ASAP?*"

She doesn't answer. Too busy emptying her tote onto the seat, the contents piling up like landfill waste—wet wipes, Haribo, makeup bags, sunscreen, flip-flops, phone chargers, and if I'm not very much mistaken, pepper spray, although I'm going to choose my battles and let that one go.

"Jesus, let me, would you?" I nudge her out the way, taking over the excavation. "You're useless at looking for things. You'd be no use at a crime scene." I unzip one compartment, then another. Ten seconds later, job done. "Here."

She snatches them off me, then gathers up her stuff. "Family's never been your priority, Cat. Are you honestly telling me you'd have come if I'd said there was no need to panic?"

"Hold on, you're saying you were *deliberately* vague?" I could cheerfully slap her, put her in the bed next to Dad. "That's cruel, Jacqs. That's not fair."

She leans in for a kiss, or rather a lazy sweep of her cheek against mine. "Look, I have to go, but I'd quit with the tone, baby sis. Manipulating you into visiting your own dad in the hospital—I think that says more about you than it does about me."

"Auntie Caaaaaat!" Finn's voice behind me, bouncy and breathless, saves me from having to admit she's probably right.

I spin around. He's had a haircut since I last saw him. He has kind of a "do" now, something styled and complicated and glistening with gel.

"Hey, Finn-bo." He gives me more of a headbutt than a kiss. "How's my favorite nephew doing?"

"Er, you've only got one nephew, *duh*." He unscrews the cap of the smoothie, slurps half in one go.

"Who knows?" I say to Jacqui, quietly. "Only one that I'm aware of. I doubt safe sex has ever been high on Noel's priority list."

Jacqui's face sours and I almost laugh. The fact she finds the idea of our brother having a sex life more unpalatable than the fact he's currently languishing in a Spanish prison on drug charges sums up everything that's wrong with our family.

Finn tugs my arm. "Hey, guess what, Auntie Cat? Two things, two things."

"Um . . . you're having McDonald's for dinner?"

"*Yeah, right*, when does Mum *ever* let me eat anything I like?"

I try another guess. "You're getting a dog?"

"No. Even better. Uncle Frank gave me £50. Fifty!"

"You just missed him," Jacqui says, as though this is a great shame. "He said to say hi."

"You said two things," I remind Finn, instantly blocking any talk of Frank Hickey. "What's the second?"

"Oh yeah!" He lets out a loud screech. "Grandad's got a girl-friend."

He's doubled over. This is clearly the funniest thing that Finn's ever heard. It's the most heartbreaking thing from my side, because despite the fact that Dad's rarely been without female action since Mum died—and let's be honest, for the most part when she was alive—they've always been abstract. He's always kept them private. If Finn knows about this one, it means this one could be serious. This could be the one who finally usurps Mum.

Not for us, obviously, but in Finn's life. Finn has no memories of Mum; he was only one when she died. And with Ash's mum dead before Ash even reached his teens, Finn's never had a grandma. Although knowing Dad, this "grandma" could still be paying off her student loan.

"Jacqs?" It's all I can manage.

"Don't start, Cat—she's called Ange and she's nice."

"I wasn't planning on starting anything." On the contrary, I want this conversation over as quickly as possible.

"You missed her as well, actually." She hoists her bag onto her shoulder, ushering Finn toward the exit. "She brought Dad in—

insisted on it, thank God. She left about an hour ago to check on the pub."

So it *is* serious.

"Wow."

"Yeah, wow. A lot can happen in six months. Maybe if you visited him more often . . ."

I ruminate on the name. Ange. Angela. I didn't go to school with any Angelas so I'll take a punt she's older than me.

"So how did he break his arm?" I shout at Jacqui's departing back.

Parting the seas? Healing the sick? Rescuing a kitten from an old lady's tree?

She stops in front of the reception desk, where an old guy with an eye patch is crying because there's no one to take him home. I want to cry too. I want to flash my warrant card, call Parnell, get this far worthier cause than Dad the help he so blatantly needs.

But blood is inconveniently thicker than water.

"Something to do with a beer barrel," Jacqui says, making a circular shape with both hands. "I said to him, 'It's ridiculous. You pay people to do that stuff nowadays.' But you know what he's like."

Yeah, *I* do, Jacqs. And it's a far cry from all the *World's Best Dad!* merchandise you bombard him with.

"OK, well, I'd better go and see the patient then. Where is he, exactly?"

She tips her head to a spot behind me. "Through the swing doors, right down the bottom. Oh, and I forgot, I got him these. There was a stall outside."

From another bag compartment, she produces an apple and a bruised pear. I know he won't eat them, but with Jacqui, that's not the point. Jacqui doesn't care about outcomes as long as she's doing "the done thing."

"Right, can we *finally* go now?" She's trying to sound put-upon, but we both know there's more to it. "It's just these places, you know . . ."

"I know. Go on, bugger off. See ya, Finn-bo."

Finn isn't listening. He's got Jacqui's headphones in, doing a little dance to some freeform jazz, judging by his complete lack of rhythm.

I blow Jacqui a kiss, feeling bad that she bore the brunt of today. Feeling sad that she's spent too much time in hospitals already. Too many nights spent carrying Finn over their aggressively lit thresholds. Timing seizures. Learning medication schedules. Basically, worrying herself old.

Hospitals don't bother me.

When you work for the dead, even the sick seem kind of fortunate.

I find Dad looking far worse than I expected on a trolley bed, sandwiched between two cubicles. To his left, there's an old lady with a beehive and a split chin. To his right, a full-scale amputation, if the noise is anything to go by. He rallies when he sees me, pushing himself up a little higher using his good arm, wincing sharply at the effort.

"Jesus, I think my ribs are in a bad way."

There's no "think" about it. His shirt is open all the way down, revealing not only his daily commitment to one hundred–plus crunches, but also a tramline bruise on the cusp of turning blue.

"Have you looked in the mirror? Your face isn't looking too hot either."

He presses his jaw. "Thanks very much, sweetheart. Good to see you too."

I stand at the foot of the trolley, center stage, so he can't avoid my eyes. "So when did this happen?"

"This morning." He looks away as he says it. Not quite the breezy liar he once was.

"I see. Morning, as in eleven a.m.? Or morning, as in two a.m.?"

His gaze lands back, unimpressed. "Does it matter?"

He can play the innocent but we both know it does. We both

know that in Dad's world, the subterranean world he's gone back to, the worst things happen once the sun's gone down. Betrayals in the dark. Lessons taught when you least expect them.

And I know that bruise is more than half a day old.

"Must have been a big barrel," I say, drawing first blood. "This barrel have a name?"

"Yeah." He smiles, then flinches, the tiny movement costing him dearly. "God's Twisted Sister. It's an oatmeal stout we're trialing."

"Fine, have it your way. But the doctors aren't stupid, you know. Forget your arm, that bruise is a dead giveaway." I lean forward, peering closer at his chest. "So, what was it, Dad? An iron bar? A baseball bat?"

I see it cross his face, that split second where he thinks about lying. Where he forgets that we know the very worst things about each other—that he's a criminal and I'm worse; I'm his protector.

"Ah, they won't bother with me. Knives and guns is all they care about." *Translation: a good old-fashioned beating isn't worth the paperwork.* "One of the nurses, Keeley, was telling me . . ."

"First-name terms already. Good work, Dad. Glad to see 'Ange' isn't cramping your style."

I can no sooner stop myself baiting this man than I can stop myself loving him. I've been doing both for so long, I don't know who I'd be if I stopped.

"Christ, not now, Cat." He sounds tired and defeated. Tired from the day's drama and tired of mine, my incessant needling. "Ange was a bloody angel today. She doesn't deserve your . . . your . . ."

"My what?"

"Your pettiness. Either be happy for me or say nothing, OK?"

"Nothing sounds fine."

He shrugs, wincing again. "Anyway, *as I was saying*, the nurse said they had three stabbings and one gunshot wound on Saturday night alone." He points at himself. "Seriously, they'll be happy to turn a blind eye to this."

"And does that mean I have to?"

That gets a laugh. "And what are you going to do? Arrest them? Go all Charles Bronson? I wouldn't waste your time, sweetheart. It's not a bad break and the rib pain will pass. A bit of sympathy and a couple of aspirin and I'll be grand."

I sit at the side of the bed; Dad's good arm side. "It must have been bad for you to come here. I was there that night you were stabbed, remember?" Paddy's Day, 1999. Dad bleeding onto the carpet, Mum screaming that she cursed the day she ever met him. "You called Dennis Foley—a frigging vet—rather than come to the hospital."

"You remember that?" He looks at a point past my head, eyes reddening. "Christ, what sort of a father am I? I wish you only had happy memories."

And I do, a whole warehouse of them. Parties, presents, pancakes on a Saturday morning. Singalongs in the pub, long after any normal child's bedtime. Sweets after mass—sometimes even popping candy if Mum's eye was off the ball.

And then Dad met Maryanne and it wrecked everything.

"Ah, don't worry about it," I say flippantly. "Jacqui's got enough false happy memories to last us all a lifetime." I take the apple out of my bag—the bruised pear's past saving. "She got you this, by the way. Hungry?"

"An apple?" He points at his jaw. "With this?"

"Can I have it then?" I take a bite, not waiting for the answer.

"She misses you, you know, Cat. I get why you can't be around me so much, not now, but there's no need to lose Jacqui too." The implication he's lost to me burns my eyes, blurring my vision. "She's got this floristry competition next month—she was just telling me about it, she's really excited—and she's desperate to invite you, but she knows you'll say no."

Dad and Jacqui, splashing about in the shallow end of conversation: floristry, X-ray results, oatmeal stouts, Finn.

Me and Dad, it's always straight into the deep end. One reckless plunge and we're off. No topic too toxic. No pain left unexplored.

"It's because of the lad, isn't it? Aiden." Talking of painful topics. "You can't hide him from her forever. Not if it's the real thing."

"So what do you suggest? I bring him round to Jacqui's for her famous beef and Guinness stew, and then she says, 'Aiden Doyle? Wasn't that the name of the lad who lived near Gran's place, you know the one? His sister went missing while we were on holiday. Come to think of it, you look a bit like him . . .' Yeah, that's really going to work, Dad."

"Then you're going to have to pick a team at some point."

I swipe the thought away. "At some point, yeah. But for now, Jacqui's too busy with her own life to worry about mine. And that suits me just fine."

"*I* worry about you."

"Says the guy with his arm in a sling and a chest like a punching bag." I take another bite of the apple, looking him over, the different shades of skin. "So is this it now? Frank Hickey pisses someone off and you pay the price? A beating every few months. Maybe a stabbing or a shooting every now and again and just hope they miss the vital organs?"

He says nothing, but I'm not letting up. "Jacqui said Frank was here earlier. Good of him to drop by. I don't remember him bothering that time you had pneumonia."

"It *was* good of him. He's a good friend."

I laugh sharply. "Oh, he's the best, Dad, the absolute best. So good he threatened to make sure my boss *and* Aiden found out about Maryanne unless I fed him information." I lower my voice. "Information that could get people *killed*. Is that what good friends do? Blackmail each other's kids? Threaten to ruin their lives?"

"And he backed off as soon as I told him to."

"*Told him to*," I scoff. "As soon as you gave him a better offer, you mean. His right-hand man, his blood brother, back in the firm, under his thumb—he wasn't going to turn that down, was he?" I pause, pretending to work something out. "Remind me, Dad, how long did you actually manage to go straight for? Eighteen months? Two years?"

He has my wrist before I blink. "You need to wise the fuck up, sweetheart." And there it is—doting father to snarling villain. Dad could always turn on a sixpence. "You wanted Frank off your back and he wanted me back in the fold, so we made an agreement and he's honored it. Now get off your high horse and stop acting like an ungrateful little bitch."

My eyes swoop over his bruised body. "I didn't want *this*. And get off, you're hurting me."

"I'm sorry . . . I'm . . ." His grip loosens. He stares at his hand, at my wrist, dazed by his own aggression. "I'm so sorry . . . but you have to understand, *this* was the only way I could stop him, the only way I could protect you. *This* is the life I lead now. And if you work for Frank Hickey, you're going to upset some people along the way. Sometimes you'll come off better and sometimes you'll come off worse. End of story. No drama."

Just par for the course. An industrial accident of sorts.

"What was it you thought I'd do, Cat?"

Even with the circus of sound behind the curtain—the shouts, the moans, the endless pairs of shoes scuffing across floors—right now, there's only us. Me, him, and the ever-present specter of guilt.

"Did you think I'd just say, 'Ah now, Frank, would you leave the young one alone? Don't be threatening her, it's not nice,' and he'd listen?"

"Don't be ridiculous."

"So what did you think . . . *how* did you think . . . ?"

Unfinished questions clog the air, a dense mist of noxious gas.

So did I want Frank Hickey dead?

Yeah, I'm not ashamed to admit I did.

I wanted him falling off a ladder, struck by lightning, maybe floored by a fatal bout of dysentery. I'd have even settled for a peaceful passing in his bed, surrounded by the acolytes he calls family, if it meant never having to fear what he could unleash ever again.

But did I want Dad to kill him?

I'm a police officer.

Of course not.

It's late when I get to Aiden's. Too late to eat the plate of picnic food he's left in the fridge, covered in tinfoil—a scrap of paper on top, speared with a cocktail stick.

You'd test the patience of a saint, Kinsella.

Not too late for an argument, though.

"Since when have you been a heavy sleeper? I rang the bell five times." There's accusation in my voice, a cherry tomato in my hand. "What did you double-lock the door for?"

He's standing in the hallway, rubbing sleep out of his left eye and looking like everything I ever wanted in a pair of white Calvin Kleins.

"It got so late, I didn't think you were coming back here. I mean, you wouldn't know if the mighty detective was going to grace you with her presence or not."

"You've been graced nearly every night for the past month. It'd have been a fair assumption."

"Yeah, your furnace of a flat isn't much fun in a heat wave, is it? Having to leave all the windows open, getting eaten alive by mosquitoes. Much cooler—more convenient—to crash here."

I give him a flat stare. "Oh, because that's the only reason I stay. I'm only after you for your floor fan."

"OK, truth?" he says, his look a little haughty. It's a look he doesn't carry well; Aiden's the living antonym of haughty. "I locked the door to piss you off, plain and simple. Was that petty of me? Yeah. Does it make me feel two percent better? Hell, yeah." He steps into the half-light of the living room. "So come on then, eyes down for a full house—Cat Kinsella Excuse Bingo. What was it tonight? Bad reception? Battery died? Too many Bad Guys to nail to spare a thought for the Good Guy at home, waiting for one lousy update?" He shakes his head. Disgust would be too strong a word, despair its closest ally. "Seriously, Cat—'Sorry, can't make picnic' and then nothing? That's lame, even for you."

I know I deserve it but his anger still stings. I'm not used to this version. Not familiar with the hard lines of his face. I pause, buying time, eating the tomato and then poking my tongue into a filling I should have got sorted months ago.

Should I say "work"—the catch-all excuse?

"My dad was in A&E. I had to stay with him. I'm really sorry."

It's out before I overthink it. Aiden bolts over, comfort always his primal response.

"Jesus, is he OK? What happened? Are *you* OK?"

I could tell him the truth. Aiden knows that Dad's "dodgy." He never presses beyond that description and I never expand on it, because "dodgy" I can live with. "Dodgy" is benign. An almost comic interpretation. It's geezers selling gold chains in pub car parks. It's not paying the VAT. Dishing out a few slaps for an unpaid debt. It doesn't touch the sides of the stuff Dad's been involved in. It doesn't come close to the death of Aiden's sister, Maryanne.

Not Dad's doing, but arguably Dad's fault.

"Broken arm. Beer barrel." I tell him, toeing the party line.

"Ouch."

A simple response and I love him for it. For not asking for details.

"Not to make this about me," he says after a few seconds, instinctively knowing I'll be only too happy to make it about him, the subject of Dad now closed, "did I ever tell you about the time I broke my arm? I was only five. I did it a few hours before *the* biggest match in Ireland's history. Quarterfinals of the World Cup—

Ireland v Italy. No one had a bit of sympathy for me. Dad had to drive me and Mam to the hospital in Castlebar and he'd had a feed of beer already—said if he got pulled over by the guards, he'd break the other arm *and* my two legs. And Mam was hopping mad about missing the game. Like, she could hardly look at me. Even the nurses seemed fecked off at having to work their shift."

Five-year-old Aiden. If he's this sweet-natured now, after all the childhood baggage of his disappearing sister, and all the crap that adulthood throws at everyone, he must have been a complete dote back then. A rush of tenderness ripples through me. I want to be back in that hospital, telling him it doesn't matter about the game because he's the most precious thing in the world. I want to make him laugh. Kiss it better.

And I guess it's never too late.

"Which arm?" I ask, taking both his hands in mine.

He wiggles his left. "This one. Hairline fracture of the radius. There was nothing 'hairline' about the pain, I tell you. Mam reckoned they heard me screaming in Mogadishu."

I kiss it better, then Aiden kisses me better. Those cushiony Doyle lips soothing away bones and Belmarsh and the bacteria of my family.

Eventually I pull away, exhaustion settling over. While Aiden fetches glasses of water, I walk into the bedroom and brush my teeth in the en suite, splashing my face, then smearing something called a "skin soufflé" across my forehead, nose, and cheeks.

The bedroom's cool, the fan whirring at breakneck speed.

"Here."

Aiden hands me my water and, bladder be damned, I slug it down in three noisy gulps.

"So how'd you do it then?" I ask, wiping my mouth. "Your arm?"

I need more soothing before I sleep. I need a bedtime story, tales of the old country.

"Ah sure, acting the eijit, what else?" He sprawls back on the bed, arms flung the entire width. "Fell off a haystack in this oul fella's field. A contrary old bastard called Pat Hannon."

I laugh, a desperate cover for the fact that I remember Pat Hannon. I remember that field. Noel promising he'd buy me a Push Pop if I touched the electric fence for five seconds. Me like a gormless fool complying.

Dad telling Noel he'd "wipe him off the face of the earth" if he ever pulled a stunt like that again.

"I should have a shower, really," I say, letting my new suit fall to the floor. "I got rained on this morning and burned alive this afternoon. Not good."

He holds his nose, pulling a face. "Well, go on, then, stinker. But for the love of God, pull the cord afterward. You cost me a fortune in electricity."

Lights, shower switches, hairdryers, phones. There's no end to the list of things I apparently don't turn off. Aiden says my only saving grace is the fact that I turn him on. That, and the fact he loves me. Unequivocally.

Naively.

"Ah no, I can't be bothered." I pointedly turn off the fan, taking a small bow. "Anyway, I had a shower this morning. We're supposed to be saving water."

"Top marks." He pulls me onto the bed. "I'll make a friend of the earth out of you yet."

I nuzzle into him, enjoying a few minutes of closeness before we decamp to opposite sides of the bed—heat waves aren't exactly great for your sex life. "So, we're good, then?" I murmur. "You're not in a mood with me about the picnic." I have to check, despite his arms around me. Aiden's moods are light and infrequent. So light, you'd hardly notice them at all if it wasn't for the stream of kisses missing from his texts. "I mean, I haven't properly explained about earlier—about the abrupt text, why I left you hanging. I was flustered, you see. I'd just come out of a meeting in prison, and I was miles from the hospital and I just wanted to get going because I didn't know exactly what was happening. And then when I got to the hospital, I was wrapped up in Dad, and . . ."

He turns on his side to face me, his cheek smudged into his offensively soft pillow. "Jesus, take a breath, stress head. I'm not in a mood. Will you promise me something, though?"

"I'm gonna say yes." I prod him on the nose. "Although it's actually impossible to promise something until you know what you're promising. Just saying."

He ignores the technicality. "Promise me that whatever happens, if you have a meeting on the moon, or your dad's decapitated in a freak chainsaw accident, you'll make dinner with The Americans on Thursday."

The Americans. A visit from Aiden's Head Office that feels papal in scope.

I adopt a pompous tone. "I hereby swear on my honor and conscience that I, Catrina Anne Kinsella, will make dinner with The Americans on Thursday."

"And you'll laugh at their jokes and not go on *too* much about bloated bodies and severed feet?"

"They might like a bit of morgue chat."

"Actually, Kyle, our Chief Ops guy, might. He's a bit of a dark fucker. Did I ever tell you about the time he . . ."

I turn my back and curl into him, half-listening and "uh-huh-ing" periodically, but mainly trying, and failing, to imagine a life without this. Without *us*. No picnics in the fridge. No spooning in the bed. No laughing until I can't breathe at his take on something utterly mundane that happened in the day.

Then again, *no lies.*

5

"Well, his arm's still broken, if that's what you mean?"

That's been my stock response to "How's your dad?" all morning, because while the team's concern has been nothing short of lovely, on the freak-out scale, I'm a little north of ten. With just one fractured humerus, Dad's gone from being someone I never talk about to everyone's favorite topic of conversation. Advice doled out. Comparisons made. Even a full-scale reenactment of Ben Swaines thundering down the black run at St. Moritz, two French girls plowing into him and his wrist cracking in two places.

We're only getting away with this, of course, because Steele's "in with Blake"—a euphemism for "the shit's hit the fan" and the main reason we're all canceling weekend plans before we even know why his polished black brogues have deigned to grace our humble floor.

"Something's up," insists Parnell, buttering toast in our store-cupboard-cum-kitchen. "I haven't heard her fake-laugh once, and she didn't send out for pastries either."

"Christ, if it's not a pastry kind of catch-up, we're definitely doomed."

I'm not joking either.

I steal a slice of toast and take myself over to the incident board, where Christopher Masters stares back at me with dark, impassive eyes. There are two photos, actually: his official mug shot and a casual snap taken on holiday or just a sunny day out. Skinny white legs poking out of green cargo shorts. Pipe-cleaner arms. A jaunty thumbs-up to the camera.

A reminder that the worst monsters are real.

"Hard to believe all the fuss," I say, taking in his middle-aged ordinariness. "He looks like a geography teacher on a field trip."

"Not my geography teacher," grins Swaines. "Miss Fenwick, or Jules once we got into sixth form. I'm telling you, Megan Fox wouldn't have got a look in . . ."

The creak of Steele's door brings a halt to Swaines' drooling. Out she motors with Chief Superintendent Blake trailing behind. There might be a foot and £25K in salary between them, but for all his self-importance, Blake always looks nervous next to Steele. Like a teenager with his mum, waiting in the queue at parents' evening.

"Morning, m'dears. So, dental records are back, ID confirmed, no surprises there." She holds up a file. "Hell of a surprise from the postmortem, though." I look at Parnell, who gives a small "told you so" nod. "Got the results late last night."

"Holly Kemp was shot in the head," interrupts Blake, his flat, officious tone neutralizing the sudden lightning-bolt energy. "No bullet or casings were retrieved from the skull or the scene, so she was either shot elsewhere and dumped in the Caxton field, or over the course of six years, a wild animal, maybe a fox, a squirrel, a rat, made off with them." I aim a childish grin at Parnell, amused by the image. "What we have is a close-range, small-caliber gunshot wound just above her left ear, about a quarter of an inch and—"

"And what doesn't need saying," Steele breaks Blake's stride, "is that this is obviously *very* different to Christopher Masters' other victims. Her hyoid bone wasn't fractured either, which doesn't rule out strangulation, but it was present in the others."

"Why bother strangling when you've got a gun?" Flowers is sensitive to the last.

"But a bullet to the head is clinical, impersonal," I say, trying to get my head around the news.

"Not Masters' style at all," adds Parnell.

Blake ignores us, bringing things back on script. "So adding this to the markedly different burial site, we're presented with something of a situation. A rather shit situation, if I'm frank." Suppressed smiles all around. "And this is why I've formally asked Chief Inspector Steele to look into Holly Kemp's case again. We need to be seen to be considering all options."

"To be seen" tells you everything you need to know about Blake. About his love of PR. His pathological obsession with the all-important "optics."

"Um, just to say, she wasn't actually buried, sir." Yes, I'm being facetious but I'm also being factual. "She was hidden. Well hidden."

"Which suggests her killer didn't have the time or strength to dig a hole and bury her," says Parnell.

Her killer. Not Masters. With one piece of news, no longer a given.

At least not for Parnell, anyway. Swaines lands a fist on Masters' photo. "Well, there you go. This guy looks like he'd have trouble digging a sandcastle, never mind a grave."

DC Craig Cooke, a little defensive, probably on account of not exactly being Mr. Muscle himself, warns, "Don't be fooled, mate. He was a tradesman, a grafter, he renovated houses. That means being on your feet all day, carting stuff in and out of the place. He might not have been Arnie, but I bet he was fit."

Renée Akwa agrees. "Fit enough to overpower three women and dump them in Dulwich Woods."

"Yeah, three naked women. Holly wasn't naked." I look over at Steele, reminding her that I said this yesterday.

Blake presses on, not comfortable with the ad-libbing, the back-and-forth. "OK, so let me be clear about something. Very clear. We are *not* suggesting that Christopher Masters wasn't responsible for Holly Kemp's death. There was a solid witness ID, remember? Someone who put Holly with Masters immediately before she van-

SHED NO TEARS | 63

ished. However, with the story due to break, we have to make sure we're covering all bases."

"Covering our arses," murmurs Flowers.

Steele's eyes flash, and if she heard it, Blake heard it. Not that Flowers will care particularly. Solid copper that he is, he doesn't have much ambition beyond a pat on the head and a token annual pay raise.

Blake's reaching the crescendo of his speech. "Chief Inspector Steele will be making a statement to the media very shortly, simply stating that we're reviewing all evidence in light of finding Holly's remains. We're holding off on releasing the cause of death for as long as we can, though, citing investigative purposes." He shifts from foot to foot. "Now, I'm sure I don't need to tell you all that with current staffing levels, we can do without chasing our tails on this one. We're implementing a full review because we have to, but the best result all round will be to prove a link to Christopher Masters so that we can put this to bed for good. Get closure for Holly's family."

"Foster families," I correct.

Blake obviously hasn't read her Social Services file, but I have. Seven a.m. this morning, with my picnic plate on my lap, I'd buried myself in "The Ballad of Holly Kemp," the story of a girl with no luck and no roots. Dad dead from a motorcycle accident before she turned ten. Mum dead twelve months later from an overdose/broken heart. A brief mention of an aunt who had neither the space nor the inclination to take her in.

"Sir . . ." Steele looks anxious, nodding to the clock on the back wall. "Not that we're trying to get rid of you, but didn't you say you were due at the Yard at ten a.m.?"

That clock has been fast since I joined MIT4. It does the trick, though. He leaves.

Steele waits until she hears the lift closing, then, "Oh, shoot me.

He's been here for nearly two hours and he was getting on my tits after one. Anyway, it'll give him extra time to sculpt his chest hair, or whatever it is that impresses them so much over there."

Flowers' voice is peak gruff. "So now he's gone, can we just say it?"

Steele beams. "Say what, Pete, my little beacon of positivity?"

"The ice queen, Dyer. Her lot did a shoddy job. Took this witness as gospel and lumped Holly in with the others."

I'm not quite sure what Dyer did to deserve the "ice queen" mantle, other than bleach her hair white-blond and be less peppy than Steele.

"I don't think that's fair," I say, calm and even—Flowers doesn't need an excuse to accuse me of being whiny. "Six years later, she can still rattle off facts, dates, even bloody CCTV timings. That case meant a lot."

Parnell nods. "I'm with Cat. Maybe Holly got kicked into the long grass eventually, but it happens. Things slide when there's no family pushing for answers, year in, year out. Doesn't mean she ran a shoddy investigation."

I look to Steele, expecting agreement, but in its place there's discomfort. Apprehension, even. She takes a seat at DC Emily Beck's vacant desk, saying nothing at first. Picking up perfumes and spraying them, straightening papers, biding time. Putting off the inevitable, although I haven't a clue what the inevitable is.

"Look, there's a few things you all need to be aware of. Things King of the Gloss Job, Blake, neglected to mention. And this goes no further than these four walls. I mean it." A communal nod, every ear pricked. "OK, so the different dump site, the different method of killing, they're both new anomalies. But there's always been anomalies in Holly Kemp's case. Her DNA was never found at 6 Valentine Street for a start."

I'd read this but hadn't broken too much of a sweat. "Every contact leaves a trace" is great for putting the wind up suspects, but it's not infallible. It's much harder to leave DNA than the cop shows would have you believe.

"Also, no pay-as-you-go number was found in Holly's phone records."

"Didn't Dyer say the boyfriend had a theory about that?" says Parnell.

"Who, the convicted burglar who took three days to report his girlfriend missing?" Steele's face could turn milk sour. "Can't say I'm wildly interested in his theories, Lu. Although I am interested in speaking to him again. Spencer Shaw will be getting a visit very soon, that's for sure."

"Already on it," hollers Swaines from behind his row of PCs. "Haven't found him yet."

"Did he give an alibi at the time?" I ask.

"For all it was worth," Steele fires back. "He was with another girl—'a friend'—the day Holly vanished and the couple of days after. But like Dyer said, it didn't really matter after Serena Bailey's ID."

Nothing mattered after Serena Bailey's ID.

"Talking of Dyer, where is she?" I look around, as though she might be hiding somewhere. "Shouldn't she be here?"

After yesterday, I'm full of good feels for Tessa Dyer. She was so kind about Dad, driving me to the station, physically putting me on the train because she thought I looked woozy, filling my angst-ravaged head with all the minor things it could be: *My mum cut the tip of her finger off, chopping a parsnip on Christmas Day.*

"No, she shouldn't be here. Like Pete said—a bit bloody loud, I might add—Dyer'll be covering her arse right now. I'm not saying she put a foot wrong, or that I'd have done anything different, but having one of your old cases looked into is a royal slap in the face, so it's natural she'll be in defensive mode, and we, m'dears, are very much on the offensive. We'll keep her in the loop, of course.

I've let her know these latest developments. But the point is, this is *our* case now."

She pauses, batting Emily's stapler between her hands, mouth twisted as though she's unsure of the wisdom of what she's about to say.

Steele is *always* sure. This feels big.

"There's something else too," she says, finally. "And this isn't fact, it's opinion, just so that's clear. But I think it needs saying, so . . ." I lean across my desk, intrigued. Parnell's stroking his chin. Swaines is practically on Steele's lap. "Tess Dyer is a first-class officer. She came up the ranks quickly but thoroughly, and she has the blessing of the best boss I ever worked for." *But?* "But the Roommate case would have been stressful for any DCI, never mind a newly appointed one—it was only her second case as an SIO." Senior Investigating Officer. Basically, the buck stops with you. The glory or the public flogging is all yours to own. "And it was a real 'camp beds in the office' case. Folk getting their heads down in half-hour snatches, caffeine and Red Bull on a drip. And then there was the other issue . . ." The real source of her discomfort, judging by her face. "Dyer's husband was seriously ill at the time. I don't know the details—some sort of heart issue." Parnell's nodding, he remembers. "And I hate even bringing it up, but what I've heard from a few people since is that she massively underplayed it. Only Olly Cairns knew the extent of what she was going through, but he backed her to get the job done anyway. That's what he was like. He'd put his faith in you, and in return, you'd give him everything."

My respect for Dyer grows even bigger, a satellite orbiting the Earth. But I sense where Steele's going with this.

Parnell does too. "That's a lot of pressure to be under. A lot of plates to be spinning. Mistakes could get made."

"They could, Lu." Steele nods her agreement, her thanks to him for pointing out what it pained her to do. "A high-profile case, the stress of her husband, two young kids . . . it *could* have affected her performance. So now with the cause of death, the Caxton site, we have to at least consider the possibility she might have got Holly wrong, neglected other lines of inquiry."

We sit with this, briefly. A minute's silence for the career of a bloody good officer.

"But Serena Bailey, the witness?" I say, the first to break the quiet.

Steele shuffles right back into Emily's chair, her feet only just grazing the floor. "Look, we're going to go through this methodically like we would any other case. First proposition—on the balance of probability, Christopher Masters killed Holly. Serena Bailey's rock-solid ID makes it almost impossible to see how anyone else was responsible, and he admitted or implied it on several occasions. So we do exactly as Blake said—we link him to a gun, or to Cambridgeshire, or to both, preferably. Seth and Emily should be arriving in Newcastle any time now, so let's see what the ex-wife says. What else?"

"Masters' bank records," I say. "We need a petrol station, a pub, anything that puts him near Caxton around the time Holly disappeared."

"You OK to get that rushed through, Benny-boy?" Steele bats her lashes at Swaines, MIT4's official blue-eyed dreamboat and unofficial data-whore. He also rarely leaves the office, which makes him an obvious teacher's pet—Steele's faithful little pup, lovely to look at and always by her side.

"Rushed through?" I'm confused. "They're not on file already?"

"No." Steele shrugs, more bemused than bothered. "I'd have probably requested them, but then it's fine saying that with the benefit of hindsight. Like Lu said, they were spinning a lot of plates and Masters admitted being at the house that day, where an eyewitness placed him, so it wouldn't have been high priority. I'd say the focus was on getting him charged for the other three—the bodies they *did* have—before he changed his mind about pleading guilty."

And somewhere along the way, Holly Kemp falls through the cracks.

Swaines is back at his desk, hand on the phone. "Boss, just so you know, I'm running a bit low on 'rushed through' favors. HSBC, Nat-West, Barclays, they've all got backlogs."

Not surprising. London murders have been off the charts this year and we're only halfway through. Which means a six-year-old case, where the *probable* killer is already dead, really won't get any hearts pumping.

Steele points at me. "Kinsella, you try. See if you can sweet-talk them. God knows you need the practice." To think, I was almost touched then. "So, anyway, moving on to evidence of gun use, or even just an interest in guns. Emily and Seth can check with the ex-wife, but who else was Masters close to? I know the media did the whole 'loner' thing, but it's usually a cliché. He didn't run a hardware store and pick up handyman work without some sort of social skills."

"Jacob Pope didn't paint him as a loner," I say. "Said he was always mouthing off, giving his opinion on things."

"There's the lad he employed at his store," says Cooke. "Poor bastard, eh? Fancy working alongside a monster like that and not realizing."

"What about his poor ex-wife?" I say. Because seriously, how do you reconcile the man who made you breakfast, made you laugh, who played "This Little Piggy" on your newborn baby's toes, with the devil who tortured and murdered three women? *Four* women, if we're sticking tight to Steele's first proposition. "Dyer said it was her engagement that might have sparked him off. Imagine that on your conscience."

Steele shudders but doesn't join in the pity party. "Craig, go back and check Masters didn't have any gun licenses that got missed the first time around, although God help us—God help Dyer, anyway—if he did. For now, though, let's assume he got the gun on the black market, which puts the chances of finding the seller somewhere around 'don't frigging bother.'"

A thought occurs to Flowers: "Farmers have guns. We've got to consider Johnny Heath, surely? The old guy who owned the land where Holly was found."

"Or the son," I add.

Steele takes a slow, deep sigh, a preface to our second—dreaded—proposition. "OK then, since you've brought up the unthinkable, let's get it out in the open. Who's going to say it?"

"The witness was mistaken and someone else killed Holly Kemp." Renée's straight in there.

Flowers taps a piece of paper on his desk. "Well, it can't have been the son. South Cambridgeshire sent over a copy of his passport. Until recently, he hadn't been in the UK since early 2011."

Cooke chimes in. "And the old boy was eighty-two in 2012, virtually crippled, half-blind. I suppose he might have been capable of shooting her, but hiding her? No way."

"Why not?" says Renée. "We said hiding over burying could suggest a lack of strength."

It's a stretch even for me. "Come on, Ren! A frail old man with bad eyesight—there's no way he could deal with the body of a what, nine stone–something woman. He'd have had to lift her, carry her to the ditch . . ."

"He had help?" suggests Flowers.

"Well, they weren't very helpful." I'm still not convinced. "Surely anyone with two brain cells would suggest dumping her farther away from the old guy's land."

"But it's a line of inquiry, it needs looking into." Steele looks wearied by her own instruction. "Get on it—friends, family, associates of Johnny Heath."

It's a wild-goose chase, that's what it is. Trying to distance myself from the task, I remind Steele, "Dyer said she always felt there was something iffy about Spencer Shaw, but that she was told to drop it, concentrate on Masters. He's got to be our main focus, surely?"

"And he will be when we find him. Right now, though, Serena Bailey is more of a priority. Her statement is what holds everything together. We need to reinterview her ASAP, see if that ID stands up to the test of time. You never know, maybe she's questioned herself over the years?" She sits forward, bringing a hand down on the desk. "But listen up, folks, we also need to do what we always do and what—I'm going to come right out and say it—probably wasn't done enough at the time. We need to find out more about Holly. Her routines, her personality. Anyone who held a grudge who maybe wasn't considered at the time because of the Masters link. Benny-boy, get the list of her friends—there were a handful who made statements—and get us up-to-date contact details for all of them. Foster parents too."

Steele's right. Holly, the person, was inconsequential to Dyer's team. Where she was last seen, *who* she was last seen talking to, was all that defined her. Being linked with Masters diminished her in every way.

Steele glances over at Parnell. "You're quiet, Lu. You've usually got more a bit more to say for yourself."

He smiles. "Just taking it all in, boss."

"Care to make any predictions?" Parnell and I are usually in tune, an ever-reliable two-part harmony.

"I'm not sure. I think I'm still on the fence."

"Same here," I say, pleased to see normal service is in operation.

"Good." Steele points to me and Parnell, a warning to the rest. "I suggest you hop on the fence with this pair. Best place to be at this stage."

"Although I will say one thing . . ." The gravity of Parnell's tone draws all eyes to him. "I heard what Dyer said about killers not always following patterns, and yeah sure, the different dump site doesn't stress me out *too* much. Even the fact Holly wasn't naked doesn't mean anything overly conclusive. I'd even roll with a different method of killing if he'd strangled the others and clubbed Holly over the head. But shooting? That's not just a different method, that's a different psychology. A different beast, entirely."

A different beast. An apt choice of phrase, but a gloss job, if ever I heard one.

Because I know what Parnell's thinking. If I'm honest, I'm thinking it too.

That's a different *killer*, entirely.

6

I try sweet-talking. I try sour-talking. When those both fail, I opt for plain old-fashioned begging. Sadly, none of these tactics mask the fact that Christopher Masters is very much dead and an immediate threat to no one, so my request for his bank records is graded "low"—otherwise known as "yeah, whatever, we'll get round to it."

It takes longer than it should to trace Serena Bailey too. Since last contact in June 2012, when she was told, "Thanks for the ID but we don't quite have the juice to charge Masters with Holly," she's moved house, changed jobs, got a herself a brand-new mobile number, and God alone knows if she even checks her email.

Parnell's not impressed. Every witness in an unsolved murder case—even one like Holly's, with its potent whiff of "We all know who did it"—is told that they shouldn't change their contact details without informing us immediately. But then this job is basically fueled by people doing things they know they shouldn't. Hell, this job is partly populated by officers doing things they know they shouldn't. I should know; I'm one of them. And it's why, unlike Parnell, I'm a little more "live and let live."

Not so much sympathy for the devil as empathy for the fuck-up.

We finally track Serena down to a mouthful of an establishment—St. Joseph of Cupertino Roman Catholic Primary School. SJC for short. "Holy Jo's" for laughs, according to Flowers, who lives three streets away in Limehouse, a few miles east of the City. There's something distinctly un-Catholic about the building. Vernacular and functional. A dour gray smudge of 1950s architecture, erected in a rush to cope with the postwar baby boom, and to hell with looking pretty.

"Miss Bailey's outside, may God have mercy on her soul." Evelyn,

SJC's barrel of a receptionist, lets rip with a smoker's laugh and an affectionate warning. "Honest to God, they go proper nutty altogether when it gets near the end of term. You'll wish you'd worn your riot gear."

She's not wrong. Walking onto the school fields is like peaking on an LSD trip. A carnival of color, shrieking, and cartwheeling limbs. Fever-pitch emotion smacking us hard from all sides.

"So this Joseph of Cupertino," says Parnell, before shouting, "Oi, steady!" at two little whirlwinds hurtling toward us on pogo sticks, "who was he, Patron Saint of Pandemonium?"

"Dunno. Sounds Italian to me."

"'Sounds Italian?' That's the best you can do?"

"Jesus, Sarge, I'm a pick-and-choose Catholic, not a Benedictine nun. I only do the guilt and the wafer and the half-arsed attempt to give something up for Lent. I don't do obscure saint names."

"Lent?" He glances sideways at me. "What've you ever given up for Lent?"

"Doughnuts. Same every year since I was five."

He loves this. "Doughnuts! Oh, that'll get you a spot in heaven, for sure."

"God loves a trier. 'S'all you can do in the end."

"Yeah, but isn't the whole point of Lent that it should feel like a sacrifice? You barely eat bloody doughnuts."

I'm saved from further interrogation by a munchkin in a tutu and a pink "Go Jetters" T-shirt.

"I love doughnuts. I love the jammy ones. I could eat ten and not be sick."

"Me too," I say, smiling at her. "But I like the custard ones." I hunker down, eye level. "Hey, can you tell me where Miss Bailey is?"

"You're a stranger. Miss Bailey says we mustn't talk to strangers."

"That's right." I take out my warrant card. "But look, do you know what this word means?"

She stares intently. "Po-lice. The police keep us safe. I've got a book about Police Officer Pippa. She's pretty, just like Miss Bailey. And she's got a dog called Banjo. Have you got a dog?"

"I don't." A sad face, then a reassuring smile. "But I keep people safe just like Police Officer Pippa, so you can tell me where Miss Bailey is."

"Are you going to run the race too?"

For a second, I'm thrown, but of course—Sports Day. I thought the mood was too anarchic for a simple afternoon break.

"I might. Or my friend might," I say, offering up Parnell. "He's very fast."

She takes him in, looking unconcerned by his paunch, unaware of his bad knees. "Is he as fast as a cheetah? That's the fastest animal on earth."

"He is. He's faster than a cheetah on roller skates."

She laughs at this before another child calls her and she instantly loses interest. "Miss Bailey's over there," she shouts, already running, her finger pointing toward a large group of kids, adults, pushchairs, and a few dogs congregating on either side of a makeshift running track—one cone marking the start, another marking the end. "But the grown-ups' race just started. You won't be able to join now."

Shame.

We move quickly, and by the time "the grown-ups" are scuttling the last few meters in their bare feet we're in prime position to applaud them across the finish line. I take a punt on who a little girl might deem "pretty" and call out to a woman in her thirties with a swingy brown ponytail—the runner-up in the race but the clear winner in the looks department.

"Can I help?" she says, breathless, twisting her skirt around the right way. Parnell shows his warrant card and she stares at it with huge green eyes. So huge that she can't help but look slightly enchanted by it, by everything around her. The perfect face for reading stories to children. "Police? What's this about? If it's safe-guarding, I was just deputizing. You need to speak to Mrs. Hawley."

"We're not here about safeguarding. We need to speak to you about Holly Kemp."

"Oh . . . right . . . wow." There's a pink tinge to her skin—understandable when you've just run one hundred meters in the punishing afternoon heat—but the name brings a deeper flush to the surface.

"You're a hard woman to track down," says Parnell, disapprov-ingly. "I'm sure you'd have preferred us not to turn up at your place of work, but we had no choice. We had no contact details."

"I'm sorry . . . I honestly didn't think to contact you. It was all so long ago."

"Is there somewhere less rowdy we can talk?" As if to demonstrate my point, a dispute over a water balloon erupts within earshot, fol-lowed by a loud bang. "Maybe we could go inside?"

She nods and puts her shoes back on. We head toward the building, chatting predictably about the heat, and by the time we've slipped through the side entrance into the blessed cool of the assembly hall, the squeals and chants and arguments from the field have faded into background noise. Serena's classroom is at the bottom of a long bright corridor—MISS BAILEY YEAR 2 stenciled on the door, along with an instruction to WORK HARD! BE KIND! HAVE FUN!

A design for life, when you think about it. Although a lot easier to abide by when you're five rather than twenty-seven.

Every infant classroom the world over has the same distinct fra-grance. Sweaty heads and blunt crayons. Disinfectant and cheese pizza. Serena clocks my wistful smile. "I'm guessing you don't have kids. This your first time back?"

"In an infant school, yeah. I did a stranger-danger talk to a bunch of Year Sixes a few years ago. Waste of time. They were more streetwise than me."

"That's a depressing thought." She sits down on the one adult chair. "So what's this about Holly Kemp? I know it sounds awful, but I haven't thought about all that in years."

Which is bullshit. I don't care what she says, the girl who you were the very last person to see alive is going to be a significant specter in your life. Almost as significant as the people hanging from the branches of MISS BAILEY'S SPECIAL PEOPLE TREE.

Poppy. Robbie. Mum. Grandma Joan. Mandy. Noah. Auntie Beverley. Peanut.

"I'm surprised you haven't heard." Parnell takes a kiddie chair. His bulk spills out of either side but the legs hold firm, prompting me to do the same. "We've found her remains. It went out on the lunchtime news."

"It's been a hectic day." Her eyes couldn't get any wider. "Where?"

"Caxton. It's a village in Cambridgeshire."

"Cambridgeshire? That's . . ."

"Different. We know. And due to a few other discrepancies . . ." That's me, queen of the understatement—a bullet to the head being a discrepancy with a capital D. "We're revisiting the case, checking our facts again. Your ID was our cast-iron link to Masters, so we need to make sure you're as cast-iron now as you were back then."

There's a sheen of sweat on her forehead, although in fairness, there's probably one on mine too. "What discrepancies?"

"We can't go into that," I say. "Sorry, I know that probably seems unfair. As soon we can share, we will, I promise."

"Christopher Masters is dead, isn't he? I read it in the papers a while ago."

"Oh, so you had thought about it in recent years?"

It's honestly an observation. She takes it as an accusation.

"What I meant was, I've *tried* not to think about it for years and I *saw* it on the front page of the paper. Well, you couldn't miss it, it was everywhere. But I don't let myself wallow anymore. I block it out as soon as it comes into my head. I've got this therapist friend who says blocking things out is the path to a nervous breakdown, but it works for me. I just don't want to think about that day. About what I could have done."

Bystander's guilt. The complex cousin of Survivor's. Because on a rational level, what could she have done? She didn't have a sixth sense or a crystal ball. Six Valentine Street was just a house like any other the day Holly Kemp trooped up its path. But then guilt is rarely rational. I still feel guilt that my mum died, and yet none whatsoever for wishing that Frank Hickey would.

I pull a file from my bag, resting it on my lap. "We're going to need you to think about it now, Serena."

She stares at the file, knowing instinctively what it is—the document that's come to define her existence as clearly as her birth certificate. "You want to go through my statement again?"

"Just tell us about that afternoon." We don't want her thinking in terms of her statement. The exact words she committed to paper. We want to see what the passage of time has added or subtracted. We want every doubt she's ever had since, every tiny detail that's emerged during the three a.m. horrors. "I'll probably take a few notes. I know that can be distracting, but honestly, don't let it put you off your stride."

"My stride? It might be more of an amble. It was a long time ago."

"It was. A long time for Holly's loved ones to be wondering what happened to her." Parnell lays the guilt on with a trowel.

"I'd say it's obvious what happened to her, wouldn't you?" A pinch short of arsey. "I saw Holly Kemp on Christopher Masters' doorstep and she was never seen again." She bobs her head from side to side, as if bored of repeating the same mantra. "That's it. That's all there is. I said it a hundred times in 2012. I can't say it any different now."

"Pretend this is the first time," I urge. "Go back to the beginning."

"The beginning?"

I smile. "I don't mean what you had for breakfast that morning. Let's start with what brought you to Clapham that day. You lived north at the time, right?"

"Yes, I was teaching in Edgware. Riverdale Primary. That was a great school. I mean, it's OK here. There's a good management team and the kids are lovely, but . . . oh, forget I said anything. It's fine, it's just different. It's an inner-city school whereas Riverdale—Edgware, really—had that sweet suburban feel. I'm just being a snob, ignore me." She flaps her hands, flustered. "Anyway, I was picking up tickets, in answer to your question. I was a real gig-goer in those days. I don't get the chance much now because of my daughter, but back then, if I didn't see live music at least once a week, I broke out in hives."

"My eldest son's the same," Parnell says. "Keeps moaning that he can't afford the deposit for a house, yet he somehow manages to keep Ticketmaster afloat."

She laughs. God bless Parnell and his universal rapport. I've been to two concerts my whole life and I was policing one of them.

"I'd bought tickets off eBay, collection only," she goes on. "Lady Gaga. They'd sold out on all the official sites, so the only option was to pay double and cross your fingers you didn't get conned. But, you know, Lady Gaga—I thought she was worth the risk and the two-hour round trip."

"And was she?" I ask.

"Er, that would be a *no*. I arranged to meet the guy in The North-cote and he didn't turn up. I waited for around forty minutes, kept dialing the number he gave me, but, of course, no answer. I was going to get another vino and wait a bit longer but then I thought, *What are you doing, you idiot? He's not coming. You've been had.* I headed off, cursing myself for wasting £180. It was nearly a week's rent."

I know The Northcote. I once dated a performance poet—*yeah, I know*—who lived fairly close by. For three relatively dull months, we got drunk on relatively good wine, drenching the fact that we didn't have anything in common in £30 bottles of The Northcote's finest Chablis. A performance poet with a gold Amex. I was going through an odd phase.

My point is, I know the area. The layout.

"OK, you said in your statement that you traveled to Clapham Junction that day. Presumably you were headed back the same way?" An immediate "Yes." "So what brought you down the side streets then? Down Valentine Street? Why didn't you just head straight back down Northcote Road?"

She suppresses a tiny grin. "I was avoiding someone. I'd been seeing this guy a few months before, and I'm not proud of it, but I'd kind of ghosted him, although I don't think we used the term back then. He worked in one of the Italian restaurants and I didn't want to risk him seeing me." A girl after my own cowardly heart. "So I cut down one of the side streets. Ended up walking a ridiculously long way around. I can't remember the name of the street now, but it led onto Valentine Street."

"And this was what time?"

"Four p.m., give or take."

Bang on, give or take.

Parnell shifts in his kiddie chair, pointlessly trying to get comfortable. "Talk us through seeing Holly. I know it's been a long time, I know it's hard, but as much as you remember."

I'm not sure she is finding it *that* hard. The reminder of what happened, yes. The detail, no. For a woman who claims she blocks out memories at whim, she's doing a remarkably good job of dragging them back front and center.

"I'd just turned onto the street. There was a great big hedge bordering the house on the corner . . ." Christopher Masters' house; the hedge acting as a shield when the time came to move the bodies. "And a girl was walking toward me—Holly Kemp, I later found out."

"That must have been fleeting," I say, scribbling furiously. "What made you so sure it was Holly?"

Parnell jumps on board. "I was thinking that. I know this makes me sound like a complete old fogy, but Holly Kemp—she was attractive, but she looked like a million other girls: the hair, the lips, the lashes. And yet you knew straightaway it was her when you saw her in the paper."

"One hundred percent." We wait for more. "There were a couple of things. First, it was raining—not heavily, but she didn't have an umbrella and neither did I and I felt bad for her. I mean, it didn't matter about me, I was my usual scruffy self . . ." Which on first impressions means she might have ditched a second coat of mascara that morning. "But she looked so glamorous. She had this blond salon-flicky hair and she was wearing this gorgeous white coat—well, it was off-white, cream, I suppose." She makes a sweeping motion with both hands. "It had this huge fur collar, belted, stunning. I half-thought about asking her where she got it. But anyway, I had a coffee in my hand; I'd bought one when I left the pub, and as we passed, I'd tripped, and a tiny bit splashed on her coat. *Tiny*, though. I'm talking microscopic. Most people would have said 'Don't worry about it' but she really scowled at me. That's why I remembered her. Anyway, I carried on walking past and next thing, I heard the gate bang."

I'm confused, my mind already in reconstruction mode. "So how did you see Masters at the door if you'd walked past by then?"

She leans forward, eyes darting between us both. "You know that sudden feeling you've forgotten something? I thought I'd left my bank card in The Northcote. I'd been distracted on my phone when I was paying, see, and it wouldn't be the first time I'd done it. I stopped dead in the street, looking in my purse, my bag, but it wasn't there. So I turned around to head back, cursing myself, and as I walked past the gate again, Holly was on the doorstep and

Christopher Masters had opened the door. He was saying something to her, smiling, sort of ushering her in."

"That's pretty observant," I say. "It wouldn't be the first, or second, or even fifth time I've left my card in a pub, so, trust me, I know the panic. I don't think I'd have been paying much attention beyond that."

"Maybe it's teaching infants. Multitasking. Eyes in the back of your head."

I nod, letting her have it, but for some vague, just-beyond-reach reason, I'm not quite sold. "So it was four p.m., late February. Was it starting to get dark?"

I should know this, but this summer has been endless. February, oh, the halcyon days of February, with its fog and its frost and its bluebells pushing stealthily through the soil, seems as alien as the Stone Age right now. A different space-time continuum.

"Not really, and there was a porch light shining on both of them anyway. I saw him as clear as I'm seeing you both now. He was wearing that red lumberjack shirt, the one in all the papers. I know what you're hinting at but *I know* what I saw."

"We're not doubting you, Serena. Not at all." Parnell's straight in with calming words, his tone slightly stilted, politician sincere. "We're just doing our job. Fresh pair of eyes. You understand?"

"Of course, but whatever your 'discrepancies' are, rest assured I *am* cast-iron." Eyes like headlights, full beam and unequivocal. "I wish I wasn't. I *really* wish I wasn't. I wish I'd never been there that day. But that doesn't change the fact that I had no doubts then and I've no doubts now."

As emphatic closes go, I don't think I've heard better. I shut my notebook and give a small smile. "Thanks, Serena. You've been really helpful. You can get back to your Sports Day now."

"My pleasure." She stands and we follow, Parnell with minor difficulty. "And apologies if I seemed a bit edgy to begin with.

Sports Day is fraught enough, making sure everyone goes home with their limbs intact, and then you turn up . . ."

Asking about a girl whose limbs are currently stacked in Tupperware boxes.

She walks us to the door, although "marches" might be a better word. "Sorry to rush you, but my daughter's in the Year One egg-and-spoon race. There'll be murder if I'm not there to watch."

I ignore the bad choice of phrase, thinking instead of poor Finn missing his Sports Day. Next year, I'm taking the day off, I decide. I'm going to be stationed at the finish line, whooping like a mad thing, showering him with high-fives and "attaboys" even if he comes last.

I'm going to be the best aunt in the world.

Because I can live with the Bad Sister tag. I've been living my whole life with the Bad Daughter tag. But the Bad Aunt tag—when it's occasionally flung—stings like a bitch.

Although not as much as the Corrupt Officer tag.

The most poisonous tag of all, known only to me.

7

"She's adamant," says Parnell between bites of a Big Mac.

"Word-perfect, I'd call it."

"You're doing your suspicious face, Kinsella. I'm not even looking at you and I *know* you're doing your suspicious face."

Steele's in her office, head bowed over something numerical and soul-destroying. But she's listening. She's always listening.

"I don't know if I'm suspicious or impressed," I reply to the top of her satiny black crown. "I mean, I couldn't tell you what knickers I was wearing on Monday, but Serena Bailey's still got it bad for a coat she saw six years ago."

"You should get some of those Days of the Week knickers then." Pen down, eyes up, Steele rolls the tension out of her shoulders. "We've got Spencer Shaw's address now, by the way. He lives near me actually, out west. Flowers went over—no answer. A neighbor thinks they might be on holiday, but they're not a nosy neighbor, sadly. Couldn't really tell him anything more than that."

"If he lives near you, Heathrow's worth a shot?" says Parnell. "If his passport's gone through, we should be able to track him."

"Ben's on it. Heathrow, Gatwick, Luton, Stansted, City Airport. 'Course they could be holidaying in the UK."

"Who's 'they?'" I ask.

"Shaw, his wife, and a couple of little ones, apparently." She drums her nails on the desk. "Now, what else did I need to tell you? Oh yeah, Cookey's working through the foster parents. He's met the last ones she was placed with. Nothing much doing. She was only with them eight months and it was 2006, a long time ago. They could barely remember the dates, never mind if anyone had a grudge against her. And they didn't hear from her again once she left."

"Where did she go?" I ask vaguely. What I'm actually wondering is what possible grudge a then-teenage girl could provoke to get herself shot in the head years later.

"A kind of hostel, halfway house thing," Steele explains. "For kids who are technically old enough to be independent but young enough to need a sharp eye on them."

"What about the aunt?" asks Parnell. "The one who refused to take her in when her parents died?"

"Remarried, living in Málaga. Renée had a call with her. She was no help either. Claims she never really knew Holly—she and her sister weren't close so Holly was pretty much a stranger. And she didn't fancy cramming a stranger into one of her own kids' bedrooms."

"A ten-year-old orphaned stranger with no other family," I say. "Warms the cockles, eh?"

"Quite." More nail drumming. "So what else . . . oh, Seth and Emily didn't get much in Newcastle, except lost on the one-way system." I imagine the polite bickering: Seth out of his comfort zone being so far from London Town, Emily blaming the layout, the ineptitude of the town planners, rather than her own inability to read a road sign. "The ex-wife could only think of one vague link to Cambridgeshire—a second cousin in Wisbech, which is still forty miles from Caxton and, in any case, he died in 2015. And on the subject of guns—'*No idea, but I wouldn't have put it past him.*'"

"I thought we were keeping guns out of it?" Parnell deepens his voice to match Blake's baritone. "*For investigative purposes.*"

"Good impression," I tell him. "Although *that* ruins it. Can you imagine Blake eating a Big Mac?"

"I don't think I've ever seen him eat," says Steele. "I don't think he's human. I think he was created in a lab in the bowels of Scotland Yard." She smiles, letting her head drop back. "Look, we aren't going to spoon-feed the media, I agree with him on that. But I'm not holding it back from people who could help us."

I look at Parnell. "Maybe we shouldn't have been so Secret Squir-rel with Bailey. The word 'gun' might have shifted something."

Steele sighs. "So, anything else to share, re Bailey, apart from her fashion taste?"

Parnell pulls a chair out—a chair befitting a thirteen-stone man, not a child with a mouth full of milk teeth. "She stands by everything," he explains. "What she saw, when she saw it. We got some details that weren't in her original statement, why she was in Clapham that day, background stuff, context. It's new but it doesn't tell us anything."

"Be nice if Masters had been standing at the door with a 9mm automatic and it'd just slipped her mind, wouldn't it?"

"Be nice to get Dyer's take on Bailey," I say.

"Her *take*? That sounds suspiciously like suspicion, Kinsella."

What the hell. She'll drag it out of me sooner or later. "Look, maybe it's me. I just find it odd that we spring all this on her at a second's notice, we tell her there's discrepancies, that we need to check our facts again, and she doesn't question herself at all. Not one little bit."

Parnell shrugs. "She saw what she saw. Nothing to question."

"Yeah, absolutely, and that's very probably the case. But I still think it'd be human nature to doubt yourself slightly, especially after all this time. Most people would have a moment's uncer-tainty, that's all I'm saying."

Steele checks her watch. "Well, look, I can tell you exactly where you'll find Dyer if you want to get her 'take.' I'm supposed to be meeting her in the H&F in half an hour." The Harp & Fiddle, just over Waterloo Bridge, is the most un-Dyer place I can possibly imagine. The most un-Steele place too, for that matter. The wine list consists of crap white or crap red, and you'd be wise to get a tetanus shot if you're desperate enough to use the loo. "Bloody Olly Cairns. Always did have dreadful taste in pubs. And wives. And music. Do me a favor and pop down and make my excuses.

You can grill Dyer, Cat, and I can get my head around this new grading matrix."

Our annual appraisal system. A batch of numbers that tell us if we're on Steele's Naughty or Nice list. As if she's shy of letting us know on a daily basis.

"Won't we be gate-crashing?" asks Parnell.

"No more than I would. Olly and Tess were always a lot tighter than me and Olly. And anyway, it's not just a social thing, it's a courtesy meet. Blake wants us 'pooling knowledge.' He thinks we'd be 'remiss' not to use her fine brain." Her tone is dry as dust. "She speaks fluent French. He gets a hard-on for that sort of thing."

"So do I." I turn to Parnell. "*Voulez-vous allez à la*—what's French for pub?"

"*Le pub.*"

"I almost married a Frenchman in my early twenties." Steele's prone to these kind of statements. You're never quite sure if they're the truth or a windup. "No, seriously," she says, laughing at our faces. "Church booked, dress picked, all sorted. I would have been DCI Dupont, which I'm sure you agree has a certain ring to it."

Parnell looks skeptical. "And what happened?"

"It's a grubby little story, really. He saw my chief bridesmaid. I saw him for what he was. Anyway, my point is I speak good, if not fluent, French too, so I'm going to ask you both now to *foutre le camp.*"

"What does that mean?" I ask, knowing for sure it won't mean anything pleasant.

She smiles. "Known on these shores as 'bugger off out of here.' But give Olly my best, OK?"

From good French to bad pubs.

It's years since I've been in the Harp & Fiddle, and in these turbulent times it's comforting to see that some things never change. Because you don't come to the H&F for the ambiance, or the Instagram likes, or the fifty different flavors of organically made gin. You come for a drink, plain and simple. You come to experience a pub run with such apathy that an artificial Christmas tree sags in the corner all year round, the angel sitting on top, completely crooked. Like she dropped in for a pint and stayed for a session.

And yet, on a glorious Wednesday evening, in a city rich with parks and pools and a million other alternatives, the H&F's rickety bar stools are full. A shoal of old men watching the racing at Sandown, and losing by the sounds of it. Tourists looking bewildered. The usual sad sacks using "a swift half" as a delaying tactic to avoid going home.

And polished, pinstriped DCI Tess Dyer.

"Sorry, not my choice," she says by way of greeting. She's sitting on a banquette in the far corner of the bar, the table in front carved with graffiti, including something not altogether courteous about the Metropolitan Police. "Bloody Olly! He and the landlord go way back. Best pint of Guinness inside the M25, apparently."

As requested, we make Steele's excuses. Dyer tuts, grins, declares it Steele's loss, then moves along the banquette, ripping a £20 from her purse. "Do the honors, would you, Lu? Mine's a Gin 'n' Slim and whatever you're both having." Parnell saunters off, knowing precisely what I'll have. "Interesting turn of events," she says, her eyes on mine as I sit down. "I'm still processing it, to be honest."

"I reckon we all are, ma'am." This is awkward. I can't think what else to say. It was good to get the landscape from Steele, of course— Dyer's husband, his illness, the diabolical pressure she was under and what that *could* have meant—but it doesn't make for a cozy tête-à-tête in the nook of the Harp & Fiddle. I look over to Parnell, willing him back to the table, but he's joshing with the barman, and if it's about football, he could be some time. "So, um, how was your day?"

How was your day? She's a superintendent-in-waiting, not your best mate or your boyfriend.

"I've had better," she says, not seeming to mind the question. Maybe she's grateful to be asked? It can get lonely at the top, or even at middle management. "I had to call the parents, warn them it was going to be back in the news. Well, I called Steffi and Ling's parents, and Sean and Linda . . ."

"Bryony Trent's folks?"

"No, Sean and Linda Denby—Holly's foster parents. She was with them the longest. Nearly two years, which is good going for a teenage placement. They aren't the easiest."

"Oh, right. I think one of our guys is working through those . . ."

"I had to make contact, Cat. It was the right thing to do—they knew *me*, not one of your guys."

Fair enough. "So why did Holly leave the Denbys? They weren't her last set of foster parents."

"I can't remember the details, but she'd been acting out, being disruptive, and they had other children to think of. It's common enough. They stayed in contact with her, though. Hadn't actually seen her for a few years before she disappeared, but they'd exchange birthday cards, the odd call now and again. They were the only ones who did."

"And Bryony's folks?"

"Both passed away now. I had no idea. Not that I should have known," she adds quickly, an unnecessary defense. "But you never stop feeling responsible, Cat. You never should, anyway."

Responsible? Responsible implies some degree of control, an ability to turn the tide, to make things better. No chance here. All the victims are dead and three quarters of them are buried. What she means is "you never stop feeling *guilty*," even if she can't bring herself to admit it.

And maybe she should? About Holly, at least. In trying to prove she was superwoman, did she let Holly Kemp become more of a footnote than a true victim?

Did she let another killer walk free?

But Serena Bailey. Serena Bailey. Serena Bailey. The pulled thread that unravels everything. The earworm that won't go away.

"We met Serena Bailey today." I'm all breezy, knowing I need to tread carefully. Steele might have said "grill Dyer" but there's picking her brain and there's picking her witness to shreds. "I've got to hand it to her, she's got one hell of a memory. She gave more detail today than she did back then."

"She's had six years to mull it over. I bet a day rarely goes by when she doesn't replay what she saw."

"Quite the opposite, apparently. She claimed she was a whiz at blocking things out, before giving us the whole thing in high definition."

And in any case, memory doesn't work like that, I want to say. Details fade the second you turn your back. Inaccuracies grow. Your hard drive gets corrupted. It's why Jacqui frames our childhood as something straight off an episode of *The Waltons*, while I seem to conjure up the bloodiest scenes from *The Godfather*. The truth is usually a gray blotch lying somewhere in between.

Parnell's back with the drinks. "Say what you like about this dive, but for Zone 1, the prices are stupid-low." He hands Dyer back her change. "What'd I miss?"

"Serena Bailey."

"Who else?"

I take a sip of 7 Up—no G&Ts for us; our day is far from over. "Do you know what else I found a bit odd?"

Parnell summarizes for Dyer. "Apart from the fact she doesn't doubt herself *at all*?"

"That she hadn't heard about Holly. The news was released at midday and it was gone three p.m. when we got there."

Parnell shrugs. "She did say it'd been hectic. It's not like teachers sit around scrolling through Twitter while the kids are doing their spelling tests."

"No, but it was a major event in her life," I insist. "You'd think *someone* she knew would have seen it and called, or at least texted, to say, *Oh my God, that girl who went missing, the one you were the last to see alive, she's been found."*

Dyer weighs it up, pushing a beer mat around the table. "If it was the evening news, I'd say sure, it's a bit odd. But who watches the lunchtime news?"

I shrug "OK" but it still grates. We live in an information age, facts, lies, "fake news" spread across multiple platforms within minutes. Surely someone from her SPECIAL PEOPLE TREE—basically, anyone except Peanut, who I'm assuming has four legs—would have come across the story *somehow*.

"What did you make of her?" Parnell asks Dyer.

"Bailey? Well, look, I was the SIO, so I didn't get too involved with witnesses." Same as Steele, more of a general than a foot soldier. "Although obviously I would have done if we'd been able to charge the bastard with Holly and she'd needed prepping for court. From what I remember from my team, though, she was near on the perfect eyewitness, and God knows, they're in short supply. No record, not even a parking ticket. Intelligent. Respectable. Solid."

File under "nice." Juries love nice.

"Seriously, is there ever a perfect eyewitness?" Like a dog hovering over a plate of meat, I glance over to Parnell to check I'm not about to get my snout slapped. He dips his head: permission granted. "I mean, did you see that case in America? Not one, *five* eyewitnesses gave a description of a thin black guy between the ages of thirty and forty, firing at an amusement arcade. Turns out the shooter was a twenty-year-old white male. Not particularly thin, either. Eyewitness accounts given under stress are dodgy. No wonder the CPS wouldn't prosecute."

I've probably gone too far but Dyer's fine. She looks almost impressed. "The key word there is 'stress,' Cat. Serena Bailey wasn't the witness to a crime, just the witness to two people talking. There was no trauma to devalue what she said."

"I'm not trying to devalue it, I'm just trying to digest it. I'm trying to get into a headspace where Bailey's ID is two hundred percent nailed on."

"Did anyone else put Holly on Valentine Street?" asks Parnell.

"We canvassed every house," says Dyer, shaking her head. "But then, nobody put *any* of the girls on the street. That four to five p.m. period is the dead zone in middle-class suburbia. The school run's done so all the parents are inside, wrestling with homework. The office workers aren't home yet, and the old biddies are watching quiz shows. Masters got lucky in that sense. Maybe he planned it that way." She stops, although there's a sense she hasn't finished speaking. Quickly, she turns her head, eyes lasering the door for a few seconds. "You're asking me what I think of Serena Bailey. You'd be better off asking me what I think, full stop."

We know. "Masters did it."

"Yeah." She takes a steadying sip of gin. "Or an accomplice."

The word oozes onto the table, mercury spreading outward.

Dyer to Jacob Pope yesterday: *"Did Masters ever talk about friends? People he was close to?"*

She'd been thinking this already.

Has she been thinking this for years?

"The match made in hell; it isn't as rare as you'd think," she says, qualifying the bombshell. "They reckon around a fifth of serial killers operate in teams."

Some would argue Masters was a spree killer, not a serial. The latter having longer cooling-off periods between murders, the former all done and dusted within thirty days. It's a contentious issue though, with no firm definition, and anyway, now's not the time for being a smart-arse.

Parnell whistles. "Jesus, that's one hell of a curveball you've just thrown."

Dyer nods. "One that explains the different dump site, though, and the different method of killing."

And still validates Serena Bailey's ID. Job done.

Except that it's a hypothesis, not even a solid theory. Four years of working for Steele has pummeled that difference into me.

"Think about it." Dyer sits forward. "Holly went missing on Thursday 23rd February. We arrested Masters on Saturday the 25th. We were never absolutely certain that the girls weren't taken somewhere else, held for a day or two, tortured, then killed—because while we found blood in the house, it wasn't awash with it. So what if Holly was being held somewhere, then Masters gets arrested, leaving his accomplice with the task of getting rid of her? If he wasn't a sadist like Masters, maybe more of a voyeur—and there's generally *some* psychological difference between most double acts—he might have found a bullet to the head easier to stomach."

"And he wouldn't have been able to use the usual dump site in Dulwich Woods, because by then they were crawling with . . . well, us." I find myself playing along despite the fact I haven't even started to puzzle this one out.

"Exactly. Good to see you're not as rigid as your boss, Cat." She adds a grin to soften the dig, then takes another hurried look toward the door. "And Lu, it's not a complete curveball. I said at the time we couldn't rule out an accomplice, but I was told to park it, concentrate on Masters. We had someone, the public felt safe—that meant good night and God bless, as far as the top brass were concerned."

"Same as when you expressed concerns about Spencer Shaw," I point out. "Tell me, what was it exactly, ma'am, that you didn't like about him—apart from the fact he sounds like a complete cretin? See, we haven't tracked him down yet, but he's definitely on the radar. Any light you could shine would be helpful."

"Hmm, well, he *was* a complete cretin, probably still is, but I don't want to over-egg that part. He didn't seem overly worried about Holly, that's all, and I had a sense he was lying about something. But people lie to us all the time, you know that. And for someone like him, it would be second nature. The idea of an accomplice really needled me, though—far more than Spencer Shaw."

"Hold on, hold on." Parnell rubs at his temples. "I get how an accomplice theory *might* have legs now, in light of what's happened, but why back then?"

"A few things. All three girls were young, fit, healthy. Relatively hard for a lean man in his fifties to move on his own, don't you think? There were no drag marks found at the dump site. No superficial wounds on any of the bodies consistent with having been dragged across a woodland floor."

"Yeah, but it's not inconceivable that he carried them," I say, remembering Craig Cooke's Defense of the Scrawny Man yesterday. "He did a fairly physical job. He was fit."

She ignores me, changing direction. "And did you ever hear him speak? I suppose not. Well, whether it was put on for effect or not, he had quite an unusual voice. Affected, slightly fey. Older than his years. He always reminded me of one of those BBC newsreaders from the 1950s." I've got an inkling where we're heading. "The advert—*Roommate wanted—female, age 20–35, for quiet, respectful, friendly house near Clapham Common*—to me, that sounds like an all-female house. You'd be expecting a female to answer when you called, or at the very least . . ."

"You're thinking a female accomplice?" Parnell isn't liking the sound of this. "No, look, there's examples, obviously, but you're talking about something extremely rare."

"You'd be expecting someone female or at the very least *younger*, was what I was going to say. Ling Chen's friend told us that Ling was being very picky. She had a nice flat with her boyfriend, and as he didn't know she was planning her exit, she wasn't in any great rush to move out. Trust me, I interviewed Masters on several occasions. A young woman would not be rushing to view that room after a few minutes on the phone to him."

"Oh, I don't know," I say, "£600 for a double room near Clapham Common is a hell of a bargain, even back then." I take a few seconds to consider the theory that Dyer's been percolating for years. "Seriously, you really think someone else took the calls, lured them to the house?"

"I thought it was a faint possibility back then." Her expression darkens. "I think it's certainly plausible now. It also explains—*could* explain—why he always refused to talk. To us, anyway."

"He was protecting someone," says Parnell.

"The silent pact," says Dyer. "We've seen it before. Often the imprisoned one cracks, but it can take years, decades. Masters didn't get the chance."

"Who then?" It's more belligerent than I intended, but as much as I respect her, Dyer needs to put her money where her mouth is. "Jacob Pope said he hardly mentioned anyone from the outside except his family."

"Didn't he inherit Valentine Street with two cousins?" Parnell says. "I'm not suggesting we do a dawn raid, but it's worth checking them both out, no?"

"You'd have a job doing dawn raids, Lu. One lives in Cape Town, has done since 2003, so they're in the clear. The other has been pushing up daisies since 2014."

"Which could still put him in the frame. *Could*," I add. While I'm happy to poke this theory with a stick, I'm not entirely rolling with it.

"*Her*, actually." Dyer clinks a nail against her G&T glass. On the other side of the bar, a roar of frustration erupts from the race watchers. Betting slips torn up, expletives coming thick and fast. We watch for a minute, probably less, before Dyer says, "There *was* the lad who worked for him—Brandon Keefe. A few people mentioned they seemed quite close. Masters' wife said he'd always wanted a son—he couldn't relate well to girls." *No shit.* "And he—Keefe—left the country not long after the trial, which in hindsight was . . ." She chooses her words carefully, lacing her fingers on the table. "Noteworthy, I suppose." She shrugs. "He could be worth another chat."

A chat. How genteel. Roughly translated as, "He could be worth fucking with, for no other purpose than shaking branches and seeing what falls."

Brandon Keefe. The name means zip to me but Parnell nods. "Didn't he do an interview with the *Mail*? A two-page spread. An 'I always knew he was evil'–type thing."

"Not a very silent pact if he's talking to journalists," I suggest.

"Wouldn't be the first time a guilty party thrust themselves into the limelight," says Dyer. "It could have been one big laugh between him and Masters."

The "coulds" are piling up. A stinking great compost heap of possibility. "So did you ever look into this Brandon Keefe?"

"There wasn't any real reason to. He was one of the few people who Masters associated with regularly, so obviously we spoke with him, but it was more to get a sense of what might have triggered Masters. It was Keefe who mentioned Masters' anger over his ex-wife's engagement." She places both palms flat on the table. "Look, it's not like I was ever absolutely sold on the idea of an accomplice. It was just something I thought needed considering. But I was alone in that view and the truth is, when I was told to drop it, I dropped it. Do I regret that now? Yes. Do I understand why the decision was taken at the time. Yes."

And is Brandon Keefe worth a chat? Sure, why not? Parnell gives me a small nod, signaling where our next stop will be.

"So how old are your kids now? Boys, right?" Parnell smiles as he takes a sharp swerve to the left, steering us away from witnesses and accomplices and the multiple kinks in this case. "I've got double the amount of boys since we last saw each other. Surprise twins, Joe and James. They're nearly eight now."

"So I heard. You were a brave man going back to dirty nappies in your late forties."

"Ah, but they keep me young. I mean, I haven't had a decent lie-in for years and my wrinkles have got wrinkles, but at least I can recite the entire script of *Lego Batman*."

She laughs. "Enjoy it. Mine are eleven and thirteen and it's all *Fortnite* and FIFA. And, of course, I'm a 'total loser' at both." Her eyes lower to the table. "Funny, the things that make them miss their dad. It's not just Christmases, birthdays; it's bloody computer games, which is ridiculous, because he was useless at anything like that."

Her kindness yesterday, her genuine concern. The bossiness, the fussing, making sure I got to the hospital in the shortest possible time. It all makes sense now.

"I'm so sorry. I had no idea. I thought . . ." I look down at her left hand.

"I should take the ring off, really. A lot of people, *widows*—God, I hate that word—they wear them around their necks, which I suppose is nice, but I don't want to." She twists it around her finger, now easily a size too big. Grief can do that to a person, strip the meat from their bones. "And anyway, the ring's handy for dealing with tradesmen. They're less likely to fleece you if they think a big bad husband might appear at some point." Before I can offer another inadequate "sorry," she's on her feet, beaming at something behind us. "Well, look who the cat dragged in."

"Do not *talk* to me about cats, Tessa Dyer. They have me lawn ruined, pissing and shitting all over the place."

Smooth, melodic tones, honed somewhere in the south of Ireland. As entrances go, ex–Chief Superintendent Oliver Cairns' is a bold one.

He's a striking man in a well-cut suit, although a thousand

miles east of conventionally handsome. Tall and reed thin, with a thatch of white hair sweeping back from a high forehead and a clutter of large features fighting for room on his lined face. I'm guessing if he was still on the job in 2012, he must be late sixties at most, although he could pass for late seventies with his papery skin and crooked gait.

Still, he smells wonderful, all musky and rich, and what he lacks in good looks he makes up for in verve.

I stand up, sticking my hand out. "Another cat, I'm afraid, sir. DC Cat Kinsella. I've never pissed in your garden though."

Why, oh why, oh why did I say that?

He roars laughing, giving me a bone-crusher of a handshake, then grabs Dyer in an embrace with the force of a prop forward.

Dyer's voice is muffled in his shoulder. "Cat works with Kate."

"*With* Kate." Steele's name has him wagging his tail even harder. "Jesus, even I didn't work *with* Kate and I was her guv'nor for five years. Dances to her own tune, that one." He looks around. "Where is the madwoman, anyway?"

"Budgets." Parnell offers a hand. "DS Lu Parnell, another of Kate's minions."

Cairns shakes it warmly. "Nice to meet you, Lu. And did I hear you right? Budgets? Kate Steele passing up a session for a spreadsheet? Well, she's changed." He empties his pockets onto the table: keys, phone, lighter, rolling papers, a pouch of Amber Leaf tobacco, and a ball of screwed-up banknotes.

"You haven't." Dyer picks up the tobacco. "I thought you'd quit."

"I did. Four long months and Christ, didn't everyone know about it? Honestly, I'm brutal without nicotine. I bit the head off my cleaner over a broken casserole dish I didn't even know I owned! Trust me, the world's better off if I'm smoking."

Parnell, predictable as the moon, says, "Have you tried the vape?"

"Ah now, Lu, there's nothing more tedious than a 'how-I-quitcigs' story. Save your breath, I've heard them all. Sure, I've told half of them meself. And yet here I am, still smoking like the Poolbeg Chimneys." He snatches a crumpled twenty off the table. "Now, what I can get you?"

Parnell calls time, shuffling out of the banquette. "Nothing for us, sadly. We're still on the clock. Things to do, people to see."

"Well, if you see your boss, tell her to get her arse down here. All work and no play makes Katie a dull girl."

Katie.

Brilliant.

Parnell's squinting at his phone, holding it a few feet away from his nose, having brought the wrong glasses. "Speak of the devil. Looks like I'm off to church tomorrow. There's some sort of memorial service being held for Holly. Steele wants someone there."

"Bloody hell, that was quick," I say. "We only formally announced ID this morning."

He scans the rest of the message. "Her friends have put it together. An impromptu gathering at All Saints in Dollis Hill. All welcome. Twelve p.m."

"And am I coming?"

Before he can answer, my phone dings: a text message from Steele.

And yes, Cinderella, you may go to the ball ☺

8

We didn't get many women in the shop, but when we did, something came over him. His eyes darkened. His posture went as rigid as a steel bar. His voice took on a rough, husky tone, like he'd entered some sort of altered state.

Bit of a windbag, Brandon Keefe. The type who'd craft a Hollywood script out of making a ham sandwich.

You hear people saying, "It's always the quiet ones you have to watch out for," but I never understood what that meant until now. Because that was what Chris was. Just a quiet, unassuming guy. Some days he was so quiet, I'd think I'd done something wrong. Maybe the till was £5 down or I'd let the stockroom get too messy. But then at the end of my shift, after he'd said no more than ten words to me all day, he'd always do the same thing—pat me on the back and say, "Night, Brandon. You're a good lad, you are." He certainly never said anything that made me think he'd do this.

"Oh, for God's sake!" I look up from the *Mail* article. "Such as? 'Hey, Chris, see the match last night?' 'Nah, mate, too busy slicing the flesh from a young barmaid's thigh.' I wonder how much he got paid for this tripe?"

Parnell's driving and only half-listening, concentrating instead on the swarm of headphone-wearing, smartphone-ogling pedestrians playing dodge-the-traffic as we muscle our way through the havoc of King's Cross.

"Seriously, how much do you reckon he got?" Being broke always makes me consumed with other people's windfalls. "The price of a holiday? A new car?"

"Maybe both, and change to spare. Gossip on Masters would have been high currency."

I attempt a vague calculation, settle on "a lot." "What are the chances we work with a serial killer? State of my overdraft, I could do with selling a story." I lean my head against the window, taking in the ever-changing face of the main hub of King's Cross, from Shitsville to Live-Work-Playville in less than a decade. "I think my money'd be on Cooke. He's a quiet one. I mean, he mentions 'his Karen' from time to time, but has anyone actually met her? And do we even know that he's got kids?"

"Sorry to rain on your parade, but I've met Karen and so have you. Steele's fiftieth, don't you remember? She did 'Ice Ice Baby' on the karaoke." A vague, Sambuca-soaked memory resurrects itself. "And it's a myth, you know—'the quiet ones' theory. Sure, some people fit the bill. Dennis Nilsen wasn't exactly Mr. Congeniality. Ed Gein, neither. But for every Dennis and Ed, you've got a Ted Bundy or a John Wayne Gacy. Gacy was a children's entertainer. You've got to be outgoing if you can face being stuck in a musty church hall with thirty preschoolers wired on cake pops and orange squash."

"I thought it was all fruit skewers and soy milkshakes these days? And anyway, it's a myth that Masters was quiet, if you believe Jacob Pope. 'Always mouthing off,' remember?"

"That happens sometimes, the personality change. Once they're convicted, the mask can come off. They can be themselves. Voice all the stuff they felt they couldn't before." He glances at my phone on the armrest. "How far now?"

"Zero point four kilometers." Not long to get our ducks in a row. "So how are we playing this? We can hardly accuse him of anything based on a bit of pub conjecture. I'd be wary of even implying anything."

"We're just gauging his reaction, that's all. Doing the same spiel—we're revisiting the case, checking the facts, fresh pair of eyes. All that jazz."

"You make it sound like we're selling him a line."

He doesn't answer, slowing and taking a right. "This is it, Gifford Way. Keep your eyes peeled for number seventy-eight."

Gentrification hasn't yet reached Brandon Keefe's neighborhood, the part some call North King's Cross and others call "The V," its shape formed by the convergence of the Caledonian Road—known locally as "The Cally"—and York Way. The prevailing narrative is that The V is a war zone, an area rife with social problems: drugs, violence, feral youth, ya-di-ya-di-ya, when, of course, what it's actually rife with is hordes of ordinary decent people living ordinary decent lives.

Although maybe not at 78 Gifford Way.

A guy, not Brandon Keefe—unless the past six years have been profoundly unkind—opens the door and eyes our warrant cards with the kind of dispassionate disgust shown by someone who likes to think of himself as an "enemy of da state," even throwing in a gold-toothed yawn for good measure. He shouts, "Brandon! Cops," up the stairs, then swaggers—a painfully practiced gangster glide, complete with false limp, the ultimate illusion of toughness—back down the hall to the kitchen, where he appears to be marinating chicken.

Thug life, with a squeeze of lime.

Keefe appears barefoot on the bottom stair within seconds, tying his long brown hair into a spindly topknot, his expression wary but unsurprised. While the years haven't been unkind, as such, they sure have been different. No longer the apple-cheeked cherub resplendent in university cap and gown, whose photo accompanied the *Mail* piece, *this* Brandon Keefe looks like his heart never left Woodstock. A thin, almost concave figure in frayed, flared jeans and a white linen shirt unbuttoned three buttons too far.

And beads. Rivers of hippie beads trickling down to his navel.

"I've seen the news," he says heavily. "I don't suppose there's any point asking what this is about?"

Parnell speaks before I can. "We want to talk to you about Christopher Masters, Brandon."

A mirthless laugh. "Who doesn't? That's all anyone ever wants. The media lost interest after a while, but it doesn't stop every other sticky-beak asking, 'What was he like?' 'Did you suspect anything?' Well, I tell them, 'He was fine' and 'No, I didn't' and I daresay I'll tell you the same." He turns on the stair. "Still, you might as well come up."

We follow him up an uncarpeted staircase, where the walls are covered with posters advertising clubs that closed decades ago. Keefe's hovel is on the right. The floorboards tremor with the sound of hip-hop from downstairs.

"Sorry," he says, stamping his foot—universal code for "turn that fucking thing down." "It's because you're here. He's actually an OK bloke, but his brother got sent down earlier this year—a terrible miscarriage of injustice, *apparently*—so you aren't exactly his favorite people." He does a 360, sweeping an arm around the pigsty of a room with the air of the dissolute thespian. "Anyway, sit yourselves down. I can offer you the armchair, although Nimbus might have something to say about that, or there's the bed or the bongos." Nimbus, a fluffy white cat, stretches her claws and says nothing. Keefe walks over to a loaded clotheshorse. "And if you don't mind, I'm going to pair my socks while you ask whatever it is you have to ask. I get quite stressed talking about Chris, even after all this time, so it's better if I have something to do." He smiles. "And I'll need socks for church later."

The mention of church brings a few things into focus. A book, *I Hear His Whisper*, on a nightstand, next to a statue of Jesus and some loose change. A wooden cross on the wall, the centerpiece among a collage of photos—Keefe in various bear hugs and head-locks with two burly, smiling men.

"My big brothers," he explains, catching me looking. "My best friends, really. I've opened my heart to God and the goodness of others in recent years, but they were the only people I trusted, apart from my parents, after that debacle with the newspaper."

"We'll come back to that." I pull up a bongo. I don't fancy my chances against Nimbus and there's something odd about sit-ting on a strange man's bed, even with Parnell leaning against the wardrobe. "First, we want to go over a few things. Things you won't think are relevant. Things that probably *aren't* relevant. But we owe it to Holly Kemp to try and get as clear a picture as pos-sible of what happened to her, OK?" He shrugs, tossing a pair of socks into an open drawer. "So how long had you worked for Mas-ters before his arrest? And how did you come to work for him?"

"Around six months. I'd just graduated with a First in art his-tory, which I soon realized qualified me for nothing, and I needed money fast. See, there was this girl I was keen on—*really* keen—and she wanted to go traveling and I was working up to suggest-ing we go together. I didn't have time to be going through lengthy interview processes and I didn't want to commit to anything long-term, so I lowered my expectations. Thought some money was bet-ter than no money." He talks quickly, almost harried, matching and balling socks with lightning efficiency. Anything to avoid eye contact. "Anyway, I saw the ad and I went in to see Chris. He said he was getting more and more renovation work and he needed some-one to keep the shop ticking over. We talked for about twenty min-utes and he offered me the job on the spot, subject to references, of course. I said I'd get back to him because I had another inter-view the next day. I got offered that job too. Data entry stuff." He finally stops moving, turning to face us with just about the saddest expression I've ever seen. "Do you know why I took Chris's offer?

I could leave at five p.m., whereas the other job was five thirty p.m. Wanting to get to the pub half an hour earlier ruined my life."

It's terrifying, the frivolous decisions that have earth-shattering consequences. You see the sliding doors in every case. The way grief could have been avoided if only the planets had aligned differently. If only fate had played fair.

If only the bus hadn't been delayed, the girl wouldn't have gotten bored waiting and accepted a lift from that guy who'd always *slightly* given her the creeps.

If only the guy hadn't had one more pint to stop his mate from texting his ex, he'd have been tucked up in bed by eleven p.m., instead of walking into the path of a fatal mugging.

Parnell takes his glasses from one pocket, a notebook from the other. After a minute of flicking backward and forward, he says, "You said in your statement that Masters told you he was going to be at Valentine Street all day, the day Holly Kemp went missing."

Keefe sits down, pulling Nimbus onto his lap, his right knee jigging like a jackhammer. "Actually, what I think I said was, 'Chris said he'd be at the house.' I didn't know the address. He only ever referred to 'the house.'"

"And you were at the store all afternoon?" I keep my voice light, cheerful. "Counting down the minutes till happy hour, am I right?"

He shifts a little. "Well, no. I shut early that day. It'd been dead since lunchtime . . . and well, I was feeling a bit down. The girl I liked had been flirting with someone in the pub the night before, and I'd mentioned it to Chris when he popped in unexpectedly that morning for tools, and he said that if the shop was quiet and I wanted to finish a bit early, go over to her place, have it out with her—basically tell her how I felt about her—I could."

"And did you?"

"No. I went home and closed the curtains and played *Call of Duty* for eight hours."

Which is an off-the-peg alibi. Then again, it could be the truth.

"Your parents must have been thrilled," I say, masking the real question. *Can anyone verify that?*

"They wouldn't have been if they'd been home, but they were in Venice. They go there every February for the carnival." He gives a sad little shrug. "Honestly, I can't believe what a video-game waster I was back then. No purpose, no energy. No wonder the girl I liked was shag— *sleeping* with someone else. Not that I bear her any ill will, of course. *The anger of man does not produce the righteousness of God*—James, chapter one, verses nineteen to twenty."

I dart a look at Parnell, who usually gets fidgety around any kind of religious fervor, but he's looking confused, not twitchy. Pulling on his right earlobe, his forehead more creased than Keefe's shirt.

"The interview you did with the *Mail*, Brandon—you implied that you and Masters barely spoke, besides pleasantries, but you just said he knew how keen you were on some girl." He adds a smile, making light of the statement, then points at me. "I mean, we've worked together for years and I still have to wrench that type of information out of this one."

Keefe nods as if to say it's a fair question. "Look, I was trying to dispel any false notion that Chris and I were mates. Can you blame me for that?" He looks down at Nimbus, rubbing and twisting her ears. "OK, we talked, but rarely about anything of substance. Just things that'd been on the news, or the weather, or bad drivers he'd encountered. Just chitchat, you know?"

"And your love life," I remind him.

His head snaps up. "Look, we weren't having heart-to-hearts. He just mentioned I seemed a bit quiet that morning and I ended up spilling more than I intended. He said he understood, that he always wished he'd fought harder to keep his ex-wife. It felt weird, to be honest. I made sure I cheered up the next day and it was back to moaning about people driving with their fog lights on."

"What about Cambridgeshire, or a village called Caxton? He ever mention them?" Keefe looks blank. An impatient tone creeps into my voice. "It was mentioned on the news, Brandon. We found Holly Kemp's remains in Cambridgeshire. So did he ever mention any links to the area? Any desire to visit? Anything?"

To his credit, Keefe gives this a damn good think. Eyes narrowed, bottom lip protruding. If he had a beard he'd be stroking it right now, but in its absence, he strokes the cat.

"I don't think so," he concludes eventually. Strangely, I prefer this to an emphatic no. I'm more inclined to believe it, anyhow. "He loved carp fishing and he used to go away at weekends sometimes. Again, we didn't get into details, he'd just say he'd been away. Could have been Cambridgeshire, could have been Cornwall. I just don't know."

"Did he ever mention guns?" It's a risk by Parnell, but one sanctioned by Steele—"*Play it straight, but play it cool*"—and in any case, I sense Brandon Keefe wouldn't flirt with the media again, not after his last "debacle." It gets less of a reaction than we expect, though. Another mull and then a slow shake of the head. Parnell nudges again. "Think, Brandon. You said you'd been working for Masters for around six months. You also said you used to talk about things in the news. Well, I don't know if you remember, but guns were big news in the second half of 2011." The shooting of a man in North London by police had sparked a series of riots across the capital, then the country. Looting, arson, the deaths of five more people. "There were riots in Battersea, less than half a mile from Masters' store. Are you telling me he never passed comment on it, on what sparked it all off?"

For crying out loud, give us something. Anything.

"Can I honestly say, hand on my Bible, that he didn't—no. Did he say anything notable enough that it's stayed in my memory—no. Why are you asking about guns, anyway? Did Chris shoot Holly Kemp?"

He asks it calmly, reasonably. To Brandon Keefe, how "Chris" killed Holly isn't of particular interest, and in fairness, why would it be? Keefe isn't thinking about patterns, rituals, a killer's modus operandi. He doesn't have to consider the murky truth that wrapping your hands around someone's throat and squeezing their life short over several adrenaline-fueled minutes provides a profoundly different pleasure to executing them with one bang.

I move on without answering. "Brandon, do you remember where Masters was the day following Holly's disappearance? Friday the 24th."

"Haven't a clue."

Parnell thumbs through his notebook again. "Well, in your statement you said he didn't get in until ten that morning, but that he stayed in the shop until closing, only going out briefly at lunch to get chips for you both."

"Well, if that's what I said, that's what happened. But, look, I can't remember all the details now. A lot has happened since."

Not helpful, but it sits better than Serena Bailey's total recall.

"Did he say why he was late in that day?" I ask. "Where he'd been?"

He's getting crabby now. "If he did, it'll be in my statement. I can't tell you anything more than what's in there. Unless you're implying I held something back?" He rises up in the chair, panicked. Nimbus jumps down and stalks off in search of a less stressful throne. "Is that what this is about? You think I withheld something? Why? Why on earth would I do that?"

That answer is for another day. A day where we have a scintilla of evidence, or at least a carefully thought out theory that wasn't sprung on us in the pub.

Parnell's voice is kind. "Hey, calm down, son. Like we said, we have to ask things that might not seem relevant." He slides his notebook back in his pocket; a gesture that says "your grilling here is done." "Why don't you tell us about the newspaper article? You said it ruined your life."

His face relaxes a little. "I shouldn't have said that. It was part of God's plan and I have to trust in that plan. I *do* trust in that plan. But the aftermath was terrible, I can't deny that. It certainly wasn't worth the £15,000 they paid me, but at the time I thought it'd help 'get the girl.' I thought I'd rock up at her house and say, 'Ta-dah, want to book that round-the-world ticket?' and she'd fall into my arms, happy-ever-after. What actually happened was that I rocked up at her house and that idiot guy from the pub answered the door in his boxers." Second time he's mentioned it—he bears her ill will, all right. Although all it does is make him human, rather than a sanctimonious prick. "It wasn't just about the money, though. I was honestly so sick of journalists knocking on my door all day and night, and then there were my friends and their friends and their friends, and basically anyone I'd ever brushed past in the supermarket asking me about Chris. I thought doing the interview might put a stop to all that. Get it on record and move on." He lets out a sharp laugh. "Well, that backfired, didn't it? It was like pouring petrol on the flames. And I was ridiculed. How could I have worked with him and not realized? As if we stood around counting stock and talking about murder. And then there were the comments about me being in it with him. Strangers making vile accusations." We smile sympathetically, like the two-faced swines we're trained to be. "I should have listened to my brothers. They warned me not to do it. I usually listen to them but, you know, £15,000."

"It's a lot of money—don't beat yourself up," I say, meaning it.

"It was. And it meant *I* could go traveling, get away from the girl I liked flaunting her new relationship, get away from all the questions. So I took the trip I'd been dreaming about—Tokyo, the Philippines, Bali, Singapore, Borneo, Vietnam. I wasn't even gone six months. Didn't stop some idiots claiming I'd 'fled the country,' though."

"So what do you do with yourself now?"

He may snipe that his art history degree rendered him unemployable, but his graduate photo looked full of promise. And he's clearly intelligent, with a supportive family to boot.

"What do I *do*? People always ask that question. Why do they never ask who you *are*?" I wait for a less esoteric response. "If you must know, I contemplate the meaning of life a lot. And I'm not being facetious when I say that—I'm heavily involved in the Alpha program. Are you familiar?"

"I am." A nod to Parnell. "He's probably not."

"You're not a religious man, Detective?" Parnell shakes his head. "So you never pray?"

"It's been known before the odd penalty shoot-out."

And when Maggie went into premature labor with the twins.

And when Steele found a lump in her breast a few years back.

Parnell's no different from a lot of people; an atheist with a very small "a." Happy to suspend disbelief when the stakes are sky-high.

"Well, you'd be very welcome within Alpha," he says, addressing us both. "We're an evangelical church who throw our doors open to everyone, all religious denominations. We run courses designed to foster discussion about the Christian faith—anything from 'Who is the Holy Spirit?' to 'What would Jesus make of Instagram?' There's a common misconception that it's all earnest debate, but we have lots of fun and great food too. I'm leading a meeting tonight." He looks at his watch. "In half an hour, actually. Maybe you . . ."

"Do you have a girlfriend?" I ask, cutting off the invitation.

He stands up suddenly, giving us a twirl and a sarcastic smile. "Oh, but of course. I'm such a catch, don't you think?"

"How about a job?" asks Parnell.

He stops, shrugs. "Here and there. I look after a friend's stall at Camden Market sometimes. I've been known to do the odd bit of decorating. I occasionally courier." He peers at Parnell with concerned eyes. "You know, it's not good for the soul to be so wrapped up in things like jobs. How I pay my rent is the least interesting thing about me. It's the least interesting thing about anyone, you included. All you need to know is that I'm a good person." He reaches under the bed and scoops out Nimbus, who doesn't appreciate the disturbance. "Nimbus here is the only rule I've ever broken in my life. We're not supposed to have pets, see, but what harm is she doing? *'For the fates of both men and beasts are the same: As one dies, so dies the other. Man has no advantage over the animals, since everything is futile.'* Ecclesiastes, chapter three, verse nineteen, if you're interested."

"Guilt?" Parnell's buckling his seatbelt, staring up at Brandon Keefe's open window. "The God thing, I mean."

"Is that a conclusion or a question?" I snap.

In my defense, the car's roasting and my seatbelt's all twisted. I'm not in great humor.

"It's an observation *and* a question." He reaches over and sorts the problem with one hand. "What do you think?"

"I suppose it could be guilt. He's looking to repent, be forgiven. It's a tidy interpretation if we're rolling with this accomplice theory." I shift around in the passenger seat. "But it could also be loneliness, family background, too much time on his hands, illness—'cos he hardly looks healthy."

"You're telling me. A strong fart could knock him over."

"It could be a need for security, control, a sense of belonging. Or it could be, have you considered this . . ." I perform a drum-roll on the armrest, "*faith*, plain and simple. Honestly, I don't think we should read too much into it. The whole Masters thing was bound to change his worldview somehow."

Parnell offers a noncommittal grunt, then, "Religion doesn't seem to have changed his life for the better, though, does it? Did you see all those photos on the wall? The 'before' photos. He looked happy then, smiley, well fed."

"So does everyone on Instagram—well, maybe not well fed—but it doesn't mean they're not lacking something. Searching for something . . ." I draw a circle with my hands, attempt a silly, mystical voice. "Something bigger."

"D'you think that would be Jesus' take on Instagram?" Parnell's voice is thick with sarcasm. I frown. "Ah, come on, Kinsella, you know me. Whatever gets you through the night and all that. If you're religious, be religious, and don't mind grumpy old me, but why, oh why, do they try to make it trendy?" He puts the key in the ignition, still puzzling over something. "So what's your gut feel? You think he's a dead end?"

"I think, statistically, most women are killed by their partners, not young accomplices of middle-aged serial killers. So if it wasn't Masters, Spencer Shaw seems like a more interesting prospect to me."

"So you *do* think Keefe's a dead end?"

I give him the side-eye. "Sarge, if you push me, you know what I'll say."

"*Yes. No. Maybe.*" Parnell mimics my usual evasive stance. "OK, give me your nos. Why *shouldn't* we rule him out?"

Across the road, a door slams. Keefe rushes down the litter-strewn path of 78 Gifford Way and turns right toward The Cally. He hasn't changed his clothes for church but he's buttoned his shirt up, at least.

"I don't know. *If* Masters did have an accomplice, I suppose Keefe's the obvious choice. I mean, something's clearly gone wrong for a first-class graduate to be eking out a living doing odd jobs—that sort of downward spiral could be a sign of guilt, of wrestling with something major, I guess?" I turn back to face the front. Brandon Keefe's now a mere sliver on the horizon. "And I'd say he's got more anger in him than he's prepared to let on. He can quote Bible passages all he likes, but he's still spitting about that girl's rejection six years on."

Parnell finally pulls off. "Hey, listen, I caught my first serious

CAZ FREAR | 112

girlfriend on the back seat of a mate's Ford Fiesta, and let's just say she wasn't vacuuming it. I'm still angry about that."

I try not to laugh for all of two seconds. "You are joking? That must have been nearly forty years ago."

"Nearer thirty, actually; I was a late developer on the romance front. And anyway, I'm not saying I lie awake plotting revenge, just that the memory still stings a bit. I wouldn't read too much into it is my point."

"Oh, I get it, so we should only read into the fact he's found God, is that it?" I shake my head, laughing again. "You're a bloody heathen, Luigi Parnell. Are you going to be OK at Holly's memorial tomorrow? Don't go freaking out when you see a crucifix. No one wants a scene from *The Omen*."

9

Sunlight blares through the stained-glass windows of All Saints Church, dappling the stone walls and making the whole world seem more vivid. The vicar's robe glows a fiery violet. An old lady's white coat transforms into a glittering, heavenly shroud. The peonies draped over every pew shimmer vigorous shades of sherbet lemon and bubblegum pink.

And, of course, every speck of fluff on my black dress appears ten times more noticeable.

"Stop picking at yourself," says Parnell out of the corner of his mouth. "You're like a monkey checking for lice. Sit still, for Christ's sake."

"Easy on the blasphemy." I nod toward poor Christ, currently nailed to a mosaic cross above the altar. "Anyway, you're just as bad. Stop pulling at your collar."

"Can't help it. It's like a bloody sauna in here."

It really isn't. All Saints is cool, almost chilly, in the way most fifteenth-century buildings are. Parnell just can't pass up any opportunity to highlight the very real male hardship of having to wear a tie.

Thursday lunchtime. Finally, Holly.

Her time to shine. Her time to leap from being the missing-presumed-dead girl, the one with the teeth and the tits and the question mark forever hanging over her head to being just Holly. Holly Matilda Kemp. Woman, daughter, foster child, friend. And in the generous spirit of all memorial services, quite simply one of the finest human beings you could ever hope to meet. In place of a coffin, a huge photo provides the focal point. It's hard to put an age on her, but judging by her softer features, her plumper face, and her noticeably thinner lips, it must have been taken a good while before she disappeared in 2012. Back when being attractive was deemed good enough and total perfection wasn't the base standard set.

Parnell and I are sat at the back, the best vantage point for people-watching. Not that there's many to watch. A disparate group of maybe twenty to thirty—old, young, ancient, middle-aged—looking more like a market research group, cobbled together to discuss the merits of a new washing powder, rather than a close-knit band of mourners united by a common grief. The only group interacting at all are the four twenty-somethings in the front row. Three girls and a boy, leaning over one another, whispering back and forth, sharing tissues and the occasional smile.

"Not many here," I whisper, doing a quick head count. "Twenty-three, including us."

"Twenty-four."

A slight, handsome man, sharp-suited, maybe forty, slides into the pew in front of us. He attempts a smile, an acknowledgment that he's cut it fine, but his heart isn't in it and his mouth quickly returns to its tight red knot. His eyes are pink and puffy, the dark circles beneath them badges of grief. When he sits, it's more of a slump. Parnell gives me a quizzical look.

For the next hour, we sit, we stand, we sing, we reflect, and we listen to the man in front sniff continuously, as if valiantly holding back tears. If I'm honest, I switch off for a lot of it. It's a skill you learn as a bored Catholic child. The ability to daydream about pop stars while reciting long, protracted devotions. To ask for God's blessed mercy while making paper planes out of the hymn sheet. I do drift back for a sweet section where each of the Front Row Friends bring one of Holly's "favorite things" up to the altar: a jewelry box, a juicer, a personalized book called *Holly Saves Christmas!*—a treasured childhood gift from her dad. And the pièce de résistance, a pair of studded suede Louboutins, which raise a laugh when the female vicar declares, "Oh my, the girl had good taste!"

The man in front doesn't laugh.

The absence of any family—there was certainly no mention in the vicar's opening welcome—means that there's an aimless feel as the last bars of "Dancing Queen," our unorthodox final hymn, subside. With no one specific to offer sympathies to, and no invite to tea, biscuits, and stilted conversation in the neighboring church hall, there's nothing but a slow, silent shuffle to the exit before everyone rushes off back to their lives. Lives clearly touched by Holly in some way, but otherwise completely unconnected.

Everyone except the Front Row Friends.

As we leave the church, they're huddled near the entrance to the church hall. Two of the girls are smoking roll-ups. The boy, a boxy, stunted figure who clearly compensates for his lack of height by gaining bulk in the gym, is enveloped around the third girl, which she doesn't look too wild about. I make a beeline for her, offering her the option of escape.

"It was a lovely service, thank you. You did well to pull it together so quickly." She looks baffled. I offer my hand. "Sorry, I'm Cat. I'm with the police. You probably know we're looking at Holly's case again."

"Oh right, hi. I'm Kayleigh." She wriggles out of the gym rat's grasp, grazing my hand with hers. "Yeah, it was nice, wasn't it? Although it wasn't a great turnout. I didn't recognize half the people. I think some of them were just regular churchgoers, people who'd come for a nose." She shrugs. "But like you say, it all happened quickly. The minute they showed us those photos of Holly's trainer and locket, we *knew*—we did the Facebook invite, the Twitter post, straight after that. That was only Tuesday, I guess. People need more notice to get time off work." She casts a glance back to the others. "We didn't want to wait, though. We'd waited long enough. We had to do *something*."

One of the smokers, a pale, sinewy girl with a red spiky hairdo that's trying to scream "no-nonsense" but actually whispers "fifteen minutes in front of the mirror" says, "I was with her the day she got those trainers. She'd designed them herself, custom-made. Two hundred quid. For a pair of fucking trainers." She takes one last pull on her roll-up, flicking the butt to the floor and crushing it under her heavy-duty biker boot. "I'm Shona, by the way." A point to the other smoker. "That's Emma." Then the boy. "And that's Josh."

I lift my hand, mouth *hi*. "So was this Holly's local church?"

Shona snorts. "I suppose you could call it that, although she was hardly a regular. She was baptized here and we all went to All Saints infant school, but I doubt she'd set foot in it for years."

"She hadn't lived in Dollis Hill for years, to be fair," adds Kayleigh. "Once her mum died and she started being fostered, she was all over the place—Enfield, Dalston, Islington, *Herne Hill*, for God's sake."

Ah, the old North-South divide—the subtext being "so she might as well have been in Finland."

"Are any of Holly's foster parents here today?"

Kayleigh gives a tight, lipless smile. "No. We only really knew Sean and Linda. Linda sent a message saying she was sorry they couldn't make it. Sean has a hospital appointment, some sort of scan, and if they canceled it, it could be months before they got another. She said they were thinking about Holly, though."

Emma changes the subject, aiming a bucktoothed grin through a plume of smoke. "Hey, don't suppose you brought that hot copper with you? The one off the telly?"

I assume she means Blake, always good for a smoldering cameo any time the cameras start rolling.

Parnell steps forward. "I'm afraid I'll have to do. DS Luigi Parnell."

Smiles and handshakes all around.

"Ignore Emma. She's always on heat," says Kayleigh. Of the three girls, she's the closest to Holly, looks-wise. Not in the doppelganger sense, more in the effort that's gone into her. Eyebrows, lashes, teeth, and possibly breasts, all bought and paid for.

Emma pretends to look offended. "I am *not* always on heat. Although, er, *hello* . . ." She cranes her neck, looking past us, one hand on her jutting hip. "Who's he?"

I follow her gaze. The guy from the church is heading this way at speed.

"You don't know him?" I say quickly, before he gains too much ground. "He seemed pretty upset in there. I assumed he was a friend."

A collective shake of heads. Complete bafflement.

He's almost parallel with us now. Parnell swivels to intercept, his warrant card outstretched at eye level. "Hey, mate, Police. Can I have a word?"

Church Guy picks up pace, waving his car keys frantically toward the road. "Yeah, sure, but can you hang on . . . I'm on a parking meter out here and I'm about thirty seconds off getting fleeced . . . I didn't think the service would be that long . . . Give me a minute, yeah?"

Parnell waves him on.

Close up, Emma isn't nearly as smitten. "Actually, he's a bit of a short-arse, isn't he? Shame. Nice face, good suit, but I'm nearly 5'11" in heels. It'd never work."

"That, and the fact you're married," says Shona.

Keeping one eye on the main gates, Parnell says, "Are any of you in contact with Spencer Shaw? We urgently need to speak to him but haven't managed to track him down yet. We think he might be on holiday—any ideas where?"

His name turns the air stale. Josh comes into his own, pumping his fist into the palm of his hand. "On holiday? Nice. I half-expected him to turn up here. I half-wanted him to, actually. Any excuse to lay the bastard out."

Shona groans. "Oh, for fuck's sake, Josh! Just for one day, can you drop the bouncer act?" She looks at Parnell. "And no, we don't have any idea where numb-nuts is. He could be dead for all I care. Sorry, but it's the truth. Last time I saw him was around a month after Holly disappeared. He was outside the World's End in Camden, dry-humping some blond chick in cowboy boots. A *month* after. A fucking month! He was blatantly seeing her before."

"Did Holly suspect he was cheating?" I ask.

"God knows. If she did, she didn't say anything. But then, that was Holly—secretive."

"Thing is, we don't know that much about Holly," I admit. "Will you tell us a bit about what she was like?"

"Why?" asks Kayleigh, an earnest crease across her forehead. "No one seemed bothered before."

"Really? What do you mean by that?"

She assumes I've taken offense. "Oh, I wasn't saying . . . I don't mean nobody cared. I just mean it was open-and-shut. That Roommate guy got Holly, end of. What she was like didn't come into it."

"The facts of her death eclipsed the facts of her life," says Shona, more eloquently, if a little pompously. "Or her disappearance, I should say. It's always been hard to think of her as dead without a body. At least we've got that now." She reaches over, giving Kayleigh's shoulder a squeeze. "But Kay's right. Christopher Masters killed Holly and now he's dead too. What else is there to look into?"

I'm not mentioning guns. This crew are a whole different ballgame to Serena Bailey or Brandon Keefe. They don't want to block things out or run away from the past. If we tell them Holly's cause of death, they'll want answers, details, things we can't or won't give yet. I look to Parnell for help dodging the question, but he's too busy glowering at the main gates. A few minutes have passed and it looks like Church Guy has given us the slip.

"Just loose ends," I say, blandly. "A few discrepancies." And before anyone can challenge my wooliness, I follow it up with the universal question guaranteed to neutralize any tricky situation.

"Anyone fancy a pint?"

It's a cheap round in The Rising Sun. Turns out Kayleigh is three months pregnant, even though, depressingly, she looks less pregnant than me, and Emma has to pick her son up later, and sporting red-wine lips at the school gates really isn't the done thing.

Parnell hasn't joined us either. He's already heading back to HQ, livid with himself for letting Church Guy fool him, and vowing to personally request, then watch, all the CCTV from the surrounding streets, so that if he did get into a car we might be able to trace the number plate at least.

Because Church Guy *was* upset, no question. And it's curious he's not known to any of Holly's friends. Could be nothing, could be everything, but it's something, and it's our job.

I'm erring toward suspicion. People don't just forget an encounter with the police, no matter how brief. We tend to be memorable for all the wrong reasons and in this case, I sniff a reason why he made himself scarce.

"So did you know Holly was room-hunting?" I ask, taking a sip of fizzy water. I already know the answer from Dyer's briefing, but it feels like a good place to start.

Emma taps the table. "See, that confused me from the off—and yeah, before anyone else says it, I know it doesn't take much to confuse me—but I thought Holly had her feet well under the table at Spencer's place. He had a really, really smart flat in Shoreditch. Tiny, but swanky. Holly loved all that leather and chrome stuff."

"That was Holly," says Kayleigh. "Fickle. One minute she loved playing grown-ups, going on about espresso machines and under-floor heating, the next she'd be saying she missed her own space, that Spencer was doing her head in. I wasn't that surprised, to be honest."

"Yeah, but *Clapham*," says Emma. "It's nice but it's not cool, you know? Holly liked edgy."

"Spencer was doing her head in how?" I ask Kayleigh, jumping back.

"Oh, just standard stuff. Nagging her. Moaning about her coming in late, waking him up, buying too many clothes."

"That could be my boyfriend," I tell her. "I haven't considered finding somewhere else to live."

"They argued—a lot," explains Shona. "Not just bickering, full-on screaming matches. Maybe they'd had a bad one that week and she thought, *Sod this, I'm off.*"

"But why did she feel she couldn't tell us?" Emma's pain is box-fresh; the flirty swagger of earlier all gone. "She could have moved in with me, then she'd have never gone near bloody Clapham . . ."

"Don't go there, Emma, not again. You know what she was like." Shona turns to me, explaining. "Holly was a chronic oversharer about some things—like, I knew that girl's menstrual cycle better than my own. But when it came to the big stuff, she was cagey. She had an agenda. She could be planning a mission to Mars and you'd have no idea."

"But you knew she was going to Clapham that day?"

She takes a slurp of her pint. "Yeah, and she was definitely hyped about something, but she wouldn't say what. I didn't press it. Holly'd tell you when she was ready, that's how she always was." She wipes the foam from her top lip. "I told her to be careful, though. It'd already been all over the news about those other missing girls. I said, 'Maybe give Clapham a swerve, babe. Surely whatever it is can wait?' And do you know what she said? 'Don't worry about me, Shone, I'm not the type to get murdered.' Can you believe that? Despite all the crap life had thrown at her—her dad's accident, her mum's overdose, the beatings she'd got in care—she *still* thought she was invincible." She slumps back. "Still can't work out if that was sweet or stupid."

Silence falls over the table. A silence bellowing with sadness and regret. I keep going before melancholy sinks its claws in too deep.

"Well, what did you think she was going for?" A shrug ripples around the table like a Mexican wave. "Oh, come on, guys. You can't tell me she said, 'I'm off to Clapham but I'm not telling you why' and you didn't speculate, either privately or among yourselves."

Eyes dart across the table. I get the sense I haven't so much asked a question as lobbed a grenade.

It's Shona, predictably, who speaks. "I had my suspicions. I always thought she was working as an escort on the sly, so I thought it might be to do with that. Maybe a high-paying client? Like I say, she was definitely hyped about something." There's a murmur of protest from Josh. Emma looks off to the side, muttering, "Not this again." There's no passionate rebuttals, though. No signs of outrage, or even surprise. "She was a receptionist in a car showroom. It wasn't even full-time; it was, like, maybe twenty-five hours a week. And yet she *always* had money. Loads of it. I mean, only a few weeks before she disappeared, her and Spencer had spent five nights at the Burj Al Arab in Dubai. I looked it up—£6,000. Come on! And there were other things. Like she'd cancel nights out at the last minute, would never give you a reason. Important nights too." She stares hard at Josh and Emma. "Remember, Kayleigh's twenty-first, the December before?" She looks at me. "Holly was a no-show but then, lo and behold, who turns up the next day full of apologies and Harvey Nichols bags?"

"A Chanel belt," confirms Kayleigh. "And definitely not fake, the receipt was in the bag. How many twenty-one-year-old part-time receptionists can afford to spend £300 on a belt? And she got me other bits too. Expensive makeup. A voucher for this fancy spa in Holland Park." A little sigh. "She was really kind, Holly. I mean, I'd have been happy with a Topshop voucher but she loved spoiling people."

"Well, you know my thoughts," says Josh, staring at Shona and Kayleigh.

I raise my hand. "Er, well, I don't. And I'd love to hear them."

Shona doesn't give him a chance. "Josh thinks Holly had a sugar daddy on the go. Or that's what he wants to think. For some reason, he finds the idea of one sad twat paying her for a blow job more palatable than the idea of several sad twats."

"Fuck you, Shone."

She's harsh, but I agree his morality's flawed. Sugar daddy or escort, it's still using sex as currency, whichever way you slice it. And you're either fine with that or you're not.

"And you never mentioned any of this to the original investigators?"

"No." Shona sits up straight, poised for battle. "For one, I didn't *know* I was right and I still don't. It's just a hunch. A strong hunch. But in any case, by the time they interviewed us, they'd already tied Holly to Masters, so they weren't really asking questions, they were just laying out the facts and asking us to fill in the blanks."

In policing, and probably in any field, it's possible to do nothing wrong and yet still do nothing right. This case is starting to feel like this. The race to the finish meant the details got left behind.

"OK, so is there anything else you didn't say at the time? Anything else that didn't seem relevant after Holly was tied to Masters?"

Everyone looks at Josh, who looks away, leaving Shona, again, to pick up the mic. "Look, *we* didn't notice anything." She draws a triangle on the table between herself, Emma, and Kayleigh. "But Josh reckons she seemed jumpy in the months before she disappeared."

"Jumpy, how?"

Josh's face is severe, staring at his amber pint.

"It'd be really good to hear it from you, Josh." I think about laying a hand on his meaty arm before deciding against it. "If it means nothing, where's the harm? If it means something . . ."

"What's it going to mean"—he looks up abruptly—"unless someone else killed Holly. That's what this is about, isn't it? Why don't you just come out and say it?"

Fair play. It hasn't escaped me that no one else has asked outright. Shona stares at me expectantly, like the question was all hers. Kayleigh and Emma are in shock, either at the notion of a different killer or the fact Josh had the balls to ask.

I'm going to have to give them something.

"It's unlikely," I say, my voice all press-conference monotony. "Masters and Holly were seen together just before she disappeared, and he made several statements that support the theory he killed her." *Not a confession though. Nor a speck of detail that confirmed any kind of vile intimacy; the mole on her right thigh, her appendix scar, the fresh burn on her inner forearm from taking a pizza out of the oven the night before.* "However, in light of a few things—the fact she was found one hundred miles away, for a start—we need to make sure we rule out all other possibilities. Honestly, that's all we're doing." Hands open, and with a little sigh, I give the impression it's probably all a big waste of time but hey, that's my problem, not theirs. "So, Josh—she was jumpy?"

"More clingy than jumpy," he says, seemingly happy to swallow my rhetoric. "Asking to stay at mine a lot." I tilt my head. *Oh, yeah.* "No, it was nothing like that. There was never anything between me and Holly." A chorus of "He wishes" from the girls. "The first few times, I thought it was because her and Spencer had fallen out—'cos that wasn't rare, he could be aggressive, possessive—but then after a while I noticed something. She always wanted to stay over when Spencer was away, or out for the night. It was like she didn't want to be at home on her own."

"Some people don't," I say. "It takes a while to get used to. The random noises. The imaginary ax murderers. Trust me, I've been there."

Kayleigh jumps in. "Nah, Holly *lived* for nights in on her own. If she knew Spencer was going to be out or away, she'd have everything planned. What films she was going to watch, which candle she was going to light, which takeaway, which bath bomb . . ."

"And, not being funny," says Emma, looking at Josh, "but thinking about it, when did she *ever* stay round yours until those last few months? It was always mine or Shona's."

"I was still living at home then," explains Kayleigh.

Josh puffs out his considerable chest. "I think she might have been scared of something—well, someone—and she felt safer staying with me."

Big, brawny, male me. Lifter of dumbbells. Protector of fair maidens.

"Any ideas who?" Getting blank faces, I prompt, "And you're absolutely certain you don't recognize the guy from outside the church?"

Another round of definitive nos.

"Maybe if she was escorting, someone got obsessed with her?" suggests Kayleigh.

"*If* she was escorting," says Emma, chiming with my thoughts.

Shona throws Josh a grin. "Or maybe she pissed off her sugar daddy?"

I pour water on their phantom bogeymen. "Tell me more about Spencer. Josh, you said he could be possessive?"

"I don't know about possessive," says Shona, cutting across. "It took him three days to realize Holly was missing. Does that sound possessive to you?"

There's no way around it. "It took you guys three days to realize too. Wasn't it odd not to hear from her at all—a text, a call, anything? You seem like you were pretty tight."

"Holly was tight with anyone who was bringing the fun and buying the drinks." Shona gets a sharp look from Emma. "Well, it's true. It wasn't unusual for her to go AWOL. You always knew she'd turn up eventually."

Until the time she didn't.

I jump back a moment. "So maybe not possessive, but Spencer *was* aggressive?"

"Fuck, yeah," booms Josh, followed by Kayleigh and Emma, his backing singers.

Shona's thinking about this, screwing her face up and teasing her spikes. "Look, I couldn't stand the bloke, but it depends what you'd call 'aggressive.' He'd get in her face sometimes, shouting at her, and maybe a bit of push and shove—her as well as him. But me and my boyfriend are like that too when the mood takes us. I don't think Spencer killed Holly, if that's what you're driving at." She points at Josh. "Issue is, *he* had it bad for Holly since way back in Year Seven, so anyone who dared look at her the wrong way was being aggressive, apparently. And they've both been with the same laid-back pushovers since we left sixth form." Emma and Kayleigh's contented smiles confirm this.

"Couldn't your pushovers make it today?" I ask them. "They must have known Holly."

"Mine's a plumber, works for himself," says Kayleigh. "We can't afford for him to have time off, what with the baby coming." She rubs a hand across her nonexistent belly. "If it's a girl, I might call her Holly. Holly'd have loved being an auntie; she was good with kids."

"And mine's on crutches," says Emma. "Although if I'd known so few people would turn up, I'd have forced him to come. Make up the numbers, at least."

"Short notice," I say again, hoping they're not too deflated.

Shona tilts her empty glass, rolling the dregs around the bottom. "Yeah, we'll keep telling ourselves that, but, truth is, Holly was good at making friends, not so good at keeping them. She was funny and entertaining, but she could be cruel. She'd use people. Put them down. And God, she was *so* materialistic."

Emma butts in. "And she could be kind and she was a great listener. She was one of the most perceptive people I knew—she'd know you were feeling down before you realized yourself."

"Emma likes to only remember the good stuff," Shona says.

"Maybe it's not a bad idea." I take a furtive look at my watch. "Anyway, she must have been OK, you guys stuck around."

Shona shrugs. "Your oldest friends forgive more. We knew the stuff she'd been through. She'd had such shit luck in her life and she just wanted attention, I think. So if being cruel would get the laugh, she'd say it, you know? But she wasn't *actually* cruel. It wasn't who she was."

"When will they release her . . . um . . . her remains?" asks Josh, keen to move on from Holly's faults. "God knows what'll happen about a funeral. Who'll pick up the cost? My uncle died last year and the headstone alone was over £2,000."

"You won't have to think about that for a while." I scrape my chair out, stand up. "Listen, thanks for being so open, and well done again on the service. It doesn't matter how many were there—*you* were there and you did her proud. I really need to get going, though. It's nearly three."

"Shit, you and me both," says Emma, bolting up and blowing air-kisses. "They practically call social services if you're not at the gate at three thirty. Laters."

Three thirty. A fairly standard school pickup time. On occasional days off, I've collected Finn and brought him for ice cream at Udderlicious. Every time, it's drilled into me.

"*Three thirty p.m., Cat. Got that? Not three thirty-ish. Not three forty-five. Three thirty—do you hear me?*"

And so now a question's forming. A question I'll keep from Steele, even Parnell, until I know it has weight. A question it should only take a quick detour to answer.

SHED NO TEARS | 127

Because shouldn't a teacher have been in school on a Thursday afternoon in term-time, not trying to buy Lady Gaga tickets in an overpriced Clapham bar?

Were Serena Bailey's whereabouts that day ever officially checked?

10

"May I ask why you need this?"

It's not the first time a head teacher has eyed me with suspicion over the rim of their bifocals. It is the first time I've had the upper hand, though.

"I'm afraid I can't discuss that." *Oh, the power. The head-spinning power.* "If you could just confirm for me, that'd be great, thanks."

Geetha Gopal, head of Riverdale Primary since 1997 ("The week after Princess Diana died," she announced grandly, as though only a human of immense spirit could commandeer a new school under such circumstances), returns to her computer screen, leaving me standing in the center of her office, staring at the busy walls. A patchwork of certificates and thank-you cards tell the story of a job well done. A photo of every current pupil, along with their name, birthday, favorite book, and piece of fruit, tells the story of a head teacher who goes way beyond the standard definition of "care."

"God, and to think I used to be scared of this office," I say, surveying one hundred–plus gummy smiles and bad fringes; a collage of heart-melting promise.

Mrs. Gopal looks up immediately, her lined face full of warmth. "You're an ex-pupil of Riverdale?"

"Ah no, sorry. I meant the concept of the head teacher's office. I spent far too much time in them, back in the day. Nothing terrible," I feel the need to add. "Just the usual swearing, scrapping, rolling my skirt up and my socks down."

"Hmm." She drags a finger across her screen, staring hard. "I'd love to say ours are still a bit young for all that, but the way things are going . . . ah, here we are. Miss Bailey, Thursday 23rd February,

2012. Yes, she was here—marked present all day." She looks up with a satisfied smile, certain she's given the right answer. I keep my face poker-straight, resisting the urge to sprint back to HQ with my finding, a cat dropping a chewed-up mouse on Steele's clean floor. "Serena was an exemplary teacher. A natural. Very bright, creative—and devoted. I was sorry to lose her."

"Why did she leave?"

"Well, it was a little out of the blue, if I'm honest, and I never quite got to the bottom of it. It was time for a change was all she said; she was quite adamant about that. She had been here a long time, I suppose. She'd arrived here as a teaching assistant and not everyone becomes part of the furniture like me."

"It's understandable, wanting to spread your wings," I say, half genuinely, half wanting to draw her out further. "I've been with the same team for most of my career and I guess I'll have to spread mine eventually. I'll miss them like crazy, though. I take it Serena, Miss Bailey, stayed in touch? Her first school must have been special to her."

"She sent a card the following Christmas."

"That was it? No reunions over the years?"

"No reunions." Her expression tightens. "People come and go, Miss Kinsella. Of course, I would have loved to have heard about her progress. I told her on her last day that if she ever needed advice, a mentor, then she could call me any time. But life takes over, things move on, especially when you're young. I don't think she even went straight into a new role. I certainly didn't receive a reference request for some time afterward—a year or so, if I remember rightly."

"When exactly did she leave Riverdale?"

"One moment." She turns back to the screen, presses a few buttons. "Just before Easter, 2012."

Which means taking into account a notice period, she must have resigned very soon after her encounter with Holly Kemp. My brain screeches "*curiously* soon after," and even more curiously—to the point of weird, I'd say—Mrs. Gopal seems to know nothing of Serena's starring role in the Roommate drama. She certainly hasn't mentioned it, and surely she would, what with it being back in the news? Surely she'd make the connection to my visit?

"Mrs. Gopal, is there any chance Miss Bailey could have been absent that afternoon and her absence *not* recorded?"

She brings her hands together, her face turning from warm to professionally stern. "Record-keeping has to be rigorous in this day and age. I'm sure you understand that more than most."

"So that's a no?"

I'm not in the habit of being snippy with kindly women in their midsixties, but this could be big. I need answers, not policy statements.

She sighs. "Miss Kinsella, in my forty years of working in education, I've learned that definite yeses or nos are as rare as hens' teeth. What I will say is that it's *unlikely* Serena was absent without it being recorded, but records are only as good as the humans who manage them. And I assume human error also exists in the police force, does it not?"

I knew it was impossible. I knew there was no way I could stand in front of a head teacher without feeling chastened.

I try another tack. "What if she'd just left a bit early—say two, two thirty? Would that have been recorded?" I'm covering all bases, preempting Steele's landslide of questions.

"Possibly not, but you must understand, teachers don't just 'leave early' without good reason, especially those as diligent as Miss Bailey. Two, two thirty, is still very much part of the teaching day. Her class would need to be covered, arrangements made for home-time supervision. Of course, teachers are human. We're not immune to needing doctors or dentist appointments like everyone else. Generally, though, staff try to schedule these outside school hours. But that's not to say that emergencies don't crop up that require someone to leave at short notice. That *could* have happened here, I suppose." She smiles. "You know, I do pride myself on my memory, Miss Kinsella—it's an important asset in this job—however, I'm afraid the exact whereabouts of an individual over six years ago are a little beyond even me." She beckons me forward, then points at the screen—at the date *23.02.12* and the blue tick right next to it. "All I can go by is the system, and the system is telling me Miss Bailey was here."

I don't have the heart to ask if purchasing Lady Gaga tickets falls under the banner of "emergency."

Somebody should have, though.

The officer who took Serena's statement.

I phone through an update and get DC Susie Ferris's name from Craig Cooke on the QT. Parnell might be the guy I'd trust with my life—let's be honest, I've trusted him with my boyfriend and it amounts to the same thing—but when it comes to things like this, boy, does he ask a lot of questions. Far quicker to call Cookey, the soul of discretion—or the king of complete apathy, depending on your view.

DC Susie Ferris isn't DC Susie Ferris anymore, in that she's no longer a DC, or a Ferris, for that matter. It's a DI Susie Grainger who sweeps into Caffè Nero, just a few minutes down from Lavender Hill Station, the place where Christopher Masters gave his fingerprints, admitted his guilt, then said no more. Detective Constable to Detective Inspector in six years is no mean feat, to say the least. She looks well on it too. Sturdy, almost stately, with a swishy auburn bob and the kind of clear, radiant skin that suggests five a day, eight hours a night, and a commitment to drinking the recommended daily water intake.

"A full-fat Coke and a caramel brownie," she says, proving my health-nut radar to be wonky. Unable to decide, I order the same for myself and after a long wait in the queue, we sit down.

"So, you obviously like it here?" I say. "Clapham, I mean, not

Nero's." She smiles but I don't sense a whole lot of warmth. "Had you been here long before the Masters case?"

I mask it as a pleasantry but—pathetic, I know—I'm trying to work out her age. Or more to the point, I'm trying to work out how far I'm lagging behind.

"No, it was only my second case," she says, which isn't conclusive, really. She could have been an early bird, or a late starter. She could have had a different career before joining up—Blake spent a whole ten years in banking before his proficiency in sums and spouting leadership shite became his fast-track ticket to superintendent. "I've only just come back to Lavender Hill, though. I followed Tess to Shepherd's Bush for a couple of years, then Southwark, Stoke Newington, I headed up a project in Cyber Crime. I've been all over."

"You're making me dizzy," I say, not sure whether to use her title. It feels odd to call someone "ma'am" when there can't be more than a couple of years between you. When you could have effectively shared a paddling pool, or a birthday party, or a first cigarette.

She twists the cap off her Coke. "Yeah, well, I'm a product of the Tess Dyer School. Never let the grass grow. Don't ever get too comfortable."

I used to think that when I joined the Met, I'd be a go-getter like Grainger and Dyer. The plucky little change junkie, never settling in one place long enough to become complacent, always looking for the bigger thing, the better thing, the chance to prove myself all over again.

You'd think with all the therapy I've had, I'd know myself better.

"So come on then, Serena Bailey?" Her manner's frank and unsparing, designed to make you feel like you're keeping her from something incredibly important. "You said on the phone you wanted to ask me about her."

I did. But I was hoping for a peer-to-peer dialogue with someone slightly less starchy. The fact she's two ranks higher has thrown a rusty spanner in the works.

"Oh, I just wanted to get your take, you know?" I know it sounds lame, but I'm not about to accuse a DI of doing a slapdash job. I do have *some* career aspirations. "You took her statement. You probably knew her best."

"My take?" She snaps her brownie in two, somehow making it a barbed gesture. "Well, it's hard to have a 'take' on someone you met over six years ago, but as I remember, she was helpful, forthcoming, articulate, a model citizen. My 'take,' as you put it, was probably that you don't get handed a dream witness like that too often, so make the most of it."

"And yet she wasn't a dream witness, was she?"

"Meaning?"

"Well, the CPS didn't think so."

I settle back for the rant. Utter the phrase "CPS" and it's like Pavlov's dogs for disgruntled officers.

Grainger shrugs, the very opposite of disgruntled. "The CPS applied the Full Code Test and decided that with no body and no DNA, the evidential standard wasn't met." She takes a sip from the bottle, staring at me, glassy-eyed. "That doesn't make Serena Bailey a bad witness."

That doesn't mean I took a half-arsed statement.

"No, of course not."

She glances at her watch, definitely a power move. "Look, Cat— it is Cat, isn't it?" Pretending to forget my name—there's another. "Much as I'm grateful for the sugar hit, I'm an extremely busy woman right now. Why don't you just come out and say what's on your mind?"

I shouldn't really. I should check in with Steele first, or at the very least with Parnell. But then, my life's rarely been governed by what I should and shouldn't do. And that's precisely why Susie Grainger's sat there with her inspector's badge, and I'm still measuring success by whether I've managed to get through the day without a bollocking from Steele.

But fuck it.

"OK, did you ever find anything off about her, Serena Bailey?"

"Off?" She thinks about this for a second, then leans right in, freckled forearms on the table. "You know, Cat, there are three things Tess Dyer taught me about getting ahead in this job." She holds up a finger. "I mentioned one of them—don't let the grass grow. Be committed, but always have your eye on the next job." Another finger. "Second—shout about your achievements, because you better be damn sure the men are going to be shouting about theirs. And three"—her wedding finger this time; a diamond the size of a Walnut Whip—"and this is what *you* need to pay attention to—say what you mean and in the shortest way possible. Don't dance around it. Don't say, 'Did you ever find anything off about her?' when what you actually mean is, 'Do you think she lied about anything?'"

"Well, do you?"

"No, definitely not." She sits back, offering another pro forma smile. "See, we got that cleared up nice and quick once you stopped pussyfooting around."

I could credit her with being perceptive, or I could take the more obvious view that Dyer's been in touch. Nothing cynical in that, of course. If one of your cases is being reinvestigated, it's only natural you'd want to get the band back together. To remind yourself that you worked with the best and the decisions you took were sound. I've absolutely no doubt that's what Dyer and Oliver Cairns were doing after we left the pub last night, and it stands to reason that Grainger needs the same assurances.

Thing is, I'm not questioning DI Susie Grainger's competence. I'm questioning wet-behind-the-ears DC Susie Ferris's experience. Her second case, working for a DCI who was under considerable personal and professional pressure, with barely time to brief her team properly, I bet, never mind babysit rookies—*that's* where balls get dropped. That's where less obvious leads don't get followed up and statements aren't taken as thoroughly as they could be.

It's nobody's fault. It just *is*. Give us the manpower and the budget and we'll be the superheroes we're supposed to be.

So again, *fuck it*.

"I went to see Serena Bailey's old employer earlier. Their absence records put her at work in North London on the afternoon of the 23rd. Way up North—Edgware." Before she can say it, I add, "They're not always one hundred percent accurate, of course, nothing ever is."

I tell her what Mrs. Gopal said, near verbatim. She listens, poised as ever, cocking her head this way and that. Interestingly, she doesn't interrupt once, and if I wasn't a lot wiser, I'd say she looks almost grateful for the heads-up.

"Wow, that's thorough work, Cat." I'm not sure if I feel patronized or galvanized by her approval. It doesn't last long, though. Her tone changes in a flash. "But it doesn't change the fact her statement was—is—foolproof. It fits with the evidence. The time she saw Holly on Valentine Street, a twenty-minute walk from the Tube station, chimes exactly with the time Holly was captured leaving the Tube. Her description fits. She described *exactly* what Holly was wearing." I nod. "And most importantly, what reason would she have to lie?"

I've got no answer for this. Her logic trumps my instinct every time.

"It doesn't change the fact her statement wasn't checked thoroughly, or held up to any real scrutiny," I say. "If Holly's case had got to court, that could have been problematic."

"But it didn't, so what's the issue?" For perhaps the first time ever, I feel like the jobsworth. The pen pusher. The whiny pipsqueak prefect. "And anyway, what do you mean by 'checked?' I ran her through the PNC, made sure she didn't have a record or any form for nuisance calling, wasting police time, the usuals. She was clean—like I say, a model citizen. What else should I have done? Give me one good reason why I should have questioned her account, or why we should question it now."

I have several but I'm taking them back to the office. Grainger stands up, clearly keen to get back to hers.

"Seriously . . ." Her voice is softer now. "It was worth following up—well done, go to the top of the class. But you heard your Mrs. Gopal. Human error. Someone forgot to mark her absent, that's all. Now if you don't mind, I've got get back and so should you. Do your career a favor, Cat—go and solve some cases that actually need solving."

11

"That was a long pint. I'm surprised you can stand."

I could twirl through this office wearing nothing but a pair of angel wings and Pete Flowers wouldn't notice. Give him the chance to clock that I'm missing, though, and suddenly he's Hawkeye. The guy doesn't miss a trick.

"Ah well, you know the Irish, Sarge. Takes more than a four-hour sesh to floor us." I turn to Parnell. "*Obviously*, I haven't been drinking. Hey, did you track down Church Guy? I double-checked and her friends definitely don't recognize him. Odd, right? Holly obviously meant something to him and yet her closest mates haven't a clue who he is? Seems fishy."

"As an old sardine," agrees Parnell. "I've only just got the CCTV, but it's a matter of time, trust me. Mags is missing her book club so I can stay late and trawl through the footage."

If it's a hint, it's wasted on me. Tonight is Aiden and the Americans. Not just a great band name, but a date I've promised to keep.

I sit down and scan through my emails. Nothing from Masters' bank yet but it's only been a day. Patience really isn't my forte.

"Cookey filled us in," says Parnell. I freeze. Filled them in on what? The highlights from Holly's friends? Mrs. Gopal? The fact I was after the name and current station of the officer who took Serena Bailey's statement? I thought I'd hinted strongly enough to keep *that* bit on the QT. Parnell sits back, swiveling in his chair. "So Holly could have been escorting, huh? And interesting about Bailey's school . . . don't know what to make of that."

Nothing about Grainger. Good old Cookey, discreet to the last.

"Me neither," I say vaguely. "Is Her Majesty in?" I try to catch a glimpse of Steele through her blinds.

"She is. And she hears you've been busy." As if in a puff of smoke, Steele's suddenly behind me. "Listen, pull your chairs around, folks. Quick catch-up while we're all here."

At least she's smiling, which must mean Susie Grainger hasn't been on the phone moaning about me. I'd have put money on her pulling rank, bleating about professional courtesy and the indignity of having your judgment questioned by an officer two ranks lower. Clearly, her self-preservation instinct is stronger than her ego—she knows she missed a flaw in Bailey's statement and she's happy to let it pass quietly.

As am I. Happy to let it pass that I met with her without Steele's say-so.

"So, team, what news from the trenches?" Steele perches against an empty desk, daintier than ever in green sparkly flip-flops. "Blake is all over this like a fat kid on a cake—and before anyone takes offense, I was a fat kid, I'm allowed to say it—so please don't make me walk into his office with nothing but my natural charm to fall back on."

"Seth's new woman has dumped him," volunteers Renée from the next desk. "Does that count as news?"

Seth nods, looking resigned. "Second time this year. I'm 'emotionally stunted,' apparently." He scratches his head. "Or was it 'emotionally frigid?' That could have been Becca, actually. Or maybe Camille?"

"It was Camille," confirms Emily, completely deadpan. "Like dating a cardboard box. Becca's was the 'beautifully fragrant robot.' I've been keeping track."

For a rich, blandly handsome, Oxford-educated man in his early thirties, who Renée and I once worked out was 257th in line to the throne, DS Seth Wakeman is woefully unlucky in love. He blames the demands of the job. The rest of us blame him for doing the job when he could be running an art gallery in Chelsea and living off his trust fund.

"We've found Holly's boyfriend," says Parnell, applying the brakes to the eternal Seth conundrum. "Well, Ben has."

"We got lucky with the airports?" I ask.

"Sod airports," scoffs Swaines. "Who needs airports when you've got social media. I've been Facebook stalking, trawling through a million and one Spencer Shaws. Found him just now. He's currently splashing in a pool in Tenerife with his wife and two kids. Due back Sunday, I think. Well, it's Thursday now and today's post says, *Only three more days*—sad face. *By current standards, I make that thirty more piña coladas!*—happy face."

"You're sure it's the right guy?" A note of caution in Steele's voice.

"Definitely." That earns him a twinkle. There's nothing Steele loves more than a "definitely." "Apart from the fact the idiot has his date of birth on his profile, he hasn't changed much, physically, and we've got his mug shot from the burglary conviction and a tabloid photo from 2012—a 'devastated partner' shot. It's him. I'd put my signed Ronaldo shirt on it."

"OK, so from his cheery piña colada comment, we deduce that he either doesn't know about Holly or he doesn't care." Steele hops up on the desk, her legs dangling. "Of course, it's feasible he hasn't seen the news over there, although you'd think someone would have called him."

"They don't want to spoil his holiday?" Parnell suggests. "Because I'm struggling to buy that he knows but doesn't care. Even if he hated Holly, even if he *killed* her, he'd be shocked if nothing else, surely? Not posting on Facebook about his binge-drinking."

"He's overcompensating," says Renée. "Trying to act normal."

"Has he posted a lot while they've been away?" Steele asks Swaines. "Because I can't believe people would comment and play along, and not one person mention that his ex-girlfriend's been found."

Swaines shakes his head. "No, that's his first update in three weeks. He's not prolific."

"OK, well, don't take your eyes off that post, Benny-boy. The minute you see as much as a *Call me, mate* in the comments section, you tell me."

"Of course. Nothing yet—just a handful of likes."

"So what are we going to do?" asks Flowers. "Let him drink himself blind for the next three days—lucky sod—or get the next flight over there?"

"Blake's not going to sign that off, Pete. We've got no grounds for arrest."

"But we're going to make contact?" Parnell says, brow furrowed.

She hesitates. "Look, I know it's frustrating, folks, but the last thing we want to do is spook him. If he knows he's going to get hauled in the minute he sets foot back in Blighty, it gives him time to prepare. It could even make him run, if he is guilty. And then we've got a European goose chase on our hands and I've got a very grumpy Blake to contend with." She nods to herself, decision made. "No, we let him keep splashing in the pool with his kids for now, we keep tabs on his social media, and then we pounce as soon as he's home."

"Can't believe he's got two kids," I say. "They don't hang around, this lot. One of Holly's friends has a school-age kid and another one's pregnant. I can't look after my Oyster card, never mind another human."

"Oh yeah, about Holly's friends, what they said about the escorting . . ." Steele's looking at me. "It's an angle, for sure—I mean, if he didn't know about it, it definitely gives Shaw a motive—but I'm reluctant to go public with something that's essentially just a friend's hunch. We'll get crucified if it's wrong, and anyway, is it really going to bring anyone out of the woodwork? Ex-clients, punters, whatever you want to call them, they're more likely to run for the hills."

"Church Guy?" Parnell proposes.

"Maybe," I say. "One of Holly's friends thought she was afraid of something—someone—in the months before she disappeared. Could have been a lovesick client, someone with a problem understanding boundaries. I kind of brushed it off, but stranger things have happened."

Steele's quick. "Why'd you brush it off?"

"The friend—he was a bit lovesick himself, apparently. I got the impression he likes thinking she was scared of something and that he was her knight in shining armor. Whether or not it was the case, who knows? The other friends didn't notice anything."

Steele nods. "OK, well, Cookey's out working through the main London agencies—not literally, I hope—but I'm not holding my breath. It's a needle in a haystack."

Parnell stands up, heads straight for the incident board. "You know, we can come up with alternative suspects all the livelong day—aggressive ex-boyfriends, obsessed punters—but it all comes back to one major problem." He points at the photo of Holly's skull, his finger over the bullet hole. "She was shot in the head. Executed. That isn't a domestic gone bad, or a stalker client. That's . . . that's different. Guns are different. I'm assuming nothing's come up on the farmer?"

"No, but how about this for a theory?" says Renée, folding her arms. Seth's nodding by her side, signaling his input. "Spencer Shaw had a record for burglary—well, conspiracy to commit burglary, right? What if he and Holly tried to burgle the farmer's house? Something goes wrong. Holly gets shot. Spencer can't admit what happened, because he's going away for a long time if he does. He agrees to bury Holly's body in return for the farmer's silence."

My reaction's instant. "But there must be thousands of farms between London and Cambridgeshire. Why that one? And in any case, if that's what happened, he'd bury her miles away, surely? Not right there at the scene of the crime. It doesn't make sense."

I sound more scathing than I mean to. It's not a bad theory, really, just freckled with flaws. Renée doesn't take offense, though.

Twenty-plus years of sitting in brainstorms like this gives you a hide thicker than a truck tire.

"Masters could have made a gun," says Flowers, tentatively, as if it's just occurred to him. "Between Google and his hardware store, he'd have the instructions and the ingredients."

"So we're back at Masters again." I say it quietly, but not quiet enough.

Steele gives me an arch stare. "Any reason we shouldn't be? This is all fun and games, but you know Masters killing Holly is still our most likely outcome."

"Because of the gospel according to Serena Bailey."

"Which, as far as we know, we have no reason to doubt."

"We do now. She wasn't marked absent from school that afternoon and her old boss said it's unlikely it wouldn't have been recorded." I could leave it at that, but Susie Grainger's words are itching my ears: *Say what's on your mind.* "Just hear me out, OK? Serena says she saw Holly at around four p.m. outside Masters' house. She'd waited in The Northcote for Mr. No-Show for around forty minutes before heading back, so that means she must have got there not long after three p.m." I pause, taking a quick breath. "Edgware, where her old school is, to Clapham, is the best part of an hour's travel, so that's her leaving school around two p.m. that afternoon. But Mrs. Gopal, the head teacher, said that would be unusual unless an emergency came up, and she also said Serena was an exemplary teacher, completely devoted. So would an exemplary teacher really have bunked off early just to collect concert tickets?" Steele's face is stony but she's taking it all in. Her eyes haven't left mine for a second. "I'm not saying she's lying about seeing Holly. I don't know what I'm saying exactly. But something smells off—not a stink, just a whiff." I bring my hands together in prayer. "Can we at least request her bank records? Pretty please. If something puts her in Clapham that afternoon, you won't hear another peep out of me, I promise."

"I should be so lucky." Steele wrinkles her nose, thinking about it. "Yeah, why not? Benny-boy, get on it."

While she's feeling generous, I keep pressing. "You know, she left Riverdale just before Easter that year. I'd need to check the dates but I guess that makes it late March, early April—a month, month and a half tops after her Holly ID. Presuming she had a notice period, she must have pretty much resigned straightaway."

Parnell shrugs. "Something like that could trigger a 'life's too short' mentality. Maybe she wasn't happy there? Just because Mrs. Gopal loved her doesn't mean she loved Mrs. Gopal."

"True. But also, I don't think Mrs. Gopal had the first clue why I was there. She certainly didn't mention Holly or Masters, and it'd be the obvious leap to make if Serena had told her about it. Or told *anyone* in the school, for that matter. Don't you think that's odd?"

Steele rubs both cheeks. "This whole bloody case is odd. This accomplice business, for one thing."

"Oh, Brandon Keefe has an aunt in Cambridgeshire," says Swaines, suddenly animated. "I've just been looking at him; good old Facebook again. It was his birthday last month and he got a message with a load of birthday cake emojis from an Auntie Mel in Yaxley, which is about twenty-five miles north of Caxton. It's a link."

"That's not a link, it's a coincidence." I check myself quickly. "OK, OK, it's a notable coincidence. But come on, if you look at anyone's Facebook . . ."

"Except yours," interrupts Emily. "I mean, Cat K? What's that all about? And you don't even have a profile picture. How's anyone supposed to find you?"

They aren't, that's the point. I spend enough of my life trying to keep my secrets secret without putting it all out there for the whole universe to see. I only really have the account for work—it's staggering how open some suspects are on social media—and to gaze at the occasional photo of Finn.

"My point is twenty-five miles isn't a solid link. It doesn't mean anything. We're a small island. Name any place in the UK and I bet I'll know someone who lives within twenty-five miles of it."

Steele swoops. "Or maybe don't. This isn't a geography lesson." She stares at me, head cocked. "You're not convinced by this accomplice theory, I take it?"

Truth is, after today—after Church Guy, after Holly's friends, after the saga of Riverdale's absence records, and the wholly unsanctioned meeting with DI Susie Grainger—I'd kind of forgotten about Accomplice Theory. Which, I suppose, suggests I'm not entirely convinced by it. While I can conceive it in my head, I don't feel it in my gut.

"I don't know, boss." I grasp around for something more constructive. "Where's this accomplice now? Why hasn't he carried on killing? I mean, isn't that the only reason Masters would keep quiet about him? For the pleasure of knowing his good work was being carried on? And have you read my report from the Jacob Pope meet? He said Masters was an independent kind of guy. *Fiercely* independent. That doesn't exactly scream 'accomplice.'"

"First, how do we know the *supposed* accomplice hasn't continued? We sure as hell don't have a consistent method of killing to work with—Holly's cause of death has blown that well out of the water. And second, would that be Dr. Jacob Pope, PhD psychology, you're referring to? Or Jacob Pope, the piece of shit who killed his girlfriend?"

"Point taken. But I'm not sure about Keefe, though. The *Mail* interview—why would he turn the spotlight on himself if he was involved?"

"He wouldn't be the first," Renée says. "Some killers can't help making themselves part of the story."

"OK, another point taken. But at the risk of sounding like a shrink, he doesn't quite fit the profile for me." I look at Parnell, now slumped against the incident board. Not a great sign given he's got a long night ahead. "Remember all the family photos, Sarge? Keefe's got a solid family unit. Older brothers he's close to. A mum and dad he spoke fondly of. Masters' ex-wife said he'd always wanted a son, but Keefe had no need for a surrogate father, or any type of male role model. I just can't see how Masters would have got *that* sort of hold over him."

Steele says to Parnell, "Didn't you say he'd been miffed about some girl he had the hots for shagging someone else? Masters might have got in his ear about that? 'All women are slags.' The usual tripe."

"He didn't actually know she was shagging him until much later," I tell her. "Not until after he'd been paid for the *Mail* interview. Masters was locked up by then."

Emily's hand shoots up. "Boss, remember Masters' ex-wife told me and Seth that he had a second cousin in Cambridgeshire?" Steele nods. We all nod. "Well, I ran him through the PNC and he has two convictions—one from 1987, the other 2001. Both for assaulting his wife."

"An associate of Masters' with convictions for violence against women," says Seth. "Add him to the accomplice roll call."

"But he's dead, isn't he?" says Parnell. "I'm sure you said he was dead?"

"Jesus Christ! Who isn't dead on this case?" Steele lifts her hands to rail at the gods as the rest of us exchange glances. After a moment, she regains composure, letting out a deep breath and dazzling us all with a slightly manic ear-to-ear smile.

"Right, my lovelies, who has plans this evening? I need to pay a visit and one of you lucky folk is coming with me."

Parnell's already out on account of his Church Guy crusade. Renée and Emily shout "Yoga" and "Mate's 30th" simultaneously, and Flowers' face makes it clear he'd rather nail his scrotum to the table.

Leaving me and Seth. And Steele isn't going anywhere with a recently dumped Seth.

"Bad luck, Cat. You're it."

"I've got to be in Soho for nine p.m. at the latest. A dinner reservation."

"Ooooooh!" Steele pulls an impressed face. "Check this one out. Picnics on a Tuesday night. Dinner reservations on a Thursday. Quite the socialite these days, aren't we?"

I don't rise to it. "So where are we off to?"

"Wait a minute, I'll tell you exactly." She checks her phone. "Langley Villa, number four Montrose Grove, South Kensington."

"Sounds posh."

Parnell whistles. "Sounds pricey. Who are you off to see? The Aga Khan?"

Steele laughs. "Not far off. Olly Cairns. I want to get this accomplice thing ruled in or ruled out, one way or the other, once and for all."

12

Dad's dirty money, his gold-plated membership to The Bad Life Inc., meant that I had A Good Life growing up, if by "good" you mean posh schools I never felt I belonged in, fancy holidays I never wanted to go on, and in later years, a £250 monthly allowance that I'd invariably blow on other people—mainly cool girls and bad boys—in a soulless attempt to buy friends.

It also means I've never been that wowed by nice houses, having lived in a fairly decent one myself from the age of ten. Ripped from the decade-long security of the only place I'd ever called home—the cramped flat above McAuley's Old Ale House—Mum and Dad had shipped us up to Hertfordshire at the turn of the millennium to live a middle-class life on a middle-class street in a middle-class village, so we could start the process of pretending to be something we weren't.

Dining room people. Conservatory people. Two en suites and an oak-paneled study–type people.

Oliver Cairns' picture-book house makes ours look like a peasant's shack.

"Fuck me," I say, not managing to phrase my awe more eloquently. "Cairns must have racked up the overtime."

Langley Villa is a detached, five-story, stucco-fronted townhouse, almost as wide as it is high, and set back from a dreamy cherry-blossom street. It could be Georgian. Could be Victorian. It could be the real deal or a new build. All I know is that it's expensive. Crazy, laughably, lunatic expensive.

Steele turns, halfway up the steps to the grand pillared entrance. "That Merc didn't come cheap either." She points behind me to the cobalt-blue status symbol. "I bet the number plate alone cost more than my car."

OL18 VER.

I scrape my jaw off the pavement and follow her to the door. "Seriously, is this the same guy? He didn't strike me as a personalized number-plate wanker."

"That's what having too much money does to you. What else is he going to spend it on?" She rings the bell, talking quickly. "His wife made a killing in plastic coat hangers—or could be coat hooks? Something deathly dull, anyway. But she sold the business for £50 million."

"I could live with deathly dull."

The door clicks open and there he is, the coat-hanger king, framed in late-evening sun and wearing his slippers and a tired smile. He'd clearly scrubbed up for drinks with Dyer last night, as it's a different Oliver Cairns who welcomes us into his hotel-lobby hall with its gleaming checkerboard tiles. In his brown slacks and brown cardigan, an errant eyebrow stuck out like an indicator, he looks more like a classics professor than a retired crime fighter.

We follow him into a sitting room the size of a small aircraft hangar. Four elegantly mismatched sofas form a perfect square around what I suppose you'd call a coffee table, even though it could easily host a state banquet. The high walls are full of high art: lines, shapes, colors, splodges, frenzied brushstrokes I can't make head nor tail of.

"Sit down, sit down. God knows I'm not short on seating." He leaves the room for a second, returning with a dining chair. "My back's playing hell at the moment and those bloody sofas are way too low," he explains. "I curse the day we ever bought them—and why we needed four is anyone's guess. Anyways, make yourselves at home. What is it they say in Spain? *Mi casa, su casa.*"

"Bloody hell, I wish your home was my home," I say, sinking, almost merging, with a leather sofa made for ten.

"A tip for you, Cat." Cairns' eyes twinkle. "Marry well, but divorce better."

"You and Moira broke up?" says Steele, looking shocked. "I'm sorry, Olly. I didn't realize."

He lowers himself onto the chair, a slow, labored effort. "Ah, 'twas no big deal. No drama."

"I just thought, the house, you know . . . it's very . . ."

"Tasteful?"

"Tidy, I was going to say. Christ, the state of your office at Chiswick."

"Ah well, that'll be Gracie, God love her. She comes in twice a week, keeps the place looking half-respectable."

We smile at the understatement. Steele sits down next to me.

"So when did you and Moira call time?" she asks.

"Oh, a while back, 2014. You hit that age when you realize you've only a limited amount of time left, and you start thinking, *Is this what I want for the rest of my life? Are* you *what I want?* Moira decided no." He scratches his jaw. "We'd had twenty happy-enough years, but sure, with no kids, no grandkids, no family to keep it together for, we'd drifted apart. Anyways, I got the house, even though it'd been Moira's big project. She got everything else and less of a guilty conscience in return. She's living in Toronto now. We speak occasionally. I wish her well." He might be braving it out but there's a hollow, forlorn look about him. Not so much a fish out of water as a pig up a tree, a man completely at odds with the surroundings he's found himself in. He eases himself to the edge of the chair. "So, enough about my woes, what'll you both drink? I've a lovely Barolo out there, although you won't mind if I don't join you. I've felt like boiled shite all day." A sheepish grin. "I may have had a bad pint last night."

I laugh. "Was it the sixth one or the seventh, you reckon?"

"Ah now, will you stop?" *Shtop*, the Irish "h." He reminds me of my grandad Pat, and come to think of it, he looks a bit like him.

"Blame that lush, Tess Dyer. I told her I'm not able for it these days, but sure, you might as well talk to the wall. She has hollow legs, that one."

Steele turns to me. "You'd never think this man used to drink ten pints in the evening, then run 10K in the morning. Isn't age a sickener?"

"You're telling me, Katie, love." I can't help it—the *Katie* kills me. Cairns clocks my grin and raises his voice, pretending to scold. "And I don't know what you're smiling at, young one. It'll happen to you, you can be sure of that. One minute it's all discos and twelve-hour shifts on two hours' sleep, the next you're eyeing up shoehorns and taking naps in the day."

Steele smiles. "And how are you, besides the bad pint? I heard you hadn't been well?"

"Rheumatoid arthritis." Not one ounce of self-pity. "'Twasn't too bad at first. I mean, sometimes I'd hardly recognize me own feet, toes pointing off in all directions, and the bunions—Christ, don't get me started. But like I said, 'twas manageable, anyhow." He sighs, pulling at the crook of his neck. "Then a few years ago, they tell me my immune system's attacking the joints in my spine, and that's a whole different ball game. I packed up the job soon afterward. Always thought I'd make it to sixty-five, but sure, like a lot of things, 'twasn't meant to be."

"Do you miss it?" I ask.

"Do I miss it?" he echoes, as though he's never actually considered it. "I miss the routine. Having a reason to set the alarm, you know? But I don't miss the job, not really. The Met runs on caffeine and goodwill these days, Cat. Good people, overworked people, doing difficult jobs for not much more than you'd pay a postman—no disrespect to them o'course, grand job they do. And I'd felt removed from it for years, truth be told. I wasn't a police officer anymore, I was a yes-man, a well-paid administrator. Do you know what made me call it a day in the end? 'Twasn't really my back." He shakes his head at the memory. "This young lad, a young DC, hands me his resignation, and as God is my witness, I'd never laid eyes on the fella. He was part of my team on a fecking wall chart somewhere, and yet I could have walked past him in the street, wouldn't have known him from Adam." He shoots Steele a reproachful look. "Christ, I should watch my mouth in front of the young one. The Met's short enough on detectives as it is. Don't want another one walking."

"Ah, don't worry. She'd never leave me, would you, Cat?"

"Stockholm syndrome," I confirm.

Cairns laughs, attempting to heave himself out of the chair. "Right, will I pour you a glass of that Barolo?"

Steele's hand's up, stopping him. "No, no, we're fine, Olly. Sit down, honestly. We can't be too long, anyway—the young one has a date."

He flashes me a crooked grin. "I'd say she's not short of them."

"And I've no idea what Barolo is," I admit. "It'd be wasted on me."

"Me too, until a few years ago, but I'm quite the wine connoisseur, these days. Sure, you have to fill the time somehow." He settles back down again, crossing his stiff long legs at the ankle, his shrewd gaze shifting from me to Steele. "So if you don't want my wine, and I doubt you want my company, what is it you ladies want, may I ask?"

For possibly the first time ever, Steele looks nervous, properly so.

"OK, so I could have picked her up wrong, Olly, and even if I've picked her up right, I'm not questioning your judgment, I want to be clear about that. I'm just picking your brains, that's all."

"Well now, that's quite an opener, Katie, love. I might need that glass of wine yet." His eyes are narrow. "But be my guest—you know me, I'm an open book."

"It's just that Tess said, *implied*, that certain avenues she wanted to explore during the Roommate case were shut down by the powers that be." Her voice is steady but she's scratching at a nail, defiling her gel manicure. "Holly Kemp's boyfriend for one, but in particular . . ."

"The boyfriend had an alibi, Kate. And look, I know we're hard-wired to always suspect the partner, but Holly was seen entering the house of a convicted serial killer and never seen again. I think that gets the boyfriend off the hook, don't you?"

"Possibly. But Tess also implied that you shut down the idea of Masters having an accomplice. Obviously it's something we're now open to considering, but I want to know why you didn't buy it. I assume you're the powers that be she's referring to?"

"I suppose I must be, although she flatters me, bless her. I was a middle-management cog in a very big wheel."

"Are you saying *you* were told to forget about an accomplice?"

"Well, no . . ." He straightens up a little, fingers drumming both knees. "I wasn't told to do anything because I didn't discuss it with anyone."

"What?" Steele's face creases. "You didn't raise it with John Turvill? He was Commander at the time, right?"

"No, I didn't."

Short. Sharp. Final. A reminder of who was once boss, who showed her the ropes, who taught her to tie her investigative shoe-laces.

"Ah, come on. *No?* That's it? Olly, this is me you're talking to. What are you not saying?"

"You need to understand the context, Kate." *Katie, love* has now left the building. "That case was two weeks of pure bedlam. Three separate incident rooms to cope with the chaos. A few thousand calls every day and three quarters of them stone mad. I don't know how many door-to-door inquiries were made, but we're talking thousands again, and God alone knows how many hours of CCTV, for all the good it did. Every day a new development, a dud lead, and constant pressure to make quick decisions. And all of this under fierce media scrutiny—*fierce*." He pauses, letting us feel the lead weight of it. "The real powers that be—Turvill, DAC Dempsey—wanted the case closed, is what I'm saying. They wanted the good people of Clapham sleeping easier in their beds."

"So *closed* was more important than *thorough*?" I ask.

At worst I sound disrespectful, at best naive. But as much as I've taken a small shine to Oliver Cairns, all wife-less and cardiganed in his unmanageably large home, he's not my old mentor. *He ain't the boss of me.*

"Oh no, thorough *is* important, Cat. Thing is, they want thorough, but they want it *now*. Same as any business. And o'course, anything this high profile, it's not just the family you're answerable to; it's the country, the politicians. Police cuts were big news back then. Rallies, marches, protests. Do you remember, Kate? *Cut Crime, Not Police. The Thin Blue Line Just Got Thinner.* And it's no better now. If it wasn't for bloody Brexit, it'd still be front-page news."

"Enough," Steele says, hands up. "Do you know, Olly, I've banned the B word in the office unless it's relevant to a case. Two years of everyone and his dog having an opinion; it's too much. The job's hard enough."

"Ah, you might be right," he says, although I get the sense that he'd gladly keep going. "Anyway, the point I was making is with all the noise around cuts, there was no way they wanted the Roommate case dragging on, giving the media more sticks to beat them with."

Steele shifts closer to Cairns, leaning over the arm of the sofa. "But cuts have always been big news. And I get it was pressurized, but you and me had our fair share of high-stakes cases. Denny Gray, the Vauxhall Bridge shootings. Christ, I didn't go home for six days when we were on the Carly Waters kidnapping . . ."

A twitch of a smile. "All right then, spit it out, Katie, love. It's been a few years, but I know that face. What's eating you?"

"It's just . . ." She stretches forward, giving him a fond prod on the leg. "The best thing about you, Olly—the best thing for my career, my confidence, was that you always, *always* trusted me. You were a guiding hand, a devil's advocate if I needed one, but you let me take the lead, follow my nose. Yet with Tess, with this case, you put a leash on her. Why?"

"Management isn't one-size-fits-all, you know that. Tess was a different copper to you. You were always by the book, very fact based, and that's easier to trust. I could give you more rope. Tess is all guts and glory, and while that can be great, it needs micromanaging." Steele throws me a pointed look—he could be describing me. "You know, I often thought if I could merge the pair of you, I'd have had the perfect detective."

She takes the compliment, smiling gently. "It must have been tough, though, overruling her. You were so close."

"And as my bitch of a hangover proves, we still are. Tess didn't take it personally. I think she was glad to have someone else make the decision."

Steele's surprised. "That doesn't sound like the Tess Dyer I know."

"You heard about Paul, I assume?"

"Her husband," I say, keen to keep a hand in the conversation, not let it fall into *The Katie and Olly Show*. "He was ill at the time."

"Very ill, which means she wasn't exactly the Tess Dyer anyone knew." He looks at the floor, forcing a quivery smile. "Paul was a great fella. Public-school lad, brains to burn, but always wore it lightly, if you know what I mean? He'd been born with a heart defect, but he never let it hold him back. Top university, top marks, top career with the Civil Service." The smile fades fast. "But he got a bad infection around ten years ago that made whatever the problem was ten times worse. He was in and out of the hospital for years, God love him. He'd get better, they'd get back to normal, and then bam, another setback. And all the while, Tess was climbing the ranks, haring up and down the motorway back and forth to the hospital while raising two kids—two fine lads, Ewan and Max. Ewan's the sportsman—he plays for Chelsea's Under 14s. Max is going to be the next Bill Gates, so they say. They're a credit to her. To them both."

"So her head wasn't in the game," says Steele airily. No hint to the fact she effectively nailed this in yesterday's briefing.

"Ah now, I wouldn't say that exactly; this is Tess Dyer we're talking about. But you can see why I went for the leash over the guiding hand. Tess downplayed Paul's illness, but I knew the score. I knew she was struggling, and good management's all about spotting when someone's vulnerable and having their back. I had yours once or twice in the early days, Katie Steele."

A beat of silence as something coded flies between them. Steele reddens, but she doesn't back down. "See, to me, Olly, 'having someone's back' means giving them the courage to express themselves, safe in the knowledge you'll listen, take it on board. Shooting down her accomplice theory straightaway wouldn't have done much for her confidence."

"Nor would Commander Turvill laughing her out of his office."

"Would he have?" I ask.

"Look, when we got Masters, we had our man, job done. It wouldn't have done Tess any favors to go off spouting half-cocked theories. She was newly promoted. It was only her second case at the wheel. There'd already been talk of whether she was ready for it, and I wasn't going to give Turvill—or anyone—the chance to doubt her. That's what 'having someone's back' means to me. Keeping a clear head when they can't. Stopping them racing off down rabbit holes. Protecting them from themselves."

I nod, unsure whether I think this is first-class management or paternalistic horseshit. I'd probably go with the latter if it wasn't for the fact that Parnell's steadying hand has kept me sane time and time again, and kept me employed on more than one occasion.

"Why did you think the theory was half-cocked?" asks Steele.

"Well, it seemed half-cocked back then, is what I meant. Pure hypothesis when we only had the time and manpower for hard facts. Tess got it in her head that Masters must have had someone else answering the calls, because no self-respecting young girl would still be interested in the room after two minutes talking to that old drone. I mean, there was *something* in what she was saying, but John Turvill would have kicked me into next week if we'd landed at his door with just that."

"What about the lack of drag marks on the victims' bodies?" I say. "Surely that was worth pause for thought?"

"Pause!" He tips his head back, letting out a laugh like a bark, a single scornful note. "I don't think any of us paused once, from the time the first call came in until Masters got sent down. And anyway, have you looked at the Dulwich Woods photos?" I haven't; Holly's my victim, Caxton, my crime scene. Luckily, Steele's head is bobbing up and down. "Well then, you'll know that Stephanie König was the heaviest of the girls, by some way. And where was she found?"

"Much nearer to the road than the others," says Steele, taking his point.

"Exactly. Masters couldn't carry her the same distance so he had to bury her nearer to where he'd parked. Two people wouldn't have had that problem, they'd have buried her near Bryony and Ling. That was my thinking."

All of a sudden, I'm not sure what's more flimsy. Dyer's reasoning for believing there could be an accomplice or Cairns' reasoning for discounting it.

"Listen, Olly, I want your opinion." Steele looks at Cairns like he holds the keys to the universe. "And I need you to be honest with me."

"Nothing but, Katie. I always was."

"You said before, 'It seemed half-cocked back then.' Does that mean you've changed your mind? I guess what I'm asking is, are we going on a wild-goose chase?"

Barely a breath. "Maybe not. Maybe Tess had something, after all."

She wanted an answer and she got one, and a more resolute one than I think either of us expected. Something's vexing her though. She turns to face me, eyebrows raised, then back to Cairns. "'Maybe not.' Seriously, Olly? The man who'd argue black was white admits he might have called it wrong, just like that."

"It's not about being wrong. I stand by my decision. I still say Tess's theory was too weak for us to have run with, based on the facts we had at the time." He bends forward, his face inches from Steele's—his shock of white hair, her raven-black bob. "But you, Katie, you have different facts. You have Holly Kemp rotting in a ditch one hundred miles from the other victims and a bullet hole in her skull, no signs of strangulation. I'd say there's a fair to middling chance you could be looking at an accomplice."

"Or a different killer entirely? What'd you think to that?" I try to keep it light, playful. My tongue firmly in my cheek.

"What do I think? I think if I was your guv'nor, I'd be putting the leash on you right now. Check Serena Bailey's statement, Cat—we got the right man."

Steele tops up her makeup in the rearview mirror, our post-match analysis more or less complete.

"Christ, though, he's aged," she says, head tilted back, mid-mascara.

"He might be thinking the same about you."

It's a joke. She knows it's a joke. While I can't quite wrap my head around the idea of Steele as a gauche young woman, the idea of her getting old doesn't seem at all possible.

"I aged in that meeting, I tell you. Don't ever turn up at my door questioning my management skills, Kinsella. There's a piece of advice for you." She drops her makeup bag in my lap. "Here, you've got a date, haven't you?"

I wasn't going to bother, bar a slick of tinted lip balm, but it'd be sacrilege to pass up a rummage through Steele's treasure trove: sleek designer brands, everything with its lid on, nothing blunt, smashed, or smeared, or well over five years old.

"So what did Cairns have your back about?" I ask, surveying something called a Parsley Seed Antioxidant Serum. I fully expect to be told to mind my own business.

"Nothing major, don't get too excited." She blots her lips, keeping them closed a fraction longer than necessary. "I made a mistake with a warrant. It could have been bad. It wasn't. That should have been the end of it, but it was 1992 and I was a woman on a murder team, same age as you are now, and Cairns knew they—'the lads'—would make a thing of it, make it the Biggest Mistake Ever, so he took the heat, said I was just following his orders. He's got his flaws, Olly, but he's a good 'un."

I bring my hands to my face. "Oh my gaaaaaawd! Kate Steele made a mistake! How can we ever trust her again?"

"That was about the size of it," she says, grinning. "You know, I don't envy your generation much—I wouldn't want to be in my twenties the way the world is now, or my thirties for that matter—but it's definitely easier to be a woman in the Met these days. Not easy, but easier. Sexism isn't as passé as they like to claim, but it isn't half as bad as it was, trust me. I mean, I know Flowers can be a bit of a relic, but he knows he's a relic, at least. And he'd have your back if you needed it. The whole team would. We've got a really nice setup."

Now's as good a time as any. I've made so many mistakes, told so many lies that would pulverize our "nice setup" if they ever came to light, that this almost seems like the least of them.

"You know the guy I'm seeing?" I pull down the sun visor, check myself out in the mirror: a nice couldn't-care-less gesture.

"Well, no, I don't. I don't actually *know* you're seeing anyone because you never talk about it, bar references to picnics and dinner dates, but, as you were . . ."

"Well, he's . . ." I challenge my own reflection. *Say it. Say it.* "He's . . ."

She reaches over, pushes the visor up with a snap. "He's what, Kinsella? A Mormon, a zookeeper, the King of Tonga . . . ?"

"He's the brother of one of our old victims." I pause. "Maryanne Doyle, remember her?"

"Of course." Her eyes are wide, but not hostile. "The Irish girl. Leamington Square. Strangled."

"Yeah. Well, him. Aiden."

And so, once more unto the breach, I tell our tall tale. The chance meeting a few months ago, the rain, the pub, the drinks, the easy chemistry. Steele listens, expressionless. She even attempts something tricksy with an eyeliner as I reach the crescendo, which I take as a good sign that she's really not that bothered.

"So what do you think?" I say finally, waiting for the verdict.

She's looking straight ahead, seemingly hypnotized by the sweeping cherry blossoms. In Japanese culture, they symbolize the fleeting nature of life. If she's contemplating this, she might be inclined to go easy.

"I think you're batting above your average, Kinsella. Good work. I remember him from court. Tall bloke, broad. Bit of a heartthrob, right?"

"Right." I allow myself a cautious smile, feeling wrongfooted but relieved. "So you're OK with it? You don't think it's a mistake?"

She turns suddenly. "Oh, I think it's almost certainly a mistake, Cat. I think you'd do well to have a life completely outside of the job, and dating the brother of one of your victims . . . well, there's something highly Freudian in that, if you ask me. But if you mean have you done anything wrong, professionally? Then no, absolutely not."

And with this steadfast vote of confidence, I become Steele's Biggest Mistake Ever.

13

I'm only fifteen minutes late, which by London standards is more like five, and knowing Aiden will be expecting far worse, I take a moment outside L'ingordo to call Nurse Jacqui and check on Dad. I could call Dad, of course, but there's a very real danger that he would actually answer, and it's not connection I'm after. It's voicemail. I want to do my duty, register my interest, cross it off the list, that's all. And since the dawn of time, or the dawn of expensive self-improvement courses at least, Jacqui has always spent Thursday evenings bettering herself somewhere, her phone switched to silent for maximum concentration.

The latest: The Art of Decluttering and Minimalism.

Sometimes I wonder if we're related at all.

As I zone out her message, I spot Aiden through the window, smiling and laughing and gesticulating with a breadstick.

My turn to speak.

"Oh hey, it's me. Just seeing how the patient's doing. I'm guessing he's still alive or you'd have called. Um . . . that was it really. Say hi to Finn and Ash. I'll try you again at some point. Love you. Bye, bye, bye."

Job done. Interest registered. I may not be a good daughter, or sister, but I'm an adequate one. Just about scraping a grade C.

The restaurant isn't what I expected. With Aiden in a flap about this visit for weeks—an Aiden flap, anyhow, which means he's been fractionally less Zen—I'd assumed a hammering of the company credit card. Low lighting and high prices. Sommeliers and smug waiters making endless interruptions to pour the wine and glorify the food. However, bustling L'ingordo is the blessed opposite. Rowdy and harshly lit, and in the corner, a large group are singing

"Happy Birthday" to an old man while the waiters mark the occasion by wrapping a raw pizza base around his head.

I relax instantly, making my way over to Aiden's crew—three men and one woman.

"Ah, here she is, Miss Marple." Aiden's smile is goofy, his eyes a little drowsy. Predinner drinks clearly started at lunch.

I roll my eyes at the others. "Charming, isn't it? That's how he sees me—an elderly spinster in a tweed suit."

"Yeah, Aiden." The woman, tattooed and lightly tanned, with coarse curly hair tied up in a paisley scarf, leans across and swipes his head with a huge napkin. "You could have said Christine Cagney. Or—or . . . Veronica Mars." To me, "Did you guys get that show over here?"

"Yeah, but she was a PI." I sit down between Aiden and an older guy in a polo shirt, who I'm guessing is Jack Denton, the CEO. Jack's an Oz-like figure, according to Aiden. A giant floating brain usually sequestered behind a bank of screens and Starbucks litter. "Veronica Mars hid in bushes rather than smashing down doors. Not that I've smashed down many doors—or any, come to think of it. Anyway, hi, I'm Cat. You probably gathered." I'm conscious I'm babbling.

"I ordered for you, babe." Aiden only calls me babe when he's tipsy. "Bruschetta and penne something. But there's a half an hour wait, they reckon, so load up on these." He drums two breadsticks on my forehead.

"Carbs followed by carbs, followed by carbs. Excellent choice, sir."

"It's penne alla vodka," says the woman. "My suggestion. I hope you like it."

"I like anything 'alla vodka.' Even 'vodka alla vodka.'"

"Girl after my own heart." We share a limp high-five in front of Aiden's face. "I'm Rosella, by the way. General Counsel." I nod—knowledgeably, I think, but she obviously sees through me. "General Fun Blocker. Chief Legal Bore," she explains. "If you've heard Aiden bitching about someone at head office, it's probably me."

"We just bitch about her love life," says a black guy in preppy glasses, drizzling oil on a piece of bread. "Work this one out, Cat. Rosella just broke up with someone because he ate an apple with a knife."

"A knife *and* fork." Rosella's face is pure exasperation. "Stop leaving out the fork, Zach. It makes me look picky."

"You *are* picky." That's the third guy: thirties, beige, unremarkable in every way except for an impressively straight side-part.

Rosella's still gunning for Zach. "And you need to get your facts right. I haven't broken up with him; I'm doing the slow fade." She looks at me. "You know, taking longer to reply to texts, dodging concrete plans, that sort of thing. I figured it's kinder than dumping him . . ."

"No way is it kinder," says Zach. "It's cruel. It gives the illusion of hope."

Rosella cringes. "I know, I know, but I just can't face 'the conversation.' He's so sensitive, he might cry." Her gaze back on me again. "Honestly, Cat, I don't know whether to fuck him or breastfeed him half the time—you know the type, right?"

I know I need wine and plenty of it. I'd been expecting small talk, a bit of shop talk, probably an inevitable stumble into politics at some point. I hadn't expected to walk straight onto the set of *Sex and the City*.

But I like it. I like them. Their abrasiveness is pure theater.

"Anyway, I'll tell you who's picky." Rosella points at Side-Part while telepathically filling my wine glass to the brim. "Kyle broke up with a guy because he called him the most brilliant man he'd ever met." She flops back in an exaggerated huff. "*That's* picky, Cat. When you can get dumped for giving a compliment, all bets are off, right?"

Kyle and his side-part are unrepentant. "That's not a compliment, it's hero worship. And I don't want to be brilliant. I don't want to be fucking Iron Man. I just want to be me. Tell me that's not weird, Cat?"

Me again, *Cat, Cat, Cat, Cat,* as though everyone else's opinions have been canvassed then discounted.

"Not weird at all." I take a large gulp of wine then turn the spotlight on Aiden. "Hey, you've never told me I'm the most brilliant woman you've ever met."

"See, your time-keeping lets you down." His goofy grin cracks wider. "And remembering to switch plugs off. And talking through films. And leaving orange peel on the sofa."

Rosella brandishes her attack-napkin. "Just say the word, Cat."

"So are you an East Londoner too?" asks the older guy, who by the process of elimination is definitely CEO Jack. "Aiden says it's the place to be."

"Aiden's been in London for two years and thinks he's an expert." A fond grin toward my London Oracle. "And sorry, to answer your question, no. I'm from North London and I live in South London. A place called Tooting—categorically not 'the place to be' but the rents are less eye-watering."

"Oh right, I thought you guys lived together?"

"As good as," says Aiden.

"He lives closer to town. It's a handy pied à terre."

That gets me a laugh from Jack and a prod with a breadstick from Aiden.

"And you're a cop?"

"Yeah, I think we established that with the Miss Marple thing." Zach's smirk dilutes the sharp tone.

"Zach gets antsy at the word 'cop' because he's got a criminal record," says Rosella.

"Aha, Perry Mason, I think *you* need to get *your* facts right." Zach pulls her headscarf down. Her curls spring up, electrocution style. "I got fired for shoplifting a pair of Calvin Kleins when I worked at Macy's," he explains to me. "But they didn't call the cops. They even paid me for the shift."

Jack pulls the conversation back. "A cop, though. That's a real vocation. Did you always want to help people?"

Kyle groans. "Jesus, Jack, she's not Miss Alabama 1993!"

Aiden roars. A sound that justifies every mistake I've ever made.

"Nah, it was the taser that sold me, Jack. Seriously, the power of taking someone down with that bad boy. Can't beat it."

His face is frozen.

"I think she might be joking," says Rosella, patting him on the shoulder.

"Anyway, isn't what you do a vocation?" I say, deflecting the question. I don't want to be Cat the Cop tonight, the romanticized public servant, protecting the mean streets of London with her steel resolve and warm heart.

"A vocation?" His tone says I'm mad. "Are you serious? Is that another joke? I was going to be a marine biologist. My life was going to look like something out of a Caribbean vacation brochure. But then I didn't get the grades in college . . ."

"But you do make triple the paycheck," Zach reminds him.

"I was going to be Sheryl Crow," says Rosella, fixing her scarf back in place.

A gut punch when I least expect it. In an instant, it's May 1998 and I'm in the back of Dad's car. Maryanne Doyle in the passenger seat, Sheryl Crow on the radio. Dad and Maryanne singing along, *badly*, to that song—that one about whatever makes you happy can't be so bad.

If there was ever a song that summed up Dad's philosophy on life.

"I wanted to design planes." Aiden's voice edges Maryanne closer. I gulp my wine, praying it does its magic quickly. "Didn't matter that I couldn't draw or that I hadn't set foot near an airport, never mind a fecking plane—I'd seen *Air Force One* a few times, that was good enough for me. I wouldn't have had a clue what a risk analyst was, though. There wasn't great call for them around Mulderrin."

I plaster on a smile. "I didn't know that, about the planes."

"Ah, there's lots of things you don't know about me."

"Lots of things you won't want to know either," adds Jack.

"Yeah, thanks for that, boss man."

Jack laughs, throwing his hands up in placation. "Well, it's the truth. Trust me, there's plenty about Amy I wish I could un-know. I won't go into it before we eat. Some of it's beyond gross . . ."

Kyle says, "Yeah, Amy's so gross, Jack only got her pregnant *five times.*"

"Wow, five kids," I say. "That's a basketball team."

"Well, four and a fetus. She's due in October . . . that's if she hasn't thrown herself in the Hudson."

"The heat," explains Rosella. "It was ninety-two when we left on Monday."

"But it feels closer to a hundred," says Jack.

"It's not the heat, it's the humidity," Aiden says with a grin, reciting the line like he's learned it in class. "Apparently, we have it easy here."

"Remind me of that next time I'm putting the bedsheets in the freezer."

"So have you ever been to New York, Cat?" It's the standard question but Rosella's tone is laden with something more meaningful.

"I've never been to America," I say before realizing I have. "Oh well, Disney World Florida when I was ten. But we never left the resort. Does that count?"

"No." Zach is quite clear about this.

"New York's definitely on the list, though." The standard response.

She hits the table, delighted, eyes shining. "Oh, you'd love it. You would. You'd absolutely love it." She's probably right, although I'm baffled at how she's arrived at this assumption, knowing very little about me, except I like pasta and vodka and Irish risk analysts. "I moved from San Jose in 2013. Always thought I was a West Coast girl, it was going to be a two-year adventure, nothing more." Her other hand comes down. "Best thing I ever did. The West Coast has got the better beaches, no two ways about that. But New York is everything. The hope, the energy, the food, the people. What did JFK say?—*Most cities are a noun. New York is a verb.*"

I'm not sure that even makes sense, but I *am* sure I'm being pitched to. It's not my spidey sense tingling, or my twitchy detective nose at full snuffle—it's more the fact that that's the longest anyone's spoken without someone else cutting in or contradicting.

"We'll get there, right?" I say to Aiden. "I've always fancied New York at Christmas."

Aiden smiles at Rosella, who smiles at Jack, who smiles at the sight of our huge, gluttonous starters finally arriving. Squeezing my hand under the table, Aiden says, "You never know, babe, you never know."

But of course I know. I'm the last person he should try to hoodwink. They haven't come all this way for the pasta, or to swap one mortal heat for another. They're talking to Aiden about a project, I know it. He said ages ago that a three-month stint might be on the horizon. That it was the norm, hard to say no to if you get the call-up.

And what's three months, anyway? It's a six-hour flight. A place I've always wanted to visit. With wine in my bloodstream and the Manhattan skyline in my head, I find myself smiling too.

And then my phone rings. Parnell. Who else?

I stand up. "Sorry, I need to take this. You all crack on." I mouth another apology at Aiden, but he doesn't notice. His chili king prawns are more than making up for me.

"Hey, Sarge, you still hard at it?" I'm on the street now. Soho is being Soho: a glorious, beer-soaked beehive, chock-full of tattoos and tourists and everything between. "Any joy?"

"I wouldn't call it joy. I've been stuck listening to Swaines and Flowers going another ten rounds over Brexit."

"Oh dear. Was the boss there?"

"No. So while the cat's away . . ."

"The mice will hurl insults at each other. What kicked it off this time?"

"Started with Swaines' mum stockpiling olive oil, finished with the Irish border."

"Oh, and they're both experts on the complexities of the back-stop, are they?"

"Hey, we're all politicians now, kiddo. Makes you long for the time that only nerds and intellectuals gave a damn. Still, it beats Flowers moaning on about his blistered feet—just."

"Urgh. Do you mind, I'm just about to eat."

Parnell's voice goes up an octave. "At nine forty-five? You'll pay for that tomorrow. You're supposed to give your food time to go down before bed. Four or five hours, they say."

Work-Dad strikes again.

"How do you know I won't be up for another four or five hours? I am a Bright Young Thing, you know."

"You'll be a Tired Young Thing. I need you in early. We have a date with Church Guy."

"Wow, you found him?"

"Of course. Was it ever in question? He turned up on CCTV a few streets away from the church getting into a very nice Lexus."

"So does he have a name?"

"Dale Peters. Car's registered to a Nottingham address. His wife was a bit stunned by a couple of Nottinghamshire's finest ringing her doorbell on a Thursday night. She was expecting a Chinese takeaway."

"For two?"

"He wasn't home. He's still down here, apparently. Anyway,

she gave us his number and long story short, he's agreed to attend a voluntary interview at seven thirty a.m. tomorrow."

Which means I'll be in for six thirty a.m, prepping. Goodnight, Bright Young Thing.

"And is this early bird lawyering up, as my New York chums would say?"

"I've done the usual. Told him he's welcome to, but it'll be quicker if he doesn't." Ah, the old favorite. You could call it a lie; we call it an intentionally false suggestion. "I doubt he will, though. He seemed more interested in how long it was going to take than his legal rights. He runs his own consultancy—something to do with ecology—and he's a very busy man, don'tcha know?"

I laugh, picturing Parnell's face. "I bet that went down well."

"I let it pass. He'll find out tomorrow he's not the only busy man in town." After four close years, I know every shift in Parnell's tone. Something's coming. I step back into the doorway, shielding every word from the babble and zing of Thursday night Soho. "You see, I've been doing a little digging into Mr. Dale Peters and guess what? He didn't have his lovely Lexus back in 2012; he had an equally lovely Saab. It got scrapped though. Scrapyard sent the details to the DVLA on 5th March 2012."

He doesn't wait for me to do the math. "Eleven days after Holly disappeared."

14

Last night wasn't a late one. Thankfully, and unusually for me, my fear of missing out was trumped by my fear of not waking up, and so it's with a clear head and a sharp eye that I sit across from Dale Peters. And he really isn't doing himself any favors.

It's the bacon brioche that gets me.

The takeaway coffee, I accept. Maybe he didn't sleep well last night. Maybe he can't function in the morning until he's popped seven types of vitamin and downed two Americanos—he looks that type. Maybe he needs something to do with his hands—he doesn't have a record so I can allow for first-time nerves; I'm not completely unreasonable. But tucking into breakfast? Saying that he knows it's a bit rude but it's the only chance he'll get? I can't accept that. Too casual. *Way* too relaxed. And it's blatantly all an act, anyway. He only manages three bites, bless him. The first a huge maul like a lion attacking a carcass, the second less voracious, the third barely a nibble. The remainder sits stinking on the table, a greasy lump of proof that behind all the superficial charm and ceaseless gibber, his stomach's tied up in knots.

"Anyway, apologies *again* for flitting off yesterday." He clears his throat. He clears his throat a lot, actually. Could be hay fever, could be a stubborn bit of bacon, could be a sign of lying. We don't know yet. "When I saw the time on the parking meter, I panicked. I had a meeting at Waterloo at two p.m., you see, and I was already cutting it fine. I fully intended to call your incident room later, but one drama led into another, you know how some days go? Then before I know it, I'm getting a hysterical call from my wife saying two policemen have been to the house. Wasn't that a bit heavy-handed?"

Dale Peters comes across as a delicate guy, the kind who'd find a raised voice hysterical and an overzealous door-knock heavy-handed. While he's certainly quite attractive—slight but athletic, with large hazel eyes and perfect capped teeth—there's something so insipid about him, so *"come and wipe your feet on me"* that you almost can't resist taking him up on the offer.

"'Before you knew it?'" I repeat, looking down at my notes. "PC Holmes and PC Thakkar arrived at your home address at just after eight thirty p.m. That's over seven hours since your 'flit,' as you call it. I'm calling it 'your refusal to answer police questions,' by the way."

His cheeks flush. "Is that an offense? Maybe I should have a solicitor."

Parnell shakes his head. "No, no offense, Dale. Completely your right. We only cautioned you as a formality, remember? Although, I'll be honest, it doesn't make us feel all warm and fuzzy toward you."

"Look, I'm sorry," he stutters. "It was a hectic afternoon. My client insisted on a drink following the meeting, and then I had to pop to Hamleys to pick up something for my daughter's birthday—she collects Steiff bears." *One drama led to another*—a fucking Steiff bear? "And after that I was starving so I went for an early supper just off Carnaby Street, and then it was gone seven before I realized I hadn't been in touch and I thought . . . well . . ."

His excuses burn themselves out. He tries a doe-eyed look instead, but he's thirty years too old for it to be anything less than embarrassing.

"And you thought what?" I ask. "That the entire Metropolitan Police would have left for the day? Put our chairs up on the desks and gone home for our dinner?" I grin at Parnell. "Chance would be a fine thing, huh?"

"You'll have receipts for those, of course?" says Parnell. "The drinks, the bear, your dinner. We can check it all on CCTV but receipts would save time. And you owe us some time back, Dale."

"I don't have them on me, but I can bring them in later." He shifts forward, shoulders stiffening. "Though why do you need to check up on me?"

"How did you know about the memorial service?" I say, ignoring his question.

"Twitter. I was following the news and I saw a post, all the details. And I was due to be in London anyway so . . ."

"And how did you know Holly Kemp?"

"Well, um, she was just a friend, an acquaintance, really. Someone from way back. I happened to be in North London so I . . ."

I put a hand up. "Right, back up a minute—how old are you, Dale?"

He's confused. "I'm not with you."

I shoot Parnell an amused glance, land it back on Peters. "A little heads-up for you here. Our questions are going to get a whole lot harder than the type a three-year-old could answer, so you might want to sharpen up a bit."

"I'm forty-five. Why?"

He looks younger. Could be good genes but my money's on a three-step skin routine.

"Well, it's just that you said you knew Holly from 'way back.' 'Way back' implies you'd known her for years, but she was only twenty-two when she died and you'd have been thirty-nine. So how old was she when you 'acquainted' her?"

"Oh, I see. Um, I'd only recently acquainted her, not long before she died." Is he for real? He really thinks I mean *acquainted* and not *shagged*. There's naive and there's gormless and then there's Dale fucking Peters. "Um, when I said 'way back,' I meant I hadn't seen her in years."

"Well, you wouldn't have done. She's been rotting in a field in Cambridgeshire."

His hand flies to his mouth. For a moment, I think he might puke, but he styles it out, massaging his velvet-smooth jaw.

Parnell offers fake censure. "OK, Cat, enough."

"What? I'm not telling him anything he won't have seen on the news."

"I don't think they put it quite so brutally," says Peters, his voice shaky and horrified, like a nineteenth-century woman amid an attack of the vapors.

"Then I apologize." There's no way I sound sincere. "Now, picking up on what you said about 'happening' to be in North London. Your wife, Debbie, is also your PA, is that correct?" *Debbie & Dale 4Eva*. I picture teenage sweethearts. The undisputed prom king and queen. Married at twenty-five, kids a few years later. And then one of them winds up in the middle of a murder investigation. "Well, Debbie ran PC Holmes and PC Thakkar through your appointments for that day." I sift through my notes, winding Peters tighter. "You had a breakfast meeting at your hotel in Earls Court at eight a.m., followed by another meeting at Brunel University at ten a.m., and then a *three p.m.* at Waterloo, not two p.m. as you said, so you did have time to stop and talk to us, after all. But anyway, my point is that's Central London-West London-Central London. You weren't scheduled to be anywhere near North London, and I'd go as far to say—as someone who knows London well—a detour to Dollis Hill would be a major pain in the proverbial. And that tells me two things, Dale." I give him a face full of disappointment. "One, you're lying to us, and two, getting to that memorial service meant a great deal to you. Holly Kemp meant a great deal to you. Can you tell us why?"

He says nothing, filling the silence with sharp little breaths, steadily growing faster.

"Because Debbie didn't know why," I go on. "She had no idea why you'd be there. Seemed quite shocked, actually, according to PC Thakkar. Needed an extra sugar in her tea. Said you hadn't set foot in a church since you got married thirteen years ago, and she'd had to nag you into that. You'd have preferred the local registry office. But you put your foot down about Maisie and Rhys being baptized, didn't you?"

Parnell chimes in. "You're a science man. A loud-and-proud atheist. You've got a blog—*Godless in Gedling*. I'm more of an agnostic, myself, but I gave it a read. It's very good. *Atheism Is a Non-Prophet Organization*—very witty."

Our tones might be blithe but the message is clear: *We know you*. We've drunk your tea, we've met your wife, we know your kids' names. We're all over your life.

So no bullshit.

"Look, I didn't know *her*, OK? I didn't know Holly fucking Kemp." The words sputter from him, a confetti of anger bursting above our heads. "I knew her as Megan. Sweet, fragile, unassuming Megan. We met in 2011 . . ."

Parnell interrupts, which is good as I'm momentarily dumbstruck. "For the tape, Dale. Are you saying you met Holly Kemp in 2011 and she was calling herself Megan?"

"Megan Moore. It used to be our joke that I always wanted 'more' of Megan. But she was so shy, so afraid to let you in." He looks down. "Of course, that was all part of the act. That's what she wanted me to think."

"Right, stop, stop, stop," I say, waving my hands. "The beginning, Dale. And the truth. One more lie and we'll charge you."

I've no idea what with, but he's remarkably easy to intimidate and I'm not looking that gift horse in the mouth.

He leans forward onto the table, shoulders hunched, eyes on his clasped hands. "We met on a night out in Nottingham. Two thousand and eleven, August, I think. I was at a god-awful stag party. It was at one of those fancy places where you go to be seen, full of footballers and glamour models, £200 bottles of vodka. Anyway, the bar really wasn't my scene. Megan, or Holly . . . can I call her Megan?"

We nod in sync. If it keeps him talking he can call her the Queen of Bloody Sheba.

"Megan looked like a glamour model, and it's weird because I don't usually go for that type, but there was something about her. A real warmth. We started chatting at the bar about how long it was taking to get served and then we didn't stop talking all night. We weren't even flirting, really. It was just like we had to know everything about each other, hungry for every little detail. Favorite films, books, foods. First kiss. First pet. Best holiday. Worst joke. I felt like I learned more about her in three hours than I knew about Debbie after nine years." *Oh, for fuck's sake.* "Anyway, there was a late-night café across the road and she said why didn't we go there, it'd be quieter. I didn't even tell anyone I was leaving, but we stayed in that café for hours. I told her all about my consultancy. I suppose I was bragging about how well it was doing, but she never seemed impressed, as such, just fascinated. She was fascinated in *me*. In every word I said."

"Pay them compliments, boost their confidence, make every one of them feel like stardust."

Advice once shared with me by a £3,000-a-night hooker.

"So did you sleep with her that night?" I ask.

"No. I walked her back to her hotel. But then we met up the next day and well . . ." He gets lost somewhere for a moment. "It was like being given the keys to paradise."

"Did she charge you?" I ask, dropping the keys down the toilet.

"No, of course not!"

Parnell speaks levelly. "It's been suggested that Holly Kemp might have been working as an escort."

Peters looks winded. "No, no, no. It was never like that. We fell in love, or at least I thought we did. We saw each other every week for the next few months, sometimes twice a week if we could make it work. She never seemed interested in money, that's why I was so trusting . . ."

"So were you going to leave your wife?" I ask. "Your children? How old were they then, by the way?"

It's not even slightly relevant but he deserves to squirm.

"Look, if anything, being with Debbie over those few months felt like cheating on Megan. Debbie and I hadn't been great for a long time. She was consumed with the children. I was consumed with the business. We were hardly talking, sleeping in separate rooms. The usual story."

The usual cliché.

It was a dark and stormy night, and the insecure man pushing forty left the mother of his kids and chief washer of his pants for the perky twenty-two-year-old who hung off his every word in her Agent Provocateur underwear.

"So yes," confirms Parnell.

"I would have left Debbie, yes, but it wasn't that simple." He sits back, planting his legs wide, a belligerent stance he fails to carry off. "Megan was with someone too, you see. All she'd say is that it was complicated. She couldn't just leave. It was obvious she was terrified, though—terrified to leave him, terrified of him finding out about me. That's why we could never spend time in London. She said he had spies all over. So she'd come up this way or we'd book into hotels across the Home Counties—she loved The Grove, Foxhills, Cliveden."

"She never seemed interested in money." The absolute mug.

"And you settled for that explanation?" Parnell leans in, tilting his bulk forward, settling in for the man-to-man. "Because, Dale—and I'll say straight up that this is all double dutch to me, I'm no expert in extramarital affairs and I don't intend to become one—but hypothetically speaking, if I've met a young lady and I'm splashing the cash in five-star hotels and telling her that I'm fully prepared to abandon my wife and two young kids, then I'm going to want a little bit more than 'it's complicated' when I ask her to show the same commitment."

"Of course I pushed her," Peters insists. "But I didn't want to end up pushing her away. I told her I had a fair idea what was going on—that she was stuck in a controlling relationship, being intimidated, being abused. I told her that I'd protect her, keep her safe, and do you know what she did? She burst out laughing. Not proper laughter, though—hyper, hysterical. She said I had no idea what I was talking about. She said I could never protect her from him."

Spencer Shaw? *Really?* I mean, I know he's clearly a shoo-in for the lead role of Scumbag Boyfriend, but Holly's friends just didn't seem all *that* rattled by him. Josh's first words on the subject were, "He knows I'd lay him clean out."

Peters is still going. "And then the name Simon Fellows changed everything."

It rings a bell for me but hits Parnell square in the nose.

"Yeah, *him.*" Peters revels in Parnell's reaction. "I didn't know who he was at first. I didn't know a lot about hardened gangsters, strangely enough. But when I googled him, it didn't take me long to get the gist."

"For the tape," says Parnell, "you're saying Holly Kemp—the woman you knew as Megan Moore—told you she was in a relationship with a man called Simon Fellows."

"An abusive relationship, yes. She said she wished she'd never got involved with him, but she was only eighteen when they met and she was bowled over by the attention, by the lifestyle: first-class flights everywhere, private club memberships, designer clothes." And the points go to Josh for his roundly mocked sugar daddy. "She was his trophy and he owned her and she knew he'd kill her if she tried to leave him. He'd threatened it often enough."

"So you finished it?" I say, more a statement than a question. There's nothing quite like the words "hardened gangster" to send most men scurrying back to the safe drudgery of their marriage.

"No, but Megan tried to. She said she'd been wrong to risk my safety, but that she couldn't bear to give me up. Every time she tried to walk away, she'd tell herself just one more night, just one more memory." He makes a direct plea to Parnell. "Do you know how

intoxicating it is to have a beautiful young woman tell you that?"
Parnell's unmoved. Peters looks at the floor, defeated. "Of course,
she was just pulling my strings. She knew *exactly* how intoxicating
it was. It made me hell-bent on keeping her, made me go along
with her plan."

Peters is on autopilot now, words spilling out unfiltered.

"She said the only way we could be together would be to leave the
country. Get as far away from him as possible. We talked about it
for weeks, whether it was feasible, whether we were mad. And eventually we decided yes, it was and yes, we were—madly in love, that
is. Australia seemed the best option. Obviously the distance was the
main thing, but I had contacts in Perth and I was fairly sure I could
get work there. But I couldn't just up and leave. I had loose ends to
sort out—my business, my marriage, my kids. Megan was getting
edgy, though. It was unbearable."

Loose ends. Two innocent children. Here's hoping one day Debbie Peters wises up and relegates this mealymouthed shite to a sad,
lonely life with only his atheist God to call on.

"When was this?" asks Parnell.

"Early January, 2012. We'd spent two weeks apart over Christmas. I knew it would be the last one I'd spend in the family unit,
so I'd gone all out making it special for the children." Just when I
thought I couldn't hate him more. "But she'd had a terrible time
with him in London. He'd thrown her against a wall on Christmas
night because she hadn't been ecstatic enough about some underwear he'd bought her. Then he'd kicked her in the stomach on New
Year's Day because she'd supposedly been flirting with someone
the night before. She was in a state. I could hardly say no."

"No to what?" I ask.

"She asked me for £10,000. Enough so she could buy a ticket to
Perth, get us a rental flat, basically live for a few months until I'd
sorted things here and could join her." The punch line is stamped
on his face. "Of course, I never saw or heard from her again. Well,

not until she was all over the news a couple of months later. Holly Kemp. The Roommate's fourth victim. I couldn't take it in. All her lies. The way she'd died. Everything."

"Hold on," I say, confused. "After she vanished, weren't you worried that Fellows had harmed her? Why did you immediately think you'd been conned?"

"I just knew." He taps his chest. "I knew in here. After she asked for the money, I said it might be tricky explaining away all that cash in one go, but that if she gave me her bank details, I'd drip-feed it in. But she was adamant. She wanted £10,000 in cash. She turned a bit . . . well, horrible, I suppose. Said that maybe she should call Debbie, if she was the one holding the purse strings."

I shrug. "So? You were going to leave Debbie anyway."

"I didn't want her finding out like *that*. I'm not a complete bastard."

"And even after she threatened you like that, you still wanted to be with her?"

"I chose not to see it as a threat. I convinced myself it was a sign of how desperate she was." He brings his palms up. "Look, I'm an idiot, I know. I realized that myself when she stopped answering my calls, then her phone stopped connecting altogether. But you have to understand, she had me under her spell. I was mesmerized."

Or pussy blind, a less starry-eyed take.

"And after you saw Holly—the woman you knew as Megan—on the news, you didn't think to contact the police?"

"God, no! Why on earth would I? It had nothing to do with what happened to her, and I had my family to think of."

The same family he'd been prepared to leave fifteen thousand miles behind.

"About 'what happened to her.'" Parnell's voice is low and calm, a sure sign he's sharpening his claws. "You mentioned at the start that you've been following the news, which means you must be aware that we're looking into what happened to Holly again." Peters looks wary. "This means looking at anyone in Holly's life who *a* had a reason to harm her, or *b* did anything suspicious around the time of her disappearance." Parnell sits back, circling his thumbs. "Now, you have to agree, Dale, you certainly fit *a*."

"What possible reason could I have had?"

I shouldn't, but I laugh. "Well, I can think of ten thousand good reasons, Dale. You must have been livid when you realized your dream woman and your money were gone. Ten thousand pounds—that's a lot of Steiff bears."

"Of course I was angry, but I could never have harmed her."

"Even after she stole from you? And, by the way, I'm pretty sure she spent it in the Burj Al Arab with her boyfriend. Not Simon Fellows, by the way. Another boyfriend."

He brings a hand down on the table. "I would never have hurt her. I loved her. And what's even more pathetic is that I probably still do—*Megan*. I know she wasn't real, but she felt real to me for four months, and nothing will *ever* live up to that again. Do you know how wretched that feels? To realize the love of your life was a complete construct?"

What I am to Aiden.

A bolt of sadness tears through me, as physical as a drop in blood pressure.

"Can you tell us about your Saab, please?" This was supposed to be Parnell's sledgehammer, but I need it to push the bad thoughts out of my head. "I'm talking about the convertible you owned in 2012, registration BD11 NCF." Peters couldn't look more perplexed. I may as well have asked about a pet rabbit he once owned, for all he sees the relevance. "It was scrapped in March of that year. Can you tell us why?"

He looks at Parnell. Maybe for an explanation. Maybe it's a caveman thing: *man must talk to man about cars.* "I had an accident. The damage was bad and it wasn't worth the repairs, especially as I'd been thinking of getting a new car anyway."

"Must have been a bad accident," I say. "Were you injured?"

"No."

"But you reported it to your insurer?"

"Well, no." He starts to fidget. "There was no one else involved and as I was at fault, I didn't see the point."

"Ever been to Caxton?" asks Parnell, deliberately changing direction, causing more confusion.

"Where?"

"Caxton, Cambridgeshire. Where Holly's remains were found." Peters blanches at "remains." "You see, I've been looking at the map, Dale, and I thought it was interesting that if you were to drive from London, where Holly lived, to Gedling, where you live, you'd *almost* pass through Caxton. It's just mile or two off the A1. Don't you find that interesting?"

"I don't understand. Why are you asking me about my car and somewhere I've never heard of, let alone been?"

"Point *b*," I remind him. "We're looking at anyone who acted suspiciously around the time of Holly's disappearance. Scrapping a car less than two weeks later is suspicious."

"Look, it was the week after the news about Meg— Holly, I mean, and obviously I was a wreck. I'd been drinking and I crashed into a ditch on a quiet road not far from home. The car was a write-off and I could hardly admit I'd been drunk driving. I called my brother-in-law and we got the car out and he towed me home. I took it to the scrapyard a few days later."

"Convenient."

It's taken nearly an hour but finally, Peters hardens—his tone, his face, his fists—although I'm not too worried about the last one. I'm fairly sure Parnell could take him down with one punch. Hell, there's an outside chance I could.

"It's not 'convenient,' it's the truth." He jabs a finger at me. 'But you aren't interested in the truth. You're only interested in twisting people's words, their intentions. I pity you, to be honest. It must be wearing to only see the bad in people."

"Only seeing the good didn't work out so well for you, did it, Dale? It might be wearing being an old cynic, but I'd have seen through 'Megan Moore' quicker than you can say 'ten thousand pounds in cash, please.'"

And I would have too.

It takes a liar to know a liar.

15

"Well, a bullet to the head is *definitely* Simon Fellows' style."

Steele's on her feet behind her desk, positively fizzing at our update.

"Allegedly," warns Parnell, popping her cork back in.

"Sorry, how very rude of me." She gives a contrite bow. "He's *alleged* to have been linked to six shootings that we know of. Better?"

"Less slanderous."

I'm going to have to take their word for it as what I know of Simon Fellows equates to a photo in a tabloid newspaper. A boorish, angry stare, his hand striking out toward the camera. A borderline-litigious byline suggesting that while he was arriving in court to support a nephew charged with a slew of drug offenses, it should be him in the dock and they should throw away the key. A vague recollection that he'd threatened to sue.

He didn't sue, and his nephew didn't get sentenced either. His uncle's expensive, double-barreled barrister made sure of that.

"Well, for what it's worth," I say, "even though I haven't a clue where Holly was blurring the lines between fact and fiction with all this 'Megan' business, it's the first lead that makes any sense." Steele pulls a face, urging me on. "If he's into guns then it explains the cause of death, and it also backs up a few things Holly's friends said—that she might have had a sugar daddy, that she was scared of someone, jumpy."

Parnell's leaning against the windowsill, eating a Kit Kat from the vending machine. He was all set to finish Peters' stone-cold brioche until he saw the look on my face and tossed it in the bin. "But without a bullet to match to a gun," he argues, "Simon Fellows could have a whole arsenal at his disposal and it still won't help us."

"OK, fair enough, but we've got repeated threats to kill made in the months before Holly died. It's something. It's a start."

"Do we have any eyewitnesses, though?" Steele's fizz wanes to a slow crackle. "The word of a dead thief—and that's what Fellows' brief will say she is—isn't going to cut it."

"There was a New Year's Eve party." Parnell's nodding at the corner of my vision. "It would have been 2011. We can dig into that. Ask around."

"Ask him first," says Steele. "Swaines is getting known addresses now."

"How does Spencer Shaw fit into all this, though?" It's been eating away at me amid all the excitement. "Fellows boots Holly in the stomach for looking at another man, but he's quite happy for her to live with one?"

"She's his regular plaything, not his live-in girlfriend. She's got to sleep somewhere." Steele doesn't sound altogether convinced by her own argument. "Or if he didn't know about Spencer, that's one big motive right there."

"Or if we're hopping back to proposition number one, that Masters did kill her," says Parnell, "it could also explain why she was looking for a new place to live. Maybe Fellows said she had to?"

Fellows. Shaw. Masters. Accomplices. My head hurts. "So what's Fellows' record like?"

Steele looks at me like I just asked if she's written to Santa yet. Four-fifths exasperated, one-fifth endeared.

"What? What did I say?"

"The Mr. Bigs don't have records, Cat. Other people get them for them."

Parnell cuts in. "Ah, but is Simon Fellows a true Mr. Big, Kate? The *real* Mr. Bigs are the ones you've never heard of. They don't come up on Google searches and they certainly don't hitch their wagons to eighteen-year-old trophies." Steele's eyebrows hit the ceiling. "Oh, I'm not saying they don't sleep with them, but what Holly described to Peters was a relationship. A twisted one, granted." He shakes his head. "No, the true Mr. Bigs live in respectable, un-showy mansions with their respectable, un-showy wives. They don't do anything to draw attention to themselves."

Like blackmailing police officers in broad daylight. My mind goes straight to Frank Hickey, the pencil-dick cipher.

"OK, so you worked this space, you clearly know your stuff," Steele says to Parnell. "What do you know about him?"

"Not that much, and it was years ago, remember? I know he isn't muscle. He's a money man, an investor." A money launderer, to give him his proper title. "And he's slick, well educated—he does the salt-of-the-earth Cockney thing, but he's public school through and through. He had a career in the City back in the nineties."

"His annual bonus wasn't enough?" I say with the requisite amount of vinegar.

"Clearly not," says Parnell. "But it was easy to stray onto the wrong side of the law back then. White-collar crime wasn't a priority—God, it barely *was* a crime. There were none of the regulations there are now, so you'd see it all the time—nice boy joins the firm, sees it's a dog-eat-dog world, spots a way to make money, and before you know it, he's gone from massaging the figures on a spreadsheet to setting up shell companies to help drug cartels or arms traffickers move money. Next stop—he wants a piece of the *real* action himself, he wants to *be* the trafficker, 'cos that's where the mega money is. Now, I'm not saying Fellows was ever a nice boy, or this is what happened in his case, I'm just saying it happened a lot back then."

"Do we know which outfit Fellows works for?" asks Steele.

"No idea. I haven't come across him for years, and to be honest, it's not that simple. It's not like the Mafia. British gangs don't have the same rank and structure. Everything's fluid, you get loose coalitions, sharing of expertise. I know he used to work under the Kirby umbrella, but that was years ago. I'm talking ten, fifteen, maybe more."

He offers me the last finger of Kit Kat, and I take it, smiling, even though my stomach has just plunged to the floor.

The phone's in Steele's hand. "Right, I'm going to make a call, do some digging. You pair, just get in his face for the time being. And watch him like a hawk—because I don't care how slick he is, he's not a robot. If he's been thinking he got away with it for all these years, he's going to have some sort of reaction."

Not necessarily.

I barely flinched at the mention of the Kirbys: Dan, Dean, Richie, and Gabe.

They'd never know that I, at the age of seven, once served Gabe sandwiches in the back room of McAuley's during one of Dad's "meetings." Or that Jacqui went on a date with Dean's son, back when Dad was still climbing the ladder and having your teenage daughter shagging a coke dealer wasn't your worst nightmare but smart play.

"Boss, before we go . . . slightly different tangent . . ." I get my mind back on the job, quick smart. "Has Cookey been through all of Holly's foster parents yet? A Sean and Linda, I can't remember the surname."

"Speak to him, but I think so." If Steele doesn't "know so" it means nothing much was gleaned. "Why, what's the problem?"

"Not a problem, exactly. I'd just like to meet them. Cookey'll have been asking them about past grudges, that sort of thing. Ticking boxes, crossing them off the to-do list."

"And what do you want to do?" Her hand's still hovering over the receiver.

"I just want to get to know Holly a bit better. Her friends . . . well, they obviously loved her, but they weren't entirely complimentary.

And now all this stuff with Dale Peters . . ." *How do I put this?* "I don't like her all that much, *that's* my problem." I've said it in the simplest way possible—*thank you, Susie Grainger.* "And I know that shouldn't matter—and it doesn't, not really—but she was with Sean and Linda Whatever-they're-called for two years, and Dyer said they stayed in touch with her, the only ones who did, so that must mean they saw something in her. Something . . . I dunno, good, worthwhile?" I'm aware this makes me sound like a tosser. "I just want to know what that was. You understand, right?"

Whether she understands or not, she barks, "Fine. I'll get Cookey to call them back, get them in. You two, get gone. Because I don't like Simon Fellows all that much and believe me, that *is* a problem."

After kicking off the day in a windowless room reeking of meat, our game of Hunt the Gangster gets some warm air in our lungs at least. Simon Fellows, unsurprisingly, isn't the easiest man to track down. We start at his known address—a chic three-story pad on a cobbled mews in Little Venice, just a stone's throw from the brightly colored narrowboats bobbing serenely on the Regent's Canal. We're greeted by a woman—Alma—wearing a tabard and a growly expression, who tells us that while Fellows lives here, he doesn't "live" here, and yes, she'll try to get a message to him but no, she'd rather we didn't come in as she's just washed the floors. Quite why the floors need washing when Fellows hasn't walked his Gucci loafers over them in weeks is anyone's guess, but she doesn't seem in the humor to be asked.

She does, however, point us to another address in less picturesque Lewisham, a haulage yard ten miles south, where we're greeted by more shakes of the head and a suggestion that as it's Friday, La Trompette in Chiswick might be our best bet, or possibly the Gaucho over east. We call both. Get nothing. Turn up at both. Still nothing. Over the course of three hours, we've been pointed north, south, east, and west, and call me paranoid—many have—but our magical mystery tour has a distinctly orchestrated feel to it. A network of lackeys playing pass-the-parcel with the police.

We're just about to head back when Parnell's phone rings. He's driving so I answer, hitting speakerphone as I say hello.

"Well, you don't sound like a Luigi Parnell, so I assume you're the other one. Sorry, darling, my cleaner didn't catch your name."

I pull a *"What the fuck?"* face, feeling caught off guard. I know Alma said she'd try to get a message to him, but I assumed by "try," she meant "I might some time this decade if I can be bothered." Parnell jerks his head toward the phone, urging me to speak.

"Detective Constable Cat Kinsella. Thanks for calling." Not for the first time, I inwardly thank myself for the decision to take Mum's maiden name after she died. A tribute to Mum. A *fuck you* to Dad. And protection against anyone—anyone of Fellows' ilk—ever connecting me to the McBride name. "We've been all over looking for you, Mr. Fellows. You've got lots of friends and employees, and yet no one seems to know your phone number. Funny that."

"Need to know, Cat, need to know. Can't be too careful with your personal details these days, not with all these cyber criminals doing God knows what with your data." Parnell shakes his head at the sheer gall of the man. "Hey, can you hold on a sec?" A shout of *"Kelsey, you little devil, get away, they're still cooling"* and then he's back with me. "So shoot, how can I help?"

Parnell jumps in. "We need to speak to you in person, Mr. Fellows. Can you tell us where you are, or you can come to Holborn station? Either way, it'll be under caution. I'm sure you know the drill."

Predictably, he wants us on his turf, and so forty minutes later, we're back where we started. Unpredictably, and what seems to be puzzling Parnell greatly as we follow Simon Fellows into an airy, sunlit kitchen at the back of the house, is that this so-called Mr. Big, or Mr. Big-ish at least, appears to be partway through baking a batch of rainbow cookies.

"Your cleaner gave the impression you don't spend a lot of time here," I say, taking in the domestic scene. The patio doors are wide open and outside a barefoot little girl is playing swingball, missing the ball every time and finding it gloriously hilarious.

"Alma, bless her heart, has been married for forty-eight years and she could tell you the exact time her husband takes a shit every day. Size and consistency too." I frown, not quite following. "My lifestyle's a bit flighty for her. She can't see the point of having a nice house if you're not sitting in it every night with your pipe and slippers."

Fellows is tall, dark, and sleek. Middle-aged, north of fifty, but with the patina of youth, or maybe botox, still gilding his features. Thickset but not fat, he looks every inch the tough guy, even with a tea towel slung over his shoulder and a glittery mermaid stuck to his cheek. He catches me looking at it, puts a hand to his face and laughs.

"Yeah, whoever told you I dine at La Trompette on a Friday has got their facts four years out of date." He points behind to the little girl. "Ever since that little lady came along, Fridays are about my granddaughter. I don't care what comes up, business, friends, lovers, Friday is Kelsey Day." He laughs again. "Although she's a right little madam. Fickle, but then aren't most women? Drives me mad saying she wants to do baking, then buggers off outside, leaving the legwork to me." He picks up a wire rack of cookies. "You want one?"

I'd love one. In fact, I'd love the whole batch. It's been a long old morning on just a quarter of a Kit Kat, and my stomach thinks my throat's been cut, as Parnell is fond of saying.

But this is about tone. And that's what Fellows is doing, he's trying to set it, knock us off-balance. Make this all casual, cozy, and by the look on his face, faintly amusing.

And Parnell's not having it.

"Mr. Fellows, can you tell us about your relationship with Holly Kemp?"

Fellows turns and starts filling the kettle, a fancy see-through number that could do with descaling. "Call me Simon," he says, over his shoulder. "You know, I think I remember your name, mate. Hardly going to forget a copper called Luigi, am I? Didn't you work for that fat prick, Butterfield?" He swings around, looking at me. "DCI from a while back, darling. Thought he was the King of Hammersmith until he got caught in flagrante with a fourteen-year-old trafficked girl."

It's a threat delivered with a hundred-watt smile. Every copper knows about DCI Steve Butterfield. About his rock-solid insistence that his drink must have been spiked, as he has no recollection whatsoever of the two hours where, according to photo evidence, he apparently lost his mind and threw away his marriage and highly celebrated career for a blow job in an unmarked police car.

Parnell doesn't blink. "I said, can you tell us about your relationship with Holly Kemp?"

Fellows leans on the kitchen island, cookie in hand. "Yeah, see, I heard you the first time, Luigi. Only I didn't answer because I haven't got a fucking clue who you're on about."

A tinkle from outside. "Grandpa, you said 'fucking.'"

Fellows laughs. "Ears like a bat, that one. Except when you're saying 'bedtime.'"

"Megan Moore," I say, scanning his face for a reaction.

"Come again?"

"Maybe you knew Holly Kemp as Megan Moore?"

"Maybe baby."

I give him a look that could bore through steel.

"Oh look, sorry, darling, I'm in a stupid mood today, ignore me. Must be all these additives." He takes a bite of cookie. "Come on then, what's this about? What's this Megan, Holly woman been saying about me? Because if it's this MeToo crap, just remember I'm a wealthy man and that makes me a target for all sorts." I keep my cool, biting down hard. "On Kelsey's life, I've never overstepped the mark with a woman, and if you think I'd lie on my own grand-daughter's life, you and me are going to fall out big-style."

He could be telling a twisted truth, of course. Maybe he never has overstepped the mark, sexually. Or maybe he's a member of that particular breed of vermin who genuinely thinks violence against their own partner doesn't count. After all, what's a throw against a wall or a kick in the stomach when they're picking up the bill and buying you nice lingerie?

"Couple of things, Mr. Fellows." Parnell ignores the "Simon" invite. "We're from Murder, so let me put your mind at rest about any MeToo 'crap,' and second, the victim, Holly Kemp, was long dead before that movement hit the headlines. She's been dead six years. Shot dead. Executed."

Murder. Dead. Shot. Executed.

Four opportunities for Fellows to show there's a heart in his chest. He doesn't. Just keeps munching his cookie, looking mildly curious at best.

I frown. "Seriously, you're telling us the name Holly Kemp doesn't mean anything at all."

"You need to get your ears syringed, darling. I said I don't have a fucking clue." He throws his head back, raising his voice. "And yes, Grandpa said 'fucking' again, Kels. Don't tell your mother." When he drops his head again, the hundred-watt smile is now a snarl. "I can't be any clearer, really. Her name means nothing. Less than nothing."

Only that last line sounds personal.

"It's just she's been on the news all week," I say, gesturing to a TV quietly playing in the corner. Another weather forecast. A place called Wisley hit thirty-five degrees yesterday, the poor bastards.

"I don't watch TV much. I only put it on for missy out there. And I certainly don't watch the news. I like to keep my worldview more positive."

"So you've never heard of the Roommate case? Several women murdered in Clapham in 2012."

"Yeah, I've heard of it." The twitch of his shoulders says, *But what's it got to do with me*?

"We believed Holly Kemp to be one of them, and her remains were found this week in a village in Cambridgeshire," explains Parnell. "This anomaly and her cause of death means we're looking into her case again, testing some earlier assumptions."

"Not got enough recent murders to keep you busy, huh? No wonder there's fucking corpses on the streets if you're raking over years-old cases. Couple of fifteen-year-olds last weekend, wasn't it? Shocking . . ."

Parnell talks over him. "And during the course of our renewed investigation, it's been suggested to us that you were in a relationship with Holly Kemp."

"Suggested by who?" He stands up, military erect. "I've told you, I don't know anything about her."

"By Holly," I say. "She gave a detailed account of a four-year relationship, in fact, to a close friend."

"Well then, correction, I do know one thing about this Holly Kemp. I know she's a fucking liar!" He pauses for a second, head tilting. "Was she a dancer, by any chance? And I don't mean quickstep, foxtrot. Did she know her way around a pole?"

"Why do you ask?"

He runs a hand over his slicked-back hair, blue-black, a *definite* dye job. "Well, I still had the clubs back then, and you smile at a dancer for more than a second, buy them a drink after a shift, and they think you're engaged, think they've got their meal ticket."

"Oh, it was a bit more than that," says Parnell, hopping up on a bar stool, uninvited. I'm not sure if it's a chess move or if his knees are playing him up. Either way, I join him. "Holly Kemp gave an account of a relationship that started when she was eighteen, which would have been in 2008, and which was still continuing shortly before she died."

"It wasn't the most flattering account either," I tell him. "She said you were abusive toward her, that you threatened to kill her on several occasions if she ever left you. She was terrified of you."

"And if she was still around now, she'd have every right to be. I don't like people spreading lies about me." His dark eyes glitter. He knows we know what happens to people who cross him. "You got a photo of this fruitcake then?"

I bring Holly up on my phone. Fellows walks around the island and stands behind me, leaning in closer than he needs to, so close I can smell the sticker adhesive on his cheek. There's a long pause before he speaks—the kettle coming to the boil, Kelsey singing a song about five little monkeys outside. "No, can't help, I'm afraid. Don't recognize her."

"Why the hesitation?"

"I see a lot of her kind, just wanted to be sure."

Parnell swivels his stool to face him. "You know we'll be showing Holly's photo to everyone in your circle, Mr. Fellows, and I don't just mean the people who sent us on a wild-goose chase around London this morning."

I have to ask, "Were you here the whole time this morning, Simon, hiding behind an old biddy? What was she going to do? Attack us with the mop if we tried to come in?"

He laughs. "I wouldn't let Alma hear you call her that! Sharp as a tiger's tooth, that one. I bought her a gym membership last Christmas—she's there at six a.m. every morning when you're still hitting snooze, darling."

"You're a good employer," says Parnell, eyes steady on his. "But you've made plenty of enemies who I daresay will be happy to help us. And then there's your neighbors, the restaurants you frequented, the pubs you drank in. If anyone so much as saw Holly Kemp within a hundred feet of you, we'll be back, and we'll be drawing conclusions about why you lied about knowing her."

"Be my guest. I can make a list if that makes your lives easier."

"No need," says Parnell. "We can access plenty of information about you."

A small bow. "I'm honored."

Kelsey skips in, smearing dry mud and twigs all over Alma's recently washed floor. There isn't a trace of Fellows in her. Pale and white blond, blue veins shining through, like a sprite from a Scandinavian fairy tale. Her grandfather scoops her up with one deeply tanned arm.

"Ever spent much time in Cambridgeshire, Simon?" I spot a missed call from Jacqui as I slide my phone back in my pocket.

Fellows pretends to spit on the floor. "Sorry, just a little joke. I was an Oxford man. Keble College. We're trained to hiss at the C word."

"You had a privileged start in life," says Parnell. "You could have done anything and yet . . ." He leaves it there. *Alleged, alleged, alleged.*

Fellows looks around, smiling. "Oh, I don't think I've done too badly, do you?"

"Let me give you a more specific C word," I interrupt, before Parnell makes an accusation that ties him up in paperwork until Christmas. "Caxton. It's South Cambridgeshire, around forty miles from the university. Do you know it?"

"No."

"You're quite sure."

"Quite sure." He looks at Kelsey. "I'm not being much help to these nice people, am I, baby? But Grandpa's trying. You should always try to help the police."

"Good of you, Mr. Fellows. Maybe you can help by telling us where you were on the afternoon and evening of Thursday 23rd February, 2012? That's the last time Holly Kemp was seen alive."

It's a question we have to ask but pretty pointless all the same. There's a vague expectation that most people should be able to recall their movements over the past month or so without too much fluster. Anything beyond that, a blank face is the norm. Six years later—forget about it.

But Fellows' face isn't blank.

"I can tell you exactly where I was. Street opened that day, I was there for most of it." We wait for an explanation. "Contrary to popular myth, I'm a legitimate businessman, Luigi. An investor. Street was a Peruvian-themed place over in Hoxton. The idea of street food was still up-and-coming then. Thought we'd catch the wave, make a fortune. It didn't work out. We got the concept all wrong, tried to make it a fine-dining experience. Turns out people don't want to pay fine-dining prices for food you'd normally buy off a market stall. We closed in 2014. You live and learn."

We. As if he was choosing the color scheme, curating the menu, rather than using the place to launder drug money.

"You've got a good memory," I say. "I couldn't tell you what I was doing on 23rd February *this* year."

He shrugs. "Street was the first restaurant I invested in. My baby. I'm into double figures now. Much less hassle than the clubs, I'll tell you. As a product, food's a lot less stressful than women."

He grins. I grin back. I won't let him faze me.

"What about New Year's Eve 2011?" I think about mentioning Holly's allegation, but let's see what he has to say first. "Can you remember where you were?"

"Bantry Bay, Cape Town. Why?"

"Quick on the draw again," says Parnell.

"It was a friend's sixtieth. An amazing night. Stays in the memory, you know? Do you want to see my passport stamp?"

"Did you travel to Cape Town alone?" I ask.

He lets out a sigh—not stressed, just bored. "If you mean did I travel to Cape Town with the woman I've told you I never met, then no, I didn't."

Parnell looks at me, then lowers his eyes. A sign we should keep our counsel. We need to figure this out first. Why wouldn't Holly have mentioned Cape Town to Dale Peters? Why would she leave that significant detail out?

I keep my voice neutral. "So come on then, Simon. Give us a theory. Why do you think Holly Kemp, a supposed complete stranger, would fabricate an entire relationship? And why you?"

"Mad as a March hare, obviously. Not right in the head."

He draws two fingers to his temple, making the tiniest of circular motions before jerking them skyward with a cold, sharp laugh.

The universal cuckoo sign, the twirl of his fingers indicating that Holly had a screw loose?

Or a finger gun?

A brazen confession. A gauntlet thrown down.

16

Linda Denby's been waiting an hour by the time we get back, although she could have been waiting since 1983 judging by the poodle perm and the oversized glasses that cover half her face. It's a nice face, though. Plump and lined and farmer's-wife rosy. And I kind of like her time-warp vibe. It makes her seem consistent, dependable, not given to flights of fancy or changes in fashion. Probably everything you want in a foster parent.

We're in the "soft" interview room, the pastel-hued one reserved for visitors, not suspects. If you're helping, not hindering us, you get a nice squidgy sofa and Van Gogh's *Sunflowers* to gaze on. You also get table service. Someone's brought Linda a mug of tea—Flowers, presumably, as it's definitely his mug, LEGEND stamped across the front.

Linda Denby seems inclined to agree.

"It was so good of that big chap to make it himself. I can't bear drinking tea out of those plastic cups. He made it just the way I like it too—milky-beige with two sugars." She smiles. "Holly always used to say I liked a drop of tea with my milk, not the other way round."

"Just like my wife." Parnell's opted to sit in.

"Hey, never mind the big chap," I say. "It was good of you to come in so quickly and to wait for us. We headed back as soon as we got our colleague's message, but you know what it's like at this time on a Friday. It'd be quicker to hopscotch across Central London than drive."

"I don't drive. I can't," she clarifies. "Four disastrous lessons in 1982 and that was me done. I don't need to, anyway, not living in Islington."

"You don't have to drive to be a foster parent?" I ask.

"Almost certainly in rural places, but in London, no. There's far more important qualities than being able to execute a three-point turn."

"Such as . . . ?"

"Oh, humor, patience, knowing how to discipline without losing your temper. And in any case, Sean drives." Another crinkly smile; I'd say she's not far off sixty. "Sean does the driving and I do the disciplining. That's another quality you need—teamwork."

"Could Sean not come?" asks Parnell.

She shakes her head; the lacquered perm stays stock-still. "No, he had to take a day off for the hospital yesterday—MRI scan, I think a knee replacement isn't too far off—so there's no way he could take another, not at short notice. No, I'm afraid I'll have to do, but I'm sure I can answer whatever it is you want to know." A curious frown. "Although we hadn't actually *seen* Holly for years before she disappeared. We'd send her a birthday card if we knew her address and she'd always call on Christmas Eve—usually drunk as a lord, but the gesture was sweet. She loved Christmas. We only had two Christmases with her, but they were certainly memorable. She made us play 'Who can keep their Christmas cracker hat on the longest.' It was a tradition when she was a child, apparently. She won both times. She was still wearing it on Boxing Day—slept in it, would you believe!"

"This is perfect, Linda," I say, encouraging her from the opposite squishy sofa. "This is the kind of stuff we're after. You see, I—*we*—don't feel like we've got a great handle on Holly yet. I met her friends yesterday, of course, but that's only one viewpoint."

"You met Emma and Kayleigh? They were nice girls. Kayleigh found me on Facebook, told me about the service. 'Course we couldn't go, what with the MRI." She tips her head, looking up at the ceiling. "There were another two, weren't there? Gosh, I forget their names now. Is that awful?"

"Shona and Josh. And no, not awful at all. It's a long time since Holly was in your care."

She reads my cue perfectly.

"Yes, she came to us in 2003 when she was nearly fourteen. She'd been in the system for three, four years by then, and in that time alone she'd already had several different social workers, two different foster families, two extended stays in a residential unit—not happy ones, either."

At ten years old, I was in the throes of loathing Dad. My trust had been broken two years earlier when Maryanne Doyle got into his car and he'd lied to the police about ever meeting her. But at least I'd been safe. Safe and warm and loved and fed in my Spice Girls–themed bedroom.

"Why weren't they happy?" I ask.

"There was a real culture of bullying in both of the homes, particularly Sycamore Croft; it had an awful reputation. And I'm not talking occasional name-calling or a bit of scrapping, regrettable as that is. I'm talking brutal hierarchies—the strong ones bullying the weak ones or the younger ones. Physical abuse, definitely. Sexual abuse . . . well, it happened." My heart sinks. "And no, Holly never complained about the latter, but I always wondered . . . she'd definitely been badly beaten several times. We knew that when we took her in. The problem was she was small, shy, weak when she first came into the system. 'Geeky,' one of her social workers called her. She was studious, loved reading, and depressing as it sounds, that can make you a target in some establishments." Regret crosses her face. "She toughened up, though, no doubt about that. There was nothing shy or weak about the girl who arrived in our home."

"She was a handful," says Parnell. A redundant observation but it keeps Linda in the flow.

"Oh, she was. A handful and a half! But then most Sycamore kids were. We were prepared for it, as prepared as you can be."

"So what did she get up to?" I ask.

She puts the mug on the floor, next to her worn sandal. "She had 'a mouth' as my mum used to say. Our children were older by then, sixth form and university, and I'm sure they'd heard worse, so I chose not to go to battle over that. But she ran away a few times. Stayed out late, drinking and smoking. Very little respect for curfews or homework deadlines. And there were other issues at school—bullying . . ."

I interrupt. "Holly was the bully, or she was being bullied?"

"The former, I'm afraid. The switch from victim to bully is really very common. And not to make light of it, but it was entirely normal, given what she'd been through." She brings her hands to her lap. "Anyway, I got through to her in the end, and she settled down after a few months. Oh, I'm not saying she was an angel, but she was a nice kid underneath all the front. Even when she was acting out, you couldn't help liking her. She was funny, sharp, and so, so interested in the world. She wanted to go everywhere, see everything. She was always asking questions. She got back into reading for a while, but it didn't last—I think she always had the bullies in her head telling her she was a loser, a nerd, a geek—as if that's a huge insult." She rolls her eyes, kindly. "No, I'm afraid it was clothes, makeup, vacuous celebrities, that became her passion. Oh, and our dog, Buster—they were inseparable."

"So why did she leave you?" I ask. "DCI Tessa Dyer recalls you saying . . ."

Linda claps her hands. "Oh, Tess, she was wonderful. So efficient, but you could tell she really cared. She was as devastated as we were when they couldn't charge that . . . *that man*, with Holly's murder."

I try again. "Tess recalled you saying that Holly had become so disruptive she had to leave." Her face changes. "Sorry, did we pick that up wrong?"

She fixes me with a bold stare—my punishment for implying

that she gave up on Holly, which, for the record, was absolutely not my intention.

"I could live with disruptive. I *had* lived with disruptive. I couldn't live with destructive, with dangerous."

"To herself or other people?"

"Both, and we were fostering another child by then, a much younger girl. It was an agonizing decision and we didn't come to it overnight. We had several Placement Support Meetings, discussed various strategies, but in the end, Sean and I had to do what was best for us." She's on the defensive straightaway. "And if that sounds harsh, you'll be surprised to know that one of the first things they tell you when you become a foster parent is to make sure you practice high levels of self-care. You're no good to your other children, or any future children, if you feel burned out and resentful."

Which makes total sense, of course. And yet you can't help but feel heartsick for a vulnerable teenage girl who's effectively been told that she's too hot to handle.

"So what was she doing that was dangerous?"

"What *wasn't* she doing by that point? Staying out until one, two a.m. Wouldn't say where she'd been, who she'd been with. One time, she staggered in, completely out of it, with her top on back to front, scratches and bruises all up her arms and legs. Next day, two men turn up at the door. They were easily in their twenties but Holly announces they're her boyfriends—both of them, as if one wasn't bad enough. Well, of course, Sean tried to warn them off, got a punch in the jaw for his efforts. Oh, and then there was the time she decided she knew how to drive a car at age fifteen. Cue a call from the police to say she's been joyriding and she's injured. We rushed to The Whittington and there she was, finding the whole thing hilarious."

Should this be a red card, or a sign she needed more help? I don't know and I can't judge.

"It was the drugs that sealed it, though—she was taking drugs *in* the house. Betsy, that was the other child we were fostering, got hold of an ecstasy tablet . . ." She shivers. "I found it just in time, but it was the last straw. We'd warned her and warned her and warned her. Of course, I often think now that if we'd handled things differently, maybe she'd have taken a different path, maybe she'd never have been in Clapham that day."

"I'm sure you made the right decision." It feels like the kind thing to say.

She shoots straight back. "Oh, I don't regret the decision, but I do regret not considering the obvious . . ." We wait for the obvious as she fiddles with her sandal. "Losing her parents in such quick succession at a young age, the violence at Sycamore, foster placements breaking down . . ." She takes a long, measured breath. "I think Holly had PTSD. Dangerous, reckless behavior is a classic symptom, but I just passed it off as teenage behavior—heightened teenage behavior, admittedly. I honestly think it could have been a mental illness, though. She just didn't seem to have any sense of danger, none whatsoever. She'd walk alone late at night. She'd pick fights with people you really shouldn't pick fights with. She'd push people to the edge, almost for fun. I think she wanted them to strike back to confirm her belief that the world was bleak and other people were the enemy." She shrugs. "I'm not a psychologist, but the more I've thought about it over the years, the more it makes sense."

It does.

And Simon Fellows is definitely someone you really shouldn't pick a fight with.

17

"Who's been sitting in my chair?" I ask, trying and failing to adjust the height back to something less suited to a giraffe.

"That'll have been DCI Dyer, Goldilocks." Ben Swaines' voice hovers above me. I look up to see him standing there, dangling a document like a dog treat. "Do you need a hand with that?"

"Nah, I'm done," I say stubbornly. "And, not to be pedantic, but it was the three bears that said that, not Goldilocks." I stand up, then sit down, try the chair out for size. It'll do until I get Parnell to fix it properly. "So what's that in your hand, then?"

"Aha, wouldn't you like to know?" Swaines jerks his arm back and forth, daring me to make a grab for it. Instead, I turn to Emily. "Ems, Ben's being a dick. What's he got that I'm supposed to be excited about?"

A bawdy laugh from Pete Flowers.

Emily and I aren't exactly friends, but we've established something of an entente cordiale of late. An acceptance that while we have little in common, bar a womb and an aversion to sushi, we're both twenty-something women who share the same cramped space for sixty hours a week, so we might as well unite against the patriarchy when the need arises. Which, fortunately for us, isn't all that often. The odd filthy laugh from Flowers, or Ben Swaines being a good-natured dick occasionally. Steele was right: we've got a nice setup.

"Serena Bailey's bank records," Emily tells me. "He's been guarding them like Gollum from *Lord of the Rings*."

"Has he now?"

I have them off Swaines in seconds, scanning the pages with

supersonic eyes. The relevant dates are lined through with green highlighter.

23 February 2012 > POS TESCO express, EDGWARE	£11.85
23 February 2012 > POS THE POST OFFICE, MILL HILL	£4.55
23 February 2012 > C/L NOTEMACHINE	£30.00

I look up. "No purchases made in Clapham the day she saw Holly."

It's a myth, or at least a misconception, that to be a good detective you need to possess the laser focus of an Olympic athlete and the doggedness of an old hack. If anything, you need the attention span of a toddler. An ability to shift obsessions at whim.

So, bye-bye, Simon Fellows. Welcome back, Serena Bailey.

Swaines is looking at Steele, who's wheeling her chair out of her office. "Doesn't look like it. Happy now?"

"Happy" wouldn't be the word I'd use. Possibly suspicious, certainly piqued.

"What was Dyer doing here?" I say, changing the subject.

"Fuck knows, but she's still here," says Flowers. "She's gone out to get a coffee. Nescafé isn't good enough for her, obviously. It must be all decaf soy lattes over in Counter-Terrorism."

Right on cue, Dyer walks in, carrying something swampy in a clear cup that suggests Flowers isn't too wide of the mark. "Hey, Cat," she says, smiling broadly. "You need to get Steele to stump up for a new chair. Yours is terrible. You'll have back problems by the time you're thirty. Leave it with me, I'll have a word."

"Cheers, ma'am!"

Swaines and Flowers glower at me. I obviously haven't read the memo that "We Don't Like Tess Dyer," although what was I supposed to do, ignore her? And I *do* like her. I see myself in her, for better or for worse. It was Cairns' "guts and glory" comment that sealed it.

And anyway, I don't go in for all that siege mentality bullshit—the idea that anyone from outside our team is automatically the enemy or stuck up their own arse.

"Right, m'dears . . ." Steele's voice draws all eyes to the front. "Any updates before we get on to the main business—Head-scratcher of the Day?"

Which one? Day four of this investigation and it's a wonder we've got any scalp left.

"What about you, Kinsella? How'd it go with the foster mum? Do you like Holly Kemp now? Can we put that one to bed?"

"I understand her more, definitely. A frightened kid trapped in a woman's body, it sounds like."

"Oh, and that excuses ripping people off, does it?" Flowers, who else?

"It explains some things. She was out for what she could get because no one ever gave her anything, not after the age of ten anyway."

Parnell protests. "Ah, come on, the Denbys tried to help her."

"Yeah, but the damage was done by then. First, her parents die, then she's plunged into the care system, then she's subjected to daily violence . . . I think Linda could be right about PTSD."

Flowers opens his mouth but mercifully, Swaines cuts in. "I've got a couple of updates," he says, walking back to his desk. "Spencer Shaw had parrot fish for his lunch—a Tenerife delicacy, apparently. No one's mentioned Holly in the comments, but thinking about it, you probably wouldn't, would you? In all likelihood, you'd private message him. I'll keep my eye on it, though." He sits down. "Second update—I spoke to the scrapyard who got rid of Peters' car. It seems to check out. They sent him a Certificate of Destruction and let the DVLA know that he no longer owned the car, so all aboveboard. That's it, though. They don't have any records of whether it was a write-off or not, so we've only got Peters' word."

"The brother-in-law confirms his story," Renée pipes up from the back. "I know he's family so he probably would, but there didn't seem to be a lot of love lost. Said he's never understood what his sister sees in him."

"Makes you wonder what Holly saw in him," says Seth.

Flowers balks. "What? A gullible fool loaded with money. Yeah, mate, what *was* the attraction?"

"She wouldn't have known that just from looking at him," I argue. "There must have been something there."

"Girls like her have a nose for men like him."

"Girls like her?" Steele's pounces with a warning. "That's our victim you're talking about, Pete. Watch your mouth."

A sulky shrug. "I'm just saying it probably isn't the first time she pulled a stunt like that. Her friends said she always had money."

"Where are we on the escort thing?" asks Parnell.

"Nowhere," says a slumped and beleaguered-looking Cooke. "I've been through all the main London agencies, the more established ones that were around back in 2012, and no one recognized her. It's a needle in a haystack. She could have been running her own ads online, working for a much smaller outfit based out of London. She could have been doing webcam stuff."

"Linda implied some risky sexual behavior, so it could fit," I say. "Her laptop was never found, right?"

Steele looks to Dyer, who's leaning against the incident board, drinking her anti-Nescafé through a straw. "No, the assumption was she must have had it with her and it was dumped with her phone and bag."

"OK, we park the escorting for now, unless we get stronger intelligence," says Steele. "Her friends were obviously suspicious of the fact she had money, but we know now that she had more creative ways of making rent."

"There is one angle we haven't thought of." I know what Parnell's going to say. We talked about it on the way back from Little Venice, after we'd called Steele with the highlights. "Escort agencies and money laundering often go hand in hand. Maybe Holly met Fellows that way? He takes a shine to her. She's effectively forced to become his girlfriend. It explains why he'd try to distance himself from her—he won't want us looking too closely at that aspect of his investment portfolio."

Renée's voice from the back again. "Well, I reinterviewed Holly's friends and they'd never heard of him. Didn't recognize his photo either. One of them—Emma—said Holly would have been bragging to high heaven if she'd been seeing a big-shot gangster, but the other one, Shona, said she could be secretive, so who knows?"

"Those friends knew nothing about Dale Peters either, so I wouldn't pay much attention to them," Flowers says, and it's a fair point. "They obviously weren't the bosom buddies they like to make out."

I go to speak at the same time as Dyer. Steele makes a split-second decision, choosing me. "Hang on a minute, Tess."

"It's just . . . Fellows was definitely up to something. He either sent us on a whistle-stop tour of London just to amuse himself, or he was giving himself time to get his story straight. I mean, he knew exactly where he was the day Holly disappeared, just like that." I click my fingers. "And he did this weird finger thing too, when he was talking about her. Like he was pretending to pull a trigger."

"Or it could have been, 'Holly was crazy.'" Parnell twirls his fingers by his temple.

"It could," I concede. "To be honest, it happened so quickly, I'm not sure what to think now. But . . ."

Steele smiles. "I'd have bet the farm on there being a *but* coming."

"*But* four years is a long relationship, even if they were on the down-low. Fellows must know we'll find out. Sure, he's got plenty of people on the payroll who'll be ordered to keep quiet, but eventually we'll find someone who puts him and Holly together, and he must realize that. Unless he knows we won't find someone because there's no one to find." I pause for a sharp breath. "Because there was no relationship."

Steele offers up a hand. "And now we go over to my learned friend, Tess Dyer, for Head-scratcher of the Day."

Dyer puts her drink down on Flowers' desk. He eyes it suspiciously.

"OK, so I think you all know, but in case anyone doesn't—before I went to Lyon, I worked for SCD7." Serious and Organized Crime Command. It still exists to do exactly the same job, although it's called something new now—the top brass love tinkering with a title. "I never really had direct dealings with Simon Fellows myself, I was more project focused, but I checked in with a couple of old colleagues and what I have found out is that Fellows is gay."

This lights a fire under every one of us. I let out a one-word shriek—*"What!"* Even Craig Cooke sits up.

"Yeah, he's been in a relationship with a man called Erik Vestergaard for over fifteen years. Vestergaard is well into his sixties . . ."

"Which makes a relationship with a young woman pretty unfathomable." I'm almost breathless as I draw the obvious conclusion.

"You said he's got a granddaughter?" Flowers points at Parnell. "Must mean he's enjoyed the pleasures of the female form at least once."

I interrupt. "Hold on. Vestergaard . . . that sounds Scandinavian."

"Danish," says Dyer. "He's a corporate finance lawyer. He got caught up in a big money-laundering scandal a few years back, so he was on Interpol's radar. I probably know more about him than I do about Fellows."

I look at Parnell. "My money's on the granddaughter being Vestergaard's. There wasn't a trace of Fellows in her. Totally different coloring."

Parnell's eyes are on Dyer. "Why didn't he tell us then? All he did was deny knowing Holly, he certainly didn't say anything about being gay. And, I mean, you'd think he would—it doesn't exactly put him in the clear but it throws her claim into huge question."

"Still in the closet?" Flowers suggests.

"Mmmm, not a hundred percent," counters Dyer. "According to my old colleagues, it isn't widely known at all, but it's not exactly top-with-a-capital-T-secret either. He's private, but it's not like he's living a lie—you saw him today, he's entirely comfortable with who he is, happy showing off his granddaughter. He just chooses to keep his private life private, and that seems to be respected."

"But your colleagues knew," I say.

"Only a select few, and they've been working that world for the best part of thirty years—what they don't know isn't worth knowing." She picks up her drink again, swirls the remnants around with the straw. "The point is, for whatever reason, it's almost certain Holly Kemp lied about their relationship."

"Maybe about a romantic relationship," insists Parnell. "But there's got to be *some* link between them. She used Fellows' name for a reason."

I've got an idea, although it's not going to make me popular. I think back to Steele's excitement this morning, her joy at something finally making sense.

Sod it, popularity's overrated.

"There might not be a link." Steele turns her chair to face me full-on, her expression curious but with a smidge of *"Why always you?"* "Holly could have plucked Simon Fellows' name off the internet to con Dale Peters into believing there was a real sense of urgency. Think about it. Is he really going to hand over £10,000 to protect her from some faceless, nameless bogeyman? But if you gave the bogeyman a name, a criminal reputation . . . can you imagine the rush he'd have got from that? Protecting *sweet, fragile*, ickle-wickle Megan from the big bad gangster man. I reckon she could have asked for three times the money and he'd still have handed it over."

A few nods in my peripheral vision: Dyer, Seth, Cooke, Parnell. Steele tips her head back, thinking about it.

"But why Fellows?" says Emily. "He might be a big cheese in certain circles, but it's not like he's a well-known name. I'd never heard of him."

Renée taps quickly on her laptop. "OK, so I've just put his name into Google and he gets a few references here and there, but he's hardly Reggie Kray."

"Well, that would be the point, wouldn't it?" Dyer's voice is snappy and I feel a surge of protectiveness toward Renée who, to be fair, is perfectly capable of fighting her own battles. "She'd need to make it believable. A high-profile name would be stretching things too far. And anyway . . ." She drags a hand through her hair, her perfectly symmetrical bob losing all shape momentarily. "All this talk about Fellows, this Dale Peters guy, aren't we forgetting the main man here? Masters. Haven't you guys found *anything* yet to link him to the dump site or a firearm? It's got to be there. We had—we *have*—an ID, for heaven's sake."

To her credit, and to my great, great surprise, Steele stays calm, even smiley, as another DCI tells *her* team how to do their job. But I know that smile. I've been on the receiving end of it enough times. And I know we won't be seeing DCI Tess Dyer in another briefing this side of the apocalypse.

Parnell's first to puncture the tension. "The dump site doesn't bother me as much as the gun."

"Yeah, well, I had a chat with Dolores, Dr. Allen . . ." Dyer gives Steele a look that says she might as well be hung for a sheep as a lamb. "She says it's possible Masters got bored of strangulation after the first three and needed a bigger thrill for the fourth."

"A shrink will say anything's possible," grunts Flowers.

"Boss," I say, jumping back to Dyer's precious ID before we

go too far down the path of Flowers' views on criminal profiling. "Serena Bailey's bank records are back. No purchases in Clapham on Thursday 23rd February."

"You pulled Serena Bailey's bank records?" Dyer's voice is incredulous.

Steele ignores her, staying entirely focused on me. "OK, well, a purchase would have been helpful to settle your nerves, but a lack of one isn't proof she wasn't there."

"Hold on." I search for my interview report. It takes me a few seconds to find it and I swear I can feel Dyer's eyes perforating my skull. "Serena said, *You know that sudden feeling you've forgotten something? I thought I'd left my bank card in The Northcote. I'd been distracted on my phone when I was paying, see, and it wouldn't be the first time I'd done it.* I checked her original statement and she said words to that effect then."

Steele instructs Swaines, "Benny-boy, pull all the CCTV on file from 23rd February."

Dyer sighs. "Kate, we went through it. It was next to useless."

She doesn't bother turning around. "It was next to useless for tracing Holly's movements beyond the station. But now we're looking for a sighting of Serena Bailey. And while you're doing that, Ben, look for a sighting of Simon Fellows. Or anyone acting suspicious, because if Simon Fellows *is* involved, I doubt he did his own dirty work."

Dyer catches me in the ladies', appraising myself under the harsh lights and wondering if I should sell a kidney to buy some Parsley Seed Antioxidant Serum. It's clearly done Steele no harm. Steele's got over twenty-five years on me, and has had more late nights than Dracula, yet I swear her skin looks fresher than mine.

She joins me at the mirror, facing the other way. "That's bad for you, you know? Pulling your skin downward like that. Trust me, you'll thank me for that advice in ten years' time."

I smile and wait for her to go into a cubicle. When she doesn't,

I recommence pulling. It feels like a tiny, moronic victory after her hissy fit over Masters. *You can tell me how to do my job but not what to do with my skin.*

She reads the subtext, a small grin tugging at the corner of her mouth. Then, "Look, Cat, I know you met with Suze."

For two seconds, I haven't the faintest idea what she's talking about.

"She called me last night, said you'd been asking about Serena Bailey's statement." Ah, DI Susie Grainger. I wouldn't have had her down as a "Suze." "Seriously, Cat, you could have warned me."

"I'm . . . I'm sorry." I stutter an apology, before deciding fuck that, this is *our* case. "But I had legitimate questions, ma'am . . ."

"Drop the ma'am, it's Tess, or T. And I'm not saying you didn't. But you didn't get Steele's permission, did you?"

The grin is still there, broader even, and her tone is warm, conspiratorial. I can't work out if I'm being chastised or congratulated. I turn to face her, chin high, confidence shaky.

"Fine, I should have checked with the boss when I realized Grainger was a DI, but I was there and she was happy to talk. And I didn't mention it afterward because I didn't want what I'd found out from Serena's head teacher to get lost under a bollocking for not following protocol."

"Steele's a stickler for that, I hear."

I'm not comfortable with this Steele-bashing, but then I'm not comfortable with being caught out either. Sitting firmly on the fence, I say, "Sometimes, but that's not a bad thing."

"No, no, of course not." She pushes herself off the sink, gives me a friendly poke on the shoulder. "Well, listen, anyway—you owe me a drink, Cat Kinsella. Several drinks. 'Cos I only narrowly avoided dropping you in it."

"What do you mean?"

"Like I said, you should have warned me. I happened to mention to Steele that you'd met with Suze, but then I could tell from her face that she hadn't got a clue what I was talking about. Lucky for you, I thought on my feet, said you'd been introduced in the Harp & Fiddle the other night."

Shit. "Oh right. Thanks. I mean it." And I do. I'm still not convinced that Steele's altogether fine about Aiden. She hasn't mentioned it since and I'd been expecting the Spanish Inquisition, or at least a bit of ribbing. So if she's feeling weird about that, I could do without this. There's no doubt about it, Dyer saved my bacon. "And look, I'm sorry if it seemed like I was going behind your back." I risk a grin. "You're not too annoyed, are you?"

"I'm annoyed Suze was upset. She might play the tough cookie, but she was shaken up. We all are. Just remember, it's easy to make judgments with the benefit of hindsight. Suze did nothing wrong, and even if she did, she was following my lead. If anything got missed, it's on me, not her, OK?" I nod, knowing Steele would say the same. She turns to face me in the mirror. "But I like your initiative. I think we're cut from the same cloth, Cat, you and me. And that was good work on Serena and the bank card too. I mean, I'm one hundred percent certain we got the right man and Bailey's sound, but it's still good work. I like that you question everything."

"So does Steele." I turn on the tap, splashing my face with cool water. "Well, she says she does after the event. At the time, I think she wishes I'd shut up."

She hands me a paper towel. "Kate's been a good mentor to you, hasn't she?"

"The best."

"She'll be retiring soon, though. What is she? Midfifties?"

"Fifty-three."

"She's done her thirty years; it must cross her mind now and again." Not once, but I don't want to quibble, not after "Suze"-gate. I crouch down and rummage through my bag for a hairbrush to avoid giving an opinion. "And you heard her, she's not interested in promotion. She's happy to sit out the rest of her career."

I shoot up. "Hold on, that's not fair. That's not *true*."

She nods, her face immediately softening. "Sorry, that sounded worse than I meant. Steele's great, she really is. It's just . . . you need to think of yourself, Cat. You need to be working with people, learning from people, who are going places. Steele's got bags of experience, but . . ." She presses her lips together, closing her eyes briefly. "But with experience comes complacency. I saw it with Olly Cairns. A reluctance to keep learning, to keep up with new technologies, new cultural and social phenomena. A desire for a quiet life, to keep the powers that be happy above everything else."

I let out a high-pitched laugh. "Have you met Steele? She's more worried about keeping the canteen staff happy than the powers that be."

Dyer laughs too, but it sounds hollow. "You're probably right, but that's not ideal either. There's an art to keeping all sides happy. I could teach you."

Suddenly, Parnell's voice in the corridor outside. "Catrina Kinsella! Come out, come out, wherever you are . . ."

I'm not sure whether I want to kiss him or kick him.

"In here," I shout. "Be out in a sec."

I pick up my bag and make a beeline for the door. Dyer grabs me as I walk past, a loose grip on my wrist.

"Look, Cat, what I've made a complete mess of saying is that I think you've got great potential, and SO15 needs officers like you. People who question everything, who think critically. I'm going for superintendent and if I get it, recruitment's going to be one of the first things I look at."

Did she just offer me a job?

"Counter-Terrorism?" As soon as the words leave my mouth, I'm embarrassed, sure that I've picked her up wrong.

"Just think about it, OK? Don't let your loyalty to Steele hold you back."

The door bangs open: Parnell.

"Whoa, where's the fire?" I say, taking a step away from Dyer. If Parnell's curious, he doesn't show it. There's something else on his face—white-hot excitement.

"We stirred up a fire in Brandon Keefe, that's for sure."

"Eh?"

That attention shift again. Peters to Fellows to Bailey, now back to Brandon Keefe.

"We've had a call from Kentish Town station. Seems Brandon Keefe had one too many and went berserk. Threw a brick through the window of an ex-girlfriend's flat in the early hours of the morning."

"Not very godly," I say, my head still swimming. "But why have they called us?"

"Because when they ran his fingerprints through the system, a big red flag popped up." Parnell's eyes gleam. "They match a set of prints taken from 6 Valentine Street. He was in that house, Cat. Funny he forgot to mention it."

18

It's late afternoon before Brandon Keefe is deemed sober enough to be interviewed—not surprising given he "couldn't see a hole in a ladder" when he was booked in to Kentish Town at four a.m., according to their custody sergeant. It's early evening before he arrives into our care, flanked by his mum and dad, a docile couple in their early sixties who appear utterly sideswiped, gawking around reception like they've just landed on the moon. It's then another two hours before the Duty Solicitor, Colin Gaffney—aka "Juicy Fruits" on account of his constant chewing—arrives to do his duty. Which effectively amounts to sharing his gum, nodding his head, and reminding Brandon that he's under no obligation to speak.

Fortunately, though, Brandon wants to speak. He's got concerns, important ones.

"Who's going to feed Nimbus? I haven't been home for twenty-four hours, she'll be in a terrible state."

I bring a hand down on the table. "Don't worry about bloody Nimbus, Brandon. Worry about yourself. Things aren't looking great, you know?" I eyeball Gaffney. "He understands why he's here, right?"

I feel bad about "bloody Nimbus." I like cats, generally—their inherent laziness, their lofty indifference. But I'm playing the bitch and Parnell's playing the charmer. Hopefully, Keefe will play ball with one of them.

"Forget why you're here for the moment, Brandon." Parnell, his voice like warm milk, slides a hand toward Keefe's—not quite touching, but the message's clear: *You can trust me.* "Tell me about last night. What was going on, son? That wasn't a very nice thing to do."

I let out a snort. "Yeah, forget 'What would Jesus make of Insta-gram?' Maybe your next Alpha chat could be 'What would Jesus make of men who throw bricks at young women?'"

Keefe looks to Parnell for backup. "I didn't throw the brick *at* her, I threw it at the window. I thought I was aiming at the living room, and as the lights were off, I thought there'd be no one in there. I didn't know she'd moved her bedroom to the front of the house. I was just trying to . . ."

Another slap of the table. "Trying to what, Brandon? Scare her? Teach her a lesson? Why? What has Josie Parr ever done to you, except dump you, and I think she made the right decision there, don't you? Is this what you're like after one too many tequilas?"

Just the mention of alcohol is enough to drain the red anger from his skin, leaving him looking once again like something that's been buried, dug up, shoveled repeatedly around the head, and then buried again.

Parnell continues his lullaby. "Look, son, we know this is out of the norm for you. I mean, it's not like you haven't faced rejec-tion before. That girl you told us about, the one you wanted to go traveling with—she was sleeping with someone else, but you didn't throw a brick through her window." Gaffney's eyebrows are pulled down in concentration, trying to gauge where this is headed. Keefe's looking like the act of concentration might kill him. "What I'm saying is we know, Brandon. We understand. We know why you acted out. Our visit on Wednesday. It brought it all back, didn't it?"

"He might have thrown a brick through that other girl's win-dow," I say, technically addressing Parnell but staring boldly at Keefe. "Maybe he just didn't get caught, or she didn't want to press charges."

Keefe issues an exhausted plea to Gaffney. "They've charged me with criminal damage, can't I just go home?"

"Criminal damage!" I offer a slow handclap. "You lucked out there.

They must be a charitable bunch over at Kentish Town. I'd have gone for assault. We've only got your word that you didn't know it was her bedroom, and your word doesn't mean a lot, given your fingerprints were all over 6 Valentine Street and you never once mentioned being there."

"All over?" says Gaffney, one brow raised.

A girl can but try. What we actually have is one matching print lifted from a sliding-glass door, another off the kitchen worktop.

"So talk us through it." I shrug my shoulders, a little less hostile.

Keefe bristles. "Could *you* talk me through a less-than-ten-minute incident from over six years ago?"

At last, some backbone, although he's picked the wrong person to challenge. I could talk him through a less-than-five-minute car journey from nearly twenty years ago. Maryanne Doyle swinging her legs into Dad's Ford Mondeo. Asking if he'd be in town that night. Asking nothing about the child in the back seat, wolfing down Taytos to soothe the tight feeling in her tummy.

"Oh, come on, Brandon. Don't tell me you haven't played it over and over in your head."

"I didn't trip over any dead bodies, I remember that much." Gaffney throws him a glare, then draws him in for a whisper. It goes on far longer than a whispered conversation really should. I'm thinking of whistling just to make a point when Keefe nods, resolutely, and looks back to the front. "I went there once. Once, OK?"

"When?"

"I don't know exactly. Months before Chris . . . well, did what he did. The Rugby World Cup was on, though, so it must have been October. I was annoyed, see, because England were playing and I thought I'd be able to have the TV on in the storeroom, but Chris said I had to come to the house. He needed me to bring some tools over and help him measure a few things. That's the only time I ever went there. That's the only way my fingerprints could be in that house."

It's plausible. And very difficult to prove or disprove. I know it, Parnell knows it, and gum-chewing Gaffney knows it. Brandon Keefe, though, with his squeaky-clean record, probably doesn't, so I take another shot.

"The bit I don't get is, if it was all so innocent, why did you never mention it?"

"Would you have admitted being there? In the place those girls were . . ." He shudders. "It was bad enough people asking me about Chris, never mind asking me about that hellhole."

"Yeah, but the papers would have loved it. You'd have probably got more than £15,000 for some 'House of Horrors' details. And you were desperate for money, so I think there must have been another reason—a stronger reason—for you wanting to keep it secret."

"I wasn't keeping secrets. I was never asked—by the papers *or* the police. If I'd been asked outright by the police, I'd have said yes, I went there once. I just didn't see why I should volunteer it. It was hardly relevant."

He's either the best liar, or he's had the worst luck. I honestly can't make my mind up.

Time for a cozy chat. I pull my chair in, lessening the space between us.

"Right, Brandon, I'm not going to keep any secrets from you, OK? We're looking into the possibility—and it is only a possibility, let me be clear—that Christopher Masters had an accomplice. Now, cards on the table, me and Sergeant Parnell here weren't convinced. Masters seemed like a lone wolf to us, a control freak. But there are a few things that have come up that mean it's got to be a consideration, at least." I give him a weak smile. "And then you come along. You worked closely beside him, you don't have an alibi for Holly Kemp—you told us last time you were at home

on your own that day playing video games—and now your fingerprints have been placed in the house where those women probably
died. You've got to see how it looks."

Another conflab with Gaffney, shorter, this time.

"I think I have alibis for the others."

"Wow, just like that?"

He sits up a little straighter. "I was staying with my brother for
most of February. He lives in Tulse Hill and I went back there
every night after work. I was there until my parents went away to
Venice—which was a few days before Holly Kemp disappeared.
They might be able to give you the exact date."

"Hang on." Parnell lifts his hand. "You lived a ten-minute walk
from Masters' store but you went to stay with your brother over
two miles away?"

"I wasn't getting on with my folks, my mum mainly. She was
disappointed about me not cracking on with a proper career. I
saw it as nagging, but of course she just cared." He slumps forward
onto the table, the effort of staying upright too much. "And my
brother had just split up with his fiancée. He was going through a
tough time and what with Valentine's Day coming up, I decided
I'd stay with him for a few weeks. Keep him company. We drank
beer and ate takeaways every night. He'd moan about Tara, I'd
moan about Izzy, the girl I liked. You can check all this with my
brother."

"We will," says Parnell. "Although I'm sure you understand
beloved big brothers aren't the best alibis, for obvious reasons."

Keefe sags. Gaffney's cautious. I take one last shot before the
words "take a break" kill the mood.

"You know what I'm thinking, Brandon? If you spend a lot of
time with Christopher Masters, a man who clearly hates women a
great deal and—"

"I never got that impression," he interrupts quietly, mumbling
more to the table than me. "He hated his ex-wife. Always going on

about her new life, her fancy car, her posh house, her new partner. He never said anything else bad about women though, not to me, anyway."

"Oh, so you were spicing it for the *Mail* then?" I flick through the file in front of me, pull out Keefe's interview. "*His eyes darkened. His posture went as rigid as a steel bar. His voice took on a rough, husky tone. Like he'd entered some sort of altered state.*"

"They twist your words."

"OK, well, I won't twist mine. I think you weren't getting anywhere with—what did you call her—Izzy?" His head bobs. "She was flirting with other people in the pub, not realizing she had a good man right under her nose, am I right? Then your brother—who you sound really close to—gets ditched by his fiancée. And on top of that, your mum's nagging you, making you feel bad about your decisions, your life choices. So I'm thinking you had a lot of reasons to dislike women around that time, Brandon, and then you go into work and there's Christopher Masters, angry at this ex-wife, bitter. And you make a connection."

Keefe looks up at me, deadbeat, but with eyes full of focus. "I know what you're getting at and I'm not going to demean myself by answering. You have nothing, so you want me to incriminate myself. Well, I won't do it. *Though they plot evil against you and devise wicked schemes, they cannot succeed.* The Book of Psalms, chapter twenty-two, verse eleven. Now I'd like to take a break."

Nearly ten, Friday night.

Brandon Keefe has gone home, bailed to return next week. Nimbus lives to eat another bowl of Whiskas. And all is not right with the world.

"Nothing more we could do," says Parnell, as Steele switches the lights out in her office. "Without his fingerprints on any of the bodies, or on a weapon, it's weak."

"Ha! A weapon. Imagine that." Steele's laugh is rueful, desperate even.

"We should get someone onto this Izzy." I slam the last of the sash windows shut. "I got the sense the first time we met Keefe that he was still smarting from that rejection. Maybe she can tell us something interesting. Violence, weird behavior . . ."

"Is that thorough investigative work or clutching at straws?" asks Steele.

"Probably the latter." I hold the door open for them both. Steele has her weekly pile of online shopping to contend with. Parnell's carrying two bags of food—dinner he promised he'd have on the table by eight. "Although I do think it's strange that a grown man like Masters would savage his wife to a young lad like Keefe."

"He didn't have many friends to savage her to," says Parnell.

"I guess."

Steele puts her hand over the lift button. "OK, we're not going anywhere until you say what you're thinking."

I shrug. "That maybe Masters saw something in Keefe? That he was testing him, seeing how he'd react."

Parnell's with me. "It's possible. It's classic predatory behavior—throw out the bait and see who bites." A quick glance at Steele. "What, you don't agree?"

Her face is buried in the yellow plastic of a Selfridges parcel. "Christ, I don't know what to think about any of this." She looks up. "We've got a witness who connects our victim to Masters, but Masters has *no* connection to guns that we can find—and now the witness could be iffy, for all we know." She nods at me, Serena Bailey having been designated my weekend project. Tomorrow should have been my first Saturday off in a month, and technically, it still will be, but with this case gathering momentum, I've agreed to some unpaid overtime. Serena Bailey, lucky her, is getting a visit. "And with Fellows, we've got a name that's *very* associated with guns, but as of yet, no provable connection to Holly." She lets out a noise somewhere between a groan and a yawn. "The only thing I'm sure of is that I'm bloody starving and there's no one worrying about when I was last fed. Remind me to come back as a cat next time around."

19

I stayed at my own place last night for the first time in weeks. Aiden grumbled, but I had reasons at the ready: mail (who gets mail?), a desire to "air the place," and a sudden and overwhelming concern that there might be some chicken slowly putrefying in the fridge. Another reason was genuine. The need to check on my neighbor, Jerry, who lives on the ground floor and in la-la land half the time. Jerry's become increasingly housebound over the past twelve months, and with not a soul in the world to care, I try to sit with him sometimes, have a cup of tea, listen to his tall tales. Last night's flight of fancy was an account of the time he caught Jimi Hendrix trying to bed his ex-wife, Beverley. It was a good story, full of detail and drama, and I'd cheerfully played along, even encouraging him to tell me more.

The main reason though, and far less entertaining than Jerry's nutty reminiscences, was that I needed to call Jacqui, and that's always easier if Aiden isn't next to me, looking wounded. Wondering if he'll ever get a mention. Wondering if they'll ever meet.

It was a typical Jacqui conversation: me asking questions, her going off at convoluted tangents.

"So is Dad in pain?"

"A bit, not really, his meds are pretty good. I tell you who is in pain, though. Do you remember Sarah Phelan? She was in the year above me. She was the first at Lady H's to get a mobile, lived in tartan miniskirts, you must remember her . . . Anyway, she had a boob job and it's gone tits-up, pardon the pun. A capsular contracture, whatever that is. I'll have to google it . . ."

And.

"How's Finn? Is he excited about soccer camp?"

"No! He's made this friend, Callum, and he'd rather be over at his. They've got a games room, if you please. A pinball machine, air hockey, giant Jenga, the lot. I mean, he does something in HR and she's a midwife—how on earth do they afford a games room?"

Funny how Jacqui never applied the same critique to our parents. *She* was a stay-at-home mum and *he* was a "driver" for a "businessman" of some sort. How on earth did they afford a five-bedroom house, two cars, three holidays a year, and a biweekly therapist for their youngest child—me?

Of course, I should have stayed at Aiden's. I hadn't really thought of this when I'd headed home last night: the fact that Serena Bailey isn't just an East Londoner, but she lives barely a mile from Aiden's place. Just a twenty-minute stroll along the Regent's Canal, which sure beats the hour of sweltering on public transport that I've just endured.

Serena's home is an ugly 1960s low-rise. A squat, gray building, wrapped in precarious-looking balconies, and as her flat is on the ground floor, she hasn't even got the perk of glistening canal views to gaze over, just boarded-up shops. Thirsty and frizzy-haired, I ring the doorbell. A serious little girl verging on the side of plump, with a ruckus of curls forming no determinable shape, answers the door wearing a Minions costume. It's like staring at my childhood self, except I'd have been Buzz Lightyear.

Serena's voice from inside. "Who's that, Pop-Pop?"

"A lady in a pretty dress." Bless her, my linen number is creased, damp, and stuck to me all over, but I thought wearing civvies might make Serena relax more. Encourage her to open up. Woman to woman. Summer dress to summer dress.

She comes out into the narrow hallway, her swingy brown ponytail now in plaits, a straw bag slung over her shoulder, car keys in her hand. It's almost painful to watch the shift in her expression when she sees me. Her realization that this isn't going to be a Saturday like all others: traffic jams, kids' parties, bathtime, wine.

"Oh, it's you," she says, hope dying on her face. "What is it? We were just on our way out."

"Can I come in? It won't take long."

"Who is it?" Another voice and then a man appears, toweling his hair as if not long out of the shower. He's hefty, wholesome, and rugby-ish. "Hello." He looks to Serena for an intro.

She comes forward, a smile painting over her panic. "Cat, come in, come in. This is Robbie." I raise my hand, completely bewildered. "Hon, this is Cat. She's been helping out at school."

She lies well, and so easily.

"God, I'd completely forgotten you were coming round," she says, hitting her forehead, then turning to Robbie. "Hon, can you take Poppy? I'm really, really sorry. I know it's a pain, but Cat and I have got to get some stuff sorted for the end-of-term assembly."

Poppy pipes up. "It's my friend's birthday. We're going to Hobbledown *again*, but only four of us this time. When we went for *my* birthday last week, the whole of Year One came. Robbie got us a coach." It comes out as one long word, one long breathless brag.

"Wow, lucky you!" I throw a "no idea" look at the grown-ups.

"A farm, way over the other side of London," explains Robbie, lacing his feet into a pair of Converse. "Another three-hour round trip. Happy days."

"You're the best." Serena hands him the car keys. "But it starts at midday, you need to go now—go, go, go!"

A minute later they're gone and it's just us. Me, Serena, and the obvious question.

She answers before I ask: "He doesn't know about all that business."

OK.

"Well, that's your decision, I suppose. Although I'm going to ask why."

"I wasn't in a great place back then. My life was a bit chaotic, just . . . well, stuff, it doesn't matter now. Anyway, I met Robbie a few years after and . . ."

"He isn't Poppy's dad?"

She shakes her head. "No. And as I was in a much better place by the time I met him, I wanted to leave the past in the past."

So the perfect witness wasn't so perfect.

The model citizen was just a schmuck with baggage like the rest of us.

And who am I to judge? But then again, it's my job to judge. It's what pays my bills, buys my takeaways, enables me to at least make a stab at clearing my overdraft every month—my ability to drag secrets out of others and make judgments on what I find.

My hypocrisy astounds even me.

"So is that why you left Riverdale? Moved east? Changed numbers? You were leaving the past in the past."

"Something like that."

We're still in the hallway, facing off like chess pieces. "Look, Serena, can we sit down? I need to go through a few things with you."

I head through the nearest door, assuming it's the living room. She follows behind, as though I'm the host and she's the visitor. The room's cheery and lived-in, coloring books on the floor, breakfast dishes still on the table. I park myself on the arm of a battered leather sofa. Serena stands behind an armchair, shielding herself.

"You seem a bit anxious," I say.

"It's just . . . I don't like having to lie to Robbie. What's this about?"

"You didn't have to lie to him." She shoots me a hot glare. "Look, I don't know what else you haven't told him, but you didn't do anything wrong by ID'ing Masters, unless there's something I don't know?" She's gripping the back of the armchair. "Well, is there?"

Quiet. Just the frenzied buzz of a fly behind the curtain and the distant hum of a lawnmower somewhere.

"Fine," I say. *Have it your way.* "So you remember I said we were looking at Holly Kemp's case again? Well, that means looking at everything. Every*one*. Reinterviewing, checking all statements again. And the thing is, Serena, something's come up. A possible discrepancy in your account."

Her face twitches. "How do you mean?"

"Well, you said to us, and to DC Ferris in 2012, that the reason you turned back and consequently saw Masters with Holly, is that you thought you'd left your bank card in The Northcote." She moves her shoulders, *yeah so?* "Well, we've checked your bank records—we can go back seven years—and there's no record of you paying for anything in The Northcote. No record of you paying for anything in Clapham, full stop. And you mentioned you'd bought a coffee too—the coffee you splashed on Holly's coat."

I brace myself for outrage, the familiar medley of "You can't do that!" and "How dare you!"

Instead, she says, "I'd have used cash for the coffee, it'd have only been a couple of pounds. I must have used cash in The Northcote too, then. I honestly can't remember."

I frown. "But you remember so much. And you were very specific about that detail."

"Like I said, there was a lot going on in my life back then. I must have got mixed up."

"No, no, no, Serena. You were adamant, then *and* now. You've never wavered, in fact. Are you now saying that maybe you didn't see Masters and Holly?"

"I did." Barely a whisper, then louder. "I did."

"We've also spoken with your old school—Riverdale Primary. According to their records, you were present that day. All day."

She pales to a shade that gives Brandon Keefe a run for his money.

"I . . . I don't know what to tell you. I left early. I said I didn't feel well. I felt bad doing it but . . ." She pauses, swallowing hard.

"Look, I don't know why I wasn't marked absent. I'd have told Mrs. Gopal's secretary I was leaving. Ask her."

It's a challenge, not a suggestion. She knows as well as I do that it's hardly worth asking someone to recall a two-second conversation they had six years ago, one that was of no importance to them at all.

"Right, so let me get this straight. You lied to your employer, dumped your lesson on a probably already overstretched colleague, and left your pupils in the lurch, all so you could bunk off to buy Lady Gaga tickets. Is that what you're saying?"

Chin high. "Yes. So?"

If she'd shown a dot of shame, I might have believed her. As it goes, her petulance makes me even more suspicious.

"Well, at least we've got that cleared up." I give a sardonic smile. "Now, back to the 'mix-up' regarding your bank card."

"Jesus Christ, sorry I'm not perfect! Sorry I got *one* detail wrong." I'm getting the full teenage temper now.

"No need to be sorry," I say, sounding how I imagine she sounds when she's ever so slightly disappointed with a pupil. "It does make me question every other detail you've given, though."

"Fine, you do that." She gestures to the door. "Now I'd like you to leave, please. I've got a busy day."

"You see, there's a lie right there, Serena. You thought you were going to Hobbledown." I throw my hands wide. "And then I turn up and get you out of it. You should be thanking me. You've got your day back."

"Believe me, I've got plenty of things to do that don't involve sitting around justifying myself to someone who only graduated last week."

While I'll take that as a compliment, I'm bored of her newfound sass already. I slip down off the arm of the sofa and snuggle among the scatter cushions, making it clear I'm not going anywhere. She stares at me with those wide green eyes. I stare back harder with my baby blues.

"What was going on in your life at that time, Serena? Because if it affects the accuracy of your statement, we need to know, and I'm staying right here until I do." Nothing. "You mentioned issues with an ex the first time we met? Were you distracted that day, maybe?"

More silence.

"I'm deadly serious, Serena. What did Robbie say it is? A three-hour round trip? Well, I haven't got plenty to do. In fact, I've got nothing planned at all, except a load of washing, so three hours doesn't bother me. More is fine. I'd rather be in here than outside, truth be told. I'm not exactly what you'd call a sun worshipper."

"I was what you'd call a prostitute."

She breaks the stare and looks off to the side, drinking in a photo of Robbie and Poppy on a waterslide, their hands thrust high in the air, loving life.

"OK . . ." I nod slowly, giving myself time to compute. "Can you put that into context for me. I'm not sure . . ."

"I was meeting a client that afternoon in Clapham." She walks around and virtually collapses onto the armchair, the look on her face pure contempt. For the client? For herself? Or maybe me, the person who dragged it all up again. "I started in my early twenties. I didn't plan it, but have you any idea how hard it is to survive on a teaching assistant's salary in London? And then by the time I'd qualified and was earning a bit more money, I'd got used to earning a lot more, so I kept doing it. Doing *them*." A sour smile. "Anyway, I wasn't doing it a lot by that time, 2012. I was completely focused on my job, but then . . ." She takes a deep sigh. "There was this one guy. He'd been a client, but then he'd moved back to America, which was gutting. He paid really well, see, and he was nice too, not like some. He was over in London that February for work and he called me up. He was staying in Clapham, but he was busy in the evenings so he asked to see me for an hour that afternoon, and I couldn't afford to turn down £500 cash. I didn't earn that in a week teaching." She draws in another breath, fixing me with a righteous glare. "Everything else was true. I cut back through Valentine Street and saw Masters and Holly, exactly as I said."

"Exactly?" I need to drill down. "So you passed Holly at the gate and then you turned around and saw them both at the door. Why? Why did you turn around?"

"More or less what I said. I thought I'd left my bank card at his place. He'd been doing coke. I hadn't—I swear on my daughter's life, I only had a couple of glasses of wine. But I'd given him my card"—she mimes a chopping action—"because his wallet was downstairs." She wraps her arms around herself, righteousness morphing into self-pity. "So you can see why I didn't admit this at the time, and why I've never brought it up with Robbie. It's just all so upsetting. I want to forget it ever happened. I wish I'd never walked down that street."

"Funnily enough, Serena, I think Holly Kemp would have said the same."

20

Victoria Park, also known as the People's Park, is the largest and most popular green space in East London, attracting nearly ten million visitors a year.

Around nine million of those visitors appear to have descended today.

At least half a million are in this queue for a burger.

Good job Aiden and I have got plenty to talk about.

"So she says to me, 'I think you've got great potential and SO15 needs officers like you,' and *then* she says she'll be recruiting once she makes superintendent. That's a job offer, right? Or do you reckon it's just hot air?"

"Search me," Aiden says, kissing me on the forehead.

I look up. "Well, that's very helpful. Thanks for your input."

"What do you want me to say? Sounds like a job offer to me, but you know the woman."

This isn't like him. Aiden's a talker, a theorist. Doesn't matter if it's job offers, betting odds, or how to get Tabasco sauce out of every known fabric, you better believe he's got an opinion on it. I let it go, putting it down to hunger. Or the fact I said I'd sort out a picnic this afternoon and instead we've been queuing for fifteen minutes for a splat of meat and processed cheese.

"That's the thing, I don't really know her. She's smart and ambitious and she's got this kind of Snow Queen vibe going on, all supercool and regal, but maybe I shouldn't be thinking about working for someone I don't know, not properly. God knows Steele can be challenging sometimes, but at least I know where I am with her."

It's hard to forget Dyer's warning, though: *"Don't let your loyalty to Steele hold you back."*

"So what's the SO stand for?" asks Aiden. "Don't tell me—Sexy Officer?"

"How did you guess?" I give him a smile. "Specialist Operations."

"Right. Very 007."

It's still there. Not a tetchiness, as such, but a sense that he's not really here. I rack my brains, panicking that I've forgotten an important date. Maryanne's birthday? The anniversary of his mum's death? Maybe even the anniversary of his dad's death? Aiden's never had a good word to say about the man who ruled with his fists and cared only about his next pint, but grief is a knotty bugger and time can gold-plate even the worst of pricks.

"Are you OK?" We're nearly at the front now and I haven't picked the best time to ask.

"I'm fine. Just starving." He catches the server's eye, turning on the Aiden razzle-dazzle. "You all right, mate? Give me one of those double quarter pounders, would ye? With cheese and fried onions. *Plenty* of fried onions—like, whatever you think is plenty, double that. Good man! And whatever this one wants."

"This one wants a halloumi burger," I tell the server. "So come on, what do you think?"

"Each to their own. I'd rather chew a flip-flop."

"You know what I mean, funny guy." Although maybe he doesn't; he hardly seems switched on today. "Do you think I should take this job?"

"So you think it *is* a job offer?" He pays with a twenty, receives a pitiful amount of change in return. "You should do what you want to do. Although as far as I can tell in your job, moving to another team just means being lied to by a different type of criminal."

"Substitute 'criminal' for 'colleague' and you could say the same about anyone's job. Do you know, over the course of a ten-minute conversation, over sixty percent of people tell at least two lies." God knows why I said that. My self-destructiveness knows no bounds. "Hey, shall we go and sit by the lake?"

So we sit by the lake. We eat our burgers. We smile at people passing by, parents chasing children, children chasing dogs, dogs chasing Frisbees, and a few blatantly stoned teens.

"Must be easier to be one of those," Aiden says, watching the ducks and geese criss-cross each other. "More straightforward. 'What can't speak, can't lie'—isn't that a quote?"

My head's on his shoulder. "Sounds like something Parnell would come out with."

"Have you talked to Parnell? About making a move?"

I haven't, and it's not like I haven't had the chance. We spent great swaths of yesterday waiting for Brandon Keefe to dry out, and I was on the phone to him only an hour ago, filling him in on Serena Bailey. He didn't sound rushed, I could have asked his advice then.

"I don't want to hurt his feelings," I explain.

"Christ, Cat, he's a grown man! He must have made a few moves himself."

"I know. It's just he'll ask why and I don't want to lie to him, but I don't want to tell him the truth either."

"Which is?"

How to put this? I lift my head and turn to face him, cross-legged. "I think I'm coasting in MIT4. It's not just what Dyer said. I met this DI this week, Susie Grainger. Aiden, she's more or less the same age as me and she's high-tailing it up the ladder while I'm just plodding along. Don't get me wrong, I'm on a great team. Everyone's competent, *highly* competent, and Steele's an absolute legend, but honestly, who gives me a run for my money? Parnell and Renée are ace but neither of them is ambitious. Seth's good, but he could give it all up tomorrow and go and live in Downton Abbey. Flowers, although it pains me to say, is good too, but he hasn't got the savvy to go far, and Cookey hasn't got the ability. And Swaines . . . well, he's just so pretty that he'll sail through life getting everything handed to him, so he's not real competition."

"That pretty, huh?"

I grin. "Don't worry, not my thing. Too vanilla flavored. Oh, and there's Emily, and I still can't work out why she applied to be a police officer. I think she's hoping there'll be a fly-on-a-wall documentary one day and she'll get spotted by Hollywood."

"You'd be good value on a fly-on-a-wall documentary."

"I'm not sure that's a compliment."

"You'd make good TV is all I'm saying."

I give him a light punch. "Oh, I get it. So while Emily's on the cover of *Vogue* or dating DiCaprio, I become a crazy cult figure. One of those late-night shows—*Z-list Celebrity Meltdowns*."

He laughs. "Not what I meant, but Jesus, I'm digging meself a hole here. Let's get back on track—you need more competition at work, that's your issue?"

"I think so. See, to Steele, I'm the star striker. I know I am." I squirm, feeling boasty, but I've got to get this out. "If I moved to Dyer's team, say, I'd be a squad player again, competing for a starting place. It'd be a kick up the arse. A *positive* kick up the arse."

"Excellent football analogy, Kinsella. I'll add it to the reasons why I love you."

I smile and look away. It's a child's drawing of a beautiful day. An almost clear blue sky, a few fluffy clouds thrown in for good measure. Lush green grass. Butterflies and sun hats. A balloon making a break for freedom in the distance.

And this man telling me he loves me.

I should be grateful for what I have. Maybe change isn't all it's cracked up to be.

"Hey, look, probably nothing'll come of it. Forget about it for now." I nudge his knee with mine. "So come on, when are you going to tell me your news?"

He looks at the ground, pulling at a clump of grass. "What news?"

"The Americans, the other night. All that I Heart New York stuff. I figured it out, don't worry. How long are they pinching you for? Will you be there around Christmas? Can we skate in front of the Rockefeller tree? Not that I can skate, mind. And I bet you're rubbish, as well. Tall people usually are . . ."

"Two years."

The words cut through my babble.

"I beg your pardon?" My voice sounds hollow, robotic.

"Two years. Well, twenty-two months, for some reason. The project starts late November and runs until September 2020." He finally looks up. "Twenty twenty sounds mad, doesn't it? Space-age."

I don't know why I'm shocked. If I hadn't been so neck-deep in this case, in *myself*, I'd have seen what was pretty bloody obvious: that special envoys aren't dispatched to London to convince someone to uproot for a few months. That kind of low-level badgering can be done over the phone, maybe Skype. But you need to see the whites of someone's eyes if you're asking them to leave their old life, or at least put it on pause.

"Jesus, late November. That's four months away."

"I haven't agreed yet."

"And are you going to?" The words curdle in my throat.

"Depends, doesn't it? On whether you come too."

My laugh is shrill. Relief, disbelief, and a burst of anger at the pressure.

"Fuck's sake, Aiden, I can't just . . . you can't just . . ." I shake my head. "This isn't fair."

"Christ, remind me not to give you bad news."

"I'm sorry. It's just all a bit sudden."

"I know, I know." He takes both my hands. "Look, it's just an offer and I'm flattered, o'course I am. But I'm not going anywhere without you, so if you can't get your head around it, it's grand, I'll say no. And that's a genuine 'it's grand,' by the way. Not a Cat Kinsella 'it's grand but I'm secretly plotting to assassinate you.'"

I stifle a grin.

"It won't look good though, will it? If you turn it down?"

"They'll get over it. Look, five minutes ago, I might have pushed a bit more, but honestly? I didn't realize you were that ambitious. I mean, I know you love your job and you're great at it . . ."

"*I* didn't know I was that ambitious until this week. But anyway, it's not just my job, it's my family. My dad, Jacqui . . . it's such a long way."

Aiden's face contorts. "Your family? Your dad? Are you actually fucking kidding me?" He drops my hands. "I'm barely allowed to go near your dad, and I've never even met your bloody sister for some reason that I can't even be bothered fighting about any more, but apparently *they're* the reason we can't go to New York. Oh, that's brilliant, Cat. First class."

"No one said *you* can't go," I fire back. "Go! I get five weeks holiday. We can have weekends. It'll be fine." It sounds about as fine as severing an artery. "It's just seeing my dad in the hospital the other night . . ."

"He's got a banjaxed arm, for fuck's sake. Oh, hold on, didn't I tell you I stubbed my toe on the bed this morning? That means you have to come with me, surely?" He's shaking his head. "No, Cat. Do *not* go all Daddy's Girl on me now. Say you don't want to come because your career's too important. Say it's too big a step for us. Say New York's too stressful. But *not* your dad. I mean, have you even called him since Tuesday? Because if you have, you haven't mentioned it. But then, what's new?"

"Don't shout at me."

"I'm not shouting."

He isn't. He's raised his voice, but he's not a shouter. I am a manipulator, though—Daddy's Girl, through and through—and accusing him of shouting beats having a serious conversation.

But I could go, couldn't I?

Because maybe deep down, I'm not thinking of leaving MIT4 because of ambition. What if it's the chance to start again I'm craving? To be someone else, somewhere else. And where better than New York, three and a half thousand miles away from all the mistakes I've made?

From the family who'll keep me making them.

"Do you really, really want to go then?" I say softly, sucking the sting out of the argument.

"Well, o'course I do."

"Must be one hell of a project."

A flat stare. "Fuck the project. Same old shite, different time zone, that's all it is."

"So why then?"

"Why?" He's trying to play it cool but his lovely face gives him away. The wide-eyed awe. The glow of possibility. "Because it's New York, baby. And because you've been to America and France and Barbados and probably South Central Siberia for all I know, and I've been to Ireland and England and three days in Prague—which I hardly saw anything of, I might add."

We share a much-needed grin, reliving our seventy-two hours of sex, sex, and room service, ending with a trip up a lookout tower, where Aiden was up for having sex again.

I can't be without him.

He either stays or we both go.

"I'll think about it, OK?"

"OK. And it really is grand if you decide no. All that matters is that we're together, Kinsella. I just want to be with you."

The rest of the weekend passes in a blur of laughs, chores, and avoiding *the* conversation. Sunday lunchtime, we roam around

Spitalfields Market, mingling with the tourists and shoppers, stopping to marvel at things we probably can't afford and definitely don't need. Aiden buys me a corsage and a candle he claims smells of fish. I buy him a Mr. Whippy and then proceed to eat half.

It's the little things, they say. And whoever *they* are, they're right.

Sunday night. I'm brushing my teeth when my phone rings.

Aiden answers, which must mean it's Parnell. I pause, trying to catch the gist of what's being said. Something about a Brazilian defender and then a few nice words about the dinner I made. I walk into the living room, still brushing. Aiden's laughing at something Parnell's said. I'd hazard a guess it's at my expense.

"Give," I order, my hand out for the phone, my mouth full of foam.

"I'll pass you over, big man . . . yeah, see you soon . . . sure, we'd love to . . ."

I take the phone back into the bathroom. "We'd love to what?"

"Come over for dinner," says Parnell. "Although from what I hear, you make a mean beef Wellington."

"I unwrap a mean beef Wellington and throw it in the oven, gas mark seven."

"Oh." He actually sounds disappointed. "Aiden seemed to think it was the best thing he's ever eaten."

I spit and rinse quickly. "He's easily impressed."

Parnell resists the obvious retort. "Anyway, Spencer Shaw lands back at Heathrow tonight. The boss wants us on his doorstep first thing."

"Yeah, fine, although I'm not sure about him anymore. The cause of death. Holly's 'Megan' stunt, Fellows' name coming into it—it feels bigger than a domestic gone wrong, don't you reckon? And then there's Brandon Keefe—we don't know where that might lead. I honestly don't think Spencer Shaw will have a lot to tell us."

"And isn't that the beauty of what we do, kiddo? Who knows what treasures lie ahead?"

"Have you been drinking?"

"I may have had a nightcap. All I'm saying is don't be so defeatist. He might solve the case for us. We might be cracking open the champagne in the Tavern tomorrow night."

"I don't think the Tavern does champagne. It's debatable whether it does wine." I walk into the bedroom, hurl myself on the bed. "So you think there's a case to solve then? You don't think Holly is one of Masters'?"

"I don't know." There's a huff of breath down the line, a sigh in the place of an impossible answer. "I do know Jacob Pope's been attacked in Belmarsh, though."

"Shit! Is it bad?" I ask, slightly thrown. I'd kind of forgotten about my prison jaunt earlier in the week. Another sign that maybe a change might do me good.

"Very bad. Critical. He's in the ICU."

"Oh wow, so not a playground spat?"

"More like a nine-inch-shank-at-lunchtime thing. A gang dispute, they reckon."

Standard.

I stare at the ceiling for a few seconds, taking it in. "Well, *clearly* I wouldn't wish that on anyone, but I'm not going to lose much sleep over him. His girlfriend didn't even make it to the ICU."

"He knew stuff about Masters though. Handy to have him around."

Someone obviously didn't think so.

21

If you didn't know much about harassed-looking Spencer Shaw—the conspiracy to commit burglary, his labeling of his ex-girlfriend as a "mad bitch" when she'd been missing for three days, his dry-humping of a cowboy-booted "blond chick" a month after Holly was presumed murdered—you could almost, *almost*, feel sorry for him this morning. The last thing he needs is us clogging up his living room.

"We didn't get home until two a.m. I actually felt sorry for my wife going into work this morning, but I think it was me who drew the short straw."

He's not wrong. There's barely a sliver of carpet to be seen under all the half-unpacked suitcases, not to mention the usual miscellanea that comes with traveling with small kids: carriers, wet wipes, devices, snacks, pushchairs, nappies, a whole host of other contraptions. In fact, we've been there a few minutes before I realize there's a child sleeping under a mound of crap on the sofa. A boy, I think, tucked under a blanket, only his sunburned forehead and socked feet on display. Another child isn't so hard to spot—a baby girl in a playpen, making some sort of cuddly toy protest, bear after bear hurled over the bars and into the mess.

Spencer Shaw stands in the epicenter, staticky dark hair sticking out at odd angles, looking for all the world like he hasn't got a clue where to start. Like domestic duty isn't normally part of his job description. And, of course, he hadn't banked on a visit from the Metropolitan Police this morning, although he knows all about Holly.

"I didn't find out until Thursday. We try not to spend too much time on our phones when we're on holiday with the kids, but I couldn't resist posting a few photos and there it was, all over Facebook."

"Not a good idea to advertise you're on holiday to the whole of Facebook," I say. "Attracts burglars. Thought you'd be wise to that."

It's cheap but he deserves it.

"Have you never made a mistake?" Shaw replies, all sad eyes and dark stubble. Personally, I can't see what Holly saw in him, although he reminds me of the type a younger Jacqui used to go for: intense and brooding, probably thinks of himself as artistic. A tendency to whisper sweet, poetic nothings while lifting a twenty out of your purse.

"Too many to count," I admit. "But we're not here to talk about me."

"Of course not. You're here to talk about the mistake I made taking up with Holly."

"And to see if you can shed light on how she ended up in a Cambridgeshire field with a bullet hole in her skull."

He should flinch. He doesn't.

"Funny," says Parnell, offering a pinched smile. "Her friends say she made a mistake taking up with you."

He bends down, doing a quick sweep of the floor for teddy bears. "Shona and Josh, I assume?"

"Mainly." I do my bit, picking up a purple penguin. "Emma and Kayleigh weren't your greatest fans either."

"Let me guess, Holly was a saint and I'm the devil."

"Got it in one, although you'll be glad to know we generally take these things with a pinch of salt." I throw the toy back in the playpen. "Smooching with another girl in the street only a month after Holly disappears doesn't exactly make you look great, though. Was that the same girl who alibi'd you, by any chance?"

A proud stare. "Yes. The girl who alibi'd me and the girl who married me two years later."

There's a photo by the TV. Blond chick in cowboy boots is now a redhead in flip-flops, one hand clasping her eldest child's hand, the other holding a bucket and spade.

Spencer catches me looking. "I love that photo. Loz was pregnant with Bonnie at the time, but we didn't realize." I take a glance at the zonked-out child under the blanket. It's hard to tell his age precisely, but I'd say Loz was expecting *him* not too long after Holly Kemp took her last breath. "Loz saved me, you know? I was a mess before I met Holly and I was an even worse mess when I was with her. Me and Holly, we were volatile, whereas things with Loz have always been brilliant. *She's* brilliant. She knows everything about my past but she's always looked beyond it." He taps his chest. "She sees *me*, the real me. Holly was always so wrapped up in herself. We might have been together for two years but it meant nothing."

His candor is helpful, but Christ, it's brutal.

"I'm not sure you meant much to her either," I say, feeling the need to offer a comeback on Holly's behalf. "Have you heard of a man called Dale Peters?"

"That poor sod she screwed for money? Yeah, that was a weird one."

"You knew about Peters?"

"Holly screwed a lot of people for money."

"You did OK out of it," I point out. "Five nights at the Burj Al Arab, we heard."

Parnell cuts in, saving Shaw his blushes. "What are you saying? Holly was a prostitute?"

"No, not like that. I don't mean 'screwed' as in *screwed*." He stiffens suddenly, staring at us with sharp, officious eyes. "Look, as soon as I heard you were revisiting Holly's case, I spoke to my father-in-law. Loz's dad is a solicitor, you see, and he knows all about the bad things Holly and I did, but he says I can't be prosecuted for anything I tell you if there aren't any complainants. And trust me, there aren't."

"Fine. Talk." I wait for Parnell to take issue, but he looks as intrigued as me.

"OK." He walks over to the sofa, quickly checking on the sleeping child. Once he's happy he's still dead to the world, he hefts a rucksack off a dining chair and sits down. "So I met Holly in 2010, in a club just off Regent Street. We got talking, drinking, and I ended up being up-front about being not long out of prison. She thought it was hilarious. She thought it was genius, actually— getting a job in an estate agency so you could effectively case the joints. I was flattered. I'd had enough of feeling like scum, so when a gorgeous girl—because she was gorgeous—is looking at you like you're this master criminal, it's hard not to play along. And then I tell her about my parents. My mum had died a couple of years before; that's what sent me off the rails, and my dad was nowhere to be seen since my sixth birthday . . ."

A flash of Serena Bailey's daughter yesterday: "*When we went to Hobbledown for my birthday last week, the whole of Year One came* . . ." My first instinct is to feel sorry for Spencer Shaw, which surprises me. My second is something else. Something I can't quite grasp hold of. Not exactly a feeling in my gut but a pebble in my shoe.

Shaw's voice quickly distracts me.

"The no-parents thing settles it for Holly. She decides there and then that we're kindred spirits. Says there's no one in the world who's going to give us what we want, so we just have to take it. And then, just like it's the most natural thing in the world, she walks off and starts chatting up this guy right in front of me. I'm so shocked, I just stand rooted to the spot. But then after about ten minutes I think . . ." He shoots a look to the sofa, lowering his voice. "*Fuck this.* So I'm just about to leave when she comes flying across, saying *we* have to leave right now, while the other guy's in the toilet." He smiles, though it's more of a grimace. "She'd stolen his wallet while she'd been chatting him up, brazen as anything.

She's waving £90 at me, saying that'll buy us a bottle of champagne in Claridge's. I was smitten."

Parnell gives Shaw a confused stare. "So you didn't steal the wallet, but you still checked that you couldn't be prosecuted for drinking 'stolen' champagne eight years later?"

That bilious smile again. "Oh, that was just the start. Nicking wallets was just a giggle. Holly wanted bigger payoffs to justify the risk." He clears his throat. "Do you know what a 'badger game' is?"

Parnell looks blank. I do my best to summarize.

"A woman gets a man—usually a married man—into a compromising position, and then a male accomplice bursts in and threatens the man with violence, scandal, the police, whatever, unless they cough up."

"It's a con trick," says Shaw. "It was small fry at first. Exactly as she said." He gestures to me. "Holly would hang around a bar, spot a guy wearing a wedding ring, and then work her magic. It didn't work every time, but you'd be surprised how often it did. Holly would bring them back to her place—we weren't living together then—and after about ten minutes of relaxing them, getting them at least seminaked, I'd burst in screaming that that was my girlfriend they were in bed with. I'd take a photo and if their phone was in sight, I'd grab it and threaten to send the image to all their contacts. If it wasn't, it wasn't a problem. Holly would usually have got enough info—where they worked, that sort of thing—so we always had something to threaten them with. To be honest, you didn't need much. Just the shock was enough to make them agree to be frog-marched to the nearest cashpoint."

And Loz and her dad still decided this louse was worth saving? He either talks a good game or they're a family of Buddhist monks.

"What's the maximum you can get from a cashpoint?" I ask. "Three hundred pounds? Maybe £500 if you're a good customer. That only equates to a handful of wallets, I reckon. Surely that was easier than pulling this type of stunt?"

"Exactly what Holly thought after a while, so she changed the rules, upped the game. She started going to the best bars—mainly Mayfair, Chelsea, the City—and she'd spend more time choosing the target. Looking at details. The watch they were wearing, their shoes. Moving on if she thought they weren't rich enough." The baby tosses another bear out of the playpen. Shaw sighs and lifts her out, jigging her on his lap as he carries on. "The idea was that these targets would pay more, so we'd get whatever we could that night, but we'd insist they meet us the next night too to hand over the same again, on the understanding that we'd then delete the photo. And we did do that, initially. We played fair if they did."

Parnell coughs—code for *"Can you actually believe this low-life?"*

"Why not ask for more?" I say. "If they were meeting you the next day, they could have gone to the bank, withdrawn any amount of cash, within reason."

"I was conscious about not being greedy—£500 to £1,000 wasn't a huge amount to most of these men. We were confident they'd pay this to make us go away quietly. If we demanded more, it could get complicated. That was my view anyway."

"Not Holly's?"

"She felt that to truly protect ourselves, we had to make the threat more severe. See, there'd been this one target who'd called our bluff, said, 'Fine, send it to my wife, she's shagging around anyway.' Holly was fuming. There was no way she was risking that happening again. So she came up with the idea of . . ." He pulls up for a moment, blinking slowly at the floor. "*She* came up with the idea of using roofies—Rohypnol—to really disable the target . . ."

"'Disable the target?' You're talking about human beings here." Parnell's voice is entirely calm but full of loathing.

"Sorry, she wanted the *men* to be completely out of it, pretty much comatose, so we could get better photos. See, the photos we'd been taking up until that point were going to get you in trouble at home, for sure, and it'd be embarrassing if your work colleagues got hold of them, but they weren't degrading, as such. Just Holly and the tar— the *man*, half-naked. Soft porn, at most. But if Holly could get them home, slip something in their drink—roofies work pretty quick— then . . ." He's struggling again, reluctant to revisit this old version of himself. "We, *she* mainly, could stage far more compromising pictures. She could tie them up, dress them up, plant drugs beside them—and God, worse stuff too. I mean, use your imagination." I glance at Parnell, who looks like he's just about given up on human nature. "And, of course, drugging them gave us time to go through their stuff, get phone numbers, find out where they worked, where their wives worked. Smartphones weren't all that common back then, but people—these types of men, anyway—still had their lives pro-grammed into their phones, their BlackBerry." He shrugs. "It was all working perfectly fine, there was no way anyone would call our bluff again, but then Holly got greedy—although she called it ambitious."

The baby squirms on Shaw's lap, getting restless. He puts her down on the floor, where she makes a beeline for Parnell's shoes. I'd make a beeline for Parnell too, if it was a choice between him and this scuzzball.

"I should have seen it coming, really. She was never going to be happy earning good money here and there. She wanted *big* money on a regular basis."

"*Earning?*" Parnell's even finding it hard to smile at the baby. "You mean stealing."

Shaw throws his hands up. "Look, I clearly don't have many good things to say about Holly, but she'd had a tough life. She was tossed around the care system after her parents died. Her aunt didn't want her. Nobody ever really helped her so she helped herself. That's how she saw it."

"And I can buy that," I say. "So what was your excuse?"

He takes it to be a genuine question, not the barb intended. "I honestly think I was having some sort of breakdown when I was with Holly. A delayed reaction to my mum dying. It's not like I even needed the money. I had my own flat. I'd been a good estate agent, despite everything. I'd paid off a decent chunk of the mortgage. And I had a job with a friend's agency that was going OK."

"So you blackmailed for fun."

"For the thrill. It helped numb the grief. But then Holly went too far."

Losing my mum made me do it.

It's not a bad line for the in-laws, but it's unadulterated bollocks. People process grief in many different ways—me through the haze of white wine, Jacqui through the treadmill, Dad through the comfort of a thousand different beds. My brother, Noel—well, who gives a fuck about Noel, to be honest? I haven't spoken to him in eighteen months and even that feels too recent. My point being that however you're hurting yourself, however you're getting through the night, grief doesn't strip you of your sense of right and wrong. If anything, it heightens it.

"You're going to have to define 'too far' for me, please," says Parnell. "Personally, I'd define stealing someone's wallet as 'too far.'"

"Long-term blackmail." We wait for him to elaborate. "See, after a while Holly started to question why she was putting herself out there, dressing up, going out, going through the same old motions two, three times a week, when if she picked the right target—the right *man*, sorry—she could spend one night setting them up, and then months, maybe even years, blackmailing them."

"She could have done that before?" I say, not quite following. "What sort of man was she after?"

"Being wealthy and married wasn't enough anymore. If she was going to play the long game, she needed men with a lot more to lose. She really thought about it. She figured that ultimately, your average forty-something banker with the wife and two kids probably wouldn't put up with being bled dry over the long run. They'd eventually crack, tell their wives, tell their HR person, maybe even tell the police if the only likely punishment was a few months in the spare room at home and a disciplinary at work. No, she needed men with standing, influence. Men whose lives would be ruined if she shared those staged photos. I know the first guy she targeted was a senior GP. He was the father of a friend—some friend, huh? He paid her £1,500 in cash every month. He had no choice. She had photos of him supposedly taking drugs, among other things. He could have lost his practice."

"So how many other men did she target like this?" I ask.

"Several, I'm not sure precisely."

Parnell's pad is out. "We need names, Spencer."

"I don't have names! She was working on her own, basically; I didn't want anything to do with long-term blackmail. Things got really bad between us after that."

"Why didn't you end the relationship?"

He looks me in the eye. "I was scared of what she might do is the truth. I'd seen her stitch up so many men, who's to say she wouldn't try to destroy me?"

I know I should do the required *And you didn't think to mention any of this at the time of her disappearance?* but frankly, it's a waste of breath. He was hardly going to incriminate himself, and anyway, he can always fall back on the now all-too-familiar stance: *And it had nothing to do with what happened.*

So much of Holly's life left undiscovered, unexplored, the second it was assumed she was Masters' fourth victim.

"So what did you do with the money?"

He startles, blinking rapidly. "I'm sorry?"

My voice was perfectly clear. He's stalling for time.

"The money, Spencer. Holly's bank account didn't show any major deposits, so I'm assuming she kept the cash at the flat?"

I'm taking a punt on this. There was a whole twenty-four hours between Shaw reporting Holly missing and Serena Bailey coming forward with her ID. Twenty-four hours of Holly being classed as a missing person. Her phone records pored over. Her bank accounts scrutinized. Surely they'd have picked up on something like this?

"There was no money in the flat."

"So where did she keep it? She was bringing in £1,500 a month from one target alone. She wasn't walking around with it stuffed in her handbag, I assume?"

He stands and scoops the baby off the floor. She kicks and wriggles, turning puce with ascending rage, but he clings to her like a life buoy. The message being: *"I'm a father now. Can't you cut me some slack?"*

"Um, well . . . the money was usually in the flat but . . . um . . . it'd been broken into that weekend."

"Broken into?" Parnell's eyebrows hit his hairline.

"I'd been with Loz all weekend—I'm not proud of that, but there you go—and when I got back, I could tell someone had been in the flat. The money was gone, some other bits too—jewelry, an iPod, both our laptops, a PlayStation Vita I'd literally just bought."

"Were there signs of forced entry?" I ask.

"No. But the front-door lock wasn't great. I'd got in once using a credit card when I'd locked myself out."

"But surely your first thought was Holly? That she'd taken these things and done a runner, especially since no one had seen her since Thursday. And yet you still reported her missing?"

"I knew it wasn't Holly. She had two wardrobes full of designer clothes, shoes, bags. All of those were still there. And personal mementos, gifts from her mum and dad. She would have taken those over my bloody PlayStation."

"How did you know she didn't have her laptop, though? What made you assume that had been stolen?"

"She never took her laptop anywhere. She never had the need, and anyway, all her bags were far too small. That's one of the million things we used to argue about—how she'd spend £300 to £400 on a handbag and you could barely fit your keys in it."

"So you told the police all this," I say, although I don't remember seeing it in the case file.

"No. No, I didn't."

"No?" My exasperation makes the sleeping child stir. "You didn't think it was important to mention it when the police arrived to talk about Holly?"

"I wanted them to concentrate on her. I thought that if I mentioned the burglary . . ."

"They'd have dusted for prints, checked CCTV. They'd have been able to do their jobs properly," says Parnell.

Dyer had said she'd known he was lying about something.

I persist. "Seriously, you didn't make any connection between your flat being burgled and Holly going missing?"

He shrugs and I could slap him. "I'd been burgled before. I kept pretty shady company back then, it could have been anyone. Look, I probably would have mentioned it eventually, but when we found out she'd been seen with Christopher Masters, everything spun in a different direction. Suddenly she wasn't 'missing' anymore. It was obvious he'd killed her. The burglary was irrelevant."

"Thing is, Spencer, for a few different reasons, it isn't so obvious now. And you've just told us a story that suggests God knows how many other people had a reason to want Holly dead. If you don't have names, do you still have any photos of the men who were blackmailed?"

The baby wails and I know how she feels. Shaw shouts over the top, making little effort to soothe her. "No, not anymore, not in a long time."

"Are you sure you don't know names?" says Parnell. "You knew Dale Peters."

"Because he was different. She wasn't blackmailing him, exactly, she was stringing him along for a payoff. I think she actually liked him, in her own way. That's why she took a different approach. She enjoyed his company for a while."

She enjoyed the five-star hotels. But still, cold comfort for the lovesick half-wit.

"Back to this GP . . ." says Parnell.

"I told you," Shaw whines, worse than the baby. "I don't know who he is."

"You said he was the father of a friend. What friend?"

"I honestly don't know. 'Friend' was a loose term with Holly. It could have been someone she met twice."

"What about Simon Fellows?" I ask, his name a hard thud. "You said Holly was 'stringing along' Dale Peters, which implies she told you what she'd told him about Fellows."

"No."

Instant. Emphatic. More a plea than a reply.

There's recognition though. It's in the pallor of his skin, the panic in his eyes. It's in the way he puts the baby down, as if fear has weakened his body and he doesn't trust himself to keep hold.

Parnell laughs. "We'll take that as a yes then, Spencer. Don't take up poker would be my advice." After a long silence, he adds, "And I'd try answering the question again. That would be my other piece of advice."

"Look, I didn't know the details but she said she'd landed a big fish—'a crook with lots of cash.' I said to her, 'What do you mean, a crook? What kind of crook?' She just laughed and said, 'The worst kind.'"

"But she didn't tell you his name?"

"I've got a family."

"Which means she did."

He looks desperate. A living, breathing, trembling definition of being trapped between a rock and a hard place. But there's only one choice he's ever going to make—self-preservation.

"I'll say it again—no, she didn't tell me his name. And it doesn't matter what you threaten, I'm not going to say that she did."

22

Jacob Pope died this morning.

Serena Bailey hasn't turned up on CCTV.

Brandon Keefe's brother backs his story up, and still nothing to connect Masters to either a gun or the Caxton site.

And then Parnell and I enter the fray, heavy on motive, light on suspects.

Or *provable* suspects, I should say.

It's fair to say Steele's frustrated, and frustration is one of her more animated states. Anger makes her motionless, arms folded, chin high, four-inch heels stamped wide, virtually drilling the floor. Disappointment has her seated, hands clasped and head dipped, reproachful eyes peering up at you beneath her Chrissie Hynde fringe.

But for the past ten minutes, she's been at full throttle. Hurtling like a roller coaster—right, left, up, down, corkscrewing around desks, trying to whip up logical debate. I've been keeping my head down, scribbling in my notebook, edging ever closer to dislodging the pebble in my shoe.

> *Finn*—*age 8. Just about to finish Year 3.*
> *Poppy Bailey*—*age 6? Just about to finish Year 1.*

Plus, a spot of personal planning:

> *NYC v SO15*—*pros/cons*
> *Check out US Visa situation*—*B2 Tourist??? ESTA?*

"So, Jacob Pope?" asks Parnell, lobbing me a warning look—*pay attention.*

I throw my pen down and sit back.

"Cardiac arrest," says Steele, currently circling Flowers' desk. "Well, respiratory failure leading to cardiac arrest. His lung was punctured."

"Boo-fucking-hoo," says Flowers. "That's karma for you. Who did the honors?"

It's not often I agree with Flowers and I'm not about to start now. While I won't be crying over Pope, his mum, who visited him regularly, undoubtedly will.

"Lad called Arlo Rollins," confirms Steele. "A gang thing, they reckon. He's saying nothing, which probably means he got his orders from the outside—they'll be looking at his visits and calls, of course. Quiet lad, by all accounts, not prone to violence. Only twenty. He's serving two years for various drug offenses, although he'll obviously be serving a whole lot more now. Another young life down the tubes."

The hopelessness seems to drain her and she finally sits down. A silence falls briefly and then a sigh that could sink a ship.

"So, you two . . ." Me and Parnell. "Good golly, Miss Holly— what on earth was she playing at? Because that's one heartbreaker of a lead you've brought back—a woman with more enemies than you can shake a stick at, but no easy way of tracking them down, short of putting out an appeal along the lines of, 'Hey, were you blackmailed by Holly Kemp? Care to fuck up your marriage and become a murder suspect in the process? Come and have a chat with the Metropolitan Police . . .'"

"We do have one suspect," I say. "Fellows."

"Er, we have two—*Masters* and Fellows," says Flowers. "And if it was Masters, I don't think we'll ever prove it conclusively, not now."

"Shall we just pack up then, Pete?" snaps Steele. "File this one under *a bit too tricky* and head over to the Tavern?" She turns her attention back on us. "So is Fellows the 'big fish' Holly landed?"

Parnell answers. "Shaw's face said yes, but do you know what I'm struggling with? Would she—would *anyone*—be stupid enough to blackmail someone like that? And he's gay. He would have hardly gone home with her, so how would she have got him into a sexually compromising position?"

"Maybe this was different, maybe she was threatening to out him?" offers Emily, breaking into a yawn.

"Yeah . . ." Parnell considers it. "But how would Holly know that? Dyer said only a select few know. So even if Holly had targeted Fellows, it's unlikely he'd say, 'Sorry, love, not interested, I'm gay' to a complete stranger."

I go out on a limb. "Look, he's *got* to be the big fish. He's a crook with lots of cash, which I know doesn't exactly narrow down the crook pool, but Holly actually said his name to Dale Peters. Although, there is another angle . . ." I brace myself, ready to set the cat among the pigeons. "What if she wasn't blackmailing him? What if she was working for him, or with him, and that's what she meant when she said she'd landed a big fish?"

Steele bounds over to my desk. "OK, this is interesting. Keep talking."

I look to Parnell for reinforcements. "Remember Fellows mentioned Steve Butterfield?"

Flowers' face darkens. "He did what? He's got some nerve, that bastard! Steve Butterfield was my DCI at Redbridge, and a top bloke. It was sickening what happened to him. Everyone knows Fellows' crew was behind that."

"OK, and so now we know what we know about Holly, doesn't the similarity seem curious to you? Forget about Butterfield being one of us, he was a man who got caught in a compromising position in a career-ending photo. *And* he always insisted he'd been drugged."

"But that was about removing an obstacle, not blackmail," says Parnell. "Steve was too good at his job. He was taking too many of them out of the game, so they took him out."

"It's in the same ballpark, though," I insist. Steele nods along. "And using Fellows' name to persuade Dale Peters to hand over £10,000—how do we know Holly didn't pull that same scam on other men? Maybe they had some sort of deal? Holly does the legwork but she gets to use Fellows' name as leverage. They split the cash."

"Five thousand pounds each," scoffs Flowers. "That'd be a pair of cufflinks to someone like Fellows. Hardly worth the effort."

"Yeah, he's not been in the four-figure game for a long time," admits Parnell.

"Or the five-figure." Steele pivots on her heel and sweeps back to her seat. "Although it's not a bad sum just for letting someone use your name. And he didn't get where he is by turning his nose up at easy money."

"Why kill her, if she's his business partner, not his blackmailer?" asks Renée. "She's taking all the risk—surely that's the best kind of business partner."

"Business partnerships go sour," I say. "And when things go sour with Simon Fellows, people wind up dead."

A chorus of "Allegedly."

"You've got to hand it to her. Whoever she was working for or against, the girl had balls." Flowers sounds genuinely in awe.

"She was scared, though," I remind him. "Nervous about staying in her own flat. And she was right to be. Her flat was broken into just after she disappeared, and I'm not buying all that 'I knew a lot of shady people, it could have been anyone' bullshit from Shaw. Her laptop was stolen, *not* dumped by Masters—another misstep by Dyer's team." It comes out harsh and I mean it to. Dyer's crown is definitely slipping. "And what do people often store on laptops? Photos. My bet is someone wanted that computer. Could have been Fellows if he knew there was something on it that connected him to Holly."

"Could have been any one of the men she was blackmailing," says Seth. "Fifteen hundred pounds a month? Not many people could keep that up for too long."

Flowers smile-snarls. "Wouldn't put a dent in your piggy-bank, I bet."

"There were no signs of forced entry," I say, coming to Seth's rescue. It's not his fault he was born with a silver spoon in his mouth and a turret over his head. "That suggests someone who knows what they're doing."

"It wasn't just Holly's laptop," Parnell says, in the interest of clarity. "They took a PlayStation, an iPod, jewelry. Shaw's laptop, as well."

I flap it away. "Par for the course, Sarge. Make it look like your average burglary to mask what you were really after."

Steele's hands are in the air, shushing us. "OK, OK, enough chat, people. We need actions. Do we have a list of the bars that Holly targeted? These beautiful-people haunts that I never get invited to?"

I nod. Spencer Shaw gave us as many as he could remember. Some of them will have closed down by now—six years is a lifetime on the ever-evolving London bar scene—but we can only work with what we have.

"Good. So we need to find out if Simon Fellows is, or was, a regular—or even an irregular—in any of these bars. And then we canvass more widely, show Holly's photo to every single bar-fly, looking out for reactions that ring alarm bells. Volunteers for tonight, please? Benny-boy? Emily?"

A spot of perfect casting. Their exquisite faces will fit right in.

"Although it's a hell of a long shot after six years," says Swaines, not moaning, just making the point.

"And it's Monday night," Emily points out. "It's not exactly going to be party central. Even I like a Monday night slobbing on the sofa."

"And every other night dancing on the tables, eh, Ems? No wonder you're always yawning."

Slightly unfair, but Flowers never passes up a chance to make someone else look bad.

Steele ignores him. "Then we go back tomorrow night and the next night and the next night and the next. It's called meticulous police work, and it'll do Benny-boy good not to be cooped up in here." She stands up. "And talking of meticulous police work, I've got a stack of appraisal forms to get back to. Work hard like me, folks; you get all the best jobs."

"Can't you just say we're all bloody brilliant and be done with it?" pleads Flowers, only half-joking.

I shout over to Swaines. "So no joy with the CCTV? You lost your game of Spot Serena?"

"Not a whisker, I'm afraid. It rained on and off most of that day, which means the quality is shite. And there're so many people under umbrellas; she could be any one of them."

"She said she didn't have an umbrella," says Parnell, well-remembered. "Nor did Holly."

Flowers joins in. "That one's said a lot of things, Lu. I mean, 'buying Lady Gaga tickets'—hell of a euphemism for screwing a punter."

An email arrives in the corner of my screen, so I leave Flowers to his guffaws and Parnell to his polite chuckle. It's an email I'd forgotten I'd requested a few days ago.

SUBJECT: Status—Actioned: Christopher Dean Masters
BANK RECORDS {RO:1182499}

I look up to tell Steele, but she's already crossing the threshold of her office. To my right, Parnell's cleaning his glasses with the sleeve of his suit jacket. To my left, Renée's opening a packet of biscuits, Emily, Swaines, and Seth not-so-subtly hovering close by.

And then with one click of my mouse, everything changes.

This case.

My career options.

My self-flagellating belief that I'm the only police officer to have ever made a grave mistake.

Everything.

"Sarge, can you come and look at this," I say, my voice shaking. "Things are about to get ugly."

23

Detective Constable Catrina Kinsella: Force Identification
Number 293CN

I spot my name at the top of an appraisal form. The boxes are still
blank so it looks like Steele hasn't tackled me yet. I'd joke, *"Saving
the best till last,"* if she looked in any way in the mood for it. Maybe
she would have been two minutes ago, before Parnell and I carried
a loaded bomb into her office.

"Again, Kinsella," she says, signaling to Parnell to close the door.
"Once more with less feeling. And slower, for God's sake."

I can try speaking slower. I can try speaking Sanskrit if it makes
what I'm about to repeat sound less catastrophic.

Ultimately though, it doesn't matter how I dress it up, we land
back at the same carnage.

"Masters was nowhere near London on the day Holly disappeared. Serena Bailey is lying."

Steele stares straight ahead. Trying to find a happy place,
maybe? Or a better place, at least. A place where the Metropolitan
Police Force aren't about to be dragged through the mud, then
thrown in the sea.

"He was in Newcastle, nearly three hundred miles away. Three
purchases prove it. A Shell garage in Jesmond, just north of the city
center, where his ex-wife lives. A fishing tackle shop called Bait's
Motel, which, you know, in happier circumstances I think we'd all
award a medal. And £8 in a Burger King."

Parnell scatters the printouts across her desk. "It looks like he
traveled up there regularly. There are numerous purchases going
back to April 2011."

"Visiting his daughters, I suppose," Steele says quietly, before fury revives her. "Then why the frigging hell didn't his ex-wife tell us he was there that day?"

"She didn't know," I say, leaping to her defense. If anyone deserves a stiff lunchtime gin it's the former Mrs. Masters, and frankly I'd been jealous when she said she was going to make one right after our call. "She told me they hadn't seen him since they left London in 2010. It's looking like he was stalking them, boss. Brandon Keefe did say he was always going on about his ex-wife's fancy new house, her new car. I think spying on his old family had become a bit of an obsession."

"We've worked through all the timings," Parnell adds gently. "He couldn't have got to Newcastle early and then back in time to meet Holly at four p.m. because Brandon Keefe saw him in the shop at eight fifteen a.m. and it's a ten-hour round trip, and that's if you're putting your foot down." A sharp look from Steele. "Yeah, don't worry, we're not just taking Keefe's word for it. There is an old statement from another witness who saw Masters dropping off tools at Valentine Street, just like Keefe said."

I take over. "But there's also no way he headed to Newcastle *after* his supposed encounter with Holly, because the fishing tackle shop shuts at five thirty p.m."

"He wasn't in London, Kate." Parnell sounds almost apologetic. "There's no two ways about it, Bailey was either lying or mistaken."

"Fuck. Fuck, fuck, fuck, fuck." Steele pretends to headbutt her desk, then lays her head down, looking up at us. "Seriously, guys, there have to be easier jobs than this. Am I too old to join the circus? I could be one of those glamorous women strapped to a big target—the ones they throw knives at. It'd be a breeze compared with broaching this shitshow with Dyer."

Dyer.

I look at Parnell, hoping he's going to say it. The words feel stuck in my throat, thickened like glue that's sat in the bottle for too long.

"Dyer knew, Kate."

"Knew?" She lifts her head slowly, dread rising in her voice. "Knew what?"

"That Masters wasn't in London. She requested his bank records back in 2012."

"They always flag two requests for the same information," I remind her. "And Dyer requested everything on 1st March—two days after Bailey came forward. They sent them to her the following day."

"But none of it's on the system?" A question. A statement. A death knell for Dyer's career.

I shake my head. "We triple-checked the physical files too, just in case. Nothing."

After another torrent of *fuck*s, Steele stands up and walks over to the blinds, peering out at the team. "Does anyone else know about this?"

"Renée knows something's up," I say. "But you know Ren—she doesn't make it her business unless you make it her business. I don't think anyone else noticed me having an aneurysm."

"OK, good, keep it that way—for now." She points a finger. "I mean it, this is confidential. In fact, it's more than confidential. It's bloody classified. Think JFK, think Watergate. Think bloody weapons of mass destruction."

We nod our understanding, respectful of the shitty privilege bestowed on us.

"So . . ." Parnell takes a deep, loaded breath. "Why would Dyer withhold information that proves Masters wasn't in London?"

"And why would Serena Bailey insist he was?"

The answer to Parnell's question borders on sacrilege. The answer to mine is plain baffling.

Steele sits down again, leaning forward onto the desk. "OK, so I'm Dyer. I've got Holly on CCTV in Clapham, I've got Bailey's doorstep ID—a rock-solid ID." She holds a hand up to stop me. "Everything's looking neat and rosy and tied up with a nice silky bow, even if Masters is playing mind games and won't admit what he did with her, and then, boom, suddenly an email from HSBC is pissing on my chips. Everything I believe to be true is called into question because of a Double Whopper and some fish bait."

"So?" says Parnell, a little tetchy. "That sort of thing has happened to me a hundred times. I didn't ignore it just 'cos it messed up the narrative."

"But you're not under the pressure I'm under," says Steele, still channeling Dyer. "Pressure from the powers that be to get the case wrapped up. Pressure to be at my sick husband's bedside. Pressure to reassure my kids it's all OK, Mummy's home. And then on top of that, pressure to keep all this personal stuff from the top brass in case they take me off the case."

I pick up the next verse. "And it makes it a lot tidier—I'll get back to my ailing husband and my devastated kids a lot quicker— if Holly is one of Masters'. If those bank records don't exist."

Parnell stares at us, open-mouthed. "Can you pair hear yourselves? She should have stepped down if she couldn't handle it—if she was that bloody stressed she was tempted to withhold information just to get a quick conclusion."

Information. He used that word before. Of course, he's dancing around using the word "evidence" because *that* word packs a far more devastating punch. That word will finish a career, ruin a reputation, show you up for who—what—you really are.

"Look, I'm not condoning it, Lu. No way! I'm just trying to step into her shoes for a bit before all hell rains down." She hesitates, tapping her foot against her chair leg. "And as for 'she should have stepped down'—well, yeah, she should have done, *obviously*. But it wouldn't do you any harm to put yourself in the shoes of a female colleague for one minute. And I know it's not the seventies. We're not still getting felt up in the lift or being told to put the kettle on. But if you think a female officer can step down due to 'personal reasons' and not have a massive blot on her copy-book, you're living in a lovely male dreamworld. Because I prom-ise you, Lu, I might be senior in rank, but if it came to it, they'd make more allowances for you than for me."

"I know, boss. I know. It's just all this . . . it's a lot to get your head around."

"What I can't get my head around is why Dyer was even request-ing bank records in the first place?" Confusion coats Steele's face. "I mean, sitting on the phone to HSBC is a hundred miles below her pay grade. I couldn't tell you the last time I did something like that. I'm talking fifteen, twenty years ago. That type of task is spadework; it's DC fodder—no offense, Cat."

"'S'OK, I know my place. Although, this lowly spadeworker was right about something. I knew there was something off about Serena Bailey, although, I admit, I didn't think she was outright lying."

"So you're not with your bosom buddy here." A thumb to Par-nell. "*Mistaken.*"

I hesitate before answering, conscious I should follow Steele's lead and plonk myself in Bailey's size fives.

And I try. I really try. However, I keep arriving back at the same conclusion.

"I can't buy that, no. Maybe if she'd shown a flicker of doubt at any point, I might feel different, but she's been unshakable, boss. And both times I've met her, particularly the first time, I all but invited her to admit that she *might* have been wrong—no reper-cussions, we all make mistakes, la-di-la-di-la—and the lady was not for turning. And there's something else . . ."

The pebble in my shoe.

Steele manages a weary smile. "There always is with you."

"OK, so it was Serena's daughter's birthday last week, and she's just finishing Year One, so that would make her six. We're mid-July now, so assuming a normal pregnancy, Serena would have been four months pregnant in February 2012. And if you're four months pregnant, you know it, right?"

"You'd be better off asking Renée," says Steele. "Or even the super stud over there." Parnell, proud father of four, grins at the moniker. "But more likely than not, I suppose. Then again, you hear the stories—women who didn't realize until they were five, six months gone, sometimes more. And most symptoms can be passed off as something else. Can't do your jeans up—one too many pizzas. Feeling a bit tired—well, frankly, aren't we all?"

"Your period, though?"

"You can still get light bleeding," explains Parnell. "Maggie did with the twins."

"OK, but if you're working as a prostitute, you're in tune with your body. You've got a vested interest in keeping it looking a certain way, especially if you're a £500-an-hour kind of prostitute, and at four months, she'd have had a bump, even just a small one. So would you *really* sell your body if you were fairly sure you were pregnant?"

I'm looking at Steele, but Parnell's always up for testing out a theory.

"I might if I was desperate," he says. "Serena's fella—he's not the daughter's dad, is he?"

"No, she met him a few years later."

"Was there any dad on the scene?"

"I've no idea, although if I were to hazard a guess, I'd say no. She said her life was a bit of a mess back then."

Parnell nods, conclusion reached. "Then, yeah, I might sell my body if I was facing single motherhood and already struggling on a low wage. Especially if I'd done it before."

"But she's got 'Special People,'" I say, earning me a strange look from Steele. "Oh, it's just this thing she had up in her classroom: MISS BAILEY'S SPECIAL PEOPLE TREE. All the kids had them.

My point is, she seems to have a decent support network, so surely someone would have helped her? Selling your pregnant body smacks of some drug-addled street girl needing to pay for her next fix, not a woman with a job, friends, family." I pause, letting them digest what I've said before going for the bull's-eye. "And I suppose with what we now know about Masters, it just makes me wonder if she was ever in Clapham at all?"

Steele flops back heavily, her eyes boring into mine. "Why though, Kinsella? Why would she lie? Is she a crazy?"

A crazy. A fruitloop. A cop-botherer. A loon. They're not nice, the labels we give to those sad, rejected creatures who insert themselves into police investigations for attention and nothing more.

But Serena Bailey isn't one of them, I'm sure of it.

"If anything, boss, she's always shied away from attention. Her partner doesn't even know about the case, and I'm pretty sure she didn't mention it to anyone at her old school."

"So I'll ask you again, if she's not a crazy and she's not mistaken, then what is she?" I hold Steele's stare but I don't have an easy answer. "I mean, are you saying *she* shot Holly and decided to blame the nearest available serial killer?" I twitch my shoulders, saying nothing. "I'm being serious, Kinsella. Are you?"

I don't think I am?

"No, of course not."

"Good. Thank Christ for that! 'Cos now Masters is out of the frame—however god awful that fallout is going to be—I say we focus solely on Simon Fellows." She thumps her reasons out on the desk. "He has access to guns. He was named by the victim as someone she knew *and* was scared of. And finally, you guys are telling me that Spencer Shaw pretty much cacked his pants when you mentioned Fellows' name, which speaks volumes."

But proves nothing.

"So what are we doing about Bailey?" I ask, intent on seeing my pet project through.

"You interview her again, of course. You tell her we have proof she's lying and throw in Perverting the Course of Justice for fun. I'd say we'd have a hard time proving it, but we can see what it shakes up, at least."

"And Dyer?" asks Parnell.

"And Dyer," she repeats with a world-beating sigh. "How do you solve a problem like Tess Dyer?" Steele's words might be straight out of a film, but her face is a gritty drama. So grave and stricken, it almost pains me to look. "Right, this is what we're going to do. Nothing. We sit tight for now—for today, maybe even half a day. I just need some time with this, m'dears. I need to work out what this means, who I need to talk to first. So top secret, you remember?"

"JFK," I say.

"Watergate," adds Parnell.

"Bloody weapons of mass destruction," we chime in unison.

Unfortunately for Serena Bailey, it's the end of the school day when I rock up at St. Joseph of Whatever-it's-called, and I strongly suspect my presence, notably my warrant card and my request that Miss Bailey come with me immediately, is going to be the talk of many a WhatsApp parents' group tonight. Fortunately for me, once we're back at the station, Serena says she doesn't want a solicitor. Or more specifically, that she doesn't have time to wait for one, as if she isn't home before Robbie at six, he'll start asking questions and that's the last thing she wants.

Apart from me asking questions. I'm fairly sure she wants that less.

"This is ridiculous," she asserts; she's been asserting all over the place since we got back. "It was him, Masters. He was standing at the door, smiling, wearing that red lumberjack shirt, welcoming her in."

"I don't believe you, Serena."

My tone is blithe, singsong: Jacqui warning Finn that she knows for sure he hasn't brushed his teeth. In contrast, Serena Bailey's like the star of a YouTube tutorial—*How to Tell When Someone's Lying*. Wild, whirling hand gestures. Feet shuffling under the table. And those eyes, those wide green eyes, darting left, right, anywhere but on mine.

"Because you can't have seen him, Serena. We've now got proof, you see. Bank records prove Christopher Masters was nowhere near London, let alone Clapham, that day."

She blushes, her skin matching with her rose-pink shirt. "Then I must have been mistaken."

"Just like that?" I half-laugh, keeping it light for now. "Six years of certainty and now 'whoops, I made a boo-boo.'"

She pulls her ponytail over her shoulder, tugging at the ends, circling it around her finger. "Look, a man opened the door. He was wearing a check shirt. He was around fifty. They showed me a photo of Masters and there really was a strong similarity." A shrug. "But if you've got proof that I got it wrong, then I'll have to accept that I got it wrong. And I'm sorry. But it doesn't change the fact that I saw Holly go into that house."

"Describe her to me again."

"Holly?" She drops her ponytail, bringing her hands to her lap. Still, almost rigid. "Salon-flicky blond hair, really glamorous. She was wearing this gorgeous white coat—well, off-white, cream, I suppose." She makes a sweeping motion with both hands. "Huge fur collar, belted, gorgeous. I half-thought about asking her where she got it."

Verbatim. A computer throwing out a programmed statement.

"Very good." I'm tempted to applaud. "Hey, what do you think of this?" I clear my throat. "*I am the star and I mark out the way. To Jesus, the Lord, as the prophecies say.*"

Understandably, she's flummoxed.

"It was my one line in the Nativity," I explain, grinning. "I rehearsed it so much, I can still recite it, word for word, over twenty years later. Amazing, right?" I tap the side of my head. "Funny how things stick when you practice them enough times." She swallows hard, getting the message, but I prattle on, leaving her to squirm. "Yeah, I was gutted, I don't mind telling you—auditioned for Mary, got cast as the bloody star! Thought I was going to be trooping around the stage, looking all noble and dignified, clutching a Tiny Tears doll. Ended up suspended on a wire, dressed in leggings and gold lamé." I sigh. "But then that's life, eh? Never quite works out the way you planned. Although you've got Poppy, of course. She seems like a sweetie—did she have a good time at Hobbletown?"

"Hobble*down*," she corrects. I laugh at my own mistake, putting her at a tiny bit of ease again. "And yes, she did. She got to walk a llama. And then she saw another llama looking after a lamb, which was the sweetest thing ever, apparently." Her eyes are shining, shoulders soft.

How to Tell When Someone's Lying: Part 2:

Displaying obvious signs of relief that the difficult subject has been dropped.

Providing unnecessary, unasked-for details about llamas.

"She went for her sixth birthday, right?" Serena nods, blissfully unaware of the oncoming ambush. "So if Poppy's six now, you must have been . . . um"—I tilt my head, pretending to grapple with the math—"*four* months pregnant when the whole Clapham thing went down?" I make a low whistle. "Christ, I bet you didn't need that. I mean, you're not long out of the hell of the first trimester, hoping for a bit of quiet time, maybe a bit of pregnancy 'glow,' and then, wham, you're in the middle of a murder investigation."

Her smile slips. "I suppose you're going to try to claim pregnancy affected my eyesight."

"No, but I think it affected your judgment." I slide her statement across, pointing to the other nugget I'd noticed as I'd trawled back through her lies. "This is what you said to me about the client you were seeing: *He'd been doing coke. I hadn't—I swear on my daughter's life, I only had a couple of glasses of wine.*" Another whistle, this one disapproving. "Hey, you know, I try to live and let live about most things, Serena, as long as they're within the law, obviously. But a couple of glasses of wine while pregnant? You do know the dangers, right?" She bristles, but it looks forced. "And—and this isn't *really* my business, but . . . sleeping with a client when you're pregnant? Isn't that a bit—" I stop abruptly, putting my hands up in apology. "Ah no, scrap that, sorry. Honestly, I'm sorry. I shouldn't have said that. It's not my place to judge, I'm only here for the facts." I give her a tight smile. "We'll need your client's details, of course."

She tugs at her ponytail again. "I don't have them. I haven't seen him since that day."

"A name would be a start."

"I only ever knew him as Dave."

Dave. She isn't even trying now. At least she used to tell a good lie, a solid eight out of ten for creativity. Buying Lady Gaga tickets from a phantom con man in a pub ranks a thousand leagues higher than *"I only ever knew him as Dave."*

"OK, how about the address of where he was staying? We might be able to trace him that way."

"I don't remember."

I give her a puzzled look. "Serena, you're not being overly helpful, given it's in your interest for us to find him. 'Dave' can corroborate your story. He can confirm you were really there that day."

"My story? And what do you mean, of course I was fucking there."

Swearing now. Interesting.

"Then why can't we find one single sighting of you on CCTV?"

"I . . ." She falters quickly. "I don't know. I can't answer that."

I rub my chin. "I suppose, in fairness, it was raining. Lots of people under umbrellas. You could have been one of them."

"Yeah, I must have been." She nods, happy that's sorted, then looks at her watch. "Look, it's gone five, I need to get back. I take it I'm free to leave?"

"Except you didn't have an umbrella. That was one of the reasons you remembered Holly, because she didn't have one either."

"I said, can I leave?" She picks up her bag, presumptive.

Problem is, it's not entirely presumptive. I can't stop her from leaving. Like Steele implied, we'd struggle to get this past the CPS at the moment, and I'm still not even sure what *this* is.

Still, might as well go for it; hurl the kitchen sink at her.

"One more question, then you can leave. But think carefully before answering, because my boss is already bandying around terms like 'Perverting the Course of Justice.'" Her breath quickens, my hoped-for response. "Have you ever come across a man called Simon Fellows?"

"No, I don't think so. Who is he?"

Face completely blank. At a guess, I'd say *genuinely* blank.

Not my hoped-for response.

"So, to be absolutely clear, a man called Simon Fellows did not pay you, or influence you in any way, to say you saw Holly with Masters? Because the type of money Simon Fellows could pay would come in very handy to someone facing the prospect of single motherhood. He'd pay a lot more than £500, if he thought you could be useful to him."

She stands, mouth puckered. "Could he? Great! Then give him my number, whoever he is. Robbie's about to be made redundant and the car needs a new gearbox."

It pains me to admit it, but for the first time I think I almost believe her.

Almost.

"*Meet me at South Kensington*" sounds more like a 1950s rom-com than an instruction from a senior officer, but less than an hour later I'm striding down Montrose Grove, heading back to Oliver Cairns' place. Up ahead, Steele's standing under a cherry-blossom tree a little way down from the house, tapping away on her phone, her small frame engulfed in pink. There isn't a breath of wind and the branches are eerily still, as if the heat has zapped all their energy and they can't be bothered to move, like the rest of us. As I get closer, I notice that two petals have dropped onto Steele's head—perfect pink on perfect black. I should probably tell her or move them. But I don't. They look pretty.

And here, my wistfulness ends. Steele's straight down to business.

"News?" she orders, sliding her phone into her bag as we start walking.

I take it from the top, filling her in on the Bailey interview. Her claims that she was mistaken. My belief she's talking bullshit. The convenient unknown whereabouts of her alibi, "American Dave." A lie about an umbrella.

"I think she was telling the truth about Fellows, though. I doubt she's going to be our link."

"That famous woo-woo working overtime, is it?"

"Depends if you think body language is woo-woo. I watched her squirm and blush and fidget with her hair for more than half an hour—except when she described Holly, then she went *totally* still, the way you do when you're having to concentrate." Steele nods, getting my point. "But when I mentioned Fellows . . . I dunno . . . it's the first time she seemed natural. Genuine confusion. Her first response wasn't outright denial, it was to ask who he was. That feels like a normal reaction to me."

She nods again.

"So what are we doing back here?"

Or more to the point, what am *I* doing back here? Don't get me wrong, I like Cairns—I've clearly got a soft spot for tall, loquacious Irish men—but I still feel like a teenager being forced to visit an aged relative with their mum.

"More context. I want to make sure I've got all my facts straight before I destroy someone's career." We walk up the steps to the front door. "And you're impartial," she adds, answering my unasked question. "I want you watching, observing. You might pick up on something I don't."

It takes two rings of the bell and three knocks on the door before "All right, all right, give a man a chance," can be heard, followed by painfully slow footsteps, shuffling closer, getting louder.

Finally, he opens the door. He's wearing a full tuxedo, cummerbund and all.

"Oh."

"Oh indeed." Steele beams. "Look at you, James Bond. Are you off out?"

"No." He winks at me. "I always dress like this for me dinner."

"Very funny."

We follow him into the aircraft-hangar living room, where there's a duvet on one sofa, an array of medications on the coffee table, and an ever so slightly sour smell in the air. Nothing horrific; it's completely bearable, but if I were to guess, I'd say he's been cocooned in here for a few days, sleeping downstairs. One end of another sofa has been elevated with cushions. Cairns lowers himself onto it, unable to hide his pain.

Forget impartial—I feel emotional. Mum's final months unwelcomingly springing to mind.

"So where are you off to, then?" asks Steele, sitting down. I follow suit.

"Nowhere. I was going to go the Emerald Society Summer Ball—big posh do at The Dorchester—but I just this minute decided I can't be bloody bothered."

"That's a shame when you're all dressed up, looking suave," I say.

I'm being kind. He doesn't look suave, he looks awful. Stooped and old, and even thinner, if that's possible. His face a triangle of bone, the dark circles under his eyes made even darker by his waxy skin.

"I'm not feeling up to it, truth be told, Cat. I've had a rough few days." A flick of his hand bats away the self-pity. "Anyway, it's too fucking hot to be wearing a tux." It's also too fucking hot to have every window closed, and for one heartbreaking second I wonder if he hasn't had the strength to open any. Sash windows can be heavy; the ones in our office are a bitch. "Now, would one of you ladies unclip this bow tie for me. My fingers are bad today. It took me nearly an hour to get the fucker on."

In the absence of any movement from Steele, I oblige.

"Look, are you sure you feel up to a few questions?" Steele nods toward the duvet. "You must feel rough if you've been sleeping down here."

"Ach." Another flick of his hand. "'Tis easier than going up and down three flights of stairs. And sure, fire away. Although I'm going to be a bad host—if either of you want a drink, you can fetch it yourself."

"We're fine. Can we get you one?" "We" meaning me, presumably. Thankfully, he shakes his head. "OK, well, if you're sure."

"Glad of the company, Katie, love. I haven't seen a soul in days. I didn't realize when we were together how many of my friends were really Moira's friends. And they fell away quick enough. Same as a lot of the old Met crowd. 'Twas nice seeing Tess again, though."

"We're actually here about Tess." Steele's face is stern, imploring. "But I need to know that I can talk to you confidentially."

"You have to ask that?"

A wry smile. "You're too fond of Tess Dyer for your own good, Olly, but I'm actually trying to help her by coming to you first, by getting all the facts straight. I want you to bear that in mind, OK? If you go running to her with what I'm about to tell you, it could prompt her to make the wrong decision, and this has to be handled properly."

"OK, now you're scaring me, Kate. What? What is it?"

"Why was Tess requesting bank records?"

"Whose bank records?"

She rolls her eyes. "The Queen of England's, Olly. Who the hell do you think I'm talking about? Masters', back in 2012. Why would she have taken on that task personally? She's heading up one of the most high-profile cases in London's recent history and she's got time to be sitting on hold to HSBC?"

He doesn't answer straightaway, looking this way and that. "Look, I really can't answer that, Kate, but you know yourself, when the case is high profile, when the stakes are that high, you want to oversee everything. God knows, I put pressure on her to oversee everything. Too much pressure. I can see that now."

"Well, I'm sorry, Olly, but first, I don't know that myself. I trust my team to do the work. I trust them with my life." A part of me dies inside. Maryanne. Aiden. My family's links to organized crime. The fact I toyed with the idea of leaving her for Dyer. The fact I'm still toying with the idea of leaving her for NYC. "And second, when we were here last time, you said something different. You said you were all about taking the pressure *off* her. Protecting her from herself, closing down 'half-cocked' theories and the like."

"And I thought I was. I thought by reining her in when it came to making the big decisions, I was freeing her up to do *actual* police work. And we needed all hands on deck, trust me."

"Requesting bank records, though. That's grunt work. I've had rookies who'd have turned their noses up."

A defiant stare. "Tess Dyer has never turned her nose up at anything she's been asked to do, and that's why she is where she is. I wouldn't put it past her to head up the Met one day, and she'll still be doing the grunt work then if that's what needs to be done."

"Well, that's quite the school report, Olly, but she's not quite the model student, I'm afraid. See, it turns out that she requested them, but didn't upload them to the system. God knows what happened to them, but there was only ever Tess's eyes on them until this week."

He doesn't blink. "So she's fallible."

"Hmm, fallible's one word. Negligent is another." What Dyer did was more than negligent, but Steele's holding back, teasing things out. "Olly, she shouldn't have been on the case at all, not with the hell she was going through in her personal life."

"No." He points a swollen finger. "No, don't use that against her, Kate. A bloody admin oversight has nothing to do with what was going on at home. Tess Dyer is a professional."

Tess Dyer is a professional.

Tess Dyer never turns her nose up at what she's asked to do.

Tess Dyer shits glitter and cries rainbows, and heals the sick in her spare time.

I've no idea why I'm being caustic. I fell for it, for a while.

Cairns isn't finished. "And whether you've a sick spouse at home or not, mistakes get made, Kate. Things get missed, mislaid. It's human error. There's only so many hours in the day."

Steele sneaks a look at me—*wish me luck.*

"Thing is, Olly, that's all well and good, but I haven't given up my Monday night crochet circle"—I have no idea if she's joking—"to come here telling tales about an admin oversight. Those bank records that Tess requested, read, and then failed to upload or report to anyone, prove that Christopher Masters wasn't in London the day Holly Kemp went missing. Which means the witness isn't credible and all assumptions fall apart. In all likelihood, someone else killed Holly and Tess has known that all along."

I expect shock, outrage, maybe a short period of silence while he struggles to digest. But the ex–Chief Superintendent comes to the fore almost instantly. His body may be crocked, but his brain is still needle-sharp.

"So, let me get this straight, Masters wasn't at the house, but Holly *was*?"

"So Serena Bailey insists," I say, finally inserting myself.

"Well then, Tess was right and I was wrong. An accomplice is the obvious explanation."

"Sir, we've got doubts about whether Bailey was even there herself. She's lied to us throughout the course of the investigation. There's no sign of her on CCTV. She wasn't marked as being absent . . ."

"Tess was *right*?" Steele cuts across me, her voice breaking the sound barrier. "Olly, she ignored crucial evidence in a murder investigation."

"How do you know that for sure?" His tone is changing, every word a provocation. "You only know Tess requested the bank records, then received them. You don't know, you can't *prove*, that she read them."

Steele's eyes widen. "I'm sorry, is that supposed to be an observation, because it sounds a lot like a challenge? A threat." She gives him a long penetrating stare, playing the tough nut to a T. "Oh, she read them, Olly, *because* she's a professional, like you say. And it's not up to me to prove anything. That'll be up to the DPS." The Department of Professional Standards, or the Department of Professional Shit-stirrers as Flowers likes to call them. "She can explain to them why she withheld potentially vital evidence."

Cairns folds his arms, lets out one short, angry breath. "She did it because *I* ordered her to." Steele audibly gasps. "I told her to delete those records out of her email and never speak of them again. And I told you, Tess Dyer does what she's asked to do."

"And that includes committing misconduct in a public office?" Steele's shock goes beyond the implications of this case. She's looking at Cairns like she's never seen him before. "*What the actual fuck, Olly?*"

"Ah now, calm down. Misconduct? I was protecting our case. We had Serena Bailey and we had *no* reason to doubt her. None. Why the hell would she lie?" The sixty-four-thousand-dollar question. "She was as solid a witness as ever I saw in my career, and that was a forty-three-year career, I'll remind you. Forty-three years of making decisions that put villains where they belong." He sits up straighter, seeming braver, even physically stronger after dropping his bomb. "And look, OK, maybe I wasn't totally honest with you. Maybe Tess' personal life was affecting her work. Maybe I should have taken her off the case. But that's my failing, not hers. *I* pushed her into tying Holly up with Masters. Blame me, not her."

Blame me, not her. The same thing Dyer had said about Susie Grainger. A warped sense of responsibility passed from mentor to mentee.

"But why?" says Steele, still wide-eyed and dumbstruck. "And what would you have done if Masters hadn't decided to play silly buggers and keep schtum? He could have given himself an alibi at any point. It's a measure of the man's lunacy that he didn't."

He shrugs. "If he did, he did. I was fairly sure he wouldn't, though—that bastard liked the control, liked giving people the runaround. As for why . . . I had pressures too, Kate. Looking out for Tess. Turvill breathing down my neck. Me and Moira on the skids. I wanted that case closed."

"So you withheld evidence. Jesus, Olly . . ."

He closes his eyes, taking a moment. "Look, those bank records weren't the be-all and end-all for me. His card could have been stolen or cloned. Jesus, my nephew had his whole bloody account emptied by someone on a spending spree in São Paulo!"

"His card wasn't stolen," I say, deadpan. "It's clear from his bank records that he used it the next day, in and around Clapham. And as for cloned—one quick call to the bank would have put that to bed."

His eyes land on mine for a second, then dart back to Steele.

"Anyway, you call it withholding evidence, I call it directing resources and attention down the most obvious path—and with Bailey, Masters *was* the most obvious path." Another shrug. "And anyway, Masters' brief could have requested the very same records at any point and he didn't. It wasn't our job to prove him innocent."

"You don't believe that, Olly. I know you don't. What happened to you?" Her eyes glitter with what could be tears. The tough nut, cracked. "You know I have to hand this over to the DPS. I should have done it already."

"Then why haven't you?" There's hope in his voice, but it couldn't be more misplaced.

"I chose professional courtesy over professional duty and I'm already regretting that decision." She stands up. "And I'd really appreciate you doing me the courtesy of not speaking to Tess about this. Let me do my job."

"I will, Katie, love, if you do me one last courtesy. Forget this last half-hour. Remember all the years, all the pints. All the holes I dug you out of. I'm begging you, don't finish her career over this. This was me, this was all on me."

I look across at Steele, not sure what to say. She hasn't spoken a word since Cairns' front door closed, apart from a muttered "bloody typical" at the dollop of bird shit on her windshield. Eventually, I break the silence.

"You look like you just found out Santa doesn't exist."

In truth, she looks worse. She looks like she just found out not only does Santa not exist, but the very notion of him has been eradicated and outsourced to an expensive app. Presents downloaded. All letters to the North Pole scrapped forthwith. No more grottoes and elves and leaving a carrot out for the reindeer. All trace of magic stripped away.

"He's dying," she replies, her tone appropriately lifeless. "Prostate cancer. And now it's spread to his spine. Good days and bad days, he says, but the upshot is it's terminal."

I think I always suspected it on some deep level. Even that first time in the pub, despite all the handshakes and wisecracks, Cairns still had that haunted, hollowed-out look of a man living on borrowed time. It's a look I saw on Mum's face enough times, even as she booked minibreaks, made plans for Christmas, tried to smile as she planted sunflowers she wouldn't see bloom.

"Right. So not arthritis then?"

"Oh, he has rheumatoid arthritis. He got a nice double-whammy." A quick glance upward. "Yep, Olly Cairns certainly did something to offend the big guy in the sky."

My buttons are pressed. "Oh, come on, that's bullshit. When your time's up, your time's up. It's down to cell mutations, nothing to do with a vengeful God."

Because if it was, it'd be Dad's grave I'd be laying sunflowers on every month. Mum never did anyone any harm.

"How long have you known?" I ask.

"A few days. I tried to get hold of him the day Fellows' name came up, just to sound him out, you know—I mean, it's been years, decades, since he worked Organized Crime, but Olly's always had his ear to the ground, always been well networked. Anyway, his phone was off for hours. He called me back that night, we talked, and he told me. He'd been in the hospital. Palliative radiotherapy. It manages the pain, slows things down, although by the looks of him . . ."

"Does he know how long?"

"If he does, he isn't saying. He doesn't want the sympathy. He's been passing it off as a bad RA flare-up as much as he can."

"Dyer knows, presumably?"

She nods. "I'd say it's hit her hard."

"We can't think about that. It's not our place to get sentimental."

"Yes, I'm aware of that, Kinsella. Thank you." She glances sideways. "God, it's come to something when I'm being lectured on empathy by you, of all people. If I said Cairns is to Dyer what Parnell is to you, or he certainly used to be, would that soften your hard heart?"

"Is her career definitely finished?" I ask, punching away the thought of a seriously ill Parnell rattling around a big, lonely house. "I mean, as in *finished* finished? If she was acting under Cairns' instruction . . ."

"That might wash if I ordered you to do something dodgy, but Dyer's a DCI. She should have known better." She thinks about it some more. "There's a small chance they could be lenient, I suppose. She might not lose her job entirely. But the career she had planned, that's finished. They'll definitely take action against her."

"And Cairns."

She turns and looks back down the road, toward the house. "Well, he hardly needs the pension, does he? And he's dying. Suspended sentence is my guess, but God knows."

Despite everything, it's hard not to feel sad about a life ending in pain, probable loneliness, and complete reputational ruin.

"So what did he have to say about Fellows?"

She looks distracted. "Who?"

"Cairns. Or didn't you get around to that? I guess, 'I've got terminal cancer' is a bit of conversation stopper."

"Oh no, we did. He didn't have a lot to say, though. He knows who Fellows is, of course—hadn't a clue he was gay, which surprised me a bit; Olly always used to have the goss on everyone. But he hadn't a clue how he'd be connected to this case either. Said his name certainly never surfaced the first time around, although can we trust anything he says now? He's a corrupt police officer, Cat. A criminal."

Which makes me what, exactly?

The lights of New York City have never burned as brightly as they do right now.

25

Thinking about Mum always drives me to Dad. Unfortunately, Dad's "recuperating" at Jacqui's and Jacqui drives me to drink. Seriously, I haven't been in the door five minutes and I've already failed my sister on a hundred different levels. The color of my top doesn't suit me. The timing of my visit doesn't suit her. I've opened the Sancerre, not the Sauvignon, and the Sancerre was for the PTA raffle. I haven't noticed she's had her hair layered but I *have* noticed the damp patch on the kitchen wall.

I'm too quick to notice faults, apparently.

I'm not what her decluttering guru would call a "natural uplifter."

Still, at least Finn is pleased to see me, barreling into me with such force that half my wine ends up on the kitchen floor.

"Hey, steady, Finn-bo. Not the precious Sancerre."

"Can I have a bit?" he says, sticking his nose in the glass. "Yuck, that smells like wee."

"Ah, give it ten years and you won't be saying that. Actually, maybe you won't be drinking wine in ten years. Vodka or cider, I reckon."

He looks up at me, hazel-green eyes just like Mum's. "What's cider?"

"It's fizzy and it tastes of apples."

"Sounds nice." Next question. "Why is Sancerre precious?"

"'Cos it costs lots of Mummy's money."

"I've got lots of money," he tells me. "I've still got the £50 Uncle Frank gave me." He races to the kitchen drawer, retrieving the fifty, then waving it in my face, "I'm gonna buy a droid gunship."

"Sounds like a plan." I pull a "WTF?" face at Jacqui, who's busy making a Stormtrooper helmet out of milk cartons.

I break into a grin.

"What?" she says, shaking a can of white spray paint. "What's so funny?"

"You know you could buy one of those for a tenner."

"Why pay when I can make one myself?"

Why take the easy option when I'd much rather martyr myself?

"'S'pose," I agree, sensing this could turn into an argument. It doesn't take us much, especially after white wine. "Hey, I was up this way last week. Riverdale Primary, just down the road near Canons Park. Did you never think of sending Finn there? It seemed nice. The head had this collage of all the pupils and their favorite books and fruits and all this other stuff."

"Cute. But I'm more interested in SAT scores. King Alfred's is much better."

"You'd hope it would be at £5K a term."

Side-eye from across the kitchen. "Can we leave the Marxism for one evening, Cat?"

"It just seems harsh that Dad's paying all that money when all he wants is for Finn to play for West Ham."

She makes a *hmph* sound. "Yeah, well, he paid enough for your education and you joined the police. I think he's used to disappointment."

"Jesus, you and Noel will never get over that, will you?"

Not the police officer thing, the private school education. Jacqui and Noel were both well into their teens when Dad "made" his Big Money, and Mum decided there was probably no point in them moving schools then. That meant no fancy school uniforms, no after-school archery lessons. It was only me who was deemed young enough to be molded into the perfect private school princess.

A failed project, if ever there was one.

"Noel might be coming back from Spain," Jacqui says with a sprinkle of barbed glee. She and Noel are hardly doting siblings, but it's payback for the reminder that Dad funds her life.

And something I could have really done without hearing.

"When? What do you mean *might*?" I look over at Finn, currently engaged in a climactic gun fight on his PlayStation. I lower my voice. "He's out of prison then?"

She sets the Stormtrooper mask aside, stands up. "He's been out for months, Cat. It was nothing . . . a few Es."

"Three-hundred, Jacqs. Remind me not to come out with you for 'a few' cocktails."

"Yeah right, like that's ever going to happen. Remind me when we last had a night out?"

To be fair, I walked straight into that one.

I quickly change the subject. "So where is he then? The one-armed bandit?"

She flicks her head toward the kitchen window. "He's in the garden. I think he likes the peace."

"He lives above a bloody pub!"

"A pub that doesn't have an eight-year-old boy constantly shouting at *Fortnite*."

"Ange didn't fancy playing nursemaid then?"

"She runs her own salon, some swish place out in Essex. Does pretty long hours. It made more sense for Dad to stay here for a week or two."

"Is there any danger of her turning up here?" If the answer's yes, if there's even the slightest chance we might be forced into a pained intro, I'm going to break the land speed record getting out the front door.

"No, she's coming tomorrow night. But there's no 'danger,' Cat. She's nice."

"I'm sure she is," I lie. "I'm just not in the mood for small talk." I pour another wine—a large one this time, a third of the bottle. "And anyway, I need to talk to Dad. Alone."

"Oh yeah, what about?"

"Work."

I leave her pondering that and head outside into the now-bearable evening heat. Dad's sitting on a wooden swing bench at the top of the garden, his head back and eyes closed, two citronella candles flickering on either side of his bare feet.

"Didn't think you were a meditation kind of guy?" I call, halfway up the path.

He stirs and looks up. A look of complete love that makes me feel five years old.

"My God, we don't see you up this way often. Did you bring your passport?" He sits up a little, smiling. "I was having a snooze, actually, sweetheart. I think my painkillers make me drowsy."

"Or it's old age."

He laughs. "You might be right. Catches up with everyone at some point."

Except in his case it hasn't. Dad's always had good genes and kept himself in pretty good shape, but I'm starting to believe that he was kissed by a fairy at birth. Even in his weakened state, he could pass for a decade younger than his fifty-six years.

"They don't work, you know—these candles. You watch, we'll still get eaten alive by mosquitoes." I sit down beside him, making myself a sitting target for the little bastards. "So how are you then?"

"I'm fine. As I keep telling everyone, I broke my arm, not my neck."

"And how are the ribs doing?"

"OK. Hurts a bit when I laugh, but you know, that's not too much of a problem around here." We share a grin. "If it's not *Fortnite*, it's decluttering." Another grin. "And then there's Ash, of course."

Strong, dependable, kindhearted Ash. One of the good guys, for sure. You just wouldn't want to sit next to him at a dinner party.

I use one foot to push us off the ground, the bench swinging softly. "So you're definitely OK?"

He looks at me, confused. "God, I knew Jacqui would flap, but I was hoping for some indifference from you."

"I don't mean the injuries. I mean how you got them." I take a sip of wine. "Is it all sorted now, all square? Another 'barrel of beer' isn't going to drop on you any time soon?"

"It's sorted."

I take his word for it, proceeding to the next headfuck on the agenda. "Jacqs said Noel might be coming back. Any idea what 'might' means? I mean, a plane *might* crash into the garden in the next five minutes, but it's unlikely—although it's preferable to Noel being back in London."

"He's coming back." Dad stares into the candle, looking solemn. Looking sorry.

"You needn't look so fucking gloomy about it. If he's coming back, it's because you've paved the way for it to happen."

"Frank wants him back."

I halt the swing, turning to him fully. "But Frank hates Noel! That's about the only thing me and Frank Hickey have ever agreed on. Christ, Dad, he had Noel beaten to a pulp for skimming off him."

He shrugs his bad shoulder. "I'm back in the firm now. He knows I'll keep him in line. And Noel's good muscle, always was."

"Give Finn ten years and he'll be good muscle too. Is that what you want? Is that the plan? 'Cos if it is, he's already coming along nicely—shooting at things and waving fifties around like a mini pimp."

"Calm down." An order, not a suggestion.

"Calm down? Are you serious? Noel being back is bad news, Dad. If he ever met Aiden, it wouldn't bear thinking about." I've never really thought about what that phrase actually means, but now I know. Now I feel it in every cell, every vein, every hair on the back of my neck. "Noel would put two and two together, I know he would. Worrying about Jacqui is bad enough, but for all her 'neglected big sister' act, she's too wrapped up in herself to bother about me. But Noel makes it his business to poke his nose into mine."

"He won't go near you, Cat. I won't let him." There's a fierceness in his eyes that says I should believe him, but I can't afford to. "Same with Frank. Frank knows the day you're hurt is the day me and him are finished, and Noel will know the same soon enough. I love my boy, Cat." He takes my hand. "But you're the good one. You're the one that proves I did something right in my life."

"I compromised a murder investigation. Your standards are pretty low."

"The people responsible went to prison, that's all that matters. And now all that matters is that you're safe and happy. I won't let Noel hurt you."

And maybe he won't, not fatally. But in the same way he always used to delight in kicking my top bunk, pulling my hair, calling me names, stealing my things, Noel's never happy unless I'm miserable. Unless the Golden Child's losing her sheen.

Another tick in the box for Manhattan.

"I might be moving to New York for a while." I didn't mean to blurt that out, but all those years of spewing vitriol at Dad means my brain-to-mouth filter can be a little leaky when it comes to him. "I guess that could solve the Noel problem."

"Wow, that's some news, sweetheart." A light's gone out in his eyes, but he still manages a weak laugh. "I can just see you now—'NYPD, open up!'"

I smile. "I wish! Aiden's been offered a two-year transfer, but I wouldn't be able to work."

"So what are the odds on you going?"

"I would have said fifty-fifty, but with Noel coming back . . ."

"Then Noel won't come back."

His response is instant, reflexive, a simple matter of fact. The sun will rise. The birds will fly south for the winter. And my son will not set foot on British soil again if it means my daughter moves thousands of miles away from it.

"I mean it, Cat. If you want to go to New York, go to New York. But don't you dare go because of Noel." He looks at me with a paternal sternness that's as unfamiliar as it is hilarious. "And don't go because Aiden's pressuring you either."

"He's not pressuring me. I've said I'll think about it and he's fine with that. If I don't want to go, then we'll stay, and he won't say another word about it." I pause, considering the truth of what I've just said. "But *that's* why I should go—because all he cares about is being with me and that type of love isn't to be sniffed at."

We share a smile that says, "Mum." God knows, she put up with a lot more than what's effectively the offer of a two-year holiday.

"Anyway, enough about me." I let go of his hand, shifting position, breaking eye contact. "Ange. I take it it's serious if Finn and Jacqs have met her?"

"Serious?" He lets out a long breath. "I don't even know what 'serious' means, to be honest with you. She makes me laugh. She's kind. She's got her own life, her own money. And before you ask, she's forty-one, two kids—twelve and eight."

"Oh God, don't get too serious then. I'm a bit long in the tooth for bratty step-siblings."

"Jesus, the thought of getting married again . . ." He turns his head. I keep staring forward. "I really like her though, Cat. And I've told her all about you. She'd love to meet you. I'd love you to meet her."

"Whoa." I put a hand up. "I'm asking about her, all right. Can we take that as progress for now?"

"I think you'd like her."

"I think I need to think about it."

"Christ's sake, I'm not suggesting a two-day summit! Just pop into the pub one night, say hello."

"Pop into the pub? And can you promise there won't be stuff

going on in the pub, or in the back room of the pub, that won't make it awkward for me—you know, a sworn police officer?" He takes too long to answer. "So that's a no."

He dodges the question again. "You won't be a sworn police officer for much longer if you go to New York."

"And your point is?"

"Just that you've always said it's what you want to do. It's what makes you happy. And you're going to give it all up, just like that?"

"I wouldn't be giving it up forever and I'd get back in easily enough." *If* we came back. "And anyway, maybe a break would do me good. It gets under your skin after a while. The horror of what people do. The flippancy they do it with."

The wine's doing its thing. I can't remember the last time I talked to Dad like this, or if I ever have, full stop.

"America's not the easiest place to get into. Have you looked into all that? Visas?" He's trying not to sound hopeful.

I nod. "Worst-case scenario, I'd have to come back to the UK every ninety days."

"And that's a bad thing? Thanks."

"Oh come on, Dad. It's not like we're . . ." I struggle to find the word. It's not "close" because holy fuck, we're close. You can't not be close to the person who knows the worst thing you ever did. "It's not like we live in each other's pockets. We go months without seeing each other."

"Your choice, not mine."

"Not a choice, a necessity. In the eyes of the law, you're an active criminal first, a dad second. And I shouldn't be fraterniz-ing with active criminals. I shouldn't be here now."

"Then why are you?"

I could say I was worried about him. I could tell him I'd been thinking about Mum and I had the sudden and overwhelming need to be near people who loved her.

I opt for the path of least vulnerability.

"I'm working a case at the moment and we've run up against a few names—people you probably don't know, but I'd say you're aware of, and I just wondered . . ."

"Well, you can stop wondering right now, sweetheart." Everything hardens—his tone, his face, the very air between us. "It works both ways, you know, Cat. I'd never ask you for information. You shouldn't expect it from me."

I twist around, frustrated. "Hold on a minute, I'm not after 'information.' Christ, I think our relationship is complex enough without you becoming my snout, don't you? I just want some context, that's all." Anger rears its head. "Actually, what I want is for what you are to work in my favor for five bloody minutes. Is that too much to ask?"

"It could be, yeah." The shutter coming down is stalled halfway. "What do you mean by 'context?'"

"I'm not asking you to implicate anyone in anything, if that's what you're worried about. Just set the scene for me."

He sighs. "And whose scene am I setting?"

It's too soon to mention Simon Fellows. His name is a total door-slammer. I need to start small, or at least small*er*. I need to win trust then build up to him.

"Do you know a man called Jacob Pope?"

"I know he's dead. Is that the case you're working?"

"No, no. He's just . . . it's complicated. How did you know he was dead? He only died this morning."

He relaxes slightly, tension ebbing from his face in small, slow increments. "Every industry has its grapevine, Cat." *Industry.* "Rival gang thing, wasn't it?"

"Too early to say." The party line is also the truth.

"From what I remember of him, it's a miracle someone didn't off him sooner."

"What? You knew him?"

"Not really, just nodding terms. I think he worked for the Pierce crowd before he got sent down, but Aaron—you know, Frank's nephew—he used to run with him. Frank used him on a few jobs but he . . ."

I cover my ears; hear no evil. "I don't want to know, Dad. I don't want to know details about anything to do with you, or Frank."

"OK, OK. Pope was a bit of hothead, that's all I was going to say."

"That's an understatement. He killed his girlfriend."

"No great loss to the world then, is he?" A pause. "He was a bright lad, though, had a sharp brain. And he used to run with a far slicker crowd than the tin-pot Pierces. He worked for this smart, dangerous bastard called Simon Fellows for years. Fellows gave him his P45 when he realized he was too volatile, too much of a liability. Is this the kind of context you're after?"

My breath catches. The man who killed Masters was an associate of Simon Fellows.

A link?

"So you know Fellows?" I battle to keep the hunger out of my voice.

"No."

"'Cos from what I've heard about *him*, Pope was lucky to get his P45, and not a bullet."

"I wouldn't know. I've never met the man."

"You know that he's a dangerous bastard."

He gives me a look: *everyone's dangerous in my world, sweetheart.*

"Oh, so you don't actually *know* anything," I sneer, hoping I'll prick his fragile yet inflated ego. "It's just tittle-tattle, the old grapevine again." With a cheap laugh, I add, "God, you're as bad as Jacqui's WhatsApp group—all the school mums bitching about teachers and other parents."

It works. His need to please me, impress me, make it up to me, wins out.

"Frank knows him. Fellows is a bit of a mercenary these days—

happy to work where the money is, and, occasionally, the money's with Frank." He raises an eyebrow, smug, superior. "Although, from what *I* hear—and this is fact, not gossip, but don't even think about asking me how I know—your lot are fairly well acquainted with Simon Fellows."

"You think? He doesn't even have a caution to his name."

A laugh. "Well, you won't have when you're on *such* good terms with the police."

Somewhere in my brain there's a sense I should be reacting right now. Asking him what he's talking about. What the actual fuck he thinks he means.

Problem is, I know what he means and we both know what he's talking about. And it's explosive and game-changing, and worst of all, in the few seconds I've had to process it, it kind of makes sense.

Dad carries on spelling it out. "Yeah, the big players, Cat—they don't get that successful *and* keep their noses clean without being hand in glove with at least one senior police officer. And Fellows certainly used to be, although I don't think the officer is on the scene now . . ."

I stare at him hard, my face frozen, my nerves rioting. "And this is fact?"

"Like I said, Frank knows him." The shutter comes down. That's all I'm getting.

"I suppose a name, even which force, is out of the question?"

"On Finn's life, I don't know, and on Finn's life, I wouldn't tell you if I did. We're straying a bit too far from 'context' here, sweetheart. Let's get back to New York, eh?"

I can't conjure up New York. I can't anchor my attention to anything remotely solid. I look around the garden, taking in objects, real life; Finn's hula hoop, a watering can, the pair of leopard-print Crocs that Jacqui always gets defensive about. I can't connect to any of it. Even Aiden's face in my mind seems fuzzy and abstract.

Dad and me. *Criminals hand in glove with police officers.*

Are these officers my enemies or my tribe?

I take one last breath, then make a decision. Pick my side.

"Dad, I need you to do something for me." My voice shakes as a nervous, shivery energy courses through me. I feel cold for the first time in months. "And your instant reaction is going to be to say no, but it'll never be traced back to you, I swear . . ."

"What won't be?" he says, panicked, my nerves infecting him. "What are you on about? What do you want me to do?"

"I can't explain why and it's better if you don't know, but I need you to phone my incident room. I need you to ask to speak to the SIO heading up the investigation, *only* her—I'm pretty sure she'll still be there—and then I need you to tell her what you've just told me about Pope *and* Fellows. I'll rehearse it with you. I'll tell you exactly what you need to say."

His belly laugh carries across the garden. Jacqui looks out the window, wondering what's going on.

"You want *me* to make an anonymous call to the police? *Me*." He turns 180 with some difficulty, determined to face me head-on. "And why do you think I'd do that? Do you think I fancy having every other limb broken? And that's if I'm lucky."

I take a few seconds to answer. I need to be calm, practical, convincing, not a cat on hot bricks. "It won't happen, Dad. You can lay your hands on a burner phone in minutes and I promise, they'll never trace it. They won't even try. All you'd be doing is pointing us in a direction, and if that direction checks out, we can get all the evidence we need. Your call will be forgotten. Just one of those mystery lucky breaks that happens more than you'd think. No big deal."

"And why would I screw over Simon Fellows? I've got no beef with him."

"Because *I'm* asking you to. And because you owe me."

I shift forward, reducing the space between us, praying that the person he's seeing in front of him is his daughter, not a cop. The little girl who sat on his shoulders and bounced on his knee. The little girl who believed him when he told her, *"There isn't anything I wouldn't do for you, sweetheart."*

"So is this going to be an annual thing?" he says eventually, when staring each other out becomes unbearable. "Last year—Frank. This year—*this*. I mean, ballpark figure, Cat—just how regularly am I going to have to compromise myself for you?"

"I think it's called parenting, Dad. You've got a lot of it to make up for."

He looks away, wounded. I'm not proud of myself, not by a long shot, but then you use the weapons you have, and my biggest weapon against Dad—my hydrogen bomb, if you like—is emotional blackmail. The reminder that he failed me. He failed all of us.

He turns back. "I want one thing in return, though. And it's not a big thing. It's me asking you to be a grown-up."

"Oh yeah, how?"

"You meet Ange. You play nice."

I guess I'd have met her eventually. Jacqui's birthday. Finn's communion. Maybe the mortal hell that is Christmas lunch. I'm not a total truant when it comes to my family. I turn up for the big stuff, the main calendar events. The occasions where my absence would cause more drama than my presence.

And so I nod. "Yeah sure, why not?"

Dad takes this in for a minute, nods back.

"Sounds as though we've got ourselves a deal then."

26

"This is big, Kinsella. It's a monster. A meteor."

It's not the lateness of the call, it's the break with tradition; Steele's somber tones echoing down the line just after midnight, when the standard run of play is that Steele calls Parnell, then Parnell calls me. As a rule, Kate Steele isn't a fan of having to repeat herself. But tonight maybe she needs to. Tonight, maybe the more she repeats it, the more she can try to make peace with it. Although I could tell her right now that hasn't worked at all for me.

It's a quick call, just a précis. Not the ins and outs—not that I need them.

"We've had a tip-off," she tells me. "Anonymous, but credible."

An allegation about a senior officer.

A link—a bit tenuous but still noteworthy—between Simon Fellows and the Masters case.

I "wow" and "uh-huh" and "oh my God" in all the right places, and then she tells me she's taking the morning to do some digging—it's best she does it on her own, keep things tight for now and *strictly* between us three. She should be back by lunchtime, she says. She'll give us the nod when she's ready. Until then, we're to act normally.

I say, "Sure, whatever that means."

She apologizes for the late hour. I tell her it's fine, we're still up anyway. We're watching one of Aiden's beloved B-movies—some utter nonsense about a vampire motorcycle that runs on blood, not gasoline.

She says that after what she's heard this evening, a vampire motorcycle doesn't sound so unbelievable.

Her last words are, "Get some sleep."

And I do. I get some. A short smudge of uninterrupted blackness, somewhere between the hours of three and five a.m.

When I wake, the birds are singing, Aiden's snoring softly, and the lady upstairs is stomping around already. And yet the world still feels off-kilter. Not changed, but charged somehow. There's a current in the air that warns I'd be better off staying in bed.

Aiden waking brings normality. A mutual analysis of last night's sleep—him "like a baby," me "ah, you know, off and on"—followed by a smooch that teeters on the edge of frisky, and then my morning cuppa, delivered promptly just before he leaves. Usually I fall back to sleep at this juncture, waking twenty minutes later, cursing myself stupid as I guzzle down cold tea. This morning, though, I stare at the ceiling, blocking out Dad and Fellows and the weight of what I've unleashed, with fantasies of me and Aiden in a chic Manhattan loft space. Mum choosing curtain fabric. Parnell now a lieutenant with the NYPD.

27

Steele gives us the fast version again, but there's definitely something brewing, something magical up her sleeve. She's got a look of supreme smugness about her. An air of knowing the gold medal is well and truly in the bag.

"Seriously though, Kate? Can we really give this much credence to an anonymous phone call?"

I nod in time with Parnell, mirroring his body language to make sure I'm coming across as suitably dubious.

"No, Lu, but we can give credence to this." She pushes a document across her desk. "'Cos I promise you, I didn't sit on the phone to HMP Frankland for over an hour this morning for the good of my health. No, I wanted *this*." She taps the document triumphantly with a ruby red nail. "Jacob Pope's visitor list in the six weeks leading up to his attack on Masters—his mum, his sister, and his solicitor." A sneer on the last word.

"Why was his solicitor visiting?" I manage a good sneer myself. "Don't tell me the bastard was appealing his murder conviction? He was edging toward 'loss of control' when I met him. Crime of passion, he reckoned—his girlfriend 'disrespected him.'"

Steele looks down, sorting through a pile of other printouts. "The more important question is, why was a solicitor who has nothing do with criminal law visiting him?"

She holds up a screenshot, a LinkedIn profile:

Nicholas Balfour. Funds Lawyer, PRF Asset Management.

Parnell and I shrug in sync.

Steele's eyes flash. "Aha, well, Benny-boy isn't the only one who can navigate his way around social media. Turns out Nicholas

Balfour is married to one Maria Vestergaard." She waits to see if the penny drops.

"Vestergaard?" I jump in, the penny clattering to the floor. "Simon Fellows' other half is a Vestergaard."

"Top marks, Kinsella. The very same. Erik Vestergaard is Nicholas Balfour's father-in-law. Balfour visited Jacob Pope in Frankland on 15th April 2017, ten days before Pope killed Masters." Another printout. "Pope then made three calls to the same pay-as-you-go number over the following ten days, including the afternoon before the attack. We know the number belongs to Balfour, as Pope had to register him as his legal representative so that the prison didn't record their conversations." She sits back, job done. "So the floor's yours, m'dears. Theories?"

There can only be one. It's been ricocheting around my skull all night, and that was before this latest windfall.

I take a breath, straighten myself up. "OK, Simon Fellows killed Holly Kemp because she either had something on him or a business arrangement had gone sour. But because of Serena Bailey's ID, Christopher Masters becomes the assumed killer. Masters then does what plenty of manipulators do and refuses to confirm or deny, which is obviously a boon for Fellows, but doesn't come with any guarantee. So when Fellows hears that his old chum, Jacob Pope, is playing house with Masters in Frankland—and let's be honest, someone like Fellows would know the roll call of most prisons better than the governor—he decides to send in his honorary son-in-law, Nicholas Balfour, under the guise of Pope's brief, to get a message to him—*kill Masters and you and me are friends again*. It's a total win-win. Having Fellows onside is valuable to Pope in prison—Fellows' name would hold a lot of sway when it comes to protection, if nothing else. And from Fellows' point of view, the threat of Masters coming clean and the spotlight coming back on Holly is gone."

"Timing though," says Parnell, scratching his head—not quite

Stan Laurel, but not too far off. "Masters was in Belmarsh for nearly a year after he was first sentenced, and being local, Simon Fellows would definitely have had his tentacles in there. Why not have Masters killed then?"

"Too hot?" suggests Steele. "Masters was still big news."

"There's that," I agree. "But also something like this, there's only a certain type of person who's going to agree to do it. You can't pick just anyone and say, 'Hey, fancy adding a long stretch to your sentence?' You need a lifer. Pope got twenty-eight years for killing his girlfriend. He'd have been over sixty before he was even considered for parole. In those circumstances, I think you'd probably stop thinking about getting out and start focusing on how to make the next twenty-eight years as comfy as possible. Being on Simon Fellows' Christmas card list is one way."

"Explain Arlo Rollins then," says Steele. "He wasn't a lifer. No history of violence at all, in fact, until he stuck a knife in Jacob Pope." She slides another document across, that ruby red fingernail primed to turn this case on its head again. "They found a phone hidden in Rollins' cell—he won't say how he got it, who gave it to him. He won't say anything, basically, but there were three calls to the same number Pope called last year—Nicholas Balfour's number. The last call was Saturday afternoon. Rollins attacked Pope the next morning."

"Got to be old-fashioned intimidation," says Parnell, sickened. "Kill or be killed—either you or someone you love on the outside."

"Fellows wasn't hanging around," I say. "Friday afternoon, we interview him and he realizes he's finally been linked to Holly Kemp, even if we've got no proof to throw at him yet. Within two days, Jacob Pope is dead, silenced. He's not taking any chances."

Parnell sighs. "We still don't have any *proof* to throw at him. We've got a load of circumstantial. We've got our victim actually naming him as someone she was scared of. And now, we've got this. But it all amounts to zero. Nothing tangible."

Steele bites. "Hey, not so gloomy, Eeyore! We've got probable cause to turn Nicholas Balfour's house upside down to find that phone, and if I can convince a judge that Balfour spends a lot of time at his daddy-in-law's place, we might get a warrant for Fellows' house too. And *that* could be a gold mine."

"And when do we turn Oliver Cairns' life upside down?"

Silence curls around the room.

I can't say I take too much pleasure in firing a direct shot at a dying man. But it's obvious, surely? *Oliver Cairns hand in glove with Simon Fellows.*

Predictably, Parnell's cautious. "Cat, it was an anonymous call. We can't be sure . . ."

"Why?" I butt in. "What the caller said about Pope was bang on. So why would they be lying about a senior officer working with Fellows?"

"Settling an old score, maybe? Either with Fellows or the Met. And as for Cairns, the caller didn't name the officer, so be careful is all I'm saying."

"Oh, come on!" It's a direct plea to Steele. I take her silence as permission to keep going. "Cairns consistently steered Dyer away from all lines of inquiry that didn't point to Masters, not to mention ordering her to get rid of Masters' bank records. He can say he was trying to protect the case, but he wasn't; he was derailing it. He played on Dyer's loyalty and the fact he knew she was needed at home and therefore desperate to get Holly's case solved too." An afterthought. "*And* the caller implied the officer's no longer 'on the scene'—well, that fits."

"But he has money. His ex-wife was a multi-multimillionaire. Accepting bribes from an organized crime boss? There's greed, then there's lunacy."

"He and his wife were already on the skids. Maybe he thought it was time to build his own nest egg." I bite my lip, knowing

I might regret my next statement. "Or maybe it wasn't about money. Maybe Fellows had something on him?"

There's a grayish undertone to Steele's skin; she knows there's a logic to what I'm saying, at least. "So come on then." She leans forward, chin in hand. "You've obviously thought about this. Talk me through what you think *could* have happened."

The urge to holler "I don't fucking know" almost overwhelms me. I feel like I don't know anything anymore. Who I am. What I want. Where to live. What my police oath is even good for.

Is there any fucking point to it all?

"As I said before, Holly was involved with Simon Fellows." My calm voice sticks two fingers up to the clamor in my head. "*Something* happens and he kills her. Worried she'll be linked to him somehow, he steals her laptop, dumps her phone, does everything he can, but he's still vulnerable. He doesn't want Holly's complicated life looked into, which he knows it will be—and it would have been if she hadn't been given the 'poor Masters' victim' tag straight off. So he calls his friendly police officer, Oliver Cairns. Says he has to help him. Holly's friends, in the meantime, have told Dyer's team—which is effectively Cairns' team—that she was headed to Clapham that day and CCTV confirms it. And by that time they have Masters under arrest and he's maintaining he was at Valentine Street all day on the 23rd—probably because he doesn't want to admit that he's just a sad old fuck who regularly drives three hundred miles north to pine over his ex-wife."

Parnell's warming up a little. "I can buy that, actually. People assuming he committed another murder—that's fine, no skin off his nose, he's going away for life anyway. But having people think he's a sad loser, hung up on his ex—there's shame in that."

"Exactly." I turn back to Steele. "So Cairns realizes they've struck lucky. If they can quickly shoehorn Holly into the Masters' case, he can pull the strings and there'll be no need to start looking into every corner of Holly's life. She's just another Bryony, another Ling, another Stephanie—she answered the wrong advert, pure bad luck. But to make it work, they need a witness. And a bloody good one. A 'model citizen.' Someone who'll be believed even if Masters starts backtracking." I gather a breath before saying the name that's become as familiar as my own. "Serena Bailey. She's always been our stumbling block. No matter how flimsy certain aspects of her story seem, we still can't ignore the fact that she gave a spot-on description of Holly, far more detailed than anything released in the media. And the only way she could have known these details is if she genuinely *did* see Holly—which I've never been less convinced about—or if they were fed to her by the real killer, or someone close to the real killer." I shrug. "Oliver Cairns."

I expect resistance, rebuttal. To be laughed at, or even kicked straight out the door. Because even to my ears, it sounds fantastical. The overelaborate product of a three a.m. restless mind.

But it fits.

With everything we know, with everything we think we know, it makes perfect, abhorrent sense.

"A model witness is perfect," says Steele, tapping her cheek. "It's strong enough to get conclusions drawn, but probably not strong enough to get to court—Olly would have known that." And with that one admission, Steele's in. She's open. She's up for the discussion. "But why would Bailey agree to be involved?"

"Money," Parnell says, in a way that suggests it's obvious. "She was pregnant, broke, struggling on a low wage."

"It seems like such an extreme resort, though," I argue. "I mean, I'd be wanting a hell of a lot of money—and I'm talking life-changing money—if I was going to tell such a whopper of a lie in a murder investigation. And her bank records didn't show anything sexy, and even if it was paid in cash, it doesn't seem to have changed her life particularly. She still has the same career.

Her flat is small—homely, I guess—but the estate's pretty grim. I suppose we need to check if it's rented or owned—if it's owned, that could be interesting." Something occurs to me. "When I interviewed her on Saturday, she did say something that . . ." I pause, trying to quickly work out if I'm reading too much into it.

Steele's patience is paper-thin. "Kinsella!"

"She said she was in a 'much better place' by the time she met Robbie. I took it to mean emotionally, but she could have meant financially, I guess . . ." I shake my head. "Oh, I dunno, boss. I'm just not feeling money. People who do things purely for money tend to crack easier—and that woman is uncrackable, I'm telling you. It doesn't matter how you catch her out, she just comes back to the same point—she saw Holly and that's the end of it. It's like she's personally invested in us believing that. But in here"—I tap my chest—"not in her wallet."

Steele takes it all in, looking right, then left, finding no easy answers. "OK, well, we need to find a link between Serena Bailey and either Fellows or Cairns. Until we do that, all of this is just hunches and guesswork."

"Do we believe her about the prostitution?" asks Parnell, looking at me. "I know you're not convinced it was her reason for being in Clapham that day, but she said she started in her early twenties and that must be fifteen years ago, give or take? Simon Fellows might be a bit more respectable now with his restaurant investments and what-have-you, but back then, brothels, clip joints, strip clubs—they were his bread and butter."

"And Cairns ran Vice in the midnoughties," says Steele, eyes flicking between us.

"But Serena doesn't have a record," I remind her.

"We don't know that for sure." Parnell offers a note of warning. "The guidelines have changed now, of course, but it wasn't so long ago a senior officer could delete a record off the system after a certain period of time, depending on the offense. If Cairns had done that for Serena, back in the day, maybe February 2012 was when he called in that favor."

"So you're on board now?" I give him a weak smile, even though there's nothing remotely heartening about it.

"I don't know, kiddo. God knows, I don't want to be." He turns away from me, looking at Steele with dead-eyed focus. "I'll tell you something though, Kate. The more I think about it, the more convinced I am that Fellows was tipped off that we were onto him—that we were coming to interview him last Friday. That merry dance all over London, for a start—that was him buying time, I'd put the house on it. And remember, Cat, he was cool as anything when we questioned him—dates, times, places reeled off, he didn't even need to think about them. And don't get me started on all that stuff with his granddaughter and the baking— that was a blatant piss-take. *You came for guns, you got cookies.* No question about it, he was ready for us, he was winding us up."

Steele's head snaps up. "Well, if he was tipped off, it wasn't Olly." One small chink of hope and we're back to *Olly.* "I did *try* to call him. I wanted to sound him out, see what he thought about Fellows' name being linked. But his phone was switched off—I told Cat all this yesterday."

I nod. "Did you leave him a message mentioning Fellows?"

"No. His phone wasn't even connecting to voicemail. It was one of those automated messages—*'This phone is switched off. Please try again later.'* And I did keep trying, but he was in the hospital for hours." She sticks her thumbnail in her mouth, biting down hard on £50 worth of manicure. "I did speak to Dyer though."

"When?" asks Parnell.

"Straight after I tried Olly. You pair had just left to go to Fellows' place. I thought she was worth sounding out too."

"And what did you say to her?"

"Exactly what I'd planned to say to Olly—what do you think about Simon Fellows' name cropping up in connection with

Holly Kemp?" She lets out two short breaths. I'm all but holding mine. "She cut me off, pretty sharp, said she was going to have to call me back. Next thing—well, an hour or so later, she turns up here, practically wearing a badge that says, I'M TESS. I'M HERE TO HELP. Remember, she was here when you got back?"

She was.

Steering us away from Fellows.

Berating us about our lack of progress on Masters.

Then accosting me in the ladies', telling me, "You have to learn to play the game, Cat. There's an art to keeping all sides happy."

All sides. The goodies and the baddies.

The cops and the crooks?

"Have we got this wrong?" I look from Steele to Parnell, waiting to be shot down, but from the looks on their faces, we're all on the precipice of the same volcanic conclusion. "Because it makes as much sense as Cairns—more, probably. I hate to say it, but a woman with two young kids and a seriously ill husband would be a lot more susceptible to bribery than a man with a millionaire wife."

"And she worked Organized Crime," adds Parnell. "I was there around the same time, remember." He pauses, tapping the desk. "You know, I did think it was odd in that meeting when she said she'd always been more project-focused in OC. I thought she was just being shy about her achievements—I mean, she brought down some big names while she was there. Terence Slevin. Lee Whittlesea."

Steele laughs, zero humor. "Oh, don't you worry, Tess Dyer isn't afraid to blow her own trumpet. If she was playing it humble, it was for a good reason."

Realization smacks Parnell. "Slevin and Whittlesea were big rivals of Simon Fellows. In fact, rumor has it, Fellows made a killing taking over Whittlesea's turf."

"And the officer not being 'on the scene' anymore *sort of* plays out." Steele's nodding, waiting for me to finish. "Dyer was in Lyon for four years. Great for the CV, maybe not so great for any arrangement she had with Fellows."

"There's something else too. It's nothing conclusive, and to be honest, I hadn't put too much weight on it, but *now* . . ." Steele's tapping her fingers together nervously. "You see, it's a small world, the Met. Dyer's old DCI on Organized Crime—Tom Halley—worked for me years ago, and I called him yesterday, just to ask about Fellows, get his thoughts, his recollections, you know? Anyway, I mentioned about Fellows being gay and it was the first Tom had heard of it. I know Dyer said only a select few were in the know, a couple of the old boys, but still—that sort of information on that sort of person, a big player like Fellows—that's not the kind of intel you keep from your boss. Tom was going to ask around, call me back when he found out who Dyer got the information from. He hasn't called yet."

"You think it's not true?" asks Parnell, but I know the conclusion Steele's reaching. "What about Vestergaard, the granddaughter?"

"Oh no, I think it's true, Lu. But what if she didn't get the information from anyone. What if she already knew?"

"Forget her never having direct dealings with Fellows." I deliver the punch line. "She's one of the 'select few.'"

Steele nods, biting her lip. "I think we have this all arseways. Olly is covering for Dyer—he's taking the fall for the bank records because he's loyal and he's dying, and what can they do to him, realistically? Whereas his precious Tess—she's on the up, she's got a shit ton to lose, not to mention being a single mum to two boys who've already lost their dad." She puts her head in her hands. "God, I really hope he's doing it because he believes she made a one-off mistake, not because he knows she's corrupt."

"So we need a link between Dyer and Serena Bailey." I sigh. "Where do we even fucking start?"

Parnell's voice is serious. "We need to hand this over to the DPS now, Kate—*that's* what we need to do. We've been sitting on clear wrongdoing for nearly twenty-four hours. It's not right, I don't like it."

"Hand *what* over, though, Lu? It's the same as linking Fellows to Holly. It's all circumstantial at the moment. We can see the picture forming, but without proof, we're not ready to move." She runs a hand down her face. "Anyway—and this is *super* confidential— but the DPS itself is about to be investigated over claims of serious corruption and malpractice. It's going to hit the news next week."

"Oh, brilliant, it gets better." Parnell does a slow handclap. "Anti-Corruption being investigated over corruption. Makes you proud to wear the badge, eh?"

"Well, maybe now you understand why I'm not keen to hand it over until we've got something watertight."

I try an idea out for size. "We pull Serena Bailey's phone records, see who she's been calling this week. If we're right about all this, there's going to have been some frantic conversations."

"If Dyer's corrupt, she'll be communicating with Fellows, Bailey, whoever, on an unregistered phone," Parnell says. "She's not stupid."

"Then we get her in here," I say. "Feign some meeting or other, and then me and Serena's phone records take ourselves off to the Tavern, and I call every single number Serena's called since this case became live again. If we're stupidly lucky, she'll answer. But even if you just hear a phone ringing, we've pretty much got her."

Steele's shaking her head. "Chances are she'd have it on silent. And anyway, it's not enough. I want something concrete."

And I want my mum choosing curtains for my Manhattan loft apartment.

"Would she even come here?" Parnell wonders. "I mean, she must realize by now that we know about Masters' bank records. Either Cairns—or Bailey, if we're right about this—are bound to have told her."

"So what next?" I snap, impatient. "Short of waterboarding her, what can we do?"

"We set a trap." Steele has that air again, that air of knowing she's got the winning ticket. "I call Dyer and tell her we're preparing to make an arrest and I wanted to give her the heads-up—feels like the right thing to do, professional courtesy and all that . . ."

Parnell and I look suitably *"huh?"*

"I say we've got proof Serena Bailey lied about seeing Holly on Valentine Street and we're going to charge her with Perverting the Course of Justice. But more than that, we suspect Holly was blackmailing Serena . . ." She's totally making this up as she goes along, but one thing's for sure: by the time she's dialing Dyer's number, it'll sound as solid a theory as evolution. "Maybe they met through the escorting scene, Holly threatened to report Serena to her school, her career goes up in flames so Serena had to stop her . . ."

"Boss, this is batshit." And I love it. And I know exactly where it's heading.

"It *is* batshit," she says. "And if Dyer had time to stop and think, she'd reach the very same conclusion. But we don't give her time. We tell her Serena's arrest is imminent, a few hours off. And then we wait for her reaction. My guess is she'll go straight to Serena's school to tip her off, and to warn her to stick to her story."

"She'll call her, surely?" says Parnell.

"She'll probably try," I say. "But the chances of Serena answering are slim. School teachers don't wander around looking at their phones all day."

"Exactly. In all likelihood, Dyer will have to make a move. She'll have to try to get to Serena before we do. And when she does, you pair will be right on top of her. See how she explains that one."

"Boss, it might sound like I'm sucking up, but you really are a fucking genius."

Sometimes there really isn't anything else to say.

28

"We're cut from the same cloth, Cat, you and me."

I think about Dyer's words as we sit in Parnell's car, a little way down from the entrance to St. Joseph of Cupertino's. It's a good time for thinking. The school is calm, as schools usually are outside the hullabaloo of break times, and Parnell's quite happy to quietly gnaw his nails as he scrolls through his phone mindlessly.

Cut from the same cloth.

What did I do to make Dyer think this? Could she see it in me? Smell it off me? Can one fraud always recognize another?

And am I any better, when you shine the spotlight on me? Without Dad's protection last year, without him offering himself up in place of me, I could have found myself in a similar position, hand in glove with Frank Hickey. A little info on a rival here. A little stack of fifties in my pocket there. I'd have torn the money up, of course, given it to a beggar, used it to clean my toilet, but I still might have done what was needed to protect myself. I still might have set fire to the last remaining scraps of my integrity if it meant Steele and Parnell and Aiden never finding out the truth about me.

See, everyone has a price. I truly believe that.

Except the price isn't always money. It's just a damn sight simpler when it is.

"How long now?" I ask, just to make a noise, to shoo away the demons.

"Nearly an hour, I'd say. Enough time for me to play three games of Sudoku and read the entire Sky Sports website."

"Some lookout you are."

"You've got better eyesight than me."

We've been parked here for nearly an hour, waiting, hoping, that Steele's trap will pay off and either Serena Bailey will bolt out or Tessa Dyer will storm in. So far, nothing. The whole street's dead, in fact. Just the odd passing pensioner and a few council workers, slowly cooking in the heat while painting zigzags on the road.

"Anyway, you're quiet," says Parnell, lifting his head from his phone. "What are you thinking about?"

"Oh, you know, life, love, and everything."

"What's the 'everything'?"

"Nothing groundbreaking. When did I last get that mole checked? What am I going to have for dinner?" I point to one of the council workers, an Adonis in a hi-vis, a Levi's advert–on-legs. "Whether he's got a girlfriend?"

How the people you love most are the easiest to lie to.

Parnell frowns. "You get that bloody mole checked, do you hear me?" He's fiddling with his phone again, ready to dish out Dr. P advice. "Ah, here it is—you've got to remember the ABCDs. Asymmetry. Border. Color. Diameter." He looks up, squinting over at the workmen. "And as for Mr. Stud-Muffin over there, he'd be nothing but trouble, mark my words. Stick with Aiden. Take the easy road."

Easy. Imagine.

"Do you know what else I was thinking about?" This part is true, in a roundabout way. "Dyer offered me a job. Well, at least I think she did."

He twists to face me, wide-eyed but with no judgment. "And would you have taken it?"

"I think I need a change of some sort. Whether that would have been it, who knows?" I shrug it off, wishing I hadn't brought it up. "Oh, I dunno, Sarge. Maybe I should get a new hairstyle, or start wearing red lipstick, or buy a flashy new suit. That's an easier way to make yourself feel like a different person, isn't it?"

"Why do you want to be a different person?" He looks genuinely perplexed. "For Christ's sake, just don't start *acting* like a different person, that's all I'm going to say. You, Steele, Renée, and maybe Seth on a good day—but mainly you, kiddo—are the people who keep me sane in this job. If you're going to go all shoulder-pads-and-attitude on me, I might as well bloody retire."

And what if I moved to New York, I want to say, *would you be sad? Would you visit? Would you send me funny emails every day, ranting about Arsenal's defense and the stinky filling in Flowers' sandwiches?*

But I don't say anything. A car's slowing down, indicating, then hovering, the driver readying to park in a ridiculously tight space. I can't see their face, although I could lay bets right now that Dyer wouldn't be seen dead in a 2013 Nissan Micra. But you never know, so we keep watching, only turning away once the driver reveals herself to be a small Asian lady with a limp.

Silence again. Parnell goes back to his phone and I go back to appreciating Mr. Stud-Muffin. It's not long, though, only maybe a minute or two, before a heavy weight descends again.

"Dyer's sons," I say. "I wonder what'll happen to them if this plays out the way we think?"

Parnell feels it like a personal ache. "Eleven and thirteen, she said. God, I remember my eldest two at that age. It's not easy. Lots of physical and emotional changes going on." He shakes his head out the window. "There's never only one victim, is there?"

"Only one we're paid to worry about." Brutal, but that's the way it is.

"She'll go to prison, Cat, which is absolutely where she belongs ... but Jesus, they lost their dad too. I could lie down on the asphalt and cry for them, I really could."

Losing both parents at a young age, just like Holly Kemp. She may have been a car crash of an adult, but I could cry for that child too.

"When did he die?" I ask. "Was it a while ago? 'Cos she's still wearing her wedding ring. It's kinda sad . . ."

Only a fraud can feel sympathy for another fraud.

"Yeah, a good while back. Not that long after the Roommate case, I think." He picks up his phone again. "I'll tell you exactly when, shall I?"

I roll my eyes. "You and your bloody phone! You're worse than a teenager. You don't have to check every single fact on the internet, you know? I was only making conversation."

He's in a Google trance already. "Now . . . where is it? Where is it? . . . I know the Met did a fundraising thing to buy a few defibrillators. It was quite a big deal, made *London Tonight*. Ah—here we go . . ."

One of the life-saving machines has pride of place just outside Elgin Library, near Gordonstoun, where Paul Dyer went to school. Paul died at the Royal Papworth Hospital on 19th October 2012, just a week before his fortieth birthday.

I let out a low whistle. "Wow, that last bit is a kick in the guts! Goes to show, doesn't matter how fancy your education is, how privileged you are, death doesn't discriminate."

"Your health is your wealth," adds Parnell, always one for a natty phrase.

Suddenly, a loud wolf whistle. I glower over at the council-workers, then turn my ire on Parnell. "Fucking idiots! Are they still allowed to do that?" My hand's on the door catch. "Actually, I don't care if they are or they aren't, I'm going to say something. I'm in the mood for a fight."

Parnell's arm flies over. "*Wait!* Don't open that." His eyes are on the rearview mirror. "Jesus, Cat, she's here! Dyer's here. That must be who they were whistling at. Look—she's heading this way on the other side of the road."

I twist around and there she is, all grim-faced and purposeful, designer bag slung over her forearm, her silver-spun hair iridescent under the blazing afternoon sun. Striding toward the school gates, she looks less a police officer, more like a hacked-off mother who's been called out of a work meeting to come and pick up a sick child.

In another few seconds, she'll be level with the car.

"Turn to me, turn to me," Parnell's saying. "Just make sure she doesn't see your face. I don't think she'll recognize my car."

A distant male shout carries up the street. "Oi, wait up!"

I risk a glance back. Simon Fellows is locking his car. Tall, dark, and ominous. No cutesy kids and plates of cookies to soften the overall effect this time.

"T—hold on," he calls again.

Dyer pivots at the sound of her nickname.

"*T.*" He knows her well.

Which means I call checkmate, Tessa Dyer.

"Holy shit." I stare across at Parnell, my breath choppy and short. "What are they planning to do? What are *we* planning to do? Do we let them get inside? We're going to have to let them get inside if we want to get anything concrete."

Parnell watches them in the rearview mirror, knocking a knuckle against his clenched jaw. Dyer's walking back toward Fellows. There's a discussion. A heated one. Fellows gesticulating, Dyer shaking her head, jabbing a finger downward, as if ordering him to "Stay here." A few more seconds and she strides off again. Fellows doesn't follow, just thrusts his hands in his pockets and circles the pavement, head bent low. I turn my face again as Dyer draws level with us, then turn back to watch her strut past the main gates and up the path that leads to the side entrance.

She's either been here before or she's been told where to go.

Parnell picks up his phone, brings up Steele's number. "You go, Cat, follow her. I'm going to have to stay here and watch Fellows. We can't let a man like that—someone we know has access to firearms—take another step closer to a school. If it looks like he's heading in, I'll arrest him."

"On what grounds? We haven't seen a weapon." A shiver crackles through my core. "And Christ, he's as bad as they come, *allegedly*, but you don't think he'd start shooting in an infant school?"

"I think I don't want to take the chance. He's here for a reason and it won't be a good one." He looks back. "Go on, now. He's got his back to us. Go. Quickly."

I dart across the road, silently thanking myself for putting my hair up this morning. Even if Fellows does spin around, he probably won't recognize me at a distance without my wild Celtic thatch. I follow Dyer's path, past the main gates and up the side entrance, figuring she's had maybe a minute on me, then possibly two, when it takes forever for the school receptionist to buzz me in.

"My colleague, which way did she go?" I say, flashing my warrant card, peering all around. There are three corridors off reception and a set of stairs leading to the second floor.

"Look, what's going on?" she demands, arms folded, significantly less chirpy than last time. "We can't have this disruption. The mums are panicking. Phoebe Denton's mum said you arrested Miss Bailey at the school gates yesterday."

Then Phoebe Denton's mum was getting ahead of herself.

"My colleague?" I repeat, trying to smile, avoiding alarm.

She leans over the counter, pointing right. "Down there, Miss Bailey's classroom."

I fly down the long corridor, past lockers and posters and summer anoraks hanging on pegs. As I near the bottom, the stenciled mantra comes into focus once again.

MISS BAILEY YEAR 2. WORK HARD! BE KIND! HAVE FUN!
Tell lies.

I knock, then open the door. A sea of sweet faces turn to gawk at me, in among them a woman in denim dungarees who looks about twelve, but who must be in charge. "Miss Bailey?" I say.

"She's gone with the lady to show her our totem pole," announces one eager beaver. "Have you come to see it too?"

I make a face that suggests I have, then look at the child-woman for confirmation.

She points a finger at the ceiling. "Upstairs in the Nurture Room. Is everything OK?"

Another reassuring smile, and then I'm back in reception within seconds, frantically shushing the receptionist as she loudly apologizes for not seeing them when they came past. I kick off my shoes, not wanting to make a sound on the stone stairs, then take two at a time up the first flight, stopping dead on the landing at the sound of muffled voices up ahead.

As lightly as I can, I take another step, then another, until finally every word is clear.

Threat after threat, echoing beautifully off the cinder-block walls.

"*We don't have time for this, Serena. Trust me, you just need to come now. It's for your own safety.*"

A laugh thick with venom. "*Safety! I haven't felt safe since the day I met you. And as for 'trust you'—I seem to remember you saying that to me ten years ago. Worked out well, didn't it?*"

"*It worked out very well for a long time. It made my career and you got to keep yours. But we don't have time for reminiscing. They're coming for you. We have to go.*"

My phone is on silent but I need to record what's being said. I turn it up to full volume, praying that Parnell doesn't choose this moment to call me. Or worse still, bloody Jacqui, ranting about the cost of kids' football kits.

"*And then what's going to happen?*" Serena's crying now. "*I go on the run? Well, let them come. I don't care anymore. Whatever they do to me, it can't be as bad as this. And maybe it's time they found out who exactly they're employing. Protect and serve? Protect and serve yourself, that's all you ever do.*"

"*I've protected you. I'm protecting you now. And no one's going on the run, Serena. We just need to get you away for a few hours while we work this all out."* Dyer's voice gets lower. She must have stepped further into the room. I move up another stair, tailing her. *"Look, what they're suggesting is madness. They're just fishing. There's no way they can link you to Holly Kemp's murder, but we . . ."*

"Of course they can't fucking link me! I've never met the girl, never laid eyes on her."

Dyer's voice is calm as dawn; a mother soothing a tantruming child. *"Listen to me, Serena. We just need to know that you're going to stick to the story, and right now you're in a state and we don't trust you to do that. We need to get you away, that's all, quiet you down."*

"We? Who's we?"

"There's a friend of mine outside. Simon Fellows. You don't know him, but he has a vested interest in you too."

"No way am I going anywhere with you, or anyone else." Terror in her voice. A realization of just how quiet they intend to make her. *"I'm staying right here. And when they come, I'm telling them the truth."*

A pause, the sound of footsteps, then something being torn from the wall.

"Well then, I'm just going to have to show Simon this photo of Poppy, aren't I? Trust me—and you can really trust me on this one, Serena—if you think you didn't feel safe before, you'll never know a day's peace again unless you come with us now."

I've heard enough. We have enough.

I race up the last few stairs onto the landing, staring straight ahead into the open-plan "Nurture" space. Serena's facing me, open-mouthed. Dyer turns to see what can possibly have turned her so anemic, so quickly. Her eyes meet mine for one second, then dart behind.

She's thinking of making a run past me.

Part of me wills her to try it. It'd actually give me great pleasure to slam her to the floor or even watch her get to the bottom of the stairs, thinking she's got away, only to meet Parnell and the cavalry who surely—*surely*—must be here by now.

She doesn't try it, though. She doesn't do anything except shake her head and smile—regret, respect, and I could be wrong, but a little bit of relief, maybe?

"Game's over, ma'am," I say, my cuffs in one hand, my phone in the other. "Turns out you were wrong—we're not cut from the same cloth after all."

And it's there and then that I realize we really aren't, for two very simple reasons.

I'd never threaten a child.

I didn't get myself caught.

29

"She called herself a 'talent spotter.' Made me feel like she'd seen something in me, something special, when all she'd seen was my address and an easy target. She knew I was desperate and she milked that desperation for years to further her own career. Acting like we were friends, equals. Like I had a choice. But I never had a choice, not in any of it."

A tap has been turned on, and over a decade of bad decisions are spilling out of Serena Bailey, an oozing torrent of self-pity, spreading like an oil slick across the carpet of Interview Room Three.

"For the tape, Serena, can you confirm that the person you're referring to is Detective Chief Inspector Tessa Dyer?"

"Yes, but she wasn't chief inspector then. She was a sergeant. An ambitious one." Her face sours on the word "ambitious," as though it's the preserve of bullies and despots and comic-book supervillains.

I'm in the viewing room. Steele's sitting to the left of me, dour-faced and round-shouldered with exhaustion. Parnell's perching on the edge of the table, shaking his head almost constantly. I'd fought hard to interview Serena myself, arguing that I'd earned it, *deserved* it even, given I'd been calling out her bullshit longer and louder than anyone else. But it's for this precise reason that Steele put the kibosh on it. And she's right, I can see that. This isn't the time for pitted wits or the standard suspect-cop arm wrestle. What we need now is a chronicle—a detailed account of the events that led us all to this train wreck.

And "Fair and softly goes far," insisted Parnell, which means there's no better person for the job than the one currently sitting across from Serena: Renée Akwa—whose approach to interview-

ing suspects is similar to that of winding a baby: gentle, consistent, reassuring, and results-driven.

"I met her for the first time in a room exactly like this." Serena pulls at the skin on her neck, unburdening herself to a bottle
of water on the table. Renée's given up on trying to maintain eye
contact. It isn't necessary, anyway. All we need are her words. "It
wasn't even her who arrested me. She'd had nothing to do with the
raid. But obviously the guy who brought me in—I don't remember
his name—must have told her they had someone in custody from
the Stockmoor and she saw an opportunity."

"Is that where you grew up—the Stockmoor Estate?"

She shakes her head, looking off to the side. "No, although not
far from it. You were always warned about the Stockmoor, growing up. My mum was a bit more broad-minded, but some people
painted it as worse than Sodom and Gomorrah. It really wasn't. I
mean, there was crime, definitely—drugs, bad boys, all-night parties, everything they said, but where wasn't there? And there were
also hundreds, well, thousands, of people just getting on with their
lives. I flat-shared with two girls—Shelley, a nurse, and Katy, she
did something in marketing. Something better paid than me and
Shelley, anyway."

"Tell me about the raid." Renée's pen is poised over her notebook. "Can you remember the date?"

Barely a breath. "Fifteenth March, 2007. I'm hardly likely to forget
it, am I? I was working as an escort—teaching the alphabet by day,
giving blow jobs by night. See, I didn't lie about everything . . ." Her
eyes flick toward the camera in the top right-hand corner, confident
I'll be watching somewhere, picking the bones out of everything she
says. "I'd been doing it for a few years. It was only occasional, but it
was easy money and my mum couldn't always work—she'd caught
glandular fever when I was in my teens, wound up with *me*—so it
was nice to be able to help her out. And she had no clue what being
a teaching assistant paid, so she never questioned it. In her mind it

was a 'good job' and 'good jobs' pay well. If only that were the case, hey?"

"I hear you." Renée speaks for the entire lower ranks of the Metropolitan Police Force.

"I loved it at Riverdale, though. I felt respected, *included*, for the first time. I hadn't had the easiest upbringing. I'd had a hard time at secondary school, dropped out of college. Mrs. Gopal took a real punt on me. I'm sure she had better applicants for the job, but she liked the fact I'd set up an after-school club on the Stockmoor, said it showed initiative, empathy. She said they'd train me on the job, help me get the right qualifications, a career path. I loved it. Thing is, I also loved being able to pay the rent, and eat, and help my mum out now and again, and £13,000 a year doesn't go very far in London. That's why I kept up the escorting, the odd booking here and there."

"The raid?" reminds Renée, no way near as sharply as I would.

Serena pulls a tissue from her pocket, crumpling it in her hand, kneading it like a stress ball. "It wasn't a booking through my usual agency. I knew someone who knew someone; you know how it is, and they asked if I wanted to do this party. A big posh place in St. John's Wood. They were looking for ten, fifteen girls, £200 fee for the night, with the opportunity to earn extra by pushing drugs onto the punters. I wasn't a big drug-taker, but they weren't exactly alien to me, and as they were threatening to cut off my mum's gas unless she settled her bill, I said, sure, why not? I was given thirty wraps of coke and I got a tenner for every one I sold. With the fee and the drugs, I stood to make £500 easily. But if I really brought my A-game to the bedroom with these rich guys, I thought I'd get nearer £1,000, if I was lucky." She lets out a snide laugh. "Turned out to be the unluckiest night of my life. We'd been there an hour and I'd only shifted three wraps when all hell broke loose. Police all over the place. There were underage girls working there, you see." She looks directly at Renée for the first time, her voice cracking, her composure starting to fracture. "I had no idea, I swear. I was twenty-three and they all looked a similar age to me."

"But you got caught with the drugs?"

She dabs at her eyes, nodding. "The duty solicitor said I was looking at twelve to eighteen months, probably. Well, I knew there and then I'd never work in a school again, never qualify as a teacher. I kept thinking about Mrs. Gopal, all the faith she'd shown in me. And, God, my mum—she'd been so proud of me for getting the TA job and I didn't know how she'd cope, physically and emotionally, if I went away for a year. So I'm crying, saying all this to the detective who's interviewing me, when suddenly he says we should take a break. And that's the last I see of him—and the duty solicitor. A few hours later, I'm put in another room and *she* comes in, says she—"

Renée interrupts. "Again, Serena, can you confirm who 'she' is, please."

"Tessa Dyer. She says she's heard I'm in a tight spot and she's got a proposition for me. I've stopped crying by then, so I laugh—I actually laugh—and say, 'Any chance you're proposing we forget all about this?' and she says, 'Yes, that's exactly what I'm proposing.' She says I can walk out of the station—no charges, no record, no jail time, no having to give up the only job I've ever cared about— on one condition: I befriend a woman called Nicola Regan on the Stockmoor." She stops, taking a long glug of water from the bottle.

"Serena was Dyer's snout," mutters Steele, more to herself than anyone else.

Her snout. Her snitch. Her snake. Her grass. Dyer's "Covert Human Intelligence Source" to use the official tongue twister.

"I knew who she was straightaway: Sonny Gibbs' girlfriend. Biggest dealer on the estate. One of the biggest in North-West London, apparently, or certainly had plans to be. I'd actually gone to the same school as Nicola, although she was the year above me, so we knew each other to say hi to. Dyer said I had to get to know her—and Sonny—a lot better. She wanted every bit of information, big and small, about his activities on the estate."

"And just like that you became an informant? That must have been tough, Serena. Frightening."

Another swig of water. "It wasn't 'just like that.' It takes months to get anything, Dyer understood that. Making friends with Nicola was easy enough. We were more or less the same age, same sort of interests—I remembered she'd been a really good singer at school, so I asked if she fancied going to a couple of open mic nights and it went from there. It helped that we'd both *hated* Risley High—the school we went to—and on top of that, I think she was lonely, looking for a real friend. You don't have many friends when you're Sonny Gibbs' girlfriend. But it takes time to earn trust, you know—*proper* trust. The kind that gets you the sort of info Dyer was after. I don't think I actually told Dyer anything she couldn't have found out herself for nearly six months.

"But then, after a while, and *a lot* of effort—teaching all day, sitting around Nicola and Sonny's flat every night, being the 'sister she never had'—I got something. The location of a small cannabis shipment. And then that was it, for five long years. I found out more and more stuff—bigger stuff. And it went beyond Nicola and Sonny too. Being close with them meant I was friends with everyone. I heard a lot. Handed over a lot to Dyer. She made her career off me; she was Inspector Dyer in no time. My nerves were shot, completely wrecked, but at least I was still teaching, doing something with my life. I qualified in 2009 and Dyer moved to Murder the year after. I thought there'd be some letup then, but if anything, it got worse. It was like she couldn't bear to be out of the loop, even though it technically wasn't her job anymore."

"More like Simon Fellows couldn't afford to be out of the loop," I mutter.

"Were you paid for the information you provided?" asks Renée.

"No," she answers, vehemently. "She offered the first time. It was only £100, but I wouldn't take it. I always had it in the back of my mind that if Nicola or Sonny ever did find out, maybe the fact I hadn't been doing it for money would count for something."

It might have done. They might have killed her quickly. Left her in a state that was still recognizably human. Something for the embalmers to work with in the Chapel of Rest.

Renée closes her notebook, straightens her blouse, rests her elbows on the table: slow, fluid movements designed to make Serena relax as much as possible. "You said 'five long years' just now, Serena. This started in 2007, so can you tell me what happened in 2012?"

The answer holds little intrigue. It's becoming so, so obvious. And yet the air in the room feels charged with a potent energy, like the second before lightning strikes.

"Dyer called me on the Monday—the Monday after Christopher Masters was arrested. It was really early, six a.m. or something. She said she needed a favor—of course, she *always* needed a favor, but she sounded different this time. Weird. A bit panicked. She says she'll come to me as she knows I have to be at school in a few hours, but there was no way I was taking that risk, so she says she'll pay for a cab to our usual place if I come right now. An hour later, we're in our usual greasy spoon café off Borough High Street and she says she's got a proposition for me."

She leans forward, matching Renée's posture, elbows on the table, their heads little more than a foot apart. "Now by this time, I'm utterly fed up with life, living the pretense, having this black cloud hanging over me every day, so I say, 'I think one proposition from you is enough in a lifetime.' But she says, 'Trust me, you're going to want to hear this one.' So I listen. She won't go into any real detail, she says the less I know the better, but there's going to be an appeal for information on a missing woman called Holly Kemp in the *Standard* that evening, and she wants me to call the police and tell them that I saw her—Holly—walking down Valentine Street, going into Christopher Masters' house. She says she'll give me all the information I need to make it sound credible, information that isn't in the public domain yet. Obviously I'd heard of Masters, he'd been all over the news that weekend, so I ask her, '*Why? Why do you want me to say that? Why would I do that?*' She says I don't need to know why. All I need to know is that if I do this one thing then we're quits. That's the end of our arrangement."

"She'd release you as an informant?" Renée clarifies.

"Yeah. All the secrets, all the looking over my shoulder, dreading our meetings every two weeks, convinced I was being followed— all that stress, gone. All I had to do was make one statement to the police and then make sure I stuck to it, no matter what. And she was clear about that—she said if I wavered at all, *ever*, Sonny Gibbs would find out about me within minutes. I knew deep down I was exchanging one risk for another, but this seemed so much more straightforward. A chance at freedom. A chance to have a normal life."

She blots her eyes with the tissue again. I lean closer to the screen, checking she's not playing to the gallery, but sure enough there's tears—plenty of them.

"And I was pregnant. I hadn't told anyone except my mum, not even Mrs. Gopal. But I'd not long had my first scan, heard the heartbeat, saw her stretching and kicking; I couldn't believe how active she was. And that's what really brought it home—it was one thing risking my own safety by ratting on Sonny, but I was responsible for another life now, so I practically bit Dyer's hand off. I said, 'Tell me word for word what you want me to say and I'll say it.' And I did. And then I repeated it and repeated it, and I never asked why again. I didn't care why. I just cared that it was over, that I could leave the Southmoor, leave the whole area behind. Get me and the baby away from danger."

"Where did you go?" asks Renée.

"My friend Mandy said I could come and live with her in

Limehouse. She'd just kicked her boyfriend out and hated living on her own, so it worked for both of us. Seriously, I couldn't get there quick enough. I resigned from Riverdale the following week. Walked away from my job, my maternity benefits—madness, but there was no way I was being tied to that area a minute more than I had to be. Obviously, I couldn't just disappear overnight; I had a notice period, and anyway, I didn't want to raise suspicion. But when I told Nicola I was pregnant and that I was moving away to be with the baby's father—it'd been a one-night-stand thing, but I said he was an old friend and he wanted us to try and make a go of things—she said she understood. She'd been a single mum herself, she knew how hard it could be. Of course, we swore we'd stay in touch, and we did for a little while—I had to, for appearances' sake—but Nicola was so wrapped up in the Southmoor, in their world, that I knew once she realized I was off the scene for good, she'd lose interest. And she did. I was free." She flops back, heavily. "Until last week."

"When did Dyer get back in contact?"

"She turned up at the school last Tuesday morning. She'd obviously been keeping tabs on me over the years."

So while Parnell and I were standing in a field in Cambridgeshire, antsy and wet and listening to a local DC's opinions on highfalutin dog names, Dyer was already taking care of business.

Serena's rubbing her chest, the memory of seeing Dyer again as real as indigestion. "She said it hadn't been released yet, but it was pretty much confirmed that they'd found Holly Kemp's body and I'd almost certainly be reinterviewed. My legs nearly gave way. I hadn't thought about it in years, see. I know that sounds bad, but I'm good at compartmentalizing—I had to be, living with the pressure of being an informant—and I'd put it all behind me. I honestly felt like a different person, and then suddenly there she was, reminding me of my past, of my bad side, the worst thing I'd ever done." Her eyes are back on the water bottle. "She was calm, but I think that was for my benefit. She said all I needed to do was stick to the story, that I'd done well back then and I'd be even better this time around. I was even more of a 'perfect witness' now, apparently—a mum, a lovely, wholesome, experienced primary school teacher. *Unimpeachable*—that was the word she used. As long as I repeated everything with complete confidence, it would all be fine, she said. But it wasn't, was it? And it never will be."

Renée opens her mouth, but Serena looks up sharply, cutting her off.

"You see, people talk about atonement, about wiping the slate clean, moving on, all that. And it sounds great, of course it does, but it's rubbish. It's just dumb denial. Because once you make one bad decision in life—and I mean a *really* bad decision—you're never really free of it. It might be manageable for chunks of time, but it's never fine. It'll always come back to bite you."

Her words punch me in the solar plexus.

Me and Serena: telling lies to save our careers, then telling more lies to protect the people we love.

"Right, I've heard enough."

I stand up abruptly, then power over to the door before Serena Bailey can make one more pronouncement that confirms, once and for all, that I've got more in common with the criminals than the victims I represent.

30

Craving solitude, I detour to the bathroom, then the vending machine, then I snag a rare patch of shade at the back of the station, guzzling down a can of Fanta while checking messages on my phone. I have two. One from Aiden—a Statue of Liberty emoji that I don't have the headspace to deal with right now, followed by a request to pick up loo roll, which I will if I actually make it home tonight. The other message is from Dad:

> Dinner with me and Ange Friday night?? You choose where.
> Up to you whether you bring A xx

The invite winds me. After the events of the day, I'd kind of forgotten about keeping that side of the bargain, and I certainly didn't expect Dad to cash his chips in so quickly. I spend five minutes writing, then deleting, various excuses before shooting back a lily-livered response.

> Maybe, I'll let you know x

I go back inside, forgoing the lift and flying up the stairs to the fourth-floor corridor. By the time I reach the incident room, bursting through the door like a cowboy entering a saloon, Steele and Parnell are back. Parnell's on the phone.

"So yeah, Serena's sob story is all well and good," Steele is saying, sitting at my desk, applying my 99p hand cream. "It lands Dyer well and truly in the frame for a whole load of serious charges, but it doesn't answer the main question—did Simon Fellows kill Holly and did Dyer help cover it up?" Her face contorts in disgust. "And seriously, if Dyer gives one more 'no comment' to that question, I might be up for a serious charge myself."

"I still can't believe it," says Flowers, as dazed as I've ever heard him. "Definitely one to tell the grandkids, that's for sure."

Cooke puts on a baby voice, *"Mummy, why do other people's grandads read* The Gruffalo *to them, but I have to listen to Grandad Pete banging on about police misconduct?"*

We've moved several levels of hell beyond mere "misconduct" in the past few hours, but it's still a much-needed laugh to buoy up the glum troops.

I walk over to my desk; Steele doesn't budge. "Is Fellows' brief here?" I ask.

"Where'd you disappear to?" It's not a question, more a gripe, and she doesn't wait for the answer. "Yes, Ms. Bickford-Jones is in the building. Fresh off the Paris catwalk, by the looks of her."

"Oh yes?" Seth doesn't even try to play it cool. "Does she want a coffee? A tour of the station?"

"She wants to find herself a new client." Steele slopes back, not planning on vacating my chair any time soon. "Because we've already got decent circumstantial for conspiracy to murder Masters and Jacob Pope. Nicholas Balfour's house is being pulled apart as we speak, and Fellows isn't going to recognize that lovely Little Venice mews once the search teams have finished. Or his yard in Lewisham. Or basically anywhere he's set foot in over the past six years. Blake's really raided the piggy bank for this one."

I grunt, dissatisfied. "And our case for Holly?"

"We've got Dyer's and Fellows' phones—sporadic calls going back months, probably years, although we'll need Forensics to dig those out—but there was a flurry of calls between them last Tuesday, the same day Dyer turned up at Serena's school and then here. And they've been communicating every day since, including this morning—there's a call from Dyer to Fellows made immediately after I told her we were about to arrest Serena."

"So decent circumstantial again." I'm not exactly punching the air. "I doubt *Ms*. Bickford-Jones' blood pressure will be spiking over that, though."

"Hey, boss . . ." Swaines calls from behind his stockade of screens.

"Hold on a minute, Benny-boy." Steele keeps her focus on me. "Maybe, maybe not, but Emily's heading over to Spencer Shaw's now. Hopefully, with all this, he might be persuaded to actually name Fellows as Holly's 'big fish.'"

I grin. "So you're hoping Emily's big-eyed, 'help a girl out' thing will crack him?"

"Hey, needs must as the devil drives."

"God, not you as well with the bloody quotes—you're as bad as him."

Him—Parnell—slams his phone down, practically salivating. "That was Forensics. They're sending over all the deleted stuff shortly, but get a load of this, for a start—a text from Dyer to Fellows, last Tuesday, seven fifteen a.m. *Not official yet but HK remains found. Answer your fucking phone.*"

Steele's look says, *"Is that enough for you?"*

Swaines shouts over again. "Boss, can you come here, I might have something."

I wander over with Steele. There's a map of Cambridgeshire on Swaines' largest screen. It's zoomed in on an area just west of Cambridge itself.

"It's kind of tenuous," he says, backpedaling already; Swaines always gets ants in his pants when Steele's focus is on him. "It's just that I've been digging around, and Erik Vestergaard's son was at Cambridge University in 2012—Churchill College. It's one of the only colleges based outside the main city center. Anyway, look . . ." We peer closer. A flash of something knocks the breath from me, but Swaines scrolls down before my mind can compute. "Churchill College is only around ten miles from where Holly was found. Ten miles—that's not much, is it? And maybe if they were visiting Vestergaard's son fairly regularly, then Fellows might know the area . . . and maybe if, um . . ." He sighs, losing his courage. "Ah look, I said it was tenuous . . ."

"Go back," I say. Steele picks up on my urgency, casting me a worried look over the top of Swaines' head. "Scroll up, I mean—the view we were looking at before."

Swaines scrolls up.

And there it is. A name on a map. A bold red "H" in a circle.

The writing on the wall, perhaps?

I swing around to Parnell. "Sarge, get that article about Dyer's husband up on your phone again. The one about the defibrillator thing. What was the name of the hospital where he died?"

And no doubt spent a lot of time in over the years.

"The Royal Papworth Hospital," he says, joining us at Swaines' desk. *I knew it*. "It's the UK's leading heart hospital."

And barely more than a mile north of Holly Kemp's six-year resting place.

My eyes lock on Steele's. "We know Dyer's husband was seriously ill at the time. And what did Cairns say—she was always haring up and down the motorway, back and forth to the hospital." I land a finger on the Caxton site. "She'd virtually drive past here on her way from London to Papworth. Can you zoom in again, Ben?" The small country lanes get bigger as our hearts sink further. "Look—if she turns off the A1198, she's at that field within a minute. And don't you think it's weird she never mentioned knowing the area? Seriously, a supposed victim of one of the biggest cases of your career ends up dumped within a mile of where your husband died—that'd come up in conversation, right? That'd be something you'd mention. Unless you had good reason not to."

"Dyer dumped Holly's body?" Parnell voices what Steele and I can't bring ourselves to say. "I mean, it's circumstantial *again*, but it's a pretty strong conclusion."

"But why would she . . . ?" My brain fizzes, thoughts whiplash-
ing in ten different directions. "It's one thing cleaning up after Fellows in terms of derailing the investigation, but *this* . . . why?"

Steele's fist is pressed to her chin. "Well, Dyer's not going to be
in a rush to tell us, so let's see what Fellows has to say. We can use
this as leverage: tell us the full extent of Dyer's involvement and
you might—*might*—just get out of prison in time to have a few
years left on your free bus pass." The thought's a sickener, but if it
works . . . "First though, get on the phone to Papworth. We need
confirmation that Paul Dyer was in that hospital late February
2012. The exact range of dates, OK, because we don't know exactly
when Holly's body was dumped, although within a day or two of
her going missing is obviously a safe bet."

I get on the phone to Papworth.

An hour later, they call back. It's confirmed—the 7th of February
2012 until the 9th of March 2012.

Holly was never seen again after February 23rd.

Dyer's husband was in that hospital.

31

I know before we walk in, we're either going to get raw hostility or stage-managed charm. To be fair, they're the two approaches we've been weighing up ourselves, eventually settling on a blend of both with one additional ingredient whisked in: belittlement. We need to make it clear to Simon Fellows that while he might be a "big fish" in his own swamp, here, in this interview room, with its sludge-green walls and cruel fluorescent lights that show up every blackhead, every blood vessel, he's just a bottom-feeder like all the others. The dental work might be a cut above and his woodsy cologne, I'll admit, is an improvement on the usual bouquet of cigarettes and BO that we often find ourselves inhaling, but where it counts, he's no better. He's just another longtime native of the sewer.

Parnell starts the recording. Fellows smiles the whole way through.

"For the tape, it is Tuesday 17th July, 2018, and the time is 20:02. Present are DS Luigi Parnell, DC Cat Kinsella, Simon Fellows, and Lorna Bickford-Jones, Mr. Fellows' legal representative. In accordance with the Home Office Circular 50/1995, I am obliged to inform you that this interview is being remotely monitored and the custody record has been endorsed with the names of the officers monitoring. I also need to caution you that you do not have to say anything, but it may harm your defense if you do not mention when questioned something which you later rely on in court. Anything you do say may be given in evidence. Do you understand?"

Fellows nudges his brief. "It's just like on the TV, isn't it?"

"Eight o'clock-long day, huh?" I say, as casual as a colleague at the end of a hard shift. "Are you feeling OK, Simon? Did you get something to eat?"

"I got something, yeah. Couldn't tell you what it was though."

"Not exactly La Trompette," Parnell says with undisguised pleasure. "By the way, you didn't mention you kept an office there. We've got a search team over there right now."

"Have you?" He adjusts his cufflinks, eyes lowered. "Well, if they're stopping for a late supper—'cos I'd say searching's hungry work—I recommend the baked lobster tails and the tarte tatin for afters. Best in London." He looks up. "Of course, what I'd really recommend is saving yourselves the overtime bill. You'll find nothing."

"Ah well, that's our funeral," I say, giving a light shrug. "And maybe we'll find nothing at your house, your yard, at your mum's place, at Erik's son's flat in Cambridge, at Erik's daughter's house—in Kelsey's room . . ." I take no pleasure in the idea of a little girl's bedroom being ransacked, but it rattles him, so job done. "We'll have fun looking, though."

"What exactly is it you're looking for?" Fellows asks.

I laugh awkwardly. "God's honest truth, Simon—I don't really know. I'm pretty low on the payroll here, they don't tell me that much. I suppose the gun you used to kill Holly Kemp would be nice, but I doubt we're going to find that tucked away in a cupboard behind a load of board games and unwanted Christmas presents, are we? And anyway, without a bullet to match it to . . . you were careful, well done."

"Anything that connects you to Holly Kemp," Parnell takes over. "And Jacob Pope, of course, and Arlo Rollins—the men you ordered to clean up after you."

"Er, can we stick to Holly Kemp, please. My client won't be answering questions about any other charges at this time."

Parnell levels one slow blink at Bickford-Jones then carries on. "Understand something though, Mr. Fellows—and I'm sure you do, because your type always knows the law inside out, even if you don't respect it—we don't *need* a smoking gun, pardon the pun. Sure, it'd be handy, *very* handy, but after this afternoon's events, we've got more than enough circumstantial evidence to make a very strong case."

"Basically, the cherry on the cake would be nice," I add. "But our cake's fine without it. Lovely and rich. Completely satisfying."

Bickford-Jones gives me a blasé stare. "The ingredients of this cake, please?"

"Well, quite apart from the fact that your client categorically denied knowing Holly Kemp, despite one witness stating that she named him as a man she was scared of, and another witness implying that she was in some sort of business arrangement with him"—it's a stretch but not a lie, and Parnell would be all over it if he thought I was pushing my luck—"we now have numerous calls and texts—previously deleted texts—between your client and Tessa Dyer, where they discuss Holly Kemp."

"These texts," says Bickford-Jones. "Does my client make any reference to being involved in Holly Kemp's death?"

"Well, let's see, shall we?" I pull the relevant page from the file. "Tuesday 10th July, 7:15 a.m. Tessa Dyer to your client: *Not official yet but HK remains found. Answer your fucking phone.* Then Friday 13th July, 9:59 a.m. Tessa Dyer to your client again, and this would have been moments after DCI Kate Steele, our SIO, made a call to Dyer to ask for her thoughts on your client's name cropping up: *Get out of house, police on way over. HK mentioned you to an old flame. You'll have to be interviewed, can't contain that. Need to brief you tho. CALL ME.* And earlier today at 13:22—not long after DCI Steele indicated to Tessa Dyer that we'd be arresting Serena Bailey—this is your client to Tessa Dyer: *Got ur msg. Meet u there. We need to sort this one, couldn't give shit about ur conscience.* Forensics are still working on the phones, but I have more if you want me to go on?"

"Tell me, how did you plan to 'sort' Serena Bailey?" asks Parnell, all feigned curiosity. Fellows smirks, shaking his head. "For the tape, Mr. Fellows is smiling at the question."

"I don't hear any admission that my client murdered Holly Kemp," states Bickford-Jones, completely emotionless: a beautifully decorated brick wall.

"Yet. Like I say, there's more coming. But in any case, inference goes a very long way, as you well know." I turn to Fellows. "You see, the problem with £1,000-an-hour briefs, Simon—although, fair play to you, Ms. Bickford-Jones, I wouldn't turn it down—is that you're paying for legal advice, sure, but you're also paying for them to blow smoke up your arse. And that really doesn't help you."

"And helping me is your main concern, is it?" It might be wishful thinking, but I think I detect a shift in his tone, a tiny hairline fracture to that imposing self-confidence. "Look, if I'm so banged to rights, why haven't you charged me yet?"

"Oh, we will be charging you, don't you worry about that. We're still gathering evidence, but all we're doing is strengthening an already strong case." I move in closer. "*This* is about giving you the opportunity to explain what happened. To make things slightly better for yourself."

"You're all heart, darling. And why would you do that?"

"Because we want everyone involved to be punished. And because right now, Tessa Dyer is down that corridor saying 'no comment' to every single question. Why is that? She knows better than anyone that there's no route out of here, but she's buying time, Simon. Trying to work out the best angle to take when she *does* decide to speak. Figuring out how to pin everything on you."

"Fuck that."

"Maybe we should take a break," says Bickford-Jones. It falls on deaf ears.

Parnell cranks up the voltage. "Did Dyer dump Holly's body? We strongly suspect she did, and it'd be far better for you to confirm that, rather than us having to find out for ourselves." God only knows how we'd do that, but Fellows doesn't know this. "Listen, *I'm* not going to blow smoke up your arse and claim there's going to be a whole lot of leniency. We *are* going to put you away for the murder of Holly Kemp, and quite probably for conspiracy to murder Christopher Masters and Jacob Pope, but trust me when I tell you, cooperation at this stage is always a good thing. There are things we could request in exchange for your statement. A prison near to home maybe, so visits are easier for your family. Or a prison miles away from London, if you're worried about safety. There are ways we can help, but you need to help yourself."

"If you keep denying everything," I say, piling on, "then you and you alone are going to go down for the lion's share of this."

Fellows looks at Bickford-Jones, then me, then Parnell. The same dead-eyed stare turning each of us to stone, before his snarl cracks wide and he bursts out laughing. "Fuck, this really is a mess, isn't it?"

"Then sort it out, tell us what happened. Take back a bit of control before Dyer gets in first." I slap every card down on the table. "Look, those texts, Simon, all they point to so far is Dyer being a corrupt officer—tidying things up, tipping you off. But we believe she played a far more active role in the aftermath of Holly Kemp's death."

"Aftermath?" His laugh dissolves with one last bark. "She didn't tidy up after me, I tidied up after her. This was all her. Dyer killed Holly. I barely knew the girl."

I feel the energy from the viewing room like a sonic pulse. Steele on her feet, the team scattering around her, chairs scraping back, expletives issued, orders bellowed. I look at Parnell to take the lead, praying Bickford-Jones doesn't insist on a break this time.

Fellows doesn't give her the chance.

"She'd been blackmailing Tess for over a year—well, Paul at first, but then after he got sick again, he had to come clean to Tess and she took care of it."

"Paul?" I pick up on the familiarity.

"I was a Gordonstoun boy too, so was my kid brother. He and Paul were best mates. Paul was like a part of the family growing up. Then Glenn, my kid brother, died in his early twenties—a horse-riding accident—and I kind of took Paul under my wing for a while. But then everything changed once his career took off. He was a real highflier in the Ministry of Justice—in the Press Office of all places, which meant he had to be whiter than white. He felt compromised knowing me, started distancing himself. I understood; it was no real skin off my nose. His wife, though, she saw the benefit of staying in touch with me."

"Can you be more explicit, for the tape, please," asks Parnell. "Can you state the nature of your relationship with Detective Chief Inspector Tessa Dyer?"

"We've been working together for years."

"Years? How many? Two, ten, twenty?"

Fellows blows out his cheeks. "Fifteen years, give or take. I didn't mark it on the calendar. You know, it wasn't just about money to begin with. She also wanted information on rival gangs. How do you think she managed to take down Slevin and the Whittlesea crew so easily? Pure luck? Fuck that, that was all me. But it was a total win-win—she got to look good and I got rid of the competition without breaking a sweat."

"And February 2012?" I say, shifting into fifth gear. While context is great, we can worry about that later. Right now, we can't risk him changing his mind, clamping his mouth shut. "How did you become involved with Holly Kemp?"

"Tess asked to meet; this was right at the end of 2011. She didn't go into lots of detail—I think she was worried I'd use it against her and Paul, which I was a bit offended by, if you must know." Rich, coming from the man currently selling her down the river on a punctured rubber dinghy. "Paul had had 'a lapse of judgment' is all she'd say, and now this woman, this girl, was blackmailing him. Threatening to expose things, *serious* things, to his employers. I mean, the Ministry of Justice—a government body setting the rules for the rest of us, and Paul, one of their main mouthpieces? He'd be finished and he knew it. Tess said he'd been paying her off for over six months, but when he'd missed a few payments because he was in the hospital—it had to be in person, in cash, you see—she'd shown no mercy at all. Paul had cracked and told Tess, and now it was her problem."

"And where did you come in?"

"Tess had met up with her, paid her, tried to reason with her. Offered her lump sums if she backed off once and for all. But she just turned the screw again, upped the payments. She knew she had a senior police officer on the ropes now, so why not?"

So Dyer was the "big fish," not Fellows.

"She knew Holly Kemp was never going to leave them alone, and with Paul ill, not working, and the medical bills . . . well, she asked me if I'd put the frighteners on her, warn her off. And for old times' sake—for Paul, mainly—I said OK. So I paid her a visit, told her to take a lump sum, quit while she was ahead. But *still*, she keeps going." He shakes his head, marveling at her stupidity. "So Tess says to pay her another visit. This time I let myself into her flat. I'm waiting on her sofa when she gets home. She bolts, but I have her around the neck before she gets to the front door. I tell her this is the last time I'll ask nicely and to stop trying to play with the big boys because she won't win. She just smiles. Fucking smiles! But then people often try to front it out when they're shitting themselves."

Linda Denby's words: *"She just didn't seem to have any sense of danger, none whatsoever. . . . classic PTSD . . ."*

"I thought it was job done," Fellows goes on. "I couldn't believe it a few weeks later when Tess says she's had the usual call—Holly wants her money." Another shake of the head. "You almost had to respect the girl. Naive as a fucking newborn, but brave."

"Did you threaten her again?" asks Parnell.

"No, that was it. I saw Tess for our usual business, but she didn't mention Holly Kemp and neither did I. Why would I bother if Tess seemed happy to drop it? Trust me, I've got more important things to be doing than terrorizing people who've essentially done nothing to me. I mean, I felt bad for Paul, *and* Tess, but it wasn't really my problem."

"So what happened? When did it become your problem?"

He folds his arms, stretching his legs out under the table. "End of February, I get a call out of the blue. Tess says Holly's at her house, she's injured—badly, she thinks—and she needs my help. I'm thinking they've fought, some sort of accident . . ."

"Where was this?" I ask. "Where was Dyer's house?"

"Can't remember the exact street, but it was a big old place set back from the road, about halfway between Clapham Common and Stockwell. They'd been renting it for a while. Tess always wanted to live near whatever station she was working at—*very* dedicated, our Tessa—so renting suited."

"Where were her kids?" asks Parnell. "Don't tell me they witnessed this?"

"Don't know where they were, but not at home." He shrugs. "Anyway, I get there and the girl's not great, but she's not *that* bad. She's lying in the kitchen, kind of groggy, half-conscious, and there's a nasty cut above her eye, but I wouldn't have said she was badly injured. I'd have been tempted to clean her up, let her go. Maybe now she's learned her lesson, right? And it's not like she can go running to the police, is it? But Tess says there's no way she's letting her go." A sharp laugh. "Turns out I underestimated our Tessa. It was no bloody accident, it'd been a trap. She had it planned all along. Genius, really."

"Had what planned out?"

"Killing Holly. Tess had lured her to Clapham—made up some bull about a business proposition, said they should be working with each other, not against each other. She said she could give her names of people to target—high-ranking Met officers, barristers, social workers—and Holly, bless her greedy heart, had fallen for it."

"CCTV has Holly leaving Clapham Common Tube and heading south before we lose her," I point out. "That's the opposite way to Stockwell."

"Tess had given her a false address. Their place was just off the main road—she knew Holly'd get picked up on CCTV heading that way, so she'd given her one of the quiet streets off the Common. She was waiting for her there, picked her up, drove her back to the house. Holly didn't even question it, she said. She was seeing pound signs, not red flags. Rookie mistake."

"Wasn't this all a bit high-risk?" says Parnell, forehead creased. "Obviously, on a logical level, I get why she wanted Holly out of the picture, but doing this on her own doorstep?"

"But *her* doorstep was also the Roommate's doorstep," I say, looking at Fellows for confirmation. He doesn't say anything, just gives me a snarl of appreciation. "Young women were going missing from Clapham—what harm in throwing another one in, eh? I mean, Dyer knew Holly would show up on CCTV at the Tube station—it was perfect." I shake my head, trying to wrap my mind around all of it. "God, she must have been praying they'd never find the Roommate; it would have been a lot easier for her. Still, she doesn't let Masters' arrest rain on her parade, does she? She just states that his silence is proof of guilt, then she pays a visit to her old chum, Serena Bailey, and bang, Holly enters the serial killer–victim hall of fame. And that means there's no real need to look into the murkier corners of her life."

Genius, really.

Fellows gives a polite clap. "You know, Tess said you were one to watch. Ten out of ten, darling."

"Oh, I think I'm more of a nine, Simon, because there's one bit I don't get. If she planned all this herself, if she'd gone as far as to actually attack Holly, why not finish the job? Why get you involved? Surely the fewer people involved, the better?"

"In an ideal world, yeah. But she realized once Holly was there that she couldn't do it on her own, so she subdued her then called me. And once I'm there, she says that if I step up, if I help her, then she's all mine from now on. She'll never say no to me again."

"Meaning?" asks Parnell. "Again, we need you to be really clear, Mr. Fellows. What was Tessa Dyer asking you to do? And what do you mean 'never say no' to you again?"

"She wanted me to kill Holly Kemp. And in return, she'd give me *any* information I wanted in the future. *Any*. See, up until this point, she was still trying to kid herself that she had some scruples, that there were certain lines she wouldn't cross."

"Such as?" I ask, completely rapt, vaguely nauseous.

"I'd always wanted to hear more about what I call 'twitchy' coppers—coppers who aren't bent yet, but who could possibly be manipulated into playing for our side. Coppers in debt, coppers with expensive tastes, gambling habits, three ex-wives, that sort of thing. Tess had always held back before, said it was a step too far, that she wasn't prepared to set up a colleague like that. But when you're desperate, your conscience goes out the window. It was a good move for me." He shifts in the chair, sitting forward a little. "See, we'd always had a slightly odd relationship up until that point. It wasn't the usual setup, where the likes of me has the likes of you by the balls as soon as you accept my money. The fact I'd known Paul from way back complicated things. Made me a bit soft, I suppose—'cos I don't let many people say no to me, I can assure you of that, especially when I'm funding their fancy holidays. But now, *this*—this gave me the upper hand at long last. If I helped her with this, I owned her, and the best thing was, it was all her idea. She was handing herself to me on a plate."

"So you killed a young woman to get access to vulnerable police officers. Quite the guy, aren't you, Simon?"

Utter disdain. "Didn't you hear me? I didn't kill anyone. I said I'd help her—I'd get a gun within the hour, I'd stay with her, help with the body, we'd get it sorted. But I also said that for this new arrangement to work—for me to really trust her to keep her side of the bargain—she had to be equally culpable. She had to pull the trigger."

"You're saying Tessa Dyer shot Holly Kemp."

"One hundred percent."

"When exactly?"

"Early hours of the next morning. See, the house was set back from the road, but it was still too risky going outside until it was properly late, so we waited. It was bloody ridiculous, Tess taking work calls while the girl was half-conscious in the kitchen, me standing watch." He ruffles his black hair; it looks oily, not lustrous, under the white-hot light of the interview room. "It was gone midnight before it felt safe enough to move her to the boot of the car."

"Whose car?"

"Tess's."

I've got to ask, although I dread the answer. "Was Holly conscious? Did she know what was happening?"

"Yeah, and I was surprised at how strong she was, actually. She'd been subdued in the house—like I said, kind of groggy. But as soon as we picked her up, she started hitting out, swearing—saying sorry, can you believe? So Tess gagged her, tied her hands and feet. She knew then. She knew this was it. It wasn't just another scare."

My stomach churns. "She knew she was going to die."

"Suppose so. She definitely saw the gun; I made sure of that. She quieted down then—guns tend to have that effect. Anyway, it must have been two, three a.m. when we got there. She was dead within minutes of us pulling up."

"Pulling up where?" Parnell asks, his voice thick with tiredness and disbelief.

"The place near Papworth. The field."

This one will haunt me. It's got night sweats written all over it. I mean, you'd have to be a saint not to think Holly Kemp deserved *some* kind of comeuppance. But *this*. This eighty-mile, two-hour reckoning. Her life not so much flashing before her as dragging, squirming. Every stupid, greedy decision she ever made, pored over and profoundly regretted in the boot of Dyer's car.

"So why there?" I ask, desperate to get out of my own head.

"We were actually heading for Epping Forest, but we hadn't even got over Tower Bridge before Tess gets a call from the hospital. Paul had taken a bad turn. I don't think they were giving the last rites or anything, but it was serious—she was panicking. I said we'll be in Epping Forest in less than an hour, we *need* to get this done, but she says no, she's heading straight for the hospital. She'd never forgive herself if anything happened and she wasn't there. Then she asks me to take the car once we've got to Papworth and sort things." He brings his hands together on the table. "Well, I saw red. I half-wondered if she was making it up, if she'd staged the call to get out of doing the deed herself, so I said no fucking way. I said we can head for the hospital if that's what you want, but we're going to find somewhere on the way to finish this thing. You're going to do what you said you'd do, or you can count me out. I said I'd get a taxi back to London and leave her at the hospital with a girl tied up in the boot. I didn't give a shit. She knew I meant it."

"But why that field?" I ask, drilling down. "It wasn't the most secluded place."

"'Round there, at that hour, everywhere's secluded. We'd hardly passed a car for miles. And we were running out of options. We were nearly at the hospital and Tess just kept stalling and stalling. Finally, I say, *fuck this*, and I order her to turn off the main drag, into the lanes. We drive for a few minutes and then I spot this track running alongside a field—a pretty overrun field. Seemed like no one had bothered with it in months, maybe years. I don't know, I'm no farmer. But I say to Tess, this is as good as it's going to get—*do it*. So she pulls over. I get the girl out, put her in the ditch, and Tess shoots her. Paul being ill probably helped, in some ways. It meant she didn't have time to think about it. She just wanted to be with him. She was worried about him dying, not that bitch." Bickford-Jones bristles. "Anyway, the ditch is deep. I reckon she'll be fine there for a few days. We cover her with whatever we can find—twigs, branches, leaves—but I tell Tess we need to buy some logs, go back the next night and cover her up properly. But then something kicks off with the Roommate case the next day. There's no way Tess can get away. I end up taking care of it."

"Could you tell us where you disposed of the gun please, Mr. Fellows?" Parnell maintains a professional air that I suddenly feel wholly incapable of.

Fellows leans in, shoulders squared. "You know, I did my degree in math and statistics. It might have been thirty years ago, but some things stick, don't they? And there was this quote from a scholar called Pierre-Simon Laplace. He said, *The most important questions of life are indeed, for the most part, really only problems of probability.* And I've always lived my life by that mantra. I always knew there was a faint probability this day would come. That I'd need more than my word to make sure Tess Dyer got her just deserts too."

"Your point?" says Parnell.

"Who said I disposed of the gun?"

32

By a strange quirk of fate, and most cases are littered with them, the gun used to kill Holly Kemp—a Russian 8mm Baikal—turns up on the Southmoor Estate, ex-home of Serena Bailey and current home of Simon Fellows' most trusted hoarder—an eighty-one-year-old live wire called Abraham Craddock, whose name belongs in a Dickens novel, not at the top of a charge sheet next to "Illegal Possession of a Firearm."

If Fellows is to be believed, and depressingly, we do, Dyer's DNA will be all over it. And so begins the wait for Forensics. Unsurprisingly, Blake hasn't just raided the piggy bank for this one; he's gone through his pockets, rummaged down the back of the sofa, swept a hand under every bed, and as a result we should have results within twenty-four hours. It's fair to say that when it's one of our own, we protect hard but we punish harder, and Blake's main priority, in fact his only priority, is to ensure that the Met's good name isn't tarnished further by accusations of a sluggish response.

Of course, DNA will only prove that Dyer handled the gun, and any first-year law student could put forward the theory that she merely held it for Fellows as he carried Holly to the ditch or bent to tie his shoelaces. Her fingerprint on the trigger would be marginally more helpful, although again, compelling but not conclusive. And in any case, usable fingerprints lifted from firearms tend to be the preserve of flashy, suspend-belief TV shows.

The exception, not the norm.

It therefore comes as a relief—and a shock, if I'm honest—when, after what I'd imagine was an exceptionally dark night of the soul, Dyer agrees to tell us everything in exchange for fifteen minutes face-to-face with her sons, Ewan and Max. A noble act, she clearly thinks, judging by the pious expression she's maintained for the past two hours, as we've painstakingly checked, then double-checked, every part of Fellows' statement against hers.

In summary: they tally. Once we're happy we've got what we need, we let silence fall over the room, giving her the space to fill it with anything else she'd like to hang herself with.

"Thanks for letting me see the boys," she says after a moment. "I know you didn't have to. They deserved to hear it from me, though, not some tabloid journalist."

Steele's leaning against the wall; she has been the whole time. As if sitting down with Tess Dyer is too civil a gesture for her to stomach.

"You lured a young woman to your house, Tess. You attacked her and you made plans to kill her in the same room where you pack your boys' lunchboxes, so spare us the Mama Bear routine, hey?" Every word laced with disgust. "Where were the boys that night? Packed off to a sleepover so you had free rein to end someone's life?"

"At my mum's. They often stay at her place during the week—so do I sometimes, just so I can sleep under the same roof as them."

It doesn't need saying that she won't be doing that again for a very long time. She bows her head, picking up her vending machine coffee, sipping it then wincing.

"You'd better develop a taste for bad coffee," I say. "They might claim prison's like a holiday camp these days, but I don't think Ethiopian blend is high on the menu."

"It's never a holiday camp for one of us, is it?"

Underneath the bravado, she's petrified and she should be. For most ex–police officers in prison, it's a case of surviving one minute to the next: zoning out the threats, turning a blind eye when your food's been spat in for the fiftieth time, rolling your eyes and requesting a J-cloth when someone's smeared shit on your cell walls.

If I could put the horror of Holly Kemp's final hours out of my mind for one single second, I might almost feel sorry for her.

"You'll get protection," says Steele, unmoved. "There's always the Vulnerable Prisoners' Wing."

Dyer makes a harsh scraping sound. "Half an hour out of the cell every day? That's not protection, that's isolation. Big difference. But thanks for the words of comfort, Kate."

"You think you deserve comfort?"

"I think you don't know a thing about me, so who are you to judge?"

"You're a corrupt officer and a killer. That's all I need to know."

"A killer." Remarkably, her tone suggests she's never seen it that way. So how has she been framing herself all these years? An avenging angel? A vigilante? "You know, I'd never been violent before that night, not ever. I'd never had a fight at school, never smacked the boys. Paul loved boxing, but I wouldn't have it on in the house. I always said violence was no way to settle anything. But then you meet someone like Holly Kemp and you realize sometimes violence *is* the only way, and that violence is *in* you. It's in any of us if we're pushed far enough." She stops, lost to herself for a moment. "I just hated her *so* much, you see. The complete disregard she had for *my* family. Her fucking greed. I hated her that much I honestly thought I could kill her with my bare hands, no problem. I mean, she was tiny. I had eight inches, probably thirty pounds, on her. But when it came to it, I couldn't do it—not on my own, I mean. See, I'd hit her and she'd fallen back, and just the sound of her head smacking on the floor . . . I'd actually puked in the sink. That's when I knew I had to call Simon."

I can't stop myself. "So the sound of the trigger wasn't so bad, no?"

"I'm not going to lie, it was easier. And I was so frantic about Paul by that point, I think I disassociated from it."

A scornful sniff from Steele. "Oh, here we go. Disassociation, that old defense."

"I'm not trying to defend myself, Kate. I'm trying to explain. Holly Kemp was bleeding us dry—£2,000 a month in the end— and she had to be stopped. I'd tried reasoning with her, begging her, I'd set Simon on her. I'd even threatened her myself. I said I could plant something on someone she loved any time I liked, but nothing worked. She was relentless. I'd even offered her a lump sum the week before—£10,000. She just laughed and said she'd spent more on a holiday to Dubai. That was what I was up against. *That* was what she was like."

"Shall I tell you what she was like?" I thumb through my file, finally landing on Holly's Social Services record. "A happy, bright, well-adjusted child, by all accounts, until her dad took a corner too fast and his motorbike collided with a lorry when she was nine. Twelve months later, her mum, who didn't touch drugs before the accident, dies from a heroin overdose—oh, and Holly found her, there's the kicker." I look up, expecting to see some flicker of emotion, some sign of humanity. All I get is indifference. "Then the only other family she has, an aunt, declines to take her in because—and the social worker made a note of this beauty—she felt it would be 'too much of a hardship for her own children to have to share a bedroom.' So that means Holly's shoved around various care homes and foster homes until she's sixteen, followed by two years in a hostel." I hold up another document. "Her medical records show evidence of several severe beatings between the ages of eleven and sixteen."

"She probably asked for them."

There's no point in arguing with her, she's too far gone. Holly was understandably cast as the villain six years ago and her legend will have been growing in stature ever since.

"Can I tell you what Paul was like now?" she asks, every word laced with indignation.

I look over at Steele, who shrugs. "Sure, why not?"

"A lot of people say about their partners, 'Oh, he's not perfect, but he's mine,' but Paul *was* perfect. He was the kindest, funniest, most down-to-earth, compassionate person you could meet. Everyone loved him—*everyone*. Old ladies, young babies, all the boys' friends, the bloody postman, you name it. I was always in his shadow, in that sense. Wherever I went, it was always, 'Where's Paul?' 'How's Paul?' 'Tell Paul I was asking after him.' And even when he was at his lowest, he'd still try to cheer everyone else up. He never complained once about being ill, and God knows he had every right to because it was so unfair. He had everything to live for, but his heart was failing him and there was nothing he could do. And then just when you think he's had enough bad luck for one lifetime, he runs into that parasite, Holly Kemp." Her chin lifts, eyes challenging mine. "Well, I might not have been able to fix his heart, but I could fix that problem for him."

"Did Paul know what you'd done?" I ask, wondering—unfairly, I admit, and without any medical knowledge whatsoever—if the shock of Dyer's "fix" could have hastened his demise.

"He didn't *know* anything, but I'd say he suspected something. The woman who'd been blackmailing us, murdered by the very person I'd been hunting? There's coincidence and there's convenience. Paul was a smart guy, he knew the difference. He never said anything, though."

Steele says, "So not quite the saint then? He wasn't too concerned about brushing a coincidence like that under the carpet."

A flare of anger. "He was too concerned with the fact he was dying, Kate. He knew by then—*we* knew—that the end wasn't too far off. He'd had infections before, but this one: subacute infective endocarditis—God, the lingo trips off my tongue even now—had weakened him so much. We didn't think it would happen so soon, though—he died in the October. I thought we'd have another birthday, Christmas, maybe one more holiday." She looks at me, then Steele. "I suppose you think that's karma."

"We're very sorry about your husband, Tess." Steele's voice is flat but genuine.

Dyer nods, staring at a spot on the table. "You know, I wasn't even angry when he told me what had happened with *her*, how he'd gone back to her hotel room." Her eyes fill but she blinks away the tears. "I was hurt, I suppose. Shocked, but not angry. He'd had some bad news from his consultant that day, you see. They'd told him he had to stop playing sport. Basically, he had to stop doing anything beyond gentle exercise. It knocked him for six. It wasn't just that he loved sport, it was that another part of him was being stripped away by his illness. The night *she* approached him in that bar, he was drunk and feeling like he needed to prove something to himself. That he still had it. That he was still a virile man. The bloody idiot." Even this is said with affection, as if his only crime was forgetting to fill the car up or put the washing on. "It was bullshit macho thinking, I know. But I got it. I understood. One moment of weakness in sixteen years and God, was he paying for it. You couldn't not feel sorry for him."

"When was this?" I ask.

"When did he meet her, or when did I find out?"

"Both."

"Twenty eleven. He'd met her early in the year—February, maybe March? He'd been paying her off for months by the time I found out. That was definitely early September—I know because he was in the hospital again. Ewan had just started school and was telling everyone on the ward about his first day." The image nearly topples me. "He told me that night—he had to. He'd missed a payment and she was threatening all sorts. That's when I took over. He didn't need the stress."

"What did she have on him that was so bad?"

"That was worth killing for?" adds Steele.

"The photos, the sex stuff, that was bad enough—S&M stuff, *dark* S&M . . ." She shudders, not wanting to go any further. "I know for a fact he wasn't into that sort of thing, but whatever she'd given him, he was out of it. He didn't know what he was doing and he didn't remember any of it. Nothing. My guess is she slipped him Rohypnol, maybe GHB. With all the medication he was taking, it's pure luck she didn't kill him."

Her rage is still raw, even six years later.

"But what was worse was that she told him afterward—when she was demanding money, laying out the rules—that she was a prostitute. She had a web page and she'd brought it up on his phone while he was comatose and taken photos—proof he'd been looking at her page, I suppose. Then she'd sent texts from his phone to her number, and taken photos of those too—more proof." She takes a deep breath. "The drugs were the worst bit though, the cocaine. Paul had never taken drugs in his life—he hardly would with his heart issues—but there were a few photos where you could see residue around his nose, wraps of coke in the background, rolled-up notes. I honestly don't believe he took any; it was staged. But it's the appearance, isn't it? He was a Chief Press Officer for the Ministry of Justice. The tabloids would have had a field day. He'd have been sacked, shamed, held up as a hypocrite and a deviant in front of everyone who loved him. There was no way I was risking the boys seeing their father like that. That wasn't going to be their lasting memory of him." That proud tilt of her chin again. "And it wasn't. Paul's last six months were peaceful, at least, because of me, because of what I did. But more importantly, he died with our boys still believing he was the best man in the world. Preserving that memory for them was all that mattered."

"God, you really don't regret anything," I say, appalled but kind of fascinated by her absolute belief that she did the right thing.

"Oh, I do, Cat. I might not have shed any tears over that two-bit con woman, but I regret dragging Olly into all this, asking him to lie for me. It wasn't fair." She slopes forward, hands tucked between her knees. "Mainly though, I regret ever asking Simon to go anywhere near Holly Kemp. He had me over a barrel then, you see—before that, it had been more or less an equal partnership, both of us getting what we want most of the time, both of us saying no to the other very occasionally, if the price felt too high. Worse than that, though, Holly had me over a barrel once she clapped eyes on Simon. She could link *me*, a senior police officer, to *him*, a serious criminal. I couldn't believe I'd made such a stupid mistake, but then I'd underestimated her. I honestly didn't think she'd do her homework on him, but she did, and then she turned around and threatened me with it. Threatened to finish my career too."

"So you were protecting yourself, not Paul's memory, when you killed her?"

"No," she jumps straight in, setting the record straight—her own warped record, anyway. "No, I was protecting my sons. They were going to lose their father soon enough. They couldn't lose me too.

"And to be quite honest with you, Cat, some people really do deserve to die."

33

One week later

I've visited worse hospitals. I've stayed in worse hotel rooms, to be perfectly frank. Even the name itself, The Earl Shilton, calls to mind Egyptian cotton bedsheets; pristine, fluffy bathrobes; and extensive room-service options—and this medical mecca has all three. You can even request a pedicure, although I don't want to dwell too much on Oliver Cairns' feet.

"Are you going to use these?" I call from the en suite, aka My Dream Bathroom, complete with enormous heated towel rail and an overhead shower fitting the size of Wales. "Seriously, I'm not joking, this is top-brand stuff."

Cairns rasps, "Knock yourself out," and Steele's in faster than a freight train.

"Bugger off," I say, laughing, quickly scooping the spoils into my bag. "You can afford to buy the proper stuff. I'm still at the pay-grade where I have to steal from hospital bathrooms."

"Dear God, Katie, love, are you trying to finish me off altogether . . . ?"

Cairns' voice pulls us back into the room. He's sitting up in bed, a hollow-cheeked stick man, his skin the same color as the plump white pillows that are keeping him upright. On his bony lap there's a carrier bag. He's not enamored with the contents.

"Christ, death can't come quick enough if this is all I've got to look forward to. Have you never heard of crisps or chocolate biscuits?" He holds a packet up to the light, squinting over the rim of his glasses. "What in God's name is a hemp seed, anyway?"

"They're high in iron," Steele says.

"And low on flavor." Cairns tosses them back in the bag, throwing me a wink in the process. "Would you be a love, Cat, and pass me those Jaffa Cakes? 'Twas far from hemp seeds I was raised, and it'll be far from hemp seeds that I die."

For a man supposedly dying, Oliver Cairns is on mighty form this morning. Cracking jokes, demanding biscuits, waxing lyrical about the thickness of the curtains.

"Hands down, that's the worst thing about most hospitals: they scrimp on the curtains. You'd think it'd be the food, or the boredom, or well, the bloody sickness everywhere you turn, but it isn't. It's the fact the sunlight's streaming in before you've even got to the end of your bedtime prayers." He points toward the window. "Now those, they're those blackout yokes. You'd swear it was the dead of night at half nine in the morning. They're worth the cost alone, I'm telling you."

I don't want to ask what the cost is, but I *really* want to ask what the cost is. Steele saves me from my inherent nosiness.

"Bedtime prayers, eh?" She sits down on the leather sofa, throwing her arm along the top, brochure-ready. "So you've found God again?"

"Never lost him, Katie, love. You don't have to go to mass every Sunday to have a hotline to the big fella. And trust me, there's nothing like facing death to make you hedge your bets."

She casts him a stern look. "Can we dial down the death talk, please? You're getting your pain managed, Olly, and about time too. But you'll be back home in no time."

"And to what?" he says, without a shred of self-pity. "Sure, I'm better off in here. I've company. The mattress is a damn sight better than the one I have at home. And I get to eat . . ." He turns slowly, very slowly, picking a fancy embossed menu off the nightstand. "Cajun-spiced chicken with corn and pumpkin hash, instead of something-on-toast every night. Only benefit of being at home is I can have a smoke without a nurse giving out shite."

Another joke cracked to stave off the inevitable. To make sure the elephant in the room keeps its back to us, at least.

Fearing we'll still be here at Christmas if someone doesn't bring it up, I bite the bullet.

"Did you ever suspect she was involved, sir? With any of it?"

If the question catches him off guard, he doesn't show it. Years of interviewing, I guess. The ability to change tack, field curveballs, deal with anything that's thrown your way, doesn't dwindle just because your cells are mutating the wrong way.

"Not for one second. I'd have sooner believed that Elvis himself had come back and killed that girl before I'd have believed Tess Dyer could be capable of . . ." He breaks off. I look at Steele, wondering if we should drop it, but then he rallies again. "I still can't believe it. I mean, I *do* believe it, o'course. I've no choice, she admitted it. But still . . ." He stares down at his hands. "I don't know why she didn't come to me back then. I'd have given her the money to pay that girl off once and for all, she should have known that. She knew she was more than a colleague to me. I'm Ewan's godfather, for crying out loud. She was always more like a . . ." He halts again.

"A daughter?" I say. It seems the logical answer.

He hesitates, his face pinched. "A few weeks ago, I'd have said yes. But the fact I can hardly say her name, hardly bring myself to think about her . . . you know, I'm almost glad I'm ill, because it gives me the excuse to stay well away, to never have to look at her again." Another pause. "And I think the parent-child bond is a bit hardier than that. Unconditional, they say."

And suffocating, in my experience. A bond so tight it makes a move across the other side of the Atlantic seem almost unimaginable, because of the base and desperate need to be near to the one person who knows you better than you know yourself.

The bad you.

The good and bad you.

The real you, not just the edited highlights.

"She said she regretted getting you involved, for what it's worth," I say.

"And she said you had a bright future, for what that's worth."

Steele jumps in. "I think in her own warped way, you meant a lot to her, Olly."

Cairns sees right through us. "Ah, you don't have to dress it up, Kate. I had a soft spot for you, but I had a blind spot for her. She knew that and she played me brilliantly. She knew I was dying and that I'd always felt guilty about giving her that case. She should have been on leave, or at least on reduced hours, while Paul was bad, but she was adamant she was fine and I wanted to show faith in her. It was a stupid decision. My loyalty was supposed to be to the victims, not to her, but like I said—blind spot." He swallows. "So I lied to you. I said I'd micromanaged her so you'd shift the blame for any mistakes in the investigation onto me. Truth is, I wasn't managing her enough. I was giving her free rein, trying to show I trusted her. And in doing that, I literally let her get away with murder. I could have gone to my grave without knowing that, I tell you."

"What she did wasn't your fault, Olly. In her mind, Holly Kemp had to be stopped and she'd have found a way—*any way*—to do it." Steele gets up off the sofa, moves to a chair next to the bed, next to me. "You shouldn't have agreed to take the blame for her, though. Your reputation, your legacy, all your cases, for pity's sake, could have been called into question if this had gone much further."

"She was desperate," he says simply. "She said you were looking into the case again and she knew you were going to find gaps. And she was good, Kate, convincing. She admitted she'd fucked up. Said her head was so full of Paul and the boys and what was going to happen to them all that she hadn't explored every avenue when it came to Holly Kemp and it was going to come back to bite her, wreck her career." He runs a hand through his white hair, his face pained, almost reliving the conversation. "Lord, I felt guilty. *So* guilty. I blamed myself for not keeping a close enough eye on her. So when she asked me, *begged* me, to say that she'd told me about other theories but that I'd ordered her to focus on Masters, I couldn't say no. And more importantly, I believed what she told me. I had no reason not to. Even when it came out about the bank records, I still believed she'd done it for the right reasons—because she genuinely believed Masters killed Holly and she didn't want the case railroaded." He shakes his head, staring out the window. "Do you know what she actually said? 'You're retired now, you don't need the pension, what can they do to you?' She might as well have said, 'You'll be dead by Christmas, take one for the team, boss.' Thing is, though, she had a point. I've plenty of money. I'm pretty much untouchable—that's one perk of dying. Whereas there she was, at the peak of her career, a whole load to lose, and two lads who've already lost their father. Tell me, Kate, what would you have done?"

Steele's saved from answering by the sound of her phone ringing. "Blake." She stands and walks into the corridor, leaving me and Cairns smiling awkwardly at each other.

"It's been one hell of a month," I say, just for something to say. I think by now I've complimented every single feature of the room, and in any case, it feels weird to be quite so enthusiastic about a place he clearly wishes he never laid eyes on.

"It has indeed, Cat, but to hell with it. Enough of this doom and fecking gloom. Tell me something happy, would you? Didn't you have a date the other week? The first night you came around to mine with Kate."

Two Thursdays ago. Aiden and the Americans. The conversation we still haven't quite had. Not conclusively, anyway.

"Oh yeah, right. Well, it wasn't a date exactly. I was meeting my boyfriend's work colleagues."

"Nice crowd?"

"Yeah. Yeah, they were."

"And your boyfriend's a nice fella?" He laughs at himself. "Lord God, would you listen to me? 'Is he a nice fella?' As if he'd be your boyfriend if he wasn't a nice fella. You lose the art of small talk when you live on your own."

"He is a nice fella, yeah. He's Irish," I add.

"Is he now?" This seems to please him. "And what part of the motherland does he hail from?"

"Mayo."

"A Mayo man. Well, then he would be a nice fella. Hang onto him."

"I'll try."

I smile, but Cairns senses something beneath the surface. Dad swears blind that Grandad Pat went like this in his last few months—beady-eyed and perceptive, like a medieval witch.

"You're not sure about him, no?"

"Oh yeah, I am, but . . ." I rack my brains for something bland. "It's complicated, that's all."

"No, it's not." He smiles, sinking down into the pillows a little; our visit has taken it out of him. "You know, I promised myself I wouldn't become one of those 'things only the dying know' bores, but I will tell you something, Cat. At the end of it all, jobs, careers, nice houses, flash cars"—he grins at my bag, at the haul of goodies poking out the top—"fancy shower gels . . . They don't mean anything. All you have are relationships. And relationships are never complicated. They either work or they don't. They make you happy or they don't. Look at me and Moira. When the fun stopped, we stopped. Life doesn't have to be any more complicated than that."

I nod earnestly, swallowing the bubble of tears in my throat.

"Even what's happening inside of me, that isn't complicated. It's just biology. Biology gone bad, some might say, but that's not how I see it. It's just the biological luck of the draw, that's all." He raises his hand, a tiny salute. "So there you go now, Cat, love. If stage four prostate cancer isn't complicated, I'm damn sure dating a nice Mayo man isn't."

What do you say to that?

How about dating a nice Mayo man whose sister died a horrible, violent death as an indirect result of your father's utter selfishness.

Oh, and he has no idea about any of this.

Complicated enough for you?

For one beautiful, liberating second, I think about saying it. I imagine splitting the vein, telling the secret, sucking the poison right out, here in the company of this kind, uncomplicated man.

But instead I tell him another secret. Something no one else knows. Something I only realized myself just now, when Cairns talked about life boiling down to who makes you happy and who doesn't.

"I'll tell you what is bloody complicated, sir. Applying for a B-2 visa." I move my chair in closer, taking hold of his hand. "I haven't even told Her Majesty, so to misquote the song, don't start spreading the news just yet. But . . . I'm moving to New York."

Acknowledgments

As always, I'm hugely grateful to the wonderful Katherine Armstrong at Bonnier and Emily Griffin at Harper US. Behind these editor extraordinaires, there are also teams of equally wonderful people working hard to bring my stories to the widest possible audience—special thanks to Ciara Corrigan, Clare Kelly, Felice McKeown, Nico Poilblanc, Alex Allden, Ruth Logan, Ilaria Tarasconi, Heather Drucker, Kristin Cipolla, and Kim Racon. High-fives are also due to Jon Appleton for his beady-eyed copyedit.

Immeasurable thanks to my agent, Eugenie Furniss, who maintains the perfect balance of passionate cheerleader and calming voice of reason in every single situation.

To Alan Howarth, for helping me keep Cat's world authentic (and for never losing patience with my endless stream of procedural questions!).

To friends and family, your continued support means everything—Mum, Dad, the Naughton and Frear families, Helen, Cat, Carla, Fiona, Steph, Lee Whittlesea (not a gangster brought down by Tessa Dyer, but a very dear friend), and many, many more. And the crime writing community—there really are far too many of you lovely lot to mention, but special air-kisses to The Ladykillers (long may we lunch).

Colin Scott too—you keep me sane, you keep me laughing, you keep me writing. Genuinely, thank you.

And of course, Neil—who not only makes me feel like the only girl in the world, but the best living writer too. It's hard to sum up how grateful I am—keep up the good work, baby. I love you.